JULIET BRIDGES

This is a work of fiction. Any resemblance to actual persons, living or dead or actual events is purely coincidental. Although real-life locations or public figures may appear throughout the story, these situations, incidents, and dialogue concerning them are fictional and are not intended to depict actual events nor change the fictional nature of the work.

First published in the United States of America April 2024 by Lake Country Press & Reviews.

Cataloging-in-Publication Data is on file with the Library of Congress.

ISBN Paperback: 979-8-9889859-6-9

Ebook: 979-8-9889859-7-6

Author website: https://julietbridges.com/

Publisher website: https://www.lakecountrypress.com

Editor: Borbala Branch

Cover Art: Dazzling Jedi

Cover Design: Emily's World of Design

Formatting: Dawn Lucous of Yours Truly Book Services

Lake Country Press
Publishing & Reviews

A NOTE FROM THE AUTHOR

Dear reader,

I began writing *Sliding Into Love* in mid-March, 2020. Everything felt like a free fall, a weird descent into a spiraling darkness, and the world needed a lot more light. This was my light for most of that year. The lost year. The darkest timeline, if you will.

Writing *Sliding Into Love* brought me out of my comfort zone, brought me new friends, brought me these two characters who hold some of the shattered pieces of myself in their fictional hands. When nothing felt real or safe, I had them.

So if events in this book are a little less than believable in some instances (like baseball games being over at a reasonable time for a five-year-old to go to bed or a woman playing for an MLB team), forgive me, indulge me, because this was what I needed to read in 2020, because I needed to find myself in a place far, far away from reality. I hope you find a little of the light I wanted to put into the world.

Please note that *Sliding Into Love* is a romantic comedy, but several themes may be concerning or upsetting for some readers, including mentions of past child abuse and neglect,

verbal abuse, manipulation, casual misogyny, brief depiction of a panic attack, and mentions of off-page homophobia and racism. In addition to these, *Sliding Into Love* also contains alcohol use, explicit language, and explicit depictions of sex between consenting adults.

If any of these upset you, please protect yourself.

Love,

Juliet

Ps. In the immortal words of Thea Guanzon, without whom I probably wouldn't have written this book, "I did this for the rats."

To those who are lost, you're not alone. Family can be those you choose for yourself, and home can be where you're going, not where you've been.

1

Worn black leather slid over scarred knuckles, and Ethan Ford snapped his fist into the pocket of his glove as he paced in the bullpen. Once it was flexible, he eased it off and dropped it in his bag, fishing around again until he found a pack of gum and a dingy tube of eyeblack. Through his headphones, a man's raspy voice sang about hiding his face. *A little too appropriate*, he thought as he slid the stick of black paint along his cheekbones, dragging his fingertips down to smear it into a grotesque mask. It was a psych-out tactic as much as a practical solution to block rays of sun and glaring stadium lights. He went through the ritual before every game the way some players had good luck routines.

Not that it ever gave him luck, but the practice remained, ingrained after years of playing.

The singer in his headphones growled about war with no home to call his own, about never finding someone new. Ethan tore the headphones off and shoved a piece of gum in his mouth, not needing to hear a musical reminder of his life.

Playing against his former coach's team was bad enough, worse when his former coach also happened to be his uncle. A complex series of emotions buzzed in his chest when he glimpsed his uncle's greying sandy hair heading toward the other team's dugout.

Ethan snapped the gum between his teeth, and the loud pop in his head was enough to break him out of the dark spiral he needed to avoid during the game.

After Ethan and his warmup partner, an outfielder named Jen, were sufficiently loosened up, he headed back to the bullpen to wait. When the announcer announced the National Anthem, the entire stadium stood and sang while fireworks exploded, but Ethan was itching for the game to end before it began. On the mound, he smacked his fist into his glove, adjusting his hat and dark glasses before setting up for the first pitch.

The first half of the first inning went quickly, with Ethan striking out two of the Tornadoes and the final one out on a pop fly that flew right at his face. Rolling his shoulders and cracking his neck as he jogged to the dugout, Ethan saw a couple of kids leaning against the rails and calling for Derek. When he saw the catcher give them a quick wave before ducking down the dugout steps, Ethan wondered if he knew them. Ethan stiffly tossed the ball in his hand to the nearest child, a boy about ten, who promptly handed it to a tiny girl beside him. The girl screamed and wrapped her arms around the boy. Ethan grinned up at the girl and winked, drawing a huge, dramatic gasp from Jen.

"Shut the hell up, *Jennifer*," he griped, knowing how much she hated her full name, and she smacked him in the arm in protest.

Derek joined them, looking unusually serious. "Hey, man, I know you probably don't care, but you just made his day. He's in foster care with my—"

It stung, realizing his teammate thought he didn't care about making a kid smile, but it was what came with keeping your team at arm's length to rise through the leagues.

"It's just a ball." Ethan cut him off and made a show of rolling his eyes and shrugging before pushing past Derek to grab his batting helmet and gloves, tugging them on before stepping out of the dugout.

Derek followed, remaining on the steps, his face still solemn, his heavy gaze lingering as Ethan spun the bat and gave a few practice swings to loosen his shoulders.

As usual, he didn't pay much attention to his teammates' at-bats while he waited for his turn, running through his ritual of tapping the bat against the instep of each cleat three times. Then his name rang out through the stadium, and the sound of wailing guitar tore through the air again.

It was only once his cleats were set and he'd given the bat a practice swing that Ethan looked up at the pitcher and recognized Isaac Reyes.

Shit. He'd known running into Isaac was inevitable, hell, he was surprised they hadn't so far. But seeing his old friend, no matter how he'd tried to prepare himself, was a jolt to his system.

They'd played Little League together and been best friends through high school. Back then, Isaac witnessed the final blow-up between Ethan and his parents when they first tried to talk their son out of taking a deal before graduation, then threatened to disown him when Ethan wanted to leave. Ethan and his old man threw punches, and Isaac tried to get between them and ended up with a black eye for his efforts. Seeing Isaac's face after half a decade brought back too many memories he'd tried to forget.

"Strike," the umpire yelled in his ear.

Fuck.

Breathing in as deeply as his rattled nerves allowed, Ethan channeled all his pent-up frustration into the ball Isaac pitched straight into the sweet spot of his bat.

A crack echoed across the stadium and a roar erupted from the fans when they saw he'd knocked it out of the park.

Ethan didn't care about the score, he just wanted to get

away from Isaac Reyes's too-familiar face. He rounded the bases methodically, imagining he heard his footsteps over the crowd.

The bases weren't loaded, but they'd scored enough to secure a lead. His teammates whooped as he neared home, and Ethan did the obligatory hand slap with the few of them who bothered to try. Jen, who'd been on third for his hit, banged her helmet into his, grinning broadly at him as the team filed back down into the dugout for the next batter. Ethan shoved through them to find his usual seat: the one farthest away from everyone else.

"Could've hit harder." The voice came from high above Ethan's head. Marshall was taller than Ethan's six feet three inches, and he glared down his crooked nose.

"I hit it out."

"You missed the first pitch. Your father would've done better."

Keeping his flinch internal, Ethan also managed not to roll his eyes. Reacting to the manager's needling would earn him extra running or weight training tomorrow. And he was too fucking *tired* to deal with Marshall's shit.

The rest of the game went by in a blur, with Ethan paying just enough attention to Derek that they made it through the next innings holding a two-point lead. Not his best game, but not his worst, either. When it was finally over, he jogged off the mound, squeezing the ball until his knuckles whitened around it. He needed to get the fuck out of here before Isaac cornered him. Or worse, Marshall.

Or worse still, his uncle.

Without thinking, he tossed the ball over the rail to the waiting kids but stopped when he heard his name.

"Mister Ford?" It was the same little girl who'd gotten the first ball he'd thrown into the stands. Her round face was so earnest and sweet that Ethan forgot to scowl and ignore her. "Will you sign my ball, please?" By now, most of the fans knew

Ethan Ford was an asshole who didn't sign things, so they didn't bother trying.

But the little girl was so adorable with her messy braids and big brown eyes, and Ethan found himself walking over to where she was leaning precariously over the rail.

"Uh, sure." His voice came out too loud, making her jump. He tried to soften it. "Do you have a pen?"

Her face scrunched up like she was about to cry. Ethan panicked, looking around for some way to help.

"Oh, hang on, Janna, don't cry!" A woman's voice came from behind them. "I've got one somewhere!" A head poked up from between two teenagers, and the woman emerged, rummaging in an enormous bag that must have contained enough stuff to feed and entertain her kids plus the entire team for a week. She held on to one handle of the leather bag and reached in with her other arm nearly to her armpit.

Seeing the strap start to come untied and slide off her shoulder, Ethan started to tell her to wait, but it was too late. The bag fell off the woman's arm and landed upside down on the grimy stadium floor, spilling its contents.

Before he was aware of what he was doing, Ethan vaulted over the rail and joined her, kneeling on the concrete to help her gather her things.

Both Ethan and the woman scrabbled around beneath the seats, retrieving everything that fell from the bag. The woman reached for the last item, a small, brightly colored box, at the same time Ethan did, and his hand closed over hers. Her hand was so much smaller than his. But he didn't have time to fully appreciate the thought as she snatched her hand away, taking the box with her. Unfortunately, it landed upside down. Small plastic-wrapped cylinders tumbled out, bouncing over the concrete to scatter beneath seats and roll down the stairs.

Ethan scooped up a few tampons to drop back into the box, but when he took a step to retrieve another that rolled under a seat, he felt one slide beneath the spikes of his cleat. When he took a step to steady himself, *another* of the damn things caught under that cleat, and down he went, both feet slipping behind him like a fucking Three Stooges movie.

And naturally, on the way down, he barreled into the woman he was supposed to be helping, his shoulder catching her in the thigh and taking her to the ground with him. Ethan learned how to fall and not be injured so long ago, he didn't remember learning. But Ethan played baseball, not football, and he'd never learned how to take someone down without injury. He tried, though, twisting his body to avoid landing on top of this woman.

And then he realized his arm wrapped around her waist to break her fall. Ethan jerked away and tried to stand without crushing her. Once he'd risen to his full height, he held out a hand to help her up.

The woman reached for his hand, but when she stood, she jerked her hand away and snatched the tampons out of the other. Looking her over, Ethan didn't see any injuries, but he needed to make sure.

"Are you okay?" he grunted at the same time she spoke.

"Sorry about that!" Her voice was high and tense, and Ethan looked at her, taking her in for the first time.

She was all golden skin and bright hazel eyes, with soft curves enhanced by denim shorts and a t-shirt she'd tied tight around her waist. An unbidden image of her in *his* shirt popped into his head.

"Sorry about what?" he blinked, trying to rid his mind of the scene. Why was she apologizing? He'd slid into her, not the other way around.

The woman gestured at the bag and went pink in the face when she noticed the tampon box still in her hand. She dropped it again, but Ethan caught it before it hit the ground.

As he stood to hold the box out to her, he looked into her face, and *holy shit*.

Freckles.

He was a sucker for freckles.

The woman's embarrassed smile was huge, and there was a smudge of chocolate ice cream in the corner of her mouth, right beside a perfect, round dimple with an identical one mirroring it on her other cheek.

Ethan wanted to press his thumb into those dimples, and–

Chill, dude, he thought. *You've said three words to her.*

She was still apologizing.

"It's fine," he said, shrugging. "It's not a big deal," he tried again, noticing how deep his voice was compared to her bright, almost musical one. "It's...natural?" He finally said, and then he blushed too, feeling his ears burn.

Why was he allowed to speak at all?

Derek chose that moment to hop over the rails and join the tableau.

"Derek!" the little girl yelled, reappearing from under a seat, with her ball forgotten in the cupholder of the seat in front of her as she launched herself at him, planting kisses on his sweaty face.

"Janna!" Derek yelled back at her, laughing and raising her over his head until she squealed with delight.

The woman hauled her enormous bag onto her shoulder and followed them, grabbing souvenirs and gathering their stuff as she went.

Ethan and the ball appeared forgotten, and he slunk off, the sound of his cleats scraping over the concrete floor of the stadium worse than nails on a chalkboard.

The scraping blended into the sound of his teammates as Ethan walked back to the locker room. Ahead of him, he saw Jen's bleach-blonde head as she ducked through the glass doors. All around him, his teammates gave him a wide berth.

Good.

The seasoned players knew better than to try to befriend Ethan Ford; they barely interacted with him other than what was required to play. Every year, some rookie or transfer tried to invite the whole team out for drinks or to a family cookout. But not the Hawks, especially not Ethan.

He couldn't remember the last time he'd gone out with friends.

He couldn't remember the last time he'd *had* friends.

Jen was a friend of sorts, but only in the stadium. Marshall made sure Ethan's focus was solely on the game, on winning. All of Ethan's time was spent building up his strength and endurance, to prove he was good enough to be a starting pitcher. Never mind Marshall's notoriety for leaving in pitchers until they dropped from exhaustion or blew out their arms; he rarely put in relief unless absolutely necessary.

Every game Ethan played with the Hawks, no matter the outcome, Marshall reminded him how much better his father had been. Would always be better, with his legendary Hall of Fame status and household name.

It didn't matter that this season was Ethan's first pitching in years. Didn't matter that pitching was all he'd dreamed of since the age of four when he declared his intention to pitch like his father. Ethan grew up on a baseball field, from his Little League days to high school through his stint in collegiate baseball.

In an unprecedented move, Marshall signed Ethan out of college as a center fielder and left him there for five seasons, dangling the potential to return where he belonged over Ethan's head with every ball he caught and every hit he missed.

And *finally*, after years of brutal training and manipulation, Marshall informed Ethan *this* would be the year. The season Ethan finally got to take the mound as starting pitcher for the Hawks. It was his dream. He was right where he'd always wanted to be, and the Hawks were forecast to have their best season in a decade.

And he couldn't afford to fuck that up.

"Ford!" Marshall's voice barked from the darkened depths of his office.

Shit. Ethan thought he'd get away without any trouble. Apparently, he'd thought wrong. Silently, he ducked into the office and stood, waiting.

"Mister Ford."

That sardonic tone was never a good sign.

"Coach."

"You seem to have found a few new fans tonight."

"Just tossed a ball to some kid."

"I see."

Unsure what to do, Ethan stared at the toes of his cleats and waited.

"You seemed quite interested in the one fan in particular. The girl."

"What girl?"

"I know what I saw, Ford." Marshall's hand slammed on his desk, and Ethan bit the inside of his cheek to keep from flinching. "No attachments!" Marshall yelled, though Ethan was only a few feet away. "You focus on the *game*. You focus on *winning*. You do *not* focus on some cleat-chasing girl with a litter of screaming brats. If you need to get it out of your system, do it. With someone *else*."

"Coach, I—"

"Go find some other piece of ass looking for one night with a pro. Now, get out."

Ethan's gut churned as he spun on his heel to leave. The woman didn't deserve the way Marshall talked about her, but he'd learned a long time ago it was best to take what Marshall threw at him without response.

But that didn't stop him from feeling like shit about it.

2

"Hey, Derek," Ethan yelled as the catcher pushed through the exit door. "Hold up a second," Ethan jogged forward, holding out a canvas tote bag toward Derek.

Derek looked at Ethan, confused.

"I didn't get to sign the little girl's ball, so I thought I'd sign a few and you can give them to—to them." He'd almost said to *your friend,* but he couldn't. Couldn't even think about her.

"Don't you want to give them to her yourself?" Derek waved toward a car a little away from the others.

Ethan froze, his whole body tensing, his face on fire. He shouldn't interact with her again; it would get him benched.

"Janna is probably asleep by now, but you can give them to Ivy."

What? Oh, Derek still thought Ethan meant the little girl.

"Ivy?"

"Yeah, my sister. Well, she's technically my foster sister, but a family doesn't have to be blood, you know?"

Two things hit Ethan at once. First, her name. *Ivy.* It evoked green and growing things, sunlight, and sweetness. Second, she was Derek's *sister*.

Ethan shook his head to rid himself of those thoughts. Thinking about her *at all* meant nothing but trouble.

"No, I can't—I mean—I have to go."

At least his car was nearby, so Ethan wrenched the door open, slid in, turned the key in the ignition until the engine roared, and left before he could make things worse.

IVY JOHNSON'S FOSTER DAUGHTER JANNA WAS SOUND ASLEEP WITH her older brother Jase nodding off in the backseat beside her as Ivy waited for Derek in the stadium side lot where the Hawks players and employees parked. The lot mostly held flashy, expensive vehicles, and Ivy Johnson's sensible sedan stuck out in its normalcy.

It would be too late to drive him home, Derek had said, but Ivy insisted. Derek had just been bumped up from the Double-A Hawks affiliate, and she was so excited that he would finally be home again, she'd practically dragged him to her car.

Those were the kinds of things family were supposed to do.

While she waited, Ivy fished through the bag that betrayed her to find her phone, debating if she should check her email for the umpteenth time that day.

What could it hurt? If nothing else, maybe there'd be a coupon in her inbox. Losing her internal battle, Ivy thumbed open the app, overlooking the three percent hovering beside the red battery icon. She'd have to be fast, but the service at the stadium was slow when she'd tried to check earlier. So slow, it hadn't updated at all, leaving her on edge for half the game. Waiting for an email she didn't even know would be coming reminded her too much of years of watching and waiting as others were chosen for foster placement and adoption.

Fuck it, she was checking.

In her inbox were four-hundred-twenty-seven unread emails, which she ignored. None of them were what she'd been waiting for.

She hadn't expected it to be nearly impossible to find work after she'd graduated with double master's degrees in Biology and Education. But she'd applied for what felt like hundreds of jobs in the months since her graduation and had no responses. Checking her email a million times a day felt more like muscle memory after so long.

It wasn't *just* about the money; she'd inherited a little, enough that she'd be okay for about a year. It was about stability. What she'd never had, and wanted, *needed* to give to Jase and Janna. But the waiting, the not knowing, had turned into something more than just annoyance. It lurked in the back of her mind, an old, familiar, nagging feeling of not belonging, of being unwanted.

Instead of wallowing in those feelings, she switched on the radio and scrambled to turn the volume down when it blasted dad rock at her. Janna gave a little grunt in her sleep, and Jase opened his eyes for a moment before they fluttered closed again. With a yawn, Ivy glanced at the exit, wondering how much longer Derek would be. As if on cue, the door opened, revealing him, and a few seconds later, a tall man in athletic shorts and a hoodie pushed through the door, calling out. Derek stopped and turned around, and the other man took a step forward.

Oh, *shit*. It was the player who'd picked up her tampons and knocked her down.

Ivy's cheeks burned as she relived the scene.

Not that she should be embarrassed—like he'd said, it was natural. Still, the whole situation had been so uncomfortable.

But him knocking her down was the closest Ivy had been to a man in...longer than she cared to think about. They'd wound up horizontal, and he'd wrapped his arms around her.

And Ivy didn't even know the dude's name.

All she knew was how gentle and tall he'd been. His gentleness surprised Ivy—he'd somehow managed to fall on her lightly, and while the skin of his hand was rough when he'd helped her stand, his touch was soft. Not what she'd expected from a man of his size.

Their interaction was so brief, his height was the only feature she'd noticed. The man was too far away for her to see much, but seeing him beside Derek put his height into perspective, with Derek only coming to the other player's shoulder.

Watching the pair curiously, Ivy wondered why the pitcher was so tense as he held out a bulging black tote bag to Derek. Was the guy blushing? Derek looked at him, peered down at the bag, then glanced toward her car.

Ivy ducked behind the steering wheel, but when she peered around it, Derek gestured toward the car. The other guy shook his head and looked away, then did a jerky half-wave in her direction and turned away to slide into a shiny black car. His tires screeched as he backed out of his spot, and the engine roared as he sped away. What was that all about?

Derek approached the car, and Ivy pressed the unlock button for him to open the door and slide in.

"So," Derek asked once he'd settled into the passenger seat, "what did you do to Ethan Ford?"

"Who?"

"Ethan Ford? The pitcher? Tall, long hair, kinda quiet? He asked me to give them to the kids. Said he didn't get a chance to sign the one you asked for." Derek tugged the strap of the tote bag.

Ivy reached inside and pulled out a baseball. And another. They were signed in an even, beautiful script that was the complete opposite of the scrawl Derek had spent hours perfecting years ago when he found out he'd made his college baseball team.

"He gave me a sack of balls?" Fumbling blindly for her water bottle, Ivy took a sip when a snort of laughter came from the passenger seat. Mid-swallow, it clicked, and once Ivy realized what she'd said, she nearly sprayed him with her water, laughing at his snorting as much as her accidental joke.

"Yeah," he said, still laughing. "I've never seen Ethan act that way before. He was nervous."

"I don't know why he would be," Ivy scoffed. "It was nice of him to send the...balls... to the kids, though. Will you tell him I said thank you?"

Derek leaned his seat back, careful not to bump Janna's knees.

"Sure thing, Ives. You know, I don't think I've seen Ethan sign anything all season. I heard he used to pick fights, and not just with the other teams." Derek paused, considering. "But he doesn't seem so bad to me, kind of the strong silent type. Grumpy, but so are you in the morning." He chuckled at his joke and ducked as Ivy flung the tote at him.

"He helped me gather up my stuff when I dropped my bag, and he talked to Janna when she asked if he could sign her ball. He was nice."

"I heard some rumors that he was a real prick a few years ago, but I haven't been around long enough to catch all the hot goss."

"Derek. I love you. You know this. Which is why I am begging you not to say 'hot goss' ever again. For both our sakes."

"Okay, fine, but do you want to hear more about tall, dark, and broody?"

"Sure." Ivy put the car in gear, driving slowly beneath the glowing halos of the parking lot lights.

"So, I found out he used to play outfield."

"Okay, good for him." Unsure where Derek was going, she waved her hand for him to continue.

"But he pitches now."

"Good for him? You know I don't speak baseball." At a red light, she checked on the kids in the mirror. Still asleep.

"People don't just change positions five years into their careers! It's only been done, like, once!"

"What's the big deal?"

"Well, I heard it's because Marshall screwed him over." Derek's voice grew low and conspiratorial.

"Really?"

"Yeah, he was supposed to sign onto the team as a pitcher, but at the last minute, Marshall changed something in the contract, and because Ethan refused to sign with an agent, he missed it and got completely fucked over."

"Maybe that explains the bad attitude." She didn't blame the guy for being pissed.

"Oh. I didn't think of that. Maybe he's not so bad. Marshall is pretty hard on him, too."

"How so?" Ivy fiddled with the AC; the vent blew cool air at her face, sending tendrils of hair tumbling from her bun and swirling into her eyes.

"It's kinda weird. Marshall makes Ethan stay late a lot, going over really old tapes. And he yells at him a lot. Way more than anyone else."

"Does he yell at you?"

"Actually, he pretends I don't exist."

"What? Why?" Ivy glanced sideways at Derek. His deep brown eyes met hers for a moment and looked away.

"I think he'd rather have Jacobs back."

"Jacobs is the guy you replaced?"

Derek nodded, his body language shifting. Reaching out, she laid her hand on his.

"He sucks, you know. Have you told anyone?"

With a dry laugh, Derek squeezed her hand. "What can I say? 'My coach pretends I don't exist?' Maybe that's better than the alternative."

Angry tears burned Ivy's eyes on Derek's behalf, and he must have sensed it because he changed the subject.

"Hey, do you want me to get you tickets for tomorrow's game too? There might be a few spots left with seats together."

"Ooh, yes!" Ivy paused, thinking. "They'll love it! Jase seemed to enjoy this game. Hey!" She squeezed Derek's hand again, excited. "When does small league start? Do you think he'd like it?" Her face fell. "Is it expensive?"

"Did you say small league?"

"Yes?"

"Ivy. Honey. It's called *Little League.* And don't worry about buying equipment." He leaned forward, resting his hands on his knees. "I've got some old stuff he can use. We'll figure it out."

"That would be awesome. You think he'd like it?" Her mind was already racing with the possibilities. Maybe he'd be less tense, more like a ten-year-old than the world-weary adult he pretended to be. *This could work,* she thought.

For a few moments, Ivy imagined Jase making new friends and coming out of his shell. Maybe Janna could find a sport too, though the gregarious little girl had no trouble making friends, like the pitcher with the balls. "Will you tell—what's his name—Ethan? Thanks for his sack of balls for me?"

"I will *not.*"

"Please?" Ivy fluttered her lashes at him, trying to look angelic but ruined it by giggling.

"Absolutely not. What I *will* tell him is my very attractive, *very* single sister is grateful for his lovely gift. And she also thinks he's super hot."

"Derek! NO!"

"Well, don't you? He blushed when I told him who you were, so he's hot for you, too." White teeth flashed in the dark car with his grin.

"Aren't you supposed to do the protective brother thing and keep me from dating your teammates?"

"That's so gross. You can date whoever you want."

"But you said he had a bad reputation!" Ivy scowled at the steering wheel.

"And *you* said he was nice."

"Ugh!" She grunted, glaring sideways at Derek.

"Uh-huh. I win. Besides, you're lonely."

"I have Jase and Janna. Lily. You."

"You know what I mean."

"And I know nobody will want a chaotic disaster like me." The car bounced as Ivy shifted to park a little too early.

"You never know," Derek said. "Maybe a little chaos is exactly what Ethan Ford needs."

ANOTHER MORNING WITHOUT THE ABILITY TO SLEEP IN. NOT THAT Ivy would trade Jase and Janna for anything; she loved them with all her heart.

What she did not love, however, was early mornings. Still, transitioning into being a full-time mom from occasional part-time emergency placement foster had been so gratifying. Ivy loved the little moments she got to share with them: helping Jase with math problems and figuring out cute new hairstyles for Janna each day. Ivy was spectacularly bad at things like organization, but she made damn sure her kids were happy, healthy, and always fed. Their short lives had been fraught with worry, and Ivy wanted nothing more than to give them all the things she never had at their age.

Like easy social worker visits.

Social worker visits never turned out the way Ivy expected. As a child, a familiar cold sense of dread trickled through her limbs, gradually gathering over days, so slowly that she didn't notice until the weight became so heavy, she nearly felt immovable with worry. She'd never had the excitement some of the other children in the system had shown when the state employee assigned to their cases appeared, brown folder in hand, and good or bad news waiting with a piece of paper. No, Ivy only ever knew the system, and there had only been truly good news once.

With that single instance, her life changed forever for the better. And she was so grateful to be able to offer it to Jase and Janna now, even if they were only placed with her temporarily. No matter how much Ivy yearned to make it permanent. For their sake and hers.

At this particular moment, the visit in question was due to happen in an hour, and Ivy, as usual, was running behind. That was something that hadn't changed with two new additions to her life. Janna, who never slept in, still lay curled up in her bed, snoring softly, and Ivy was loath to wake her. A moment of peace was rare in the mornings, and if she hurried, maybe she'd have time to whip up a nice breakfast to start the day off strong. She might be a terrible cook, but scrambled eggs, toast, and instant oatmeal were typically manageable. Beside her, Jase stood quietly at the toaster, waiting for the next two slices to pop up.

"Do you want jam?" Ivy asked, opening the fridge. "We have strawberry and grape."

He remained silent as he pushed the button down again.

"Jase?"

With a startling crash, Jase dropped his plate on the fading vinyl countertop. Wide-eyed, Ivy stared at the usually reserved little boy, truly looking at him for the first time that morning. Dark circles lay beneath his eyes, a stark contrast to the unusual pallor of his skin.

"I don't want to leave." His voice was small, and his eyes flitted away before they met hers.

Time blurred, and Ivy stood in another dingy kitchen, the same words leaving her mouth. But hers were too quiet to be heard. She'd had no one to fight for her, to hold on to her, keep her safe. No one *understood*. Not like she did.

Setting the skillet on the back burner, Ivy switched off the stove. Gently moving the plate aside, she leaned her hip on the counter, close to Jase but without touching him, her hands held out if he wanted to take them.

He didn't.

Swallowing past the tightness in her throat, Ivy said, "I think it's a regular visit. Ms. Nayomi is just coming to check on us. It'll be okay." That sounded real enough, she thought. No reason to add her anxieties to his.

"But what if it's not?"

Maybe he wasn't happy living with her? But no, he'd said he didn't want to leave. No one ever reassured her when she'd been in his position, so how was she supposed to help him?

"Jase, I'm not—" No, that wasn't right. "I don't know—" Her thoughts wouldn't come out through the buzzing in her head. A whooshing breath left her lungs. "Okay. I'll be real with you, buddy. This is hard for me, too. But we can get through it together. Ms. Nayomi is just coming to make sure everything is going well. That's all."

A jerky little nod was Jase's only response, but he held her outstretched hands for a second before darting to the table with a plateful of toast.

There was no time for her to check her email, but she opened the app without thinking. Her heart soared when she saw one from a local school district. After reading through the message five times, her heart rate returned to normal. The high school where she'd completed the student teaching component of her degrees would have a new spot available for the next school year; one of their beloved Bio teachers planned to retire after the current school year. The assistant principal remembered Ivy and requested that she apply, implying that the job was hers in all but paperwork, and once the budget revisions for the next year were approved, they'd extend more official news. Because she had no time to respond, she set four reminders on her phone before racing to Janna's room to get her out of bed.

Elation skipped through Ivy's limbs right up until Nayomi knocked on the door half an hour later. Then dread settled in its place, leaving her drained before the meeting began. She was relieved to have gotten both kids and herself presentable in that short amount of time. Ivy opened the door and ushered Nayomi in, marveling as always at how *beautiful* the other woman was. A few inches taller than Ivy, Nayomi had medium-brown skin that turned luminous in sunlight, with dark hair she usually wore spiraling out from her head in a pretty halo of curls. Soft-spoken and gentle, the social worker had a smile that Ivy was certain would have landed her a modeling gig on the spot if she'd ever come across an agent.

The two women sat at the table for coffee as they ran down the checklist they covered with each visit.

"Do you have any concerns? Has anything changed since I saw you last?" Nayomi held her pen poised over her legal pad, ready to jot down any misstep Ivy made.

"No!" Ivy blurted, then backtracked trying to soften her answer. "I mean, no. Everything is great!"

"Is Jase having any problems at school?

"His grades are great!" Shit, surely she knew words other than great? Why couldn't she think of any?

"Has he made any friends?"

Remembering her conversation with Derek, Ivy hedged. "I've been thinking of signing him up for baseball. Umm, Little League?"

Nayomi tapped her pen on her chin, looking thoughtful. "You might want to ease him into it since he's still seeming uncomfortable around his peers, but I think that could be a great idea."

A little whoosh of air escaped Ivy, grateful that her idea had gone over well.

After a few more moments running through Nayomi's checklist, she requested to speak to the kids, and Ivy shuffled them into the kitchen. Janna, of course, was always excited and happy. Jase, though, still had that hard set to his jaw, as though bracing for the worst. It pained Ivy to see it still there, and no matter what she ran through in her mind, nothing magically came to her to ease his worry.

Her past and less-than-pleasant memories of the same process kept replaying on a loop in her head as she tried to listen to the kids' conversations with Nayomi. Even though Jase was generally quiet, his tone was clipped, his sentences nearly monosyllabic as he spoke to Nayomi, and Ivy watched in horror as the social worker took more notes than usual.

Breathe in deep. Now, hold it. Breathe out. It's going to be okay, Ivy had to remind herself. She *knew* it was a regular visit, but she couldn't still the anxiety swirling through her, telling her to *run*, to *get out* before they made her leave.

Breathe.

And then it was over, Nayomi saying she'd check back in soon, smiling as she rose from the table. Jase squeezed Ivy in a blink-and-you'd-miss-it hug, then scampered out of the kitchen, as if moving faster than the speed of light would keep Nayomi from changing her mind. Even though Ivy had reassured both Jase and herself before the meeting, his relief was palpable, though Ivy tried to keep a lid on hers, at least until the other woman left.

"So, are you okay?" Nayomi hitched her purse higher on her shoulder as she walked toward the door but paused on the faded rainbow rug Ivy had found abandoned in the stairwell.

"Me?" Ivy's voice came out in a squeak at the unexpected concern. "Derek is back in town, so we get to hang out more. And I see Lily almost every day." She paused, remembering. "Oh, and I just heard from Central High. They have a teaching position opening up this fall."

But she didn't mention that it wasn't official. Didn't mention that she knew how bad it looked to be jobless, particularly to the social worker assigned to ensure the wellbeing of her foster kids. Didn't mention how much the waiting felt too familiar, a longing ache for acceptance and belonging.

Nayomi chuckled softly. "That's not what I meant. You're so dedicated to the kids and your friends; I wonder if you're as dedicated to yourself. Taking care of *you*."

Ivy bit her lip. "I take care of myself. I always have." She hadn't meant for it to sound quite so snappish.

For a few moments, Nayomi considered her. "I just mean... you seem lonely. That's all."

"Lonely?" She tried not to think about it. The loneliness. The *wanting*. For stability.

For family.

Sure, there were Derek and her upstairs neighbor turned best friend Lillian, and now Jase and Janna. They were the closest she'd probably ever have to a whole family.

Still, the idea of stability, of permanence, hung over her head like a dream just out of reach. Even though the kids were with her long-term, the possibility was there that they'd move on. That they'd *choose* to.

And as she'd told Derek, no one would want a chaotic disaster like her.

Why would they?

Breathe. She wouldn't do that to herself. She didn't expect to find someone who would want a partner who came with her baggage and two children to boot. And that was okay. She'd be okay.

"Ivy?" Nayomi peered at her, and she realized she'd zoned out.

"Sorry. I'm...okay. Things are different now, but good different, you know? The kids are great."

"That's wonderful. I'm glad you're all doing well, and please let me know if there's anything you need. I'll see you on the next visit!"

In another life, if Nayomi hadn't represented everything Ivy was afraid of, maybe they could have been friends. But Ivy couldn't find it in her to befriend a person with the potential to take half her life away, no matter how unlikely it was. Besides, memories of social workers in the days before she'd lived with Maya and Derek still colored her opinion of the profession as a whole. To most of them, she'd been just another number on a piece of paper, an inconvenience in their own uncaring, unfeeling, soul-sucking days. If she thought about it, Ivy almost understood where they'd come from. It must have been awful, seeing so many lives uprooted and ruined, that after a while, a certain amount of desensitization would be required.

Still, as a child, their lack of compassion had left a scar that never really healed, and Ivy did her best not to be another statistic, another mark on an endless sheet of them.

And she wouldn't let herself be a burden to anyone else.

3

After counting the tickets for the fourth time, Ivy held Janna's hand while they stood in line with Jase to enter the stadium. Yesterday, one of the tickets fell out of her pocket, but Jase snatched it out of the air before a gust of wind blew it away. This time, Ivy decided to delegate and handed the tickets over to Jase. She leaned down so he could hear her over the din of excited fans.

"Can you hold onto these?"

He nodded solemnly, clutching them tightly to his chest.

"Thanks, buddy! I don't want to drop them again, and I know they'll disappear if I put them in my bag."

He nodded again, and Ivy thought she saw the hint of a smile pass over his lips.

The sensory overload of the stadium assaulted Ivy as they waited in line; the sheer volume of conversations happening around her plagued her ears, and she expected Jase to be on edge, too, but he seemed fine, glancing around excitedly as they waited, bouncing on the balls of his feet and taking in the chaos. To avoid the onslaught as she walked, Ivy tugged her phone out of her bag, thumbing open the email app on muscle memory more than actual intent. As soon as Nayomi left, Ivy scrambled together copies of her pertinent documents and forwarded them to the assistant principal with a little note saying how excited she was to be working with them and how she couldn't wait to get started. They hadn't forwarded the paperwork she needed to fill out, but it had only been a few hours. Still, only seeing a lengthy post from a recipe blog left her feeling defeated and empty, and she refreshed the app one more time just to be sure.

Nothing.

It's fine; budgets take time, she reminded herself for the millionth time as she shoved her phone into her purse, shoving her building anxiety down with it.

After they were seated, the scent of hot dogs and popcorn reached Ivy's nose, and she couldn't resist the salty siren call. As they found their seats again, the starting lineup was called, and Jase sat up straighter, training his eyes on the field. Derek's name echoed through the stadium, and pride for her brother flooded through her as she took in the clean lines of his black and red jersey, and the crispness of his white pants. Jen followed, and Ivy watched in awe as the blonde's long legs ate up the ground as she jogged to center field.

"And starting pitcher for the Hawks tonight is number five, Ethan Ford," boomed over the speakers, and Ivy recognized the name, turning to the enormous screen as the camera showed him jogging to his place on the mound, his long dark hair rippling. Black paint striped down his cheeks into short-trimmed hair that was more like long, dark scruff than a beard, his eyes hidden by sunglasses, and Ivy found him a little imposing. *I wonder what he looks like under all that black stuff.* His full lips twisted into a scowl as he rolled the ball between his fingers and glanced toward the opposing team's dugout, quickly snapping his attention back to Derek, who squatted behind home plate, ready to catch the first pitch.

Finally, the game was underway, and Ivy followed to the best of her ability without knowing the rules. Two seats down, Jase watched intently, elbows on knees and chin in hand, his eyes darting back and forth, nodding or scowling at the calls. Sitting between Jase and Ivy, Janna seemed more interested in her popcorn and candy, or the occasional dancing mascot.

This time, their seats were further down the third-base foul line, so Ivy knew they probably wouldn't be able to catch Derek's attention to get another ball. Not that they needed one now. Ethan Ford gave them so many signed balls, Ivy probably could have sold them to pay for both kids' college tuition, though Jase would never let her. And he'd signed in such neat calligraphy, not a messy scrawl like Derek's. She was still astonished by how kind and thoughtful he'd been. Cute, too.

An overpowering scent of body spray and body odor announced the arrival of a high school baseball team several seconds before they stormed the stands near the dugout, and Ivy decided she wasn't brave enough to fight the smell and the screaming. Jase's shoulders ratcheted up to his ears in disappointment, and she decided right then to bring him back more often, even if Derek couldn't get them more tickets. The thought must have summoned him because a moment later, his head popped out of the dugout, and Janna screeched in glee when he waved at her.

Derek walked to the barrier, looking over his shoulder. Behind him, Ethan Ford walked toward the dugout with Marshall close on his heels. Ethan's dark brows pinched together, and he ducked his head as the older man talked, folding in on himself in a way that didn't seem possible for someone his size. Odd, since Derek said he had a bad reputation. Between the guy announcing fireworks and both kids talking to Derek at once, Ivy only caught a fragment of the conversation.

"—your pitches lost speed after the fifth. Do better or you're off the team. Or I could send you back to center field. In the minors." Surely it wasn't normal for a coach to speak to his players that way. When she realized she was staring, her face burned, and she looked away. Should she say something, or would her interference make it worse?

"—staying for the fireworks, right?" Derek tapped her shoulder, pulling her attention away from her eavesdropping.

"Fireworks?" Ivy stared blankly at him, wondering if the coach spoke to him the same way he had to Ethan, her gut churning at what she'd witnessed.

"Please, Ivy? They do fireworks every Friday!" Jase tugged her hand; his excitement had her reluctantly agreeing to stay.

"Awesome!" Derek's thousand-watt smile lifted some of her concern, but Ivy couldn't stop herself from looking past him to see if Ethan and the coach were still arguing. "Follow the directions to the berm, and I'll meet you after I change."

"The what?" Ivy asked, but Derek had already disappeared into the dugout.

"The berm," Jase offered. "It's the grassy area past the outfield, where the scoreboard is." He pointed to where fans were gathering, setting blankets on the grass.

Lifting Janna onto her shoulders, Ivy followed Jase as they picked their way through the milling crowd and found a space.

THE BASEBALL IN HIS HAND WEIGHED A MILLION POUNDS AS Ethan tried to block out the old man's barked stream of bullshit, but the words kept pouring from the old man's mouth. It didn't matter how many times he'd heard it, it never got easier to block out.

Never good enough. Worthless. Marshall's words turned into Ethan's inner monologue. It had been a long time since Ethan bothered fighting back, and what was the point in fighting back if he believed the words were true?

The nearer they grew to the stands, the louder the roaring grew in his head. A Brewers fan with a blue foam finger leaned over the railing, heckling Hawks players as they entered the dugout, and before he thought about what he was doing, Ethan snapped the ball toward the man, ignoring the stiffness in his arm. If the fan hadn't whipped his gloved hand up in time, the ball would have hit him in the face, and Ethan almost enjoyed it.

Almost. But that, at least, he knew was wrong.

"Save your arm, Ford. Maybe if you spent more time on your pitching instead of on fans who don't even support your goddamn team, you might do a decent job."

It was on the tip of his tongue to mention that before the last game, Ethan hadn't so much as looked at a fan since his rookie season. Marshall made sure to punish it out of him. Memories of aching muscles and burning lungs rose to the surface, and Ethan shoved past a teammate to the dugout.

"Don't mind me, dude! I'm just standing here."

Ethan turned with fire in his throat and a need to lash out.

"Maybe you should stay out of my way." He didn't bother to see who he'd pushed aside and kept going.

"What the fuck? Are you okay?"

The three words were a knife in his stomach.

Blinking, Ethan's mind cleared enough to recognize Derek looking at him in a mixture of concern and annoyance, twisting the knife.

"Why do you care?"

"I heard what he said to you. I've heard it all season. Is that normal?"

With a barely contained flinch, he glanced over his shoulder to be sure the coach wasn't around to hear the rookie speak. But the old man disappeared. Probably went home to get drunk.

"Dude." Derek stepped closer. "*Are* you okay?"

Ethan took a step back, clenching his fists at his sides to keep them from rising to a defensive position.

"Whatever. Fuck off."

Derek's smile faltered.

"Ethan, do you want to—"

"Whatever you're about to say, don't." He let himself tower over Derek, glaring at his teammate in his best approximation of Marshall.

"But—"

"I said fuck. Off." The words soured as he said them, but he spat them anyway.

His shoulder caught Derek's again as he went through to the locker room, but the clicking sound of cleats behind him alerted him Derek still wouldn't be put off.

"Look." Ethan spun, holding his arm out to stop Derek before they crashed into each other. "I don't know what you think you're doing, but you need to stop. It's best for me and for you if you just...don't."

"See, I think you're wrong." Walking past him, Derek gestured for Ethan to follow. Annoyed but bewildered, Ethan followed.

The muscles in Ethan's jaw ached as he clenched his teeth, and he wanted to shove Derek into the wall. Get in his face and yell. Ethan *should* walk away. But it was Friday night, and the fireworks were the one thing from the past he let himself remember.

"So?" He realized he wanted to hear what Derek had to say.

"Ethan." Derek's bright demeanor dropped, and Ethan saw the person beneath the grin. "I know what it's like to be talked down to. Probably more than you do."

He began walking away but paused again. Chagrined as Derek's meaning caught up to him, that Derek as a Black man put up with shit he hadn't faced, he nodded for the other man to continue, letting his eyes track the seams in the concrete flooring.

"As I said, I know. Snide remarks and worse. And I'm not saying what we're experiencing is even remotely similar. But I get it. I'm here if you want to talk about it." Before Ethan could react, Derek reached out and chucked him lightly on the shoulder, with a sympathetic tilt of his head.

Then Derek's bright grin was back in place, and he whistled as he strode toward his locker.

Marshall and Derek took more time than Ethan would like, so he threw on fresh clothes and a plain hat before slipping out a side door to pass the last concession stand to the berm.

Hundreds of people were already gathered beneath the scoreboard, waiting for the show to begin, though he paid little attention to them as he picked his way through their camp chairs and blankets. The lights switched off as he found a seat. Far enough away from the bulk of the fans, but still a good vantage point to see the scintillating sparks and brilliant colors of the fireworks.

Movement caught his eye as the countdown began. Derek's sister and her foster kids were settling on the grass, and the boy waved in Ethan's direction. He waved back on autopilot, a little stunned that he did so, and the boy grinned, turning to speak to the woman, pointing to Ethan. The countdown reached two when she leaned around the boy, and when she saw Ethan, she paused, turning to face him. The first streak of light lit the sky as a smile crossed her face, dimpling her cheeks and shining brighter than the cascade of silver erupting overhead. The sky darkened as she turned away, but the flash of the next shot illuminated her again, revealing them walking his way.

Confusion and maybe a hint of panic set in as he watched her grow closer, the colors overhead casting her in green, then red, then gold. She stopped a few feet away, yelling over the loud music and booming.

"Hi! I'm Ivy! I don't think we officially met the other day."

"Ethan," he said warily.

"This is Janna, and that's Jase."

Ethan nodded to them, then turned his attention back to Ivy, wondering why she'd come over.

"I wanted to thank you." Ivy's face was tilted toward him, not watching the show, and she was cast in shadows.

"Thank me?"

"For your, umm, for the balls." Her voice pitched higher; the way it had the first time they'd met.

Confused, Ethan blinked, then bit back a laugh.

"Oh. It was nothing." He shrugged, tilting his head back to the sky. A twangy country song played in the background, mostly drowned out by the thunderous fireworks.

"It's not *nothing*. It meant a lot to him." Ivy nodded to Jase, who stood still, enthralled by the exploding lights above. "I don't think I've ever seen him so excited."

Ethan's throat tightened, self-conscious but pleased.

"Do you want to sit? The view is good here." Was his voice always so croaky?

Ivy nodded, folding to sit beside him, but leaving a healthy distance between them, he noted. Then she folded her legs and placed the little girl in her lap. Jase glanced between Ivy and Ethan, and without letting himself consider the consequences, Ethan patted the grass on his left. Jase's eyes widened, but he sat.

If Marshall saw him with them, there'd be hell to pay. But

maybe he could get away with it. Just this once. He'd dressed incognito on purpose, to avoid fans and the coach.

Jase offered Ethan a shy smile, then tugged his knees to his chest as he turned his face skyward.

Time shifted, and it was like looking at himself at that age, a dark-haired boy with his hat shoved back on his head, feeling the booming shots in his bones, sitting so close to the lit-up sky he imagined if he reached out, his fingertips might brush the stars. Awe wreathed Jase's face, and Ethan's chest ached for days past. When he'd been so young and in love with the game. Nothing to worry about, no pressure.

Ethan fell back into the grass, exhausted, and let himself enjoy the show. After a few minutes, a round face appeared in front of his, and Ethan started at the little girl's closeness.

"Why are you on the ground?"

"Umm. I like to watch the fireworks."

"They're too loud." Janna's face scrunched up; her hands pressed firmly to her ears.

"Can I?" he asked Ivy, to be sure it was okay. She angled her head and furrowed her brows but nodded. "Do you think this will help?" He held out his hands to Janna and mimicked putting his hands over hers without touching her.

Janna looked thoughtful for a moment, then grabbed his wrists in her hands and clapped his palms over her ears. Her grin lit her whole face as she looked up. Joy radiated from her, and if he didn't exactly feel the same, he at least appreciated how much fun she was having, and he was glad to share the experience with the three of them. Ethan glanced at Ivy before turning his attention back to the show, and her expression was confused and intrigued, before she, too, looked up.

When the lights came on, Ethan dropped his hands from Janna's ears and turned to Ivy, who was standing to leave.

"Do you want to come to the game tomorrow?" Maybe it was loneliness, wanting to see them again; maybe he just wanted to give the kids something special, maybe it was both. His heart pounded in his throat as he waited for her answer.

Ivy glanced at him, perplexed.

"I have tickets. And if you come early, you can come to the pre-game warmup. If—if you want."

"Can we, Ivy?" Jase's voice sounded small, trying to hide his hope in case Ivy said no.

"That would be nice." A wide smile split Ivy's face, and it outshone the stadium lights.

4

Panic set in the next morning when Ethan woke and remembered he'd invited Ivy and Jase to the stadium. If Marshall had a problem, Ethan would play it off somehow. For public engagement or social media. Something.

It was all for the kid, he told himself. It was definitely not about seeing Ivy again.

It was sad, Ethan thought, how excited he was. For Ethan, so many firsts, like watching his first game, happened when he was too young to remember, and after a while, he didn't get excited by those things the way most kids would have. Eventually, he'd lost all the joy in the game.

Ethan's shoulders tightened at the thought of his childhood and his parents, but he was glad for the opportunity to show Jase how the game should be.

Nervous, excited energy spread through him as his mind cataloged what to teach the kid about technique, to help Jase figure out which position he'd play if he joined Little League.

Putting thoughts of Ivy out of his mind, Ethan focused instead on the third and final game against the Tornadoes. While he sautéed peppers and onions for his daily omelet, Ethan tried to block out what Marshall wouldn't let him forget.

The outcome of this game is entirely on me. Every mistake is my fault because I *am leading this team. We only win if* I *am good enough.*

With those words on repeat in his head, Ethan finished cooking and scarfed down his food before showering. As the hot water poured over him, burning his skin, he allowed his body to sag under the spray, trying to ignore the ache in his chest. The cool bite of eucalyptus and mint shampoo on his scalp broke him out of the loop in his head, and he wondered fleetingly if Ivy would like the scent. If it would smell differently on her if she used it after—

But no. Ethan shoved all thoughts of Ivy aside.

Besides, he wouldn't allow himself to focus on anything but winning this game. And the next. And this season. And the next.

Ethan sighed, turning up the water temperature until it was just on the wrong side of unbearable.

After a few moments' thought, he decided to fully shave for the first time in years. Normally, he hated the process; staring at himself so long in the mirror left him too unsettled. But Derek said Jase was skittish and shy, and the deep shadow across his cheeks and jaw gave him an air of intensity. The last thing Ethan wanted was to come across that way, so the scruff had to go. As he went through the motions, he let his eyes track the movements of his hands, following the path of the razor through the white froth on his face rather than meeting his own eyes. Would Ivy notice the difference? How would it feel for her fingers to trace across the newly revealed skin?

Shit. He was doing it again.

Thoughts of Ivy made Ethan notice his surroundings as if through someone else's eyes. For the first time, he saw the frayed ends of the towel he'd wrapped around his hips. The ones on the shelves were threadbare, too. Ethan made a note to order new ones and wondered what other details he'd missed in his own life. Swiping his hand through the gathered steam revealed his reflection. When he finished, the face staring back at him was his own, and yet, it wasn't. It was the face he'd seen before the split from his family and joining the Hawks. Younger, less worn, and less angry.

It made him want to smash the mirror.

He didn't do it.

This time.

A month ago, he would have. He'd rather the pain of split knuckles than see what might have been. What he used to be.

When he arrived at the stadium, he bypassed the locker room and went straight to the gift shop to purchase a gift card. Maybe he'd want a hat or a jersey; at ten years old, Ethan had loved everything he could get his hands on from his favorite teams. He wasn't sure if Jase would want any of those things, but the gift card worked at concessions if he didn't want souvenirs. Ethan tucked the plastic card in his pocket and shoved a hand through his hair, holding his hat under his arm. From several yards away, a wolf whistle shrieked through the air. Jen strode toward him with raised eyebrows.

"What's with the face?" Jen said, gesturing to her own, miming the shape of a beard.

Of all his teammates, Jen was the only one who bothered speaking to him. Her snark had enough bite to it that Marshall let her get away with it. Derek was okay, but the rookie was happy all the time, and Ethan was suspicious of anyone so *happy* all the time. Besides, he was still new. He'd learn soon enough to leave Ethan alone. Jen dished out shit, but she took it as well as she gave it, and her brand of cynical humor went well with his, well, *lack* of humor.

"Shut it, Jen," he snapped, but his words weren't venomous. With as little inflection as possible, he told her about Jase and Ivy coming for pre-game, trying to keep a lid on his simmering excitement so she wouldn't catch on.

She smirked. "You gave a kid tickets? That's... different."

Ethan shrugged her off like it was no big deal. Like he wasn't excited to see Jase.

And Ivy.

"He's a foster kid from the rookie's old foster home. Derek said he likes baseball, and he's having a hard time adjusting."

"You going soft on me, Ford?"

"Fuck off, Jennifer."

Jen laughed at him as he walked away. She probably saw right through him.

As Ethan passed beneath the overhanging upper seats, he paid new attention to the stadium itself. The slap of his running shoes was loud, even in the general noisiness of employees readying the stadium for the coming game. Oil hissed in the fryers as frozen chicken strips and French fries were dropped in, and Ethan heard the sounds as if it were the first time. As a kid, he'd loved the emptiness of the stadium seats and the flurry of people making food and prepping the field.

Ivy and Jase waited near the closed entrance gate, and he took the time to observe them from a distance. She stood on her toes peering between the bars, but Jase stood with his hands jammed in his pockets, head down, shoulders jacked up to his ears. With Jase's dark hair and tanned skin, Ethan jolted at yet another version of his younger self, and another rush of memories threatened to overtake him. But Ivy's golden, freckled face turned toward him, and she waved excitedly. He had to resist the urge to respond in kind.

"Hi!" Ivy called out and reached out to hold Jase's hand as Ethan approached, swiping a keycard on the reader to let them in. Jase held Ivy's hand tightly as they passed through the security gate. "Thank you so much for this!" she gushed at Ethan, giving him an enormous smile.

"You're welcome." Ethan's voice came out rougher than he'd intended, and Ivy looked up at him, all big hazel eyes and dimples. He cleared his throat and looked at Jase instead. "Hi, Jase, good to see you again." Ethan stuck out his hand for the boy to shake.

Ivy had to nudge Jase forward, but after a moment, he looked up and shook Ethan's hand. Poor kid's hands were sweating and shaking. Ethan hoped he hadn't scared him.

"Hi," Jase whispered and turned beet red.

An awkward silence stretched between them.

"Oh, um, let's take a tour before we go down to the field."

Jase nodded quickly, but he remained tense.

The stadium was still mostly empty, and Ethan took his time showing them the various concession stands and taking them up the stairs to the tiers of boxes above the regular seats. The announcer's box was empty except for Ryan, one of the announcers, who introduced himself and showed Jase a few of the sound effects and musical cues used during the games. Jase's eyes went wide, and he quietly thanked Ryan as they left. Ivy remained silent throughout the tour, mostly hanging behind Jase and Ethan, and Ethan wondered if she was avoiding him. As they neared the end of the tiered rows of seats where the gift shop was tucked in a corner, Ethan reached into his pocket and fished out the gift card.

"Umm. I don't know if you want this, but I thought you might like to get a hat or a jersey or something at the shop."

The kid's eyes went round and his mouth fell open as he looked up at Ivy, his arms twitching at his sides as if he wanted to take the card but didn't think he should.

"Is it all right?" Jase whispered to Ivy. "Can I keep it?"

Ethan shot a look at Ivy, and her cheeks were stained pink too, her eyes tear-bright as she glanced between Jase and Ethan.

Ivy nodded at Jase, and the boy grinned for the first time since arriving at the stadium. The tension lurking in Ethan's chest loosened the tiniest fraction.

They finished the tour and went into the shop, where Ethan showed them the racks of gloves and helped Jase try on a few to find his size. Jase also chose a hat and a Hawks jersey and immediately pulled them on over his clothes. The hat was several sizes too large, but it was the same kind the players wore for home games, and he'd insisted.

When they left, the boy's steps were considerably lighter, but they slowed as Ethan led them to the field house. Derek poked his head out and called for Jase to join him. Ivy watched Jase jog over to Derek, who promptly took the kid's hat off, ruffled his hair, and put the hat back on his head backward. Jase and Derek pushed through the field house doors, and suddenly, Ethan found himself unable to take a breath. He looked down to find Ivy with her arms wrapped tightly around him, squeezing surprisingly fiercely for someone so much smaller than him.

It was...nice. Unusual, but nice. How long had it been since someone hugged him?

And because he was some kind of colossal idiot with a single brain cell, he froze beneath her touch. She backed away quickly, and he bit the inside of his cheek to stop himself from telling her to come back or reaching out for her. Brushing tears away, she turned back toward the doors where Derek and Jase disappeared, and her shoulders slumped before she looked back at him.

He should've wrapped his arms around her. Comforted her.

"Thank you for this," she said, brows pinching. "He's been having a hard time."

"I'm glad I can help." Ethan willed more softness into his voice than he'd probably ever possessed.

Maybe it worked because she peered back up at him, eyes still shining with tears, and offered him a watery smile.

"Is there...anything else I can do?" God, he wanted her to

stop crying. Wanted to reach out and brush the tears away, wipe away the hurt that haunted her eyes. "To help, I mean."

"This means so much. More than you know." Her arm disappeared up to the shoulder in her enormous bag, and after a few seconds of digging, she'd fished out a tissue. "Jase..." A deep, exhausted exhale left her lips as she blotted beneath her eyes. "Jase is having a hard time adjusting to a new environment, I think. I mean, he's a perfect kid, almost too perfect, you know?"

Ethan wondered what his story was. He knew Ivy was fostering him but not much else.

"But I think this is going to be good for him. He's had so much fun at these games, and I know he doesn't look it, but he's so excited to be here."

"I'm glad. I loved stuff like this at his age." Shit, he shouldn't have shared that tidbit. Now she'd probably ask personal questions he didn't want to answer.

Or...maybe he did?

To his surprise and disappointment, she didn't pry.

During the tour, he'd noticed her checking her phone a few times, scowling at it each time. Again, she tugged it from her back pocket, deftly scrolling for a few seconds before locking it with a frown.

Ethan hesitated. She seemed upset, but it wasn't his business. In the few seconds it took him to have this internal debate, she pulled it out again.

"Is everything okay?"

"What?" Ivy looked up from her phone in confusion. "Oh. Yeah, just waiting on an email." She made a point to lock her phone and drop it in her bag. "I guess I should..." With her thumb, she gestured to the door Derek and Jase went through and gave him a blistering smile that sent shockwaves from the top of his hat to the bottom of his shoes, keeping him rooted to the spot.

Once Ethan recovered enough to follow, he found Jase shyly showing Derek the glove and jersey he'd bought. Derek glanced at Ethan with a rare serious expression on his face, but then he grinned and raised his brows as though he knew something Ethan didn't. Then the catcher shook his head and helped Jase put on his glove, telling him how stiff the leather would be at first and how to break it in to make it more flexible. While they talked, Ethan found his bag and hunted out his glove and dark glasses, unsure if he should interrupt Derek to take Jase to the practice area.

Down the hallway, Ivy wandered back and forth, looking up at the photos and memorabilia of past teams. She was so pretty wearing that look of fascination, and he watched as her nose scrunched up in concentration. So pretty and so sweet, and it was so wrong for him to even look at her.

But he did anyway.

He couldn't help it. He'd tried to give all of his attention to Jase, but now he was with Derek, Ethan wasn't able to keep his eyes away from Ivy.

Long, tanned legs with a few constellations of freckles dotting her skin. Wavy brown hair in a ponytail that swished when she walked. An oversized black Hawks tee tied in a knot at her waist accentuated the stark contrast between the shirt and shorts. The white shorts pulled taut over her rear as she leaned forward to look at a plaque beneath a photo, and shit, he shouldn't be looking at her that way, but he wanted—

A tug on his sleeve broke his attention, and Ethan saw Jase standing there looking up at him.

"Ready to go, kid?" The voice coming from Ethan's mouth was his father's, and for a moment, Ethan was frozen, transported back in time.

"Mr. Ford?"

"You can call me Ethan." He shoved his hands in his pockets to stifle the urge to ruffle Jase's hair. "Let's go." He already sounded like his father; he might implode if he started acting like him too.

Most of the team hadn't found their way out of the locker room, which was how Ethan preferred to warm up. Outside, it was quiet save for the sounds filtering out from the stadium, and the near silence was usually a balm for the constant roaring in his head. Now, though, he heard too much silence and wondered if maybe he should play music or something.

Or do what they came to do and play ball.

Together, Ethan and Jase walked to where the balls were kept. Ethan filled a small bucket and held one out to Jase. For some reason, his face had gone red again.

"Got your glove?" Ethan asked and started jogging backward to toss the ball back and forth.

Jase nodded, adjusted his hat, and shuffled his feet in the clay, sending up a puff of red dust.

"Go on, throw one to me. I'm ready when you are," Ethan called.

Jase remained silent, and though Ethan wouldn't have thought it possible, his face turned a shade redder.

As Ethan remembered what he'd learned about the kid, realization jolted through him. Jogging over, he got down at eye level with him.

"Jase, have you ever thrown a baseball before?" Ethan asked, lowering his voice. He fought to keep his voice steady at the answer he already knew was coming.

With a tiny movement, Jase shook his head and looked down, scuffing the toe of his shoe. "My—nobody ever taught me."

Well, that he could do. "I'll teach you." Ethan held out one of the balls from the bucket. "Hold it like this."

For the next fifteen minutes, Ethan showed Jase how to hold a ball properly, and they started with easy underhand throws and quickly worked up to overhand. Ethan had just begun to teach Jase how to throw a real pitch when Derek and Ivy came over to watch. Jen followed them with raised brows.

Ivy gave Jase a big smile and a wave, and Derek did a double thumbs-up. Jase waved back and turned to face Ethan, and while he wasn't smiling, exactly, a lot of the tension in his face had disappeared. Ethan's own anxiety had nearly drained away, and the realization was... interesting.

Shoving his hand into his glove and flexing it, Derek joined Jase and Ethan before calling Jen over too.

"Hey, buddy, do you want to throw with me and Jen?"

Jase looked at Ethan as though he were asking for permission, which completely bewildered Ethan.

"Go ahead," Ethan said. "I'm going to go...over there."

Derek, Jase, and Jen tossed the ball in a triangle formation, and Ethan tried not to think about what kind of shitty parent wouldn't even spend the time to teach their little boy how to throw a ball.

"Ethan?" Ivy's voice cut through the rage pulsing through him.

He stopped pacing but didn't look at her, gnawing on the inside of his cheek instead.

"Is he okay?" she asked. "Did he have fun?"

"Yeah, I think so," he said between clenched teeth, still not looking at her. "He's doing pretty well for someone whose parents wouldn't teach him."

"Oh," Ivy said. "I didn't know." Her voice cracked, sadness wreathing her soft features.

"At least that's the impression I got. But he's having fun now. Look." Ethan pointed to where Derek was dancing around, pretending to drop the ball Jase threw at him. Jase wore a proud grin, while Jen egged him on, yelling mild insults at Derek.

Once again, Ethan's breath was knocked out when Ivy wrapped strong arms around him. This time, when she squeezed him, he awkwardly patted her back until she let go.

He tried not to notice how perfectly her soft curves fit against his hard planes.

"I'm sorry." Ivy took a step back. "I'm a hugger. Derek and Lily are too, so sometimes I forget other people...aren't."

Is she apologizing for hugging me?

"No, no, it's okay," he stammered like an idiot. "It's nice."

She dimpled up at him.

"Thank you, again," she said, stopping him before he responded. "I know I've said it a lot, but as a former foster kid myself, you making time to spend with him is incredible, and it means a lot to him. And to me."

Ethan remembered Ivy and Derek were foster siblings, but it hadn't clicked for him until then that her history might be similar to Jase's. The anger Ivy helped fade away came roaring back. How much hurt had she experienced?

He *should* avoid her, then, so he wouldn't put her through more.

"It's nothing," he grunted.

"It's not nothing, not to me. Or to Jase." Her face was more serious than he'd seen it in their short interactions.

A knot formed in Ethan's throat, and he mumbled about water and shoved through the glass doors. When he returned with an armful of bottles, he found Ivy had joined the game of catch and was spectacularly bad at it. Derek tried to help her, showing her how to toss a ball, but her aim was terrible, with everything she threw going wild. For a few moments, Ethan watched them all until Jase waved him over. Ethan joined in the game to make a large circle, tossing the ball back and forth between them.

Watching Ivy was... incredible. Her face lit up with an enormous smile as she watched Jase, and she was so sweet and encouraging, with nothing but good things to say to him, even when he made mistakes. Sometimes Ethan watched Jase, with his nose and brows scrunched up the way Ivy's had earlier, and

Ethan wondered if either of them realized Jase had adopted that little mannerism.

More players left the field house, and Jase seemed to pull back in on himself. His movements went jerky, and his legs wobbled. When Marshall came out, he tripped over his own feet, though Ethan didn't blame him. The old man's face was scarred and scowling, and when he strode over to talk to their group, Jase hid behind Ivy.

Derek led Ivy and Jase back to the field house before Marshall made any snide remarks to scare Jase further, and Ethan watched as Ivy leaned down to speak to Jase. Ivy and Jase waved as they left the field, and Ethan did a weird half-salute. *What the hell was that?*

Ethan threw himself into stretching and warming up with the rest of the team, and for once, when he pulled on his uniform, he skipped the black grease paint he normally smeared over his face, finding his usual need to hide behind the mask absent.

The usual pre-game bullshit started, with a bunch of sponsor ads and antics before the game finally began. Probably because it was their last game of the set, the Tornadoes put up more of a fight than in the previous two games. On Ethan's second at-bat, he hit a grounder, landing him on first. While Jen was setting up to bat, Ethan saw a greying, sandy head come out of the dugout to replace the Tornadoes' first base coach. Shit.

"Hey, kid," his uncle said conversationally, "how's it going?"

Ethan readjusted his helmet and chewed the inside of his cheek to keep silent.

"Your mother misses you," his uncle continued.

But Ethan ignored the old man; he wouldn't allow himself to be thrown off his game. Bracing his hands above his knees, Ethan leaned forward, watching Jen set up to bat. She cracked one out right between the left and center fielders, which was enough to get Derek home and Ethan to third.

Isaac's catcher called a time-out and went out to the mound to confer, and Ethan straightened. Beneath his helmet, his hair was plastered to his forehead, so he took it off, running his hands through it and letting the slight breeze cool his sweaty face. He was close enough to see Jase and Ivy behind the third base line, and he jerked his chin in a nod when Jase waved. Beside him, Ivy was oblivious to Ethan's attention because her focus was entirely on an enormous basket of nachos balanced on her knees. She was *devouring* them. After shoving each chip in her mouth in one bite, she would pause, her eyes rolling back, and if Ethan were closer, he thought he might be able to hear a blissful moan.

He wanted to see what else made her moan.

Nope.

Get back in the game, Ford.

He heard Marshall yelling at him to put his helmet back on before the crack of the bat echoed across the field. The second baseman caught it midair, and Ethan jogged back toward the dugout. Marshall grabbed the front of Ethan's jersey as he passed and snarled in his face.

"Did you think I wouldn't see the girl and her brat?" Marshall spat. "Get your head out of your ass, Ford. Do better. Your father— "

For the first time, Ethan was able to block out the old man's vitriol, the words getting lost in the sounds of the stadium. Shrugging, Ethan walked away, though he didn't look toward the stands again.

When the game ended, the Tornadoes walked away with the win. Four to three was close, but it was still a loss, and Marshall railed at the entire team afterward about not getting a shut-out.

Although the old man's words typically left him with a

nagging sense of guilt that somehow the loss of the game was entirely on him, it was unusually absent.

After he showered and changed, Ethan was leaving, his bag slung over a shoulder when he heard Derek call out.

"Hey, Ethan, wait up!"

Instead of his usual grimace, Ethan schooled his features into something less angry and waited for Derek to catch up to him.

"I'm going to grab some food and head to Ivy's. Want to come with?" Derek was nonchalant, but Ethan wondered again if the catcher had guessed what Ethan had thought about his sister.

It had been so long since anyone bothered inviting him out that Ethan didn't know how to respond. *Are we friends now? This is what friends do, right?*

"Umm. Yeah, sure, I'll come with you."

And just like that, Ethan Ford found himself hanging out with his teammate, on his way to see the girl he couldn't think about yet couldn't *stop* thinking about, and he was terrified.

5

"Ivy!"

Derek's sing-song voice echoed through the apartment, and Ivy was grateful for his post-game ritual of bringing home takeout because she was exhausted. Seeing how Jase's tension eased with Ethan and how much he'd enjoyed the game had completely wiped her out. The surges of sadness, anger, and the tiny ray of hope she'd experienced were enough to knock her off her feet. Janna's stomping little feet echoed through the hall as she scampered toward Derek, and Ivy heard Jase follow.

Derek called her again, and she yelled at him, "Dude, I'm coming, give me a minute!"

She was in her room, checking her email on her ancient laptop hoping that a different browser would magically send a confirmation through. Not knowing was starting to get to her, wearing her patience thinner than a croissant layer, and annoyance began building in the back of her skull, though she tried to ignore it.

"I brought extra, so Lily is coming, too," Derek yelled back.

Ivy pulled out her softest, most worn Central University tee shirt, and dug around in a drawer for leggings. Yanking on the clothes, she yelled for them to save her some food and searched the floor of her closet for her favorite fuzzy socks.

Hopping on one foot down the hallway, Ivy pulled on one sock as she emerged into the living room and noticed a significantly different energy in the room. It stopped her in her tracks.

Standing on one foot in the entrance to the living room, Ivy stared, gaping, at an uncomfortable-looking Ethan Ford. Even curving his shoulders inward and ducking his head, his presence permeated the room. Although, after a second glance, Ivy decided he might have seemed larger than life because of tiny Janna clinging to one of his muscular thighs.

And seeing him again reminded her of seeing him that afternoon for the first time without the scruffy beard and that black stuff on his face. It had been a shock at the stadium, and she was struck again, now that he stood *in her living room*, by just how attractive Ethan Ford was. Maybe his nose was a shade on the large side, and his brows were kind of thick, but damn, his jawline was a study in perfect angles. Deep brown eyes that lightened to amber in the center and tended to look sad, no matter what he did. And those flawless, 'girls would kill to have this shade of lipstick' pink lips. And all those features added together were... intoxicating.

Not that noticing his face led to Ivy noticing the rest of him. But if she had, *wow.* Of course, she hadn't noticed those muscles earlier when his attention was on Jase. Or the way his tight white uniform pants had clung to those muscles.

And his ass...

Nope, she hadn't noticed any of that.

And she certainly hadn't wondered about what else his uniform might be hiding.

With a very loud internal reminder that it was rude to stare, Ivy realized she should greet her guest, until he turned the full force of his unwavering attention on her, his dark eyes taking her in. Under his gaze, Ivy's face burned as she remembered what she was wearing, so she grabbed Derek by the arm and dragged him back down the hallway to her room without even speaking to Ethan.

"Derek..." she hissed, but he stopped her.

"Yeah, I know, I should've told you I was bringing him, but he and Jase got along so well, and I thought it might be nice."

"Oh." He was right, and they both knew it.

"Yeah, and I did not miss how you looked at him either, ma'am."

"I— what?" she squawked, her face flaming even hotter.

"Mhmm." Derek said. "You are not sneaky, Sis."

"Yeah, well, I don't think he's interested in me," Ivy sighed, sliding her closet doors open. "I hugged him earlier, and he just sort of stood there, so...yeah." Frowning, Ivy ducked back into her closet to change. Was a dress too much? Probably. Shit. *Shit!*

Ivy thought she heard Derek say, "I'm not so sure," but when she came back out, he had left to join the kids...and Ethan.

A deep rumbling erupted from her stomach, and Ivy was grateful for the distraction. Holding her breath, she walked into the kitchen, finding everyone already tearing into the food. Lily had arrived, turning the small kitchen into a disaster scene.

Ivy was delighted to find enough *birria* tacos, salsa, and queso dip to feed an army, or maybe just the small group in her apartment, and once she'd loaded her plate dangerously close to disaster, she turned to find a muscular mountain blocking her way. Ethan spun a paper plate between his large hands and stared at Ivy's heaped plate with his head angled to one side. There was no judgment on his face, so she took a massive bite, feeling the rich juice from the meat drip off her first taco onto her second before responding to his curious look.

"I'm hungry," she mumbled around the taco before sitting at the small table in the kitchen. The others had already taken up residence on the couch or the living room floor. Ivy saluted

Lily with her half-eaten taco, and she waved back with a guac-laden chip.

Surprise nearly choked Ivy when Ethan sat across from her, settling into the small chair and folding his long legs beneath the table.

They ate in silence for a few minutes until Ivy noticed Ethan watching her. Embarrassed, she swiped at her face with her napkin and asked what was wrong through a mouthful of cheese.

"It's just... I don't think I've ever seen anyone enjoy their food quite as much as you do," Ethan said.

Cheeks burning, Ivy met his eyes only to find that he'd blushed too.

"No, sorry, that came out wrong," he amended quickly. "I mean, you seem to really *enjoy* it. That's all. It's not a bad thing. It's nice," he punctuated the last sentence with a nod as though his thoughts on the subject made it official.

Uncertain how to take Ethan's observation, Ivy stared at him for a moment, and when she realized he wasn't making fun of her, she decided to be candid. "I try to enjoy everything as much as I can. I had a... weird childhood."

Ethan's thick, dark brows nearly met in the middle as he scowled.

"But I'm a well-adjusted adult now, see?" She rose and lifted one leg, wiggling her toes to show him her fuzzy socks with little cartoon spaceships printed all over them. But when she tried to sink back into her seat, her foot landed square on the napkin that had fallen from her lap. Her foot slipped, sending her careening toward the table. Until Ethan's hand darted out, wrapping around her upper arm to steady her. Then he let his hand slide down the length of her arm, his fingers rough but warm and barely touching her. When he reached her wrist, he jerked his hand away, flexing it as if only just realizing he'd touched her.

Ivy tried to remember to breathe.

"That's twice you've caught me. Maybe I should keep you around for insurance purposes." Her voice came out hoarse.

Dark, faintly startled eyes met hers. And Ivy thought he might say something, flirt back a little. But he let out a stiff laugh and continued eating with no other response.

"I'm sorry," he said after a few moments.

"For what?" she asked, nonplussed. Had he disliked touching her *so* much?

"I hate for kids to be in shitty situations."

Oh.

Oh.

"OOOOOH!" came a chorus from the dining room. "Swear jar! Swear jar!" Jase and Janna chanted.

Ethan looked incredibly confused, and Ivy refused to acknowledge how adorable it made him.

"Oh, we have a jar for when we swear," she explained. "A quarter per word."

"Hmm." He fished in his pocket and pulled out a dollar, handing it to her. "Here, for my next ones too. I have a dirty mouth."

Ivy wouldn't let herself imagine what she'd like Ethan to do with that mouth, though her cheeks turned pink again.

When she returned, Ethan was still eating, but Lily had joined him, and he had a deer-in-headlights look. In the thirty-odd seconds Ivy was gone, Lily had managed to find out his age (27), sign (Scorpio), and where he was from (Indianapolis, though his family had moved a lot). She was a master at getting people to talk, even if they didn't want to. Ivy thought it was because she had poreless skin (she'd been adopted as a child, so she claimed it wasn't from good genes, just a strenuous ten-step Korean skincare routine), falsely guileless eyes, and she tended to wear her shiny black hair in youthful styles to trick people into a false sense of security without realizing they were really dealing with a she-demon.

Ivy *adored* her.

From a distance, Ivy watched Lily drawing more information out of Ethan as he finished the last of his tacos. What else might be hiding beneath the surface, if only she could draw it out?

But he flinched away from you, Ivy reminded herself. *He doesn't want to be close to you.*

And then she told herself to shut up before she followed that train of thought right off a broken track into a ravine.

Ivy found her half-empty plate, shoved another taco in her mouth, basking in its drippy glory, and left Ethan to Lily, who was asking him what it was like to be a famous baseball player.

"Oh, I'm not famous." His face went white. "I'm only there to play," he said, ducking his head so his long, dark hair hid his eyes.

Oh, that hair. In the limited interactions they'd had, Ivy had only seen him with a hat covering his hair, but with it off, Ethan's hair was...pretty. Though it felt odd to think of any feature on such a large, solemn man as pretty, it was the best descriptor. Dark and shiny, his hair looked so soft, Ivy longed to card her fingers through those perfect shoulder-length waves. Maybe she should ask Derek to find out what products Ethan used.

Rolling her eyes at herself, Ivy went in search of Derek, who lounged on the sofa. With him sat Janna, whose face was smudged with salsa.

"So," Derek deadpanned, "did you thank him for his balls?"

Ivy choked on a chip loaded with queso and salsa.

"Ya know, since he signed all those for you?" Derek wasn't looking at Ivy, but she heard the smirk in his voice.

"I said thank you very much," Ivy said primly. Or as primly as she could while shoving another chip into her mouth.

"Oh my god, you thanked him for his balls?"

"Shut up, you know what I meant. I think I annoyed him so much, he hates me now."

"I don't think so," Derek countered. "I have an idea."

And then Derek disappeared into the living room, hollering about a Wii bowling tournament *right now*, and for everyone to *hurry up*.

Lily appeared, abandoning her torture of Ethan, who followed Jase as the boy was talking non-stop. While she didn't understand their baseball speak, she'd never seen him so animated, and she considered asking Ethan about his secrets to sad kid wrangling when Lily sauntered over and pulled on Ethan's arm.

"Ethan, you have to go first! You're our guest!" Lily said, dragging Ethan forward.

The tiny woman looked even tinier next to him, but a very bewildered Ethan did as she commanded.

"I don't know how to play," he said, his ears and cheekbones stained red. They'd stopped in the cleared space in front of the TV.

"Ivy will show you. She's our best player." Lily looked over and waggled her eyebrows at Ivy.

Confused, Ivy raised her brows in question. She always lost bowling tournaments, real or otherwise, and she was certainly not the best player.

"I guess I can." Ivy glared at Lily in suspicion.

Ivy took the controller and slipped the cord over her wrist, adjusting it to fit. Then she swung her arm wildly, jerking her body forward to send the digital ball on the screen flying off into the gutter. She took her second shot and only knocked down three pins.

"See? It's pretty easy," she told Ethan, whose face had gotten redder. "You just kind of sling it. Nothing like the real thing, though."

"Oh, um, sure," he replied, not meeting her eyes.

When Ivy tried to take the controller strap off her wrist, the plastic adjuster clip, which had a piece missing due to someone (Ivy) getting too ambitious during a tennis match, got stuck, and she couldn't pry it open.

"Let me help." Ethan's deep voice came from a mile over her head. God, he was so tall.

Ethan stepped closer, taking Ivy's forearm in one hand and the thin white strap in the other. His thumb brushed over the tender skin on the inside of her wrist as he flicked the clip open, and his touch was like electricity shooting up her arm straight to...nowhere. Because he didn't want her that way. His hand was huge covering hers, and his fingers barely touched her palm as he slid the cord over her hand. It was too small to fit over his.

They still stood so close that Ivy wondered if the same rush of heat staining her skin burned him when he touched her. If she tipped her head back, it would be the perfect angle for him to lean down and kiss her, and no—*just stop.*

"Thanks," she croaked and edged away, desperately trying to decide if she wanted to avoid brushing against him as she escaped, or if she wanted to touch him on purpose.

Choosing the safe route, she retreated to the familiarity of the couch, observing the game.

Little Janna had latched onto Ethan like a barnacle, following him around and asking the kinds of questions only small children thought to ask.

"Why is your hair so long, Mister Ford?" Janna asked.

"You can call me Ethan, Janna."

"Nuh-uh. You are Mister Ford," the little girl replied, scowling up at him. "Why is your hair so long?" Janna repeated as she climbed on his lap, trying to reach his shoulders to tug on a wave.

Ethan tried to duck away, but Janna's fingers were caught in his hair, and the little girl looked satisfied to sit beside him and twirl her fingers in it.

It did not escape Ivy's notice that while Ethan untangled Janna's fingers from his hair, he talked to her, engaging with her in a way many people didn't with children so young. Her heart squeezed at the sight of them together.

After the game ended, and Lily left, Derek popped up between Ivy and Ethan, wrapping his arms around them both. Ivy noticed Ethan flinching away from Derek a lot more violently than he had from her, and that was... something. Maybe?

"We better go, dude, or she might put us in bed too!" Derek said before making T-Rex arms and chasing Jase and Janna, who shrieked, pretending to be afraid of him as they fled his roaring.

"Thanks for having us, Ivy. I hope I'll—umm— never mind."

Holy shit, the way Ethan's voice dropped when he said her name scorched her skin, and the flames still smoldered long after the kids had gone to bed.

6

Ivy had no idea that she did an adorable little moan while she ate. Because she had no idea she did it, she had no idea what it did to him.

And he hoped no one caught him staring at her ass while she'd done an adorably awkward bounce when she'd taught him how to play the bowling game.

Groaning, Ethan banged his head on the steering wheel of his BMW. Derek had dropped him off at his car, but Ethan sat frozen for several minutes, trying to get Ivy out of his head.

"Ethan! Hey, Ethan!"

Was that…? It was. Isaac Reyes, Ethan recognized the voice.

Ethan didn't look at him and didn't know what to do with the warring emotions flooding through him. Should he flip Isaac off and drive away? Ignore him until he went away? Isaac decided for him.

"I wanted to say hi. It's been a while," Isaac's voice was muffled through the car window, and Ethan turned, seeing his old friend up close and personal for the first time in almost a decade.

The same lingering sense of the past, or maybe fate, that haunted him since he had seen his uncle at the first game came up behind him and laid icy fingers on the back of his neck.

Ethan rolled down his window.

"Hi, Isaac."

His former friend leaned down, resting his forearms in the open window.

"It's good to see you. You got some good hits in! How's it going?"

"Pretty good, I guess," Ethan was uncomfortable making small talk with anyone, but especially anyone who'd known him before. "How are you? How is Zara?"

Isaac ducked his head and stuck his hands in the pockets of his worn leather jacket.

"I'm great! And Zara got serious with her journalism and moved to New York to work for a news agency. It's cool, though. Been a while." Isaac didn't seem bothered, but guilt washed over him for bringing it up. "You seeing anyone?"

Ivy crossed his mind, but before he let himself think too long about her, he shook his head.

From across the parking lot, the Tornadoes bus honked, its lights flashing.

Isaac scowled. "I better go, but we should hang out soon."

"Maybe in the off-season," Ethan said and tried to smile. It was stiff and unnatural, but Isaac didn't seem to notice.

"Well... see ya!" Isaac began to turn away.

"Isaac," Ethan said just loud enough to be heard. "How are they?"

"Good! They're good!" Isaac shot over a shoulder and jogged toward the bus.

Ethan's shoulders slumped as he pressed the button to roll the window up and ground the key in the ignition harder than necessary.

. . .

A BEEPING BUZZ STARTLED ETHAN AWAKE, AND HE SLAMMED HIS hand down on his nightstand, searching for his phone. It continued beeping, the shrill alerts growing louder.

Memories of the previous night flooded his mind, and he let himself revel in how much he'd enjoyed himself. There had been no pressure, no ire, just playing the silly game, just hanging out, and... Ivy.

His blood heated at just the thought of her.

Unbidden, Marshall's voice echoed in his head. *I made you. I gave you everything you wanted. If you fuck this up, I* will *take it away. Don't fuck this up for me—for us—over some* girl.

Sullenly, Ethan banged around the kitchen, his mug clattering on the stone countertop as he began the day in a foul mood.

What did you expect, dumbass? Marshall was right. Focus. On the game. Not...not her.

Ethan tried distracting himself by packing for the week-long trip, haphazardly tossing clothes, shoes, and toiletries into his suitcase. Then he raided the bathroom for the travel versions of all his favorite hair products. Those he carefully placed into the suitcase, ensuring everything he'd need would be there.

It took five minutes, leaving Ethan with time to kill before he had to be at the stadium.

Maybe Ethan was a glutton for punishment, but after thumbing open his phone, he clicked on Instagram for the first time in months to clear out notifications. He rarely checked the app, but the Hawks media manager suggested all players have a page for visibility. There was no point. Not for him anyway. He hadn't had a normal interaction in a while.

Irate messages from fans and truly horrifying DMs didn't count.

But he was surprised to find notifications once the app had updated. Derek forwarded inane videos like sports fails and puppies, and Jen tagged him in a few articles and photos of the team.

And one new follower request.

From Isaac Reyes.

Before he changed his mind, Ethan clicked accept and spent the next hour scrolling through his former friend's life.

THE SHUTTLE BUS TOOK UP ABOUT TEN PARKING SPOTS IN THE stadium lot, and Ethan saw his teammates milling around outside, so he decided to wait in his car until most of the team had boarded before he joined them. Pulling up his travel playlist, he set it to shuffle and let his head fall back on the headrest, closing his eyes and feeling the bass pummeling his body. The music was so loud, he almost ignored the tapping sound, but something made him open his eyes. Derek stood at the passenger side window, bedecked in a matching lounge set, with an enormous coffee cup in hand. An unfamiliar car was parked beside his, with a woman, Ivy, in the driver's seat.

The sight of her sent Ethan's heart rate skyrocketing. Shit. But he had to board the bus, which meant getting out of the car. Maybe she'd stay in the—nope—Ivy opened her door and climbed out, walking to meet Derek. Ethan watched Ivy lean down and peer into the window, a confused look on her face. Her smile as she recognized him sent him scrambling to switch off the music and slide out of his car.

"Hi!" Ethan and Ivy said at the same time.

Derek looked between the two of them. "Neither of you are this happy in the morning. This is weird."

Ivy elbowed Derek in the ribs, but he laughed and squeezed her in a side hug, bopping her lightly on a bun that flopped to one side. *Why is she so fucking cute?*

"I have a question," Ethan blurted out.

Ivy and Derek waited for him to speak, and Ethan realized he had nothing to say.

"Umm..." Ethan took his hat off, ran his hand through his hair, then replaced the hat. "Is it okay if I give you guys my tickets for the season?" He hadn't planned it, but once the words left his mouth, he was surprised he'd had such a good idea. It seemed like the right thing to do. "And I thought maybe Jase would like to learn more about baseball. I could teach him how to pitch, or—"

"YES!" Ivy interrupted. "Oh, god, sorry, go on —I—Jase would love that."

"Oh. Awesome." Ethan hadn't expected her to be so enthusiastic. Unsure what else to say, he met Ivy's eyes, then looked away, trying not to stare. But the early morning sun cast her in soft light, turning the hints of amber in her eyes so bright, they were nearly golden. "Do you want my number? So, you can text me." Her eyes grew wide. Shit. "About the tickets, I mean. For Jase. Or if he wants to learn more about pitching. Or batting. Or...whatever." And now he was babbling like an idiot. "You can get it from Derek if you'd rather, or..." Ethan trailed off, watching as Ivy bit her bottom lip. Belatedly, he realized Derek was talking with a few of their teammates, leaving him alone with Ivy. Leaving him alone to make a total fucking idiot of himself.

"Give me your phone."

"What?"

"Your phone." Ivy laughed and waved her hand at him across the roof of the car. "I can put my number in for you."

Oh. Ethan did as he was told, trying not to think of the softness against his callused fingers when her hand brushed his.

"Jase will be ecstatic." Ivy ducked her head as she typed on his phone, then handed it back to him. "It'll mean a lot to him. It's so kind of you, everything you've done for him."

Ethan shrugged her off.

"No, really. It may not mean much to you, but Jase has never had anything like this before, and it's not something I can give him. It...it means a lot to me too, and I just want to—"

"Ethan!" Derek's voice cracked the space between them, and Ethan blinked, realizing he'd leaned over the roof of the car to get closer to her. "It's time to go!" Derek called out.

"Shit," Ethan muttered. "Sorry, I've got to—" he gestured to the bus.

"Have a good trip."

Ethan slung his headphones around the back of his neck, grabbed his bag, and boarded the bus. Travel days were the worst. Everyone wanted to either talk shop or talk shit, and Ethan wanted none of it. He and Jen usually found seats at the front and listened to their loud music in grumpy solidarity. Ethan had timed his arrival so he would be one of the last to load the shuttle but not *the* last, to avoid Marshall's attention and annoyance. Although they were generally the same thing, at least in Ethan's case, but Derek saved him by ensuring Ethan had boarded the bus before Marshall.

And there was Derek, dropping his bag into the space between Jen and Ethan, grinning past his oversized coffee cup.

Ethan attempted to match the expression but felt more like a dog baring its teeth. He wanted to curse Derek for interrupting his conversation with Ivy and himself for being so dense. There was no way Marshall wouldn't notice if Ivy, Jase, and Janna began appearing in the stands for more games. But it was a problem for Future Ethan to deal with.

Because Present Ethan had to deal with Ivy putting her number into his phone, but he hadn't done the same for her.

Which meant he had to text her first.

Shit. Fuck. Shitfuck.

Slipping the headphones over his ears, Ethan composed a message to her in his mind. "Hi, this is Ethan, and I think you're wonderful, but my coach won't let me date so I'm trying to see you any way I can without getting kicked off the team?" Maybe, "Hi, this is Ethan, and while I truly want to help Jase learn about baseball, I also really want to see you, and this is the only way I can think of?"

Shit, he was so fucked.

Once the bus had deposited them at the private airport to load the charter plane, Ethan plunked his bag on the floor and sank into one of the oversized seats. Jen and Derek took the seats nearest him.

"So, what did you and Ivy talk about?" Derek nudged him with a shoulder.

"Uh. Baseball."

From the seat past Derek, Jen leaned over and snickered at Ethan. Derek smirked. Ethan flipped them off and pulled his headphones back over his ears, still typing imaginary texts.

Fuck it all. Ethan pulled his phone out of his pocket.

Ivy

Hi, Ivy.

Ethan Ford, here.

You gave me your number, but I forgot to give you mine.

So, you have it now.

Okay. Bye.

Have a nice day.

Bye.

What the hell had he done? Instead of looking at the

messages, Ethan closed the app and put his phone on airplane mode.

At cruising altitude, Ethan opened his window shade and stared at the ground beneath, trying to forget how *awkward* he'd been. The verdant, rolling landscape below slowly transitioned to a reddish, rocky desert, and he imagined traveling through the rock formations and sliding over sand dunes. The hours-long trip passed by in a blur, and when the pilot announced landing, Ethan had to pull himself from a daydream about freckles and dimples and sparkling eyes.

The moment the wheels hit the tarmac, Ethan found his phone, turning off airplane mode and anxiously waiting for it to connect. Disappointment curdled through him when he saw no new messages. He should've known better.

Before the shuttle deposited the team at the hotel, some of the players requested to stop in a convenience store, and Ethan followed his teammates, grabbing things off the shelves at random.

On his return to the bus, Derek seized the bag, pawing through its contents.

"Oh, man. Ivy must be rubbing off on you!"

Ethan choked on his water.

He wished Ivy *would* rub off on him.

Shit, no, don't think about her that way, he had to remind himself. *You're just going to help her kid to play ball. That's* it.

Derek pulled the items out of the bag one by one: a bag of chili lime Cheetos, chocolate and peanut butter coated Chex, a pack of apple pie flavored gum, cinnamon sugar cashews, ranch-flavored corn nuts, yogurt-covered pretzels, mango-chili flavored chewy candy, a sharing size bag of crispy M&Ms, pizza-flavored Combos, and white cheddar popcorn. At least he hadn't forgotten to buy his regular large pack of spearmint gum and salt and vinegar potato chips, or the trip would've been a waste. The apple pie gum seemed particularly disgusting, and Ethan flicked it at Derek with his fingertips.

"What did you mean about Ivy?" Trying to be nonchalant, Ethan twisted the cap on his water bottle and ducked to place it in his backpack. The tips of his ears burned beneath his hair.

"She has this thing about trying new food, so whenever we travel, she always buys snacks she's never tried. And it's always random shit like this." Derek tapped the package of atrocious gum.

"Weird. You can give her all this then; I don't know why the fuck I got it." Ethan pulled out the things he wanted and shoved the bag at Derek.

"She'll love it!"

Upon their arrival at the hotel, Ethan dumped his bag in the hotel room he would be sharing with Derek and headed straight to the hotel gym. Chlorine and detergent filled the air of the tiny space, and the mirrored walls reflected far too many versions of himself for his liking. The pounding of his shoes on the treadmill helped him lose a little of the tension that settled in after he'd seen Isaac the night before, and for the hundredth time, Ethan willed himself to avoid checking his phone to see if Isaac had reached out. Or do a Google search for his parents. And, no, he didn't wonder if Ivy had texted him back. Definitely not. Breathing hard, he upped the speed on the treadmill and ran until his legs were jelly. When he stopped, he saw Marshall reflected in the mirror, glaring at him. Ethan ignored him and chugged his water.

"Something is off about you. Get your head on straight and *focus*," Marshall snapped before storming away. "Meeting in ten. Don't be late.

Ethan didn't bother to keep a scowl from twisting his features as he watched Marshall walk away. When had he ever been late? When had he ever done anything but what he was told?

. . .

"THEY DIDN'T EVEN GIVE US *GRAVY?*" DEREK LOOKED DOWN, dejected, splatting the potatoes on his plate with his spoon.

Ethan snorted; he was used to it. "Got to eat healthy before the game tomorrow," he said sardonically around an unpleasant bite of overcooked chicken.

"I bet your snacks are sounding pretty good right about now, huh?" Jen quipped.

Ethan noticed her pushing the food around on her plate but not eating it.

"Shouldn't you eat?" Ethan stabbed the air between them with his fork.

Jen just grinned.

"Come to my room later, and you'll see why I didn't," she said, lifting one eyebrow mischievously.

Derek and Ethan eyed her.

"I'm getting Thai food delivered once we're released from *hell,*" she said in a low voice. "There's still time to add to my order. You guys want in?"

The answer from both Ethan and Derek was an emphatic, if quiet, *yes* as they listened to Marshall's droning speech.

When they returned to their room, Derek immediately changed from his suit into a matching pajama set with rubber ducks printed on a royal blue background.

"Nice ducks, dude." Ethan's laugh was a bark, hoarse and rough from disuse, but he got it out without dying or spontaneously combusting, which was a surprise.

Derek shoved his hands in his pockets making wings and spun around quacking and waddling before strutting down the hall like it was a runway. "Thanks! The kids gave them to me for Christmas." Derek's perpetually smiling face lit up even more.

"You really love them." A statement, not a question.

"Yeah, I do." Derek shrugged. "When you don't have a blood

family, the family you build for yourself means that much more. Those kids are like nieces and nephews to me. Ivy's like a sister." He gave Ethan a side-eye when he mentioned Ivy. "Come on, let's go eat some *good* food."

When the delivery arrived, Jen placed it in the middle of the small hotel table to share it family style. It was unusual to have a meal with his teammates. Or were they friends? But it was nice not to eat alone, Ethan realized, as he swiped one of Jen's chicken satay skewers. Ethan had just opened the container of the mango sticky rice and was avoiding Jen and Derek's duel over the last dumpling when his phone vibrated in his pocket. He ignored it, probably just an automated message reminding the team about the wake-up call for the next morning.

It buzzed again.

Ethan's brows furrowed as he reached into his pocket for his phone, and it vibrated a third time. He was going to send a strongly worded email to whoever oversaw the technical stuff to *get their shit together*. Annoyed, he shoved a spoonful of mango and rice into his mouth and checked the screen.

Chunks of the food went flying as he saw who the texts were from, and he immediately choked.

> Ethan! Sorry it took so damn long to text back, my phone died again, and I couldn't find a functional charger. Mine are all broken. Anyway hi!

> Thanks again for all the stuff for Jase and for agreeing to work with him! He's so damn excited he can't stop talking about it.

> When I told him you messaged me, he freaked the fuck out.

> In a good way!

> He says hi, btw.

Ethan looked up from his phone to find Derek and Jen staring. They simultaneously jumped up and scrambled around the table, reaching for his phone. Ethan was a lot taller than Derek, but Jen was Ethan's height, so they ganged up on him, with Derek tackling him around the waist and Jen reaching high where the phone dangled out of reach.

"Got it!" Jen sang triumphantly and started reading the messages aloud. "Ethan Ford here? What, are you a scarred firebender prince who saw the error of his fiery ways?" She rolled her eyes at Ethan but kept reading. "You texted her seven times but managed to say nothing at all? Damn, dude, you've got it bad."

"Who is it? It's Ivy, isn't it?" Derek was much too excited about the new development.

"Yes, damn it, now give me the fucking phone." Ethan grabbed for it, but Jen ducked away.

"Hmm, no, I don't think so." She began typing a message, singing about trees and kissing. Derek joined in.

"Jen. We are *adults*," Ethan snapped.

"Could've fooled me." Jen laughed, waving the phone in his face. "When was the last time you had a conversation with a woman who wasn't me?"

Ethan's face burned, giving him away.

Derek was still singing, and he'd begun twirling around the room with a pillow.

"I thought so," Jen said. "I'm going to help you."

"Help me how? She just said 'hi' and 'thank you' and that's it."

"I think she likes you too," Derek piped up.

"What?" If his voice weren't so deep, Ethan would most definitely have called the sound he'd made a squeak.

"Just her reaction to seeing you last night." Derek shrugged as if it were obvious. "She went and changed out of comfy clothes because you were there. *Nobody* can get the girl out of her pj's, that's for damn sure. Except she changed her clothes when you showed up."

The world stopped spinning.

The world stopped spinning and chucked him off it.

Shit shit *shit*.

He'd shoved thoughts of her aside because he'd assumed she wasn't into him, but if she was...

But no. He couldn't afford to get close to her. Anyone. Marshall would bench him.

But texting didn't count, did it?

"Give me the goddamn phone, Jen." The growling voice was one he hadn't used since the team learned to leave him alone.

Jen scowled but handed it back.

"I'm not scared of you, Ford," she said, standing up to her full height to look him dead in the eyes.

"Good." Her statement was jolting. Ethan hadn't wanted to be the person he'd become under Marshall's influence; it had just been easier to become something he wasn't. To let himself believe it too.

Scowling, he turned and walked back to his and Derek's room, slamming the door behind him.

Tell Jase I said hi. And you don't have to keep thanking me. It was fun.

And I never have fun.

Shit, why had he said that?

I do have to thank you! I've been having such a hard time getting him to relax and open up and he's had the biggest smile on his face the past few days. if you stick around us, you'll probably have more fun than you'll know what to do with lol.

Unsure how to reply, he scrolled back to her first messages, amused to find the cursing. He'd missed it before, and he immediately fixated on the image of her pretty mouth saying the filthy words.

What did she mean by 'if you stick around us?' Did she expect him to come around a lot? What did any of it mean?

I'm happy to help.

It must be hard seeing someone you care about struggling so much.

That's sweet of you!

It has been hard, and it's harder for me because I feel like I know what he's going through more than most but I just...can't get through to him.

Ahhh sorry you don't even know me and I'm laying this heavy shit on you.

The burning anger from last night roiled through his gut again. He didn't know her full story, or Jase's, but he knew no one deserved anything like whatever they'd been through.

No, it's okay. I understand about weird childhood shit.

That sounded weird.

I don't have a great relationship with my family, is all.

Yeah I understand! I never had good relationships with the people who fostered me until I was older.

You do have that. Derek told me how you guys basically made your own family.

We'll take you in! we take all the misfits and lost ones around here.

Well thanks. Maybe I'll take you up on that. :)

Wow did you just old-school emoji me, Grandpa?

Watch it, you whippersnapper.

You can't be much younger than me, though.

I'm 26, but at least I'm hip with the emojis the youths are using these days ;)

Ethan had no idea how to respond, so he plugged his phone in and went into the bathroom to shower. By the time he returned from the tiny steam-filled room, Derek had returned and was lounging on the bed, flipping through channels.

"This is usually the part where the misogynistic, patriarchal, but supposedly good-intentioned brother says, 'She's too good for you'."

"I know," Ethan agreed, shoving his wet hair back from his face.

"But I'm not going to. I can tell you like her, and I think you might be good for each other."

Ethan's head whipped around, wet hair stinging his cheekbones and flinging droplets.

"She's sweet and I love her, but she gets too caught up in her head sometimes, you know? It's hard for her to let people help her. I'm telling you this," Derek continued, "because I think you have that in common. And I think you would be good together."

Derek was much more perceptive than Ethan gave him credit for.

But was he right?

Small hands jostled Ivy awake, and she looked up to find Jase staring down at her, his face serious and distraught.

"Ivy, the game is going to start soon. Is it cool if I use your phone to text Ethan? I want to tell him good luck." Anxiety rolled off his narrow frame in waves.

"Sure, Jase. Isn't it kind of early for a game, though?"

"The Raiders are in another time zone. It starts at twelve their time."

Huh. After the games they'd attended and the practice with Ethan, Jase had become obsessed with the Hawks, so she shouldn't have been surprised. Ivy handed Jase the phone and rolled back over. Sleep had been elusive the night before, and Ivy was loath to get up and face her day.

"I sent him a message, but your phone is almost dead. I think you need a new charger." Jase held out her phone. The plug-in bit of the charger was barely attached, and the tape she'd wrapped around it in a last-ditch effort to save the damn thing was already coming unraveled.

In the haze of being half-asleep, she reached for her phone automatically, swiping open her job-hunting app *before* her email. That was progress, right? Still nothing from the school district, but she told herself it was okay. The assistant principal was obviously a very busy person. Switching back to the job app, Ivy scrolled postings for a few minutes, pausing to peruse the same ones she'd already read a hundred times.

Ivy groaned internally as her phone dinged with a low battery alert. She needed a new charger. *Add it to the never-ending to-do list, right after finding a job and achieving self-actualization.*

Jase returned to send another message. "He said thanks!" His grin lit up the room more than the sunlight streaming through her curtains. Ivy watched him scamper off with her phone just as she remembered the last text she sent Ethan was vaguely flirty with an old-school winky face emoji. She groaned again, out loud this time.

"I'll make you coffee!" Jase called from the kitchen.

Sweet boy, she thought.

If he woke up before she did, he always set up a mug and coffee pod for her, even though at ten, he wasn't old enough to drink the coffee he made. But every time he made her coffee, Ivy's heart squeezed in affection.

The sound of her phone drew Ivy out of her bedroom to join Jase where he sat at the kitchen table, going back and forth between staring at Ivy's phone and scribbling in the program he'd gotten at the first Hawks game.

"What's that?" Ivy tapped the screen.

"It's the stats for the Raiders." Jase didn't look up from his note-taking.

"Do you want to see if we can find the game on tv?"

"Yes!" Jase jumped up and hugged Ivy, and her heart burst at the uncommon display.

When her phone vibrated where Jase had left it, Ivy picked it up and thumbed open her messages, reading the exchange between Jase and Ethan.

Hi, Ethan. It's Jase. I wanted to tell you good luck before you play the Raiders today.

Hi, Jase. Thanks! I'll try; the Raiders are pretty good this season.

Ivy snorted into her coffee over Ethan using a semicolon in a text. He'd probably even used it correctly.

Well I'm sure you'll beat them! Go Hawks!

Thanks, buddy.

Hey, tell Ivy she owes the swear jar from last night.

What?

Scrolling further back to reread their texts, Ivy saw that yes, dammit, she'd cursed a lot last night. She texted him back.

This is Ivy. I refuse to put money in the jar for swearing over text lol, but you still have three curse words left from last time.

Ivy's phone made a sad chirping sound to let her know the battery was even closer to dying, so she rummaged through the end table catch-all drawer.

"Hey, Jase, did you see my other charger?" she called when she didn't find it.

"Yeah, but it was missing the base." Jase's eyes were glued to the tv screen, watching someone talking about RBIs and stolen bases.

Maybe Lily had a spare cord.

Rustling came from Janna's room, and Ivy set out cereal and milk for her. Jase followed Janna into the kitchen while Ivy ignored the sugar content on the side of the box as she shoved a handful of the sweet, crunchy goodness into her mouth. Ivy was eternally grateful for kids who, like her, would eat anything put in front of them. Even Ivy's truly horrific cooking.

Besides, weekend mornings were for sugary cereal; everyone knew that.

When the National Anthem played over the TV, Jase jumped to attention with his hand over his heart. He'd gone into his room to grab his Hawks hat, and he held it behind his back like the players on the screen. Ivy snapped a picture of Jase with the TV showing the game in the background to send to Derek...and maybe Ethan, too, but her phone died as she pressed send, so there was no way of knowing if it made it through.

As the game progressed, Ivy found herself seeking out Ethan's tall frame on the screen. Jen and a few other players were as tall as him, but Ethan was so...broad. The camera panned over him leaping to catch a ball, and Ivy wondered how the buttons of his jersey held together as he reached up and snatched it out of the air. Beside her, Jase jumped up and cheered.

"Did you see that catch?" he yelled at her.

Ivy gulped. "Oh, um, yes." Heat flooded her as she remembered Ethan's touch on her wrist and how gentle his large, calloused hands had been on her skin.

Ivy wondered how gentle he would be if he touched her... elsewhere. And then her dreams from the night before returned in a flood of images.

Rough hands touching and teasing. Soft, full lips burning a path over her skin. A deep voice rumbling in her ear as a dark-haired man moved over her. Her cheeks burned hotter as her thighs clenched, but she silently scolded herself, wondering if it would be a mistake to let him into the life she'd built for herself and her kids.

But Ethan had been so kind to Jase, that despite how uncomfortable he seemed around her, she thought maybe...

Derek would know what to do. She should text him.

Except her fucking phone was dead, so Ivy headed upstairs

to borrow a charger. Lily answered the door and retrieved the cord with a knowing smirk.

"This isn't about the job. You're all red. What gives?" Lily asked, dangling the cord in front of Ivy's nose.

"Well..." Ivy began, "Jase was texting Ethan, and he got so excited about the game, and I thought he might want to text Ethan after the game."

"It's for Jase, huh? Damn, that's shady, blaming it on him," Lily chuckled.

"I don't know what you're talking about." Ivy looked away from her friend's dark, scrutinous eyes that saw straight through the lie.

"Uh-huh. I saw Ethan Ford, and I saw you *looking* at Ethan Ford. You looked like you wanted to climb him like a tree. He's definitely tall enough," Lily said, arching a brow.

"I do *not!* It's just that he was so sweet with Jase and Janna. But he was kind of weird around me."

"Maybe you should get to know him." Lily shot her a feral grin. "I hear a great way to do that is to—"

"Bye, Lil!" Ivy called over her shoulder as she slammed the door closed. "How's the game going?" she asked Jase as she reentered her apartment.

"It's okay, but not great. We've only got a two-point lead, and the Raiders have caught up every time we get a run." Jase didn't turn away from the screen.

"How's Derek playing?"

"Pretty good."

"And Ethan?"

Jase wouldn't read into her ulterior motives in asking about Ethan; he was Ethan's biggest fan, after all.

"Ethan's doing great! He's had a couple of good hits."

As the final inning began, Ivy took the borrowed charger into her room and plugged her phone in before plopping down on the couch beside Jase. The camera caught a good angle behind Ethan, showing again how broad his back was. He gave the bat a couple of loose practice swings, then squared up his feet and shoulders, readying himself for the first pitch. The pitch was called a strike, and Ivy held her breath as Ethan reset his feet, tapped the bat on his shoe, shook his shoulders, and lifted the bat. After a breath, he settled deeper into his stance, and not that Ivy was looking, but the camera angle perfectly caught how well those white pants fit. Her mouth went dry, and she thought about sinking her nails into his ass *without* the tight white pants. The next pitch was a foul; so was the third. The fourth went right beneath the shortstop's glove, allowing Ethan to make it to second base.

A player Ivy didn't recognize stepped up to the plate, but she stayed in her seat to watch him bat. The first baseman caught the second hit, and Jen stepped up to the plate. The camera caught her steely gaze as she rolled her shoulders before jamming the batting helmet over her platinum hair. She was a lefty, so the camera caught her face as she swung, and it was a terrifyingly beautiful thing to behold as she hit her first pitch out between center and left. Ethan made it to third; Jen made it to first. Derek batted fourth, and he hit what Jase called a sacrifice fly, allowing Jen to run to third and Ethan to make it all the way home. Ivy's excited shrieks turned to gasps of shock as she watched it happening as if in slow motion: the other catcher didn't move out of the way fast enough, and as Ethan's legs slid toward the plate, he angled his upper body, as if in an attempt to avoid the collision. It worked, barely, except the angle twisted his leg in an unnatural direction, and pain crossed his sharp features as he skidded to a stop.

He didn't stand, and Ivy pressed her hands to her mouth in horror, unable to look away from the screen.

It took a few moments for his teammates to notice since they were congratulating each other for the win and not him for scoring the winning run, which Ivy found odd. After a few seconds delay, Derek jogged toward him at the same time the umpires gathered around Ethan's prone form. A staff member jogged toward the knot of people, squatting beside him. Eventually, a stretcher appeared and EMTs loaded him on it. A cold pit formed in Ivy's stomach as she watched the stretcher carry him away.

8

I have three swear words left? How bout fuck, fuck, and fuck.

YES, PLEASE, IVY THOUGHT. *WAIT WHAT?*

It was a glorious, sunny day, flitting between spring and summer, never choosing between the two, and Ivy walked with Janna and an anxious Jase to a nearby park.

Fuck is my favorite.

Is it your favorite?

It's my favorite. I think I said that already.

You're so pretty.

What. The. Fuck. What was happening?

Are you okay? Jase and I saw you get carried off the field.

Ivy ignored the other messages he'd sent because what the hell? She hadn't known him long enough to know him well, but the man had been terrified when she'd hugged him and now, he was...flirting?

You guys watched me?

That's so nice.

You're really nice.

I'm okay. Dislocated my knee. Doctor gave me drugs before they popped it back in!

Did I say you're nice? And cute? Cause you are.

I like your freckles. And dimples.

Unsure how to respond to him, Ivy pocketed her phone and found a swing beside Jase. When she told him Ethan's injury was a dislocated knee, Jase seemed relieved it wasn't worse.

"Will he be able to play anymore?"

"I don't know. I'll ask him."

Jase wants to know if you'll be able to keep playing.

So sorry about your knee!

I think so. I'm getting an x-ray now, but I definitely can't play anymore this week.

Which fucking sucks.

Ivy texted Derek to find out what was happening.

DEREK

Derek! We watched the game! Great job! Is Ethan okay?

Yeah, he's good. A little loopy now, though.

Yeah I noticed...

A picture of Derek giving a thumbs up and a confused-looking Ethan doing the same beside him appeared on Ivy's screen.

You're so pretty!

Umm thank you?

It's Ethan.

I stole Derek's phone! He said to stop saying how nice you are. But I wanted you to know!

The bright opening notes of "Happy" by Pharrell played as Ivy's phone lit up with a FaceTime call. Ivy wasn't certain what to expect as she accepted the call.

A dark blur covered the screen, and Ivy saw glimpses of both men's faces. They were...wrestling? A flash of blonde hair crossed the screen, then both men yowled in pain as Jen yanked them apart by the ears. She squinted at the phone for a moment, and Ivy waved at the other woman.

"Behave, children." Jen's stern voice seemed to chasten the two men, but only for a second.

"Ivy!" Derek and Ethan shouted at the same time. Derek sounded exasperated and Ethan sounded...different.

Jase's ears perked up.

"Is that Ethan?" he asked.

"Yes, but he's tired, I think. He got meds for his knee." Ivy was trying not to laugh at the silent conversation Derek and Ethan were having behind Jen's head.

"Hi, Jase!" Ethan yelled.

Derek grabbed the phone from Jen, holding it in front of his face and silently laughing, pointing over his shoulder at Ethan, who was making grabby hands at the phone. "Hi, Jase! Heyyyy Ivy!" His voice deepened when he said her name. "How you doin'?"

He did *not* do the Joey at her. Ivy snorted but tried to cover it with a cough. Derek abandoned containing his laughter and nearly howled.

"Ethan! We saw the game! It was awesome! You were awesome!" Jase's excitement bubbled over as he rushed to get his words out.

"*I* got more hits than him," Derek said, sounding miffed, and Ivy couldn't resist needling him.

"But Ethan broke the tie," Ivy added with a smirk.

"But but but— *I* hit the one that got him home!" Derek spluttered, and Ivy grinned at him.

"You did well, D," she said fondly.

The screen went dark again, with a hand holding a pack of gum sliding past the camera for a few seconds until Ivy saw half of Derek and Ethan's faces.

"How was the trip?" Ivy was unsure if she should try to carry the conversation or hang up.

"Good, good," Derek said absently, trying to dodge Ethan, who was trying to hide behind him. "Ethan, what the shit!"

"It's Ivy!" Ethan said in a stage whisper. "She's so pretty!"

"Yeah, so why don't you *talk* to the pretty girl?" Derek spoke as though to a small child, and he looked simultaneously exasperated and as though he would have entirely too much fun torturing Ethan about this later.

"Nuh-uh," Ethan said.

"Derek!" Ivy hissed as she rejoined Jase and Janna near the swings.

Derek made pointed hand gestures between Ivy on the phone and Ethan behind him.

"Ethan? Are you feeling okay?" Ivy said when she got tired of trying to decipher Derek's gesturing.

Ethan's dark head slowly rose behind Derek's shoulder, and he nodded without speaking. Absently, he chewed a piece of gum, his jaw flexing, his lips falling open, the tip of his tongue poking out the tiniest bit, trying to blow a bubble.

Oh.

I'll give you somewhere to put your tongue, a voice said in her head. *Nope. Nope. Do not go there,* she told the voice. *Now is not the time.*

Derek was talking, but Ivy only had eyes for Ethan and his sinful mouth. He kept blowing bubbles, and Ivy's eyes kept returning to his lips. Ethan took a huge gulp of air, and with a look of concentration so intense his eyes nearly crossed, he blew an enormous bubble right beside Derek's ear. It popped so loudly that Derek jumped, swearing at Ethan, who doubled over giggling.

"Ivy, we're at the hotel now, so you're going to have to talk to *those two* later." Jen reappeared on the screen and jerked her thumb toward Derek and Ethan, who were grappling for the phone again.

"It's okay, my phone is going to die again, anyway." Even though she'd *just* charged it. Shit. "Bye, guys!" she trilled and ended the call.

Loud, snorting laughter erupted behind her, and Ivy nearly fell out of her swing. Lily had arrived.

"Ivy's sooo pretty!" Lily put on a mocking deep voice and pretended to swoon and fan herself.

"Shut up. Asshole." But Ivy grinned too. Medicated Ethan was... interesting, and Ivy wondered how to get him to open up without resorting to narcotics.

. . .

THE NEXT DAY, THE DOORBELL RANG RIGHT AFTER IVY SETTLED IN to eat her lunch. Naturally, she stuffed half her sandwich in her mouth before answering the door and was surprised to see a uniformed delivery driver through the peephole. Still chewing, she opened the door. The driver held up a clipboard and asked her to sign before handing her a box. Inside the box were two smaller boxes, and Ivy opened the smaller first. Inside was a portable battery charger with a solar panel. Huh. Nifty.

The second box contained five extra-long charger cords. Also useful, but odd. Her sleep-shopping was usually more random, impractical things like matching unicorn onesies for the entire family or turkey-and-dressing-flavored soda.

At the bottom of the second box lay a note.

To: Ivy

This is for you. I thought I heard you say your phone was dying again, and I wanted to be able to talk to you more and I thought if you had a better charger, it wouldn't die so much.

From: Ethan Ford

Pinching the bridge of her nose with her fingers, Ivy tried not to freak out. On the one hand, his wanting to talk to her was sweet. But on the other… it wasn't like he'd crossed a hard line, but it was so unusual. Ivy couldn't accept it.

A loud groan escaped her lips, and she clapped her hand over her mouth so she didn't wake Janna, who had fallen asleep for a rare midday nap.

Jase popped his head into the kitchen. "You okay?" He sounded worried.

"Yeah. Yeah, I'm okay."

"You don't sound okay," Jase said, coming into the room and sitting across from her.

"Well... it's kind of complicated."

"Oh." He sounded hurt and turned away.

"It's Ethan," she explained, not wanting him to feel like it was something he'd done. "He sent me a bunch of chargers. It's kind of weird, right?"

A sense of unease Ivy hadn't suffered in years resurfaced, bringing with it a multitude of other unpleasant sentiments. Gifts didn't always come with strings attached, but what if this one did?

Before Ivy began spiraling, Jase spoke. "I'm ten. Everything grownups do is weird. But Ethan is nice, and he was probably trying to be helpful." He shrugged. "Ask him about it or send it back if it bothers you."

Ivy released a pent-up breath and closed her eyes.

"You're right. He seemed a bit off yesterday."

"That was great!" Jase laughed. "He's funny. And he thinks you're pretty."

Had *everyone* heard their exchange?

"That's not a good reason to buy someone a gift." Ivy bit her lip, trying to keep the memories at bay.

Jase lifted one shoulder in another shrug.

"Ask him about it." And then he seemed finished with the conversation. "Can I look up more stats on your computer?"

"Yeah, go ahead." Ivy considered what to say to Ethan as she finished her sandwich.

Hi, Ethan. Thanks for the chargers. It was nice, but I can't keep them.

Wait, what?

You sent me phone chargers.

Ah, shit.

This is awkward. I don't remember doing it.

Those were good pain meds, huh?

Um. Should I give a blanket apology for anything else I did yesterday? Damage control?

You don't remember anything else?

Well… I'm reading my texts now. And I'm sorry if I made you uncomfortable.

The unease lying heavy in Ivy's chest since reading the note loosened slightly.

It's ok. Nobody ever calls me pretty.

It was kind of weird, but it's returnable.

Shit, I'm sorry.

It's fine! pain meds make everyone act a little weird.

I really am sorry about all of it.

I do think you're pretty, though.

But that's not how I wanted to tell you.

SHIT. But I guess now you know?

Sorry.

I think you're pretty too.

Can you do the return process and forward the label to my email so I can send it back?

I don't think anyone has ever called me pretty before.

It's true. But focus.

Your phone seems unreliable. You should keep the chargers. Think of it as a safety measure if nothing else.

I don't have the chance to buy gifts for anyone.

New pain formed in Ivy's chest at his words. Maybe...maybe it wouldn't be so bad to accept a gift. This once.

I guess the chargers are okay. thank you. is there something I can do for you?

Ivy thought of *several* things she'd like to do *to* him, but maybe she should keep those to herself.

I looked back at my account and pain-meds Ethan is right.

I would like to talk to you more. If that's okay.

It's been great texting you.

Ivy's heart broke a little more. Ethan was lonely.

I can do that.

Are you... okay?

The three little dots appeared and disappeared so many times, she put her phone down and left the room for a while.

I think I'm better since I met you.

9

"Ethan!" A voice chirped. An Indian woman in a white coat approached Ethan as he sat in a chair outside an exam room, scrolling through his messages with Ivy. "Are you ready?"

Inside the room, Dr. Chadna sanitized her hands and patted a paper-covered examination table in a silent order for Ethan to sit. Last night, he'd refused to accept the crutches Dr. Chadna had offered, so he limped over to the table and boosted himself up with a crunch of paper. He backed up so his leg was propped up enough for the doctor to roll up his sweatpants and hiss. Black and purple stained his knee, and it was swollen to more than twice its normal size. Gently, the doctor rotated his leg and poked and prodded the swelling.

"How bad is it?"

"I've had worse injuries." Ethan shrugged, avoiding the doctor's assessing gaze.

"Tough guy, huh?" Dr. Chadna stared at him for a moment before pressing down on the worst of the swelling.

Ethan jerked his leg away and resisted the urge to snap at the doctor.

"I thought so. You need to be honest with me," she said coolly, "or I can't do my job."

"Fine," Ethan grunted. "It hurts." He crossed his arms over his chest and stared at the ghastly bruise.

"Right." Dr. Chadna sounded exasperated. "I'm sending you for an MRI to be sure nothing is torn. Given your range of movement, I don't think you did any serious damage, but better safe than sorry. Ice it and stay off it, and you'll be fine to play again in a few weeks.

"But—" he started to speak, but the doctor interrupted, holding up a hand.

"No buts. If you play on your knee, the probability of severe injury increases. I'll check it again once you're back home."

Ethan scowled and shoved off the table, leaving the room and slamming the door behind him. Marshall waited, leaning back. He didn't say a word, just tapped a bent, arthritic finger on the arm of the desk chair like a king on a throne, instead of a warped old man.

"Can't play." Ethan crossed his arms over his chest. "For the next week."

"*Pathetic*." The old man spat the word like poison. It was one of his favorites.

"I dislocated my knee last night when I scored the *winning* run. Remember?" Ethan bit the words out just short of a snarl. Marshall always brought out the worst in him, all the anger he always kept pent up, but it was rare for him to speak up, no matter how angry he was.

Marshall snorted.

"Wrap it and pop a pill. Or better yet, play through the pain. You'll never get better if you can't play through it. Focus on the pain, and maybe you'll throw a half-decent game for once."

Ethan took a step forward, settling into a stance like he was bracing for a punch.

Or about to throw one.

"You'll never live up to your name. You're nothing like your father or your uncle." Marshall's voice cracked through the air like a whip.

Not many people would ever measure up to Ethan's father, a Hall-of-Fame, god-tier pitcher. And Ethan bit his tongue to keep from retorting about never wanting to be anything like his uncle.

"So, you *will* pitch tonight." Marshall sounded smug. "Or you can warm the bench for the rest of the season. Maybe I can reconsider your place on the roster if you'd prefer."

Ethan hung his head, defeated, his dark hair concealing his face as his hands clenched into fists at his sides at the command.

Slowly, he limped away, the pain shooting like fire through his leg. Every door he found, he slammed. In the locker room, he tossed his bag with a crash onto the wooden bench in the center of the room, and it tipped over, spilling its contents on the floor.

"Fuck. *Fuck*."

Half his shit rolled out of the bag, and Ethan groaned at the pain shooting through his leg as he knelt to retrieve it. He'd neglected to take the pain medication the doctor had given him the night before; it wasn't the same thing, but he didn't want to risk embarrassing himself again. How ridiculous he'd been with her flashed through his mind, and he threw his cleats onto the bench with a satisfying crash. For good measure, he slammed his batting helmet back into the bag with all the force a six-foot-three professional athlete possessed. A few slams. More like ten. Once he'd replaced everything he'd dropped, Ethan threw the offending bag into the locker he'd chosen, pulled a stretchy bandage and tape out of his pocket, and sank uneasily onto the bench to attempt to stabilize his knee.

"Need a hand?" Derek's bright voice cut through the silence in the room.

"I've got it," Ethan snapped without meaning to. Another fuckup.

"Shouldn't you be somewhere with ice on that?" Derek asked, sitting next to Ethan and pulling a bag of sunflower seeds out of his pocket before dropping a handful in his mouth.

"Coach says I'm playing." Ethan pulled his foot on the bench, rolling up the leg of his sweats. His knee was still purple and swollen to triple its usual size. Derek reached out as if to poke it. Ethan swatted Derek's hand away. "It's fine."

"Yeah, but won't you make it worse if you run on it?" Derek said around a mouthful of seeds, spraying a few shells.

"Maybe." Ethan shrugged. "Nothing I can do about it." *Why do you care,* he wanted to ask.

"*That* looks frightful." Jen entered the room and leaned on the bank of lockers opposite Ethan and Derek, holding her hand out to Derek for the bag of seeds. They were dill pickle-flavored, and Ethan was simultaneously repulsed and intrigued. He wondered if Ivy would like them. "You're playing?" Jen put a single seed at a time between her teeth, the cracks of the shells audible as she bit down.

Ethan nodded, adjusting the position of his leg before slowly wrapping the elastic bandage around it.

"That's bullshit," Jen muttered, cracking another seed between her teeth. "Has he made you play injured before?"

"Once or twice." Ethan gritted his teeth and tugged the bandage tighter.

"Really?" Derek sounded concerned.

"Yeah. It's fine." Ethan kept his head down, wrapping tape over the elastic to keep it in place.

"Ethan." Jen said his name gently. It was startling coming from her. "How many times has Marshall made you play with an injury?"

Ethan finished with the tape and pulled his pants leg down.

Gingerly, he stood and tested putting weight on his knee. It still hurt, but at least it was stable.

"Doesn't matter." He'd resigned himself to playing through anything after the second time Marshall put him back on the field immediately after an injury. He'd played with the flu once, vomiting between innings and sweating buckets with a 103 fever.

Needing to be away from their concern, Ethan limped out of the locker room in search of solitude, and when he found a place, he pressed his back to the wall and sank to the floor, unable to hold himself up any longer. In the silent, abandoned hall, he braced his hands on his knees with his head in his hands, trying to calm the roaring in his head.

On a whim, Ethan pressed the green symbol beside Ivy's name, regretting it instantly. He shouldn't bother her. But she answered before he hung up or blamed it on a butt dial.

"Hi!" Ivy's voice was warm and soothing. Did she sound excited to hear from him? When Ethan didn't immediately respond, she asked, "Did you need something?"

Shit.

"Oh, umm sorry if it's a bad time. I just...wanted to talk to someone."

"Okay! About what?"

"Literally *anything*. Just not baseball." Ethan looked up at the walls and ceiling for inspiration. Nothing. "Umm... what's your favorite food?" *Dude. You are so lame,* he thought.

"Anything!" Ivy laughed. Her laugh was champagne bubbles popping on his tongue. It was watching the Friday night fireworks at the stadium. The first rays of the sun beating down on him after months of winter. "But I *love* pasta. With lots of garlic and butter. Horrible for dates, but good for the soul." She laughed again. "But I'll eat anything that doesn't eat me first. What's your favorite?" Ivy asked.

"Huh?" Ethan was distracted thinking about dates. "Oh. I

think...spaghetti carbonara with *Pancetta* instead of *Guanciale.* Not traditional, but..."

"I don't know what any of those things are, but I bet it's *amazing*." Ivy's voice turned wistful.

"I'll make it for you. If you want."

"You COOK?" she squawked. "Marry me?"

Ethan's heart stopped beating.

"Oh shit." Was it possible to hear a blush over the phone? Ethan thought he heard the most delicious pink tinge creep over Ivy's cheeks. "I meant more like... I need a personal chef. I'm a horrible cook. Like, *so* fucking bad."

Ethan heard a yell from Jase about the jar, then rustling and a muffled retort from Ivy.

"Tell me another favorite. Dessert this time."

Ivy was silent for a few seconds, and Ethan heard birds chirping and what he thought was the creak of chains on a swing. He imagined being at the park with her family, little wisps of her hair blowing in Ivy's face as she played with Janna. Janna screeching with glee while he and Jase played catch nearby. Teaching Janna to play catch too. Stealing a kiss when the kids weren't looking.

The scene in his head was so cinematic and vivid and so heartbreakingly unattainable, he was jolted when she spoke again in his ear.

Ethan shouldn't let himself imagine her, *them*, together, but...

"You tell me yours, and I'll tell you mine," Ivy said.

Holy shit, Ethan needed to get a grip because the innocuous words sounded incredibly suggestive on her lips.

Ethan wondered if she'd said it on purpose. He hoped she had.

"Chocolate soufflé straight out of the oven with fresh whipped cream," he replied without having to think about it.

"Yes! That! That's mine too! I've never eaten chocolate soufflé, though. I tried to make whipped cream once, except it turned into butter. But we've already discussed my love of butter, so it worked out! Warm chocolate soufflé, though, mmm."

The moan Ethan had first heard her make while eating came through the speaker, and he imagined her eyes rolling back in bliss.

He wondered what it would take for Ivy to moan for him.

"I can make that for you too?" His breath caught.

"Really? I've seen the Great British Bake Off. It's tricky!"

"I took some cooking classes in college." Ethan shrugged, forgetting Ivy couldn't see him. "I like it. I don't cook much anymore because I don't like to cook just for myself. I'd cook for you, though."

"That would be nice," Ivy breathed.

Ethan wondered what her whisper would be like ghosting over his skin.

"I've got to go. Janna has to go potty."

He laughed out loud after she broke the silence.

"Of course, she does. Tell her I said hi." Ethan was disappointed to go, but duty called them both.

"Yeah! Bye, Ethan."

Was Ivy as disappointed as Ethan was?

"Bye, Ivy."

About an hour later, Ethan was in the locker room in his uniform, adjusting the wrapping on his knee when his phone buzzed a few times inside his bag.

He popped a couple of Advil and joined the rest of his teammates as they filed out onto the field for the anthem. An MRI had confirmed that there were no tears, and he'd played with worse than a sore knee. But Ethan was pissed about Marshall playing him despite the injury.

Think of the devil, and he will appear.

Angry eyes burned into the name emblazoned on Ethan's

back as he passed the old man on his way out of the dugout. Ethan ignored whatever the man whispered at him for the first time in years as he stalked toward the mound.

The first pitch flew straight down the center for a strike, and Ethan shifted his weight, trying not to injure himself further. He bit the inside of his cheek until he tasted blood, focusing on the batter. The new pain helped, but not enough. The first half of the inning passed in a blur as he concentrated on making it through to get a few moments of respite in the dugout.

Ethan made it through six more innings, but during the seventh inning stretch, Dr. Chadna stormed into the dugout and pulled him aside.

"Ford, I thought I told you not to play on that knee."

"It's fine." Ethan resettled his hat on his sweaty hair, looking past the doctor to Marshall, who'd come up behind her.

Dr. Chadna narrowed her eyes at him, glancing between Ethan and Marshall.

"You're done here. Come with me." Dr. Chadna grabbed Ethan by the front of his jersey, and with surprising strength for such a small person, dragged him toward the stairs.

"Where the hell are you going?" Marshall pushed himself between Ethan and Dr. Chadna, completely disregarding the doctor.

It was a mistake.

Dr. Chadna spun around, getting in Marshall's face, shaking her finger at him.

"You went against my orders and made Ford play after he blew out his knee. He would have been fine if he stayed off it for a few weeks, but now he's probably damaged it further."

"It's not the first time!" Derek piped up.

"Ethan's played injured before." Jen stood from her seat on the bench.

"Is this true?" Dr. Chadna's voice was low.

Marshall sputtered but no words came out.

“I’m reporting you to the League. You’ll be suspended by the end of the week. Sooner. And that’s *if* you even have a job. Now get out of my way.” Dr. Chadna shouldered past Marshall, still dragging Ethan by his jersey.

Bewildered, Ethan followed along.

“This should never have happened,” she muttered once they were in the hallway leading beneath the stadium.

Ethan coughed.

“I read your file, you know.” The doctor looked sideways at him. “I’m not sure I understand why you’re here and not with—
“

“Don’t. Please.”

“All right, all right.” Dr. Chadna raised her hands in a placating motion. “We’re getting you an ice pack, then you are going straight back to the hotel. Looks like I have several phone calls to make.” She still looked angry, but her face softened when she looked up at him. “I’m sorry you went through this, but I’m going to do everything I can to make it right. And to make sure it doesn’t happen again.”

Ethan nodded. Having someone stand up for him to Marshall left him shaken.

When Ethan was ensconced in the hotel bed with the ice pack wrapped around his knee, his phone vibrated once, again, then the screen lit up with notifications, nearly buzzing itself off the table as messages kept coming in.

Derek texted him, then Jen, and then Isaac messaged him on Facebook, and more from Derek and Jen. Ethan elected to check Instagram first; he’d see the other two in person later anyway. Emails from journalists, a text from the Hawks’ team publicist informing him of a press conference.

Ethan groaned. He didn’t feel like talking to anyone.

The phone vibrated again, and grumbling about nosy teammates, he looked at it.

Okay, so maybe he wanted to talk to one person. He

thumbed open the call.

"What the hell happened?" Ivy's voice was shrill.

Ethan spoke when she paused to take a breath.

"What do you mean?"

"Don't play dumb, Ethan."

"I should've realized Derek would rat me out."

"He was worried! And Jase showed me some articles. How often do you play when you're not supposed to?"

Her voice still held that edge of worry, and an unfamiliar warming sensation spread through his chest.

"Ivy." His voice went deeper when he said her name, and he thought he heard a gasp on her end. "I'm fine. Really. You seem upset, though."

"I am upset!" Ethan imagined Ivy crossing her arms over her chest and huffing at him. "Jase saw you on tv and freaked out about your knee. And then the cameras caught what happened with you and your coach, and we saw some woman pull you out of the dugout, and Jase was so worried you were in trouble for something because we didn't know she was the doctor. All we saw was yelling! I tried to calm him down, but he wouldn't listen. I think he wore himself out worrying so much, and he's passed out in his room now. He'll be happy to hear you're okay, though. And you really are okay?" The rant left Ivy sounding a bit breathless.

"I really am okay."

"I'm glad. I was worried, too." Her voice sounded small.

"Why are you so worried?" Ethan didn't know if he wanted to hear the answer to that question. It seemed dangerous.

"Dammit, Ford, I—"

For a moment, he wondered if he should've told her his real name. What would she think of him if he did?

"Dirty mouth, Ivy." He couldn't control the quirk of his lips or the way his voice dropped when he said her name.

Why was he so awkward? *Why*?

After a few seconds of silence, Ethan thought she'd hung up on him when—

"Oh, you have no idea." The words left Ivy's lips in a purr evoking silk sheets and silkier bare skin.

What.

WHAT.

The sound that came out of Ethan's mouth was more dying animal than grown-ass man.

"You okay over there?"

"Sorry. You were saying? About your dirty mouth?"

Ivy Johnson was going to kill him.

"Oh, I swear a lot. That's all. Why? What did *you* mean?" Her voice was too high, her words a tiny bit too fast. Ethan would have put money on her fluttering her lashes at the phone, she sounded so falsely innocent.

"Hmm... is that all?" Was he doing this? Flirting? What was happening?

"Is what all?" Ivy giggled again, and he heard a clink of glass and a pouring sound.

He couldn't help but say her name. It came out somewhere between a groan and a growl.

"Damn, your voice is so *deep*." Ivy's voice was breathy in his ear.

That gave Ethan an idea.

"Do you like my voice, Ivy?"

"Mhmm. Do you like my dirty mouth, Ethan?"

"I think you know I do, Ivy."

"Is there anything, in particular, you'd like me to do with my dirty mouth?"

Ethan's body jackknifed, and he nearly fell off the bed. The phone fell out of his shaking hand and hit the floor with a thud.

"Ethan? Ethan! What happened?" Her voice sounded far away.

Pull yourself together, dude, for fuck's suck.

SAKE.

For fuck's sake.

Oh, hell's bells and Freudian slips. He was in trouble.

He fumbled around for his phone. When he found it again, she was breathing hard in his ear.

"Are *you* okay?" he asked.

"Yep!" Her voice was overly bright again. "Just spilled some wine is all."

"Oh, okay." His voice was shaky. "So, you were saying. About your dirty mouth?"

"Do you want to find out how dirty it is, Ethan?" The words sounded like cursive script, the syllables too close together. He realized she might be a bit tipsy.

"Believe me, sweetheart, there is nothing I'd like more than to find out more about your dirty mouth. But you've been drinking, and I don't want you to regret this tomorrow. I don't want you to regret anything you do with me. Even this...whatever this is."

Ivy sighed. "Fine. You're probably right."

"I think you should get some sleep."

"Good night, Ethan," she mumbled.

He imagined her mouth curving into a sleepy smile.

"Good night, Ivy." But she'd already disconnected.

He let his head fall back against the cheap hotel headboard and sat in silence for a while, contemplating the day.

Dr. Chadna meant well, but Ethan was still only a player if he could actually play and Marshall always made sure he did just that, despite how much he belittled his supposed star pitcher.

The only silver lining to this shitshow and his throbbing leg was her. Ivy. Her laugh and that mouth. Dirty or not, Ethan let his mind wander to what he wanted to do to that mouth. The way he'd run his thumb along her plush lips or how they'd look around his—

A beep at the door whipped him back to reality, but the rest of him missed the memo, and he scrambled to adjust the thin hotel comforter over his lap, nearly toppling over again. He knew his face was red and guilty, but he'd pretend it was just from pain.

Derek dropped a bag onto the nearby desk, giving him a once-over. "Is... everything all right? You look like I caught you with your hand," Derek paused, making pointed eye contact, "in the cookie jar."

Ethan breathed a sigh of relief. He hadn't noticed.

"No. I mean—yeah. Don't worry about me, dude. I'm good." Ethan wasn't good, and it had little to do with his knee, but he had no intention of telling Derek anything about his conversation with Ivy and definitely not about the erection he was currently concealing, especially since the man's sister had caused it.

Fuck. Ethan was a mess.

"If you say so. You just look, I dunno. More uptight than normal." Derek wasn't wrong. Ethan knew his face was pinched. The vein in his forehead likely more prevalent than normal.

"Just tired. I'm gonna sleep." With that, Ethan abruptly clicked off his bedside lamp, hoping Derek might take a hint and not ask him anything else. And now that he thought about it, Ethan was tired.

So fucking tired of all of it.

Was this really what he wanted? After years of working his body past its limits, did he truly want *more* of the same? His entire career had been that way, always working through pain. But what else could he do? Because running back to his family with his tail tucked between his legs was *not* an option. So, he'd play through the pain, physical or otherwise.

Because he *should* keep going the way he always had—alone.

10

Ivy awoke to a tiny, warm body snuggled up against hers, and a headache. She cracked one eyelid to peer at Janna, whose sleep-tangled hair tickled Ivy's nose. Gently, she smoothed Janna's hair down and tucked the little girl's head under her chin. She didn't go back to sleep, but she appreciated the comfort of another person beside her, even if it wasn't quite what she'd dreamed of waking up to.

The doorbell rang, and Ivy groaned as her headache split her head in two. Dragging herself out of bed, she tucked the blanket over Janna and headed to see who the hell needed her at such an ungodly hour.

Bleary-eyed, she looked through the peephole to see a delivery driver in a bright yellow uniform, so she peeked out, hiding her faded Star Wars pajamas behind the door.

"Ivy Johnson?"

"That's me," she said hoarsely.

"Got a delivery for you from Ethan Ford." The driver handed over a large box and a cardboard drink holder.

Ivy took the box and drinks inside, and when she opened the box, she nearly swooned. Fresh-baked pastries. The scent of flaky, buttery crust and rich chocolate made her mouth water. The drinks in the carrier were marked as one coffee and two hot chocolates. Ivy was seriously considering making Ethan a real marriage offer if he sent her breakfast when they weren't even...anything.

Maybe he sent breakfast to a lot of girls, though.

But he'd remembered to send food for Jase and Janna, too.

Ugh. It was too early for her to get confused over his thoughtfulness, but she was dangerously close to embodying the heart eyes emoji.

"Guys, come here!" They trooped into the kitchen. Jase had the comforter wrapped around himself like a cape, and Janna followed, dragging a well-loved teddy bear by an ear. "Ethan sent us breakfast!" Ivy said, pulling her coffee out of the carrier and taking a small sip. It was *amazing* and exactly what she needed. She snagged two chocolate croissants out of the box and went to text Ethan, but he'd beaten her to it.

Good morning, Ivy.

I hope you don't mind, but I ordered breakfast delivery for you. I thought you might need it after last night. It's not chocolate soufflé, but it's a close second. The bakery has a pastry chef who trained in France.

ETHAN YOU SENT ME BREAKFAST?!?!! 
THANK YOU!!!

How are you feeling?

Much better now thanks to you

Umm. Sorry if I got a bit... forward last night...

Hope I didn't offend you.

Thanks again for the food! You've elevated yourself to god status to the kids.

Then Ivy muted the phone and buried it in her bag before she could thumb open the email app. Tendrils of anxiety spread down her neck, tightening in her lungs. How many days had it been? She'd lost count at this point.

Better to focus on something else instead.

Focus on something she *could* control. Like breakfast. And after that, she'd call the assistant principal. Why hadn't she thought of it before?

The croissants were lovely and flaky, with heavenly, rich chocolate. When she ventured back to the kitchen, the other pastries had been devoured, with only crumbs remaining in the box.

By the time Ivy worked up the nerve to check her phone again, she saw with a pang of disappointment she had no new notifications. Maybe she *had* scared Ethan off. Resisting the urge to go back and reread the articles she'd read about him, she pulled up the number for the school instead. A tired-sounding receptionist informed her that the school administration was in meetings all week, but if she left a message, they'd get back to her. The phone call accomplished nothing, but taking charge made her feel better. Now there were two balls in the other court, so to speak, and her hope was bolstered just enough to take the edge off the tightening knot of worry forming in her throat.

To walk off her nervous energy, Ivy took the kids to the park, remembering how Ethan said her name on the phone instead of worrying over what felt like a nonexistent job.

At the entrance to the park, Jase and Janna made a beeline for the swings, while Ivy went to the water fountain to refill her water bottle. Keeping her eye on the kids while her bottle filled, Ivy watched them crowd around a large, dark-haired man in a backward baseball cap sitting on a bench near the duck pond.

Ivy's heart stopped beating.

No. Fucking. Way.

The man turned to face her, and it *was* him.

Ethan Fucking Ford was sitting on a park bench, with Jase and Janna climbing onto the bench beside him. Ethan gave Ivy a crooked, shy smile, and oh, *God*, it did things to her.

Water trickled over her fingers and Ivy realized her water bottle was overflowing. Swearing under her breath, she twisted the cap on and slowly walked to where Ethan was talking to Jase and Janna.

"–and and and we saw you get pulled away by that lady, but we didn't know she was a doctor, and I thought you were in *trouble*!" Jase was distraught. His dark brows pulled so low, his eyes were barely visible.

"I'm fine, buddy." Ethan gestured at his wrapped knee, and Ivy's stomach twisted at the sight of the tape.

Janna settled herself on his knee and twisted her fingers in his hair. Ivy tried to gently detangle Ethan's hair from Janna's fingers because if he didn't stop her, Ivy knew from experience Janna would unintentionally pull it. Ethan's hair was every bit as soft as Ivy imagined, and for a moment, Ivy considered taking Janna's place on his lap.

"What are you doing here?" Her voice was entirely too breathless. Yes, she'd wanted to see him again, but he'd caught her off guard. And so soon after her drunken attempt at phone seduction.

Oh, *God*.

"After last night, team management gave me the week off, so I caught an early flight home. The assistant coach is taking over for the rest of the away games until the team is back here, and then whoever they hire for Marshall's replacement will start soon." Ethan's voice sounded lighter than Ivy had ever heard.

"But why are you *here*?"

"Oh." The tips of Ethan's ears and his cheekbones turned pink. "Derek told me you might be here. And I wasn't ready to go home yet. I needed time to think about...everything."

"Good!" Jase interjected. "He sucks."

"Jase!" Ivy had never heard him say anything so vehemently.

"Well, he does. And you say worse all the time, Ivy." Jase wrinkled his nose at her.

"Yes, but I'm a grown-up. You're right, though. He does suck."

Ethan huffed a laugh, turning to look at her, and Ivy realized she still had her fingers in his hair. Oops. When she removed her hand, Ethan looked disappointed.

"So, Jase, want to play catch?" Ethan pointed to a gym bag on the ground at their feet.

Of course, Jase wanted to play, so he and Ethan went to the big open field adjacent to the park while Ivy played with Janna in the sandbox. They weren't close enough to hear, but Ivy watched Jase and Ethan, and what she observed cracked something in her heart. Jase stared wide-eyed at Ethan, nodding and serious as if it was the most important thing he'd ever heard. Ethan couldn't run, but they tossed the ball back and forth, and Ivy saw how much Jase and Ethan enjoyed it. Both man and boy seemed so at ease, and watching them left her close to tears.

She swiped at her eyes for the hundredth time when she heard a familiar voice call her name. It seemed that Lily had come to join the shenanigans.

"Poison Ivy!" Lily's short, blue-black bob appeared in Ivy's vision. "*That* is Ethan Ford."

"Thank you, Lil. I hadn't noticed."

"What's he doing here?"

"Playing ball with Jase. Duh."

"And why aren't you over there with them?"

"I wasn't invited," Ivy said.

"Hmm. You're welcome, by the way."

"For what?"

Grinning evilly, Lily answered. "Oh, for casually mentioning to Derek about you wanting to date tall, dark, and bandaged over there. He might have said Ethan was flying home early, and I might have told him to tell Ethan to come here. So, you're welcome." Lily narrowed her eyes and looked between Ivy and the far-off Ethan. "Hey, what are you doing tonight?"

"Tonight? I thought about taking the kids to a movie."

"Wrong. You're going on a date." Ivy tried to speak, but Lily cut her off. "I have spoken." She held her hand up and gave Ivy a *look*.

Ivy gave her the side-eye. "Except for the part where he didn't ask me out."

Lily scoffed. "Not a problem." Another evil grin adorned Lily's face before she took off toward the field, her black hair fanning out behind her as she went.

Ivy broke out in a cold sweat, knowing exactly what the other woman was about to do.

Oddly, Lily did not go directly to Ethan. Instead, she paused to lean against a tree trunk and made a quick phone call, and Ivy wondered what could possibly require a phone call in the midst of her nefarious plans. Lily's evil grin flashed again as she jogged up to Ethan. Even from a distance, Ivy saw Ethan's emphatic, *yes*, and she couldn't hold back a smile. Lily returned with Jase and Ethan in tow, and Ivy had to turn away to hide her grin. Smirking at Ivy again, Lily herded Jase and Janna to the duck pond, abandoning Ivy and Ethan.

Alone with Ethan for the first time, it occurred to Ivy how large the man was. His muscular body completely engulfed her line of sight, and she drank in the sight of his plain black tee stretching across broad shoulders and curving over deliciously defined biceps. And his chest. Her breath hitched as she took in the outline of what was sure to be an incredible amount of muscle beneath his poor, straining shirt. Her eyes went up to the column of his throat, where she followed it up to his face, settling on his eyes. Without the hat blocking the sunlight, they turned brighter, almost amber instead of their usual deep, earthy brown. He peered down at her with a smirk on those damn kissable lips.

"So, Lily has informed me she and Derek have very generously offered to hang out with Jase and Janna tonight." Ethan's voice was a low rumble, and Ivy wanted to be closer, close enough to feel it vibrate against her skin.

"Oh, have they?"

He chuckled. "It seems Lily and Derek are practically forcing us to go out. Together. You and me. If... you want to?"

"Busybodies." Ivy scowled.

"So, you don't want to?" His shoulders sagged, and—

Oh, no, she hadn't meant—

"No! I mean, yes! I want to." She paused, searching for words.

At his sides, Ethan's hands clenched into fists, and Ivy wanted to hold them in her own. She shoved her hands in her pockets instead.

"Oh." He ran a hand through his long, dark hair, leaving it adorably disheveled. She wanted to card her fingers through it to set it right. "I haven't, ah, dated in a while. Fucking hell, Ivy. I don't know what to say."

"Ethan, would you like to go on a date with me?"

"Yes, I would."

"Good. Pick me up at seven. I'll see you then."

Ethan gazed down at her for a moment, his eyes intent on her face, a muscle ticking in his jaw. At his side, his hand twitched. Ivy's breath caught, anticipating the touch, but his hand stilled before he reached through the inch of space remaining between them, grazing his thumb over her cheekbone. Their eyes locked, and electricity coursed through Ivy's body.

Lily shoved herself between them.

"I see my plan worked!" Lily cackled and rubbed her hands together like a movie villain. "When are you picking her up?"

"Seven." Ethan didn't break eye contact, but he dropped his hand as if it burned.

"Good. She'll see you then." Lily looked at Ivy. "We've got work to do."

"Bye," Ivy breathed, still not wanting to look away.

"I'll see you later."

Lily broke their eye contact for them, tugging on Ivy's arm until she moved.

"Lovebirds. You'll have all night to make googly eyes at each other. Now, go on, Sasquatch, before I change my mind." Lily made shooing motions at Ethan, who did as he was told, waving goodbye before walking to a shiny black sports car in the parking lot.

"Lily," Ivy began, but Lily interrupted.

"Nope. I knew neither of you was going to make a move, so I did it for you. You're welcome. Let's get these two home, and then we're digging in your closet because you can*not* wear leggings and a tee on a date."

Ivy groaned. Lily was right.

"Fine. Lead the way, tiny bossy one."

Lily found a rarely worn green satin tank in the back of her closet and shoved it in Ivy's hands with a demand that Ivy wear her "butt jeans", the high-waisted skinny jeans that fit just a hair too tightly, but admittedly made her butt look incredible, and a pair of Lily's chunky-heeled shoes that were a near-perfect match to the shade of the top. After applying mascara and lip gloss, Ivy was ready about an hour early.

Waiting was...strange. Not in a bad way, but she hadn't had time to process the whole 'date' situation, and before she knew it, it was six forty-five and all the feelings that should have been spread out over the entire afternoon crashed into her all at once. Excitement and nervousness and trepidation. What if Ethan changed his mind? What if she changed her mind? What if it was terrible? What if it was amazing?

What if, what if, what if...

A small hand slipped into Ivy's, and Jase squeezed her fingers. He leaned his head against her arm, and her breath caught in an entirely different way. Affection for the sweet little boy overtook everything else, and she was grateful for him.

Janna stared up at her with eyes as big as saucers. "You look so pretty! Like a princess."

Ivy leaned down and scooped them both into a hug. "Have fun with Lily! I'll be back after you go to bed, but I'll come in and check on you, okay?" She pressed her forehead to each of theirs in turn.

Jase looked at her, biting the inside of his cheek.

"I'm coming back," Ivy whispered in his ear. "I promise."

Jase nodded solemnly, looking too old for his ten years. Ivy's heart ached for him, but he seemed happy enough with her answer.

A knock at the door, and all the air escaped the room, taking Ivy's breath with it.

Jase grinned at her and ran to open the door.

The sun was too bright and low behind him, so all she saw was Ethan's shoulders taking up the width of the door frame and his head nearly brushing its top. But then he stepped over the threshold and *holy shit*.

It occurred to Ivy that she'd only ever seen Ethan in his baseball uniform or athletic wear. Her brain short-circuited seeing him now. He wore a black button-down shirt with rolled sleeves, dark jeans, and motorcycle boots. The sleeves of his shirt molded to the outline of his muscular shoulders, and the buttons of his shirt looked like they'd split at the seams if she stared at them too long.

Janna ran at Ethan, and he gathered her up in a hug. He

limped as he carried her and looked at Ivy in bewilderment when Janna refused to climb down. Jase did a shy half-wave, telling Ethan he'd tried to practice pitching, but Ivy had forbidden it inside the apartment.

When Ethan turned to face her, she saw his eyes travel up and down her body the same way she'd drunk him in, and heat gathered in her cheeks and between her thighs.

Lily appeared and pushed Ivy and Ethan out the door with promises of hyping the kids up with sugar and scary movies and other lies.

"But," Lily said, stopping them on the way out, "I want your address and a promise nobody gets axe murdered. I don't know you, Sasquatch, so if Ivy doesn't check in at least once an hour, I'm coming for you."

"Right, uh, I'll send it to you."

Ivy was amused to note how much her tiny friend terrified enormous Ethan Ford.

Phone numbers and addresses were exchanged, and when Lily was satisfied, she roughly shoved them out the door.

"You look... incredible." His voice, as always, startled her in the best way. He reached out like he wanted to touch her but pulled his hand back.

"Thanks." Ivy laughed. "Lily practically attacked me once we got home. I'm lucky she found this in my closet, or she would have dragged me shopping." She shuddered. "You look nice too."

"Thanks." His voice was gruff like he didn't know what to do with the compliment. Shall we?" When he offered her his arm like an old-fashioned gentleman, she melted.

Placing her hand in the crook of his elbow, Ivy wanted to sneakily slide it higher to see if his biceps was as hard as it looked. But for now, she'd have to settle for the softness of his shirt, which was smooth and warm under her fingertips. She wondered if he'd like how she looked if *she* wore it.

Heat flooded her veins.

But they'd reached his shiny black car, and he opened the door for her. The interior gleamed in black and chrome, with smooth seats, their leathery scent mingling pleasantly with his cologne. He ran his hand through his hair, and it occurred to Ivy he might be as nervous as she was.

"So, I thought we'd try to cook together? Since you seemed to like the idea yesterday?" Ethan seemed unsure.

"I'll help you, but only if you give me the least important job. I am a shit cook; you can ask anyone."

His lips twitched.

"Can you boil water?" Ethan asked.

"Only on days with an 'r'."

"We'll start there."

Once he parked outside his apartment building, he raced around to open her door again, and she bit back a laugh at how hard he was trying to be a gentleman. It was so unexpected and sweet, *which sums him up in three words,* she realized.

His apartment was large and open, and very neat, with mostly black furniture and no decorations on the walls.

It was sad and cold and...lonely.

She followed him inside, leaving her purse near the door as Lily instructed, in case she needed a fast getaway. For a few seconds, she hesitated, not wanting to check her email on a date, but not able to resist the habit. She'd just silence her phone so it wouldn't be a distraction. Except, when she unlocked the screen, a tiny red dot glared at her from the email app. A rush of hope flew through her chest; usually, she didn't let herself get excited–too many disappointments taught her that lesson at a young age. But something about Ethan, maybe the possibilities of whatever was happening between them, or maybe even just...him, gave Ivy a sliver of hope.

Ms. Johnson,

I'm writing to inform you that Mrs. Niman's official retirement date is May 25th. After that time, we will review the budget and your paperwork. If we decide to move forward, someone will contact you.

J. Simpson

Ivy dropped her phone with a thunk, excitement swiftly curdling to disbelief and annoyance. They couldn't even manage a 'sincerely'? A 'best'? 'Fuck you very much'? The entirety of the email was just repeating what she'd already known, without providing the paperwork she needed, and it made Ivy want to scream in frustration.

It was fine, this was fine. She was on a *date*, for fuck's sake.

"Is something wrong?"

Shit.

Ivy squeezed her eyes closed, loosing a long, beleaguered sigh. "I've been waiting on paperwork for a job for several days, and at this point, I feel like they've changed their minds." Frustration escaped her in a dry laugh. "With budget cuts, there just aren't that many jobs available, and this is the only thing I've found. I thought it was mine but now I'm not so sure. It almost feels like betrayal."

Ethan held out a hand to help her up from where she'd knelt by her bag. "Is there anything I can do to help?"

"Not unless you know anyone on the school board."

"I don't, but I can offer a large donation with a few stipulations." He gave her a cute, crooked little grin.

"God, no." It struck her then just how different their worlds were. How different they still were. It was sweet of him to offer. "I mean, thank you, but no. It's just a waiting game now. At least I hope so. So anyway, I heard something about dinner?" She peered past him to the minimalist kitchen.

Ethan entered the kitchen and pulled two aprons out of a drawer. Ivy raised her eyebrows at him.

He grinned at her.

"I thought we'd make pasta alfredo. You said you like garlic and butter, and it only takes a few ingredients. It's really simple, but it's one of my favorites." With a few quick movements, Ethan had his apron over his head and tied around his waist, holding his hands out in an offer to tie hers. Ivy turned for him, and the feeling of his fingers brushing over her waist sent a shiver down her spine. The heat of his body behind hers was enough to send her heartbeat into outer space, and they were barely touching.

Without thinking, Ivy spun around to face Ethan while his hands remained on her waist. He twitched as if he would pull away, so she grabbed his hands and held them in place. Above her, his eyes widened as he tentatively moved his hands to bracket her hips and stroked his thumbs over her hips. Ivy took half a step back, pressing against the counter, and Ethan followed her like he couldn't let go once she'd let him touch her. He leaned forward, his hair a dark curtain framing his face. Ivy slowly reached up, afraid to spook him, and slid her fingers through his hair. For a moment, his mouth fell open, then he moved to close the distance between them.

And then Ivy's stomach growled.

11

Ethan backed away from Ivy, amazed and a little dazed she'd let him touch her.

He couldn't breathe, not when she was looking at him the same way she'd eyed her nachos. He didn't deserve it, didn't deserve *her*. He should never have agreed to the date.

But since she was already in his apartment...

"So, dinner?" he asked.

Ivy's lips formed a pout, but she nodded. Ethan leaned forward again to brush his lips against her temple and whisper in her ear, the scent of her perfume nearly making him lose himself again.

"We're making pasta. With garlic and butter."

Ivy perked back up, giving him that sunshine smile, the hints of gold in her eyes sparkling.

It didn't take Ethan long to find out Ivy really was a shit cook. First, he gave her the knife to chop fresh parsley while he peeled and chopped garlic, but when she squeezed her eyes closed before making the first cut, he put the knife aside, vowing to teach her to chop safely. Next, he put her in charge of melting the butter, but she got so distracted talking to him that she nearly let it burn. He'd been trying to explain baseball's rules to her, but he watched as her eyes slowly glazed over.

He didn't mind though; it was fun just talking to her, and he found himself continually distracted. Hence the slightly browned butter. Grating the Parmigiano Reggiano went far better than the garlic or butter, and when she thought he wasn't looking, she stole bites of cheese. When she wasn't looking, he glanced at her, taking in the sparkle of her eyes and the way she spoke with her whole body. She valiantly spread the loaf of Italian bread with butter and garlic, proclaiming that garlic bread was impossible to screw up. Finally, Ethan put Ivy in charge of boiling water for the pasta. He was mesmerized as she hopped up on the counter beside the cooking range, glass of wine in hand, and watched him stir more garlic and butter together.

"Fuck, that smells heavenly." Ivy inhaled deeply and took a tiny sip of her pink wine. Rosé was what she preferred, but when he hadn't had any, he'd opened a bottle of red and a bottle of white and mixed them, rather than see her be disappointed. The wine gods probably hated him, but Ivy didn't, so he didn't care.

"I don't know what it is about garlic and butter," Ethan tilted the pan, watching the bubbling concoction, "but it's always been one of those things that remind me of home. My mom wasn't much of a cook, but my dad was, and he cooked all the time. I used to come home after practice and smell this and..." he stopped talking.

"Oh, I'm so sorry, are they..." Ivy trailed off.

"No." He sighed. "We just don't talk anymore. Have you ever heard of Jimmy Fisher?"

"Sounds familiar, but I can't place him. Why?"

Ethan was surprised, and Ivy's lack of knowledge about his family was refreshing. Encouraging. He continued.

"He's... my dad. He pitched for the Tornadoes in the nineties." Ethan didn't look at Ivy as he whisked heavy cream into the butter and garlic. "He was inducted into the Baseball Hall of Fame a few years ago."

"How cool! Was it more like a party or just a bunch of dudes in expensive suits shaking hands? I always wonder about those sorts of things."

"I don't know. I didn't go." The sting of regret still rose inside him when he thought about it, and no matter how much he tried, he couldn't make himself forget. But they wouldn't have wanted him there anyway.

"Why not?" Her hazel eyes grew shadowed, her brows pinched. Ethan looked back at the pan as he whisked the sauce.

"It's a long story. Do you want to hear it?"

Ivy gave Ethan a long, searching look. "I do. But this sounds like a conversation to have over dinner. Let's finish this first."

"It's not my finest moment."

"If you're okay sharing with me, I'd like to hear it. I'd like to know more about you." Silently, she nodded, her eyes never leaving his.

"I think it's time to add the cheese, anyway."

The mountain of Parmigiano Reggiano slowly disappeared as Ivy sprinkled it into the sauce while Ethan stirred until it had incorporated into the creamy mixture. When Ethan pronounced the sauce done, he pulled the bread from the oven and showed her where the plates and utensils were. They loaded up plates with pasta, sauce, and bread, and he showed her out onto the balcony where he'd set up a small metal table and chairs.

Ethan chose the balcony rather than the dining area because it looked out over a park dotted with clumps of trees and a few hills sloping down to a lake. He'd never seen it until that afternoon when he had been panicking over figuring out what to do *on a fucking date*. During the panicky trip to the grocery store, and subsequently the mall because he somehow only owned a couple of suits and gym wear, he'd been wracking his brain for what to do. He'd thrown open the balcony doors for fresh air, and the green of the park had calmed him; he'd thought Ivy would appreciate the scenery.

Taking a huge, fortifying gulp of wine, Ethan decided it was best to get it over with. Let her decide if she still wanted to be around him once he'd finished.

"My mom inherited ownership of one of the largest sports agencies in the country after my grandfather died. He played baseball too before he became an agent, but things went south for him pretty quickly. Drugs and bribes. Gambling debts. When I was younger, when my dad was still playing and my mom was trying to rebuild the agency, they weren't around much. In high school, I got the chance to live with my uncle who coaches for the Tornadoes. I thought I'd have the chance to train with one of the best coaches in the country. Thought even if my parents weren't around, at least I'd be with family. And I guess I learned a lot from him, but he traveled too, with his team, so I was still on my own a lot. But when he was there, it was all training, all baseball, all the time. I barely had time to go to school, much less finish my homework or have friends."

Pausing for a breath, Ethan looked at Ivy, whose green-gold eyes were wide and sad as she listened to him, her fork forgotten in her hand. "After high school, my parents planned for me to sign with the agency, but I didn't want anyone to think I had my place handed to me because of who my parents were. I wanted to earn it. To be good enough on my own."

Not good enough. Half the player your father was. Ethan had to fight to push Marshall's voice out of his head.

"Before all that, though, Marshall found me through a scouting program and started trying to recruit me early. He kept in touch, coming to some of my college games too. Halfway through my sophomore year, when Marshall offered me a place with the Hawks, it sounded amazing. Like everything I wanted. Going straight to the big leagues without playing my way through the minors." Ethan let out a laugh devoid of mirth. "But when I told my parents about the deal, they said it sounded too good to be true and Marshall had a bad reputation in the League. But I didn't care because it was all I'd ever wanted. They wouldn't even try to listen; they tried to shove me in the direction they'd chosen when I graduated. My dad and I...well...I regret the fight now, but I stand by not wanting anything handed to me. They didn't understand, so I got the fuck out and signed with Marshall to play for the Hawks.

"Once I'd signed the contract, Marshall was completely different. Always telling me I was worthless. He wrote into my contract that I'd play center field, even though I'd pitched my entire career. My first season was rough. I had to pivot to the outfield but still keep up with the pitchers, 'just in case', Marshall always said. He threatened to break my contract constantly, pushed me to get into fights...

"But I didn't question it. I have been lately, though. All the injuries he made me play through and the way he talked to me... Always telling me I wasn't good enough, how I'd never make it ... Now, I think his hiring me was some misguided revenge against my uncle. And maybe the agency. Marshall and Lawrence played together in the minors and had some weird rivalry, and the agency didn't sign him. I think Marshall blames my family for keeping him from getting further in his career."

Ethan trailed off, realizing he'd probably spoken more in the past twenty minutes than he had in a year. Longer.

A sniffle sounded from Ivy's direction. She wasn't crying, but her eyes were lined with unshed tears.

"I'm sorry," she whispered, looking away. "I understand your issues with them. But for me, it was the other way around. My mother left me outside a hospital when I was little–three– I think. I have vague memories of my mom, or maybe they're dreams. I don't know. I don't know if she didn't want me, or couldn't take care of me, or..." With a huge gulp of air, like she was preparing herself, she continued.

"Anyway, once it was clear to the authorities she wasn't coming back, I became a ward of the state, and I bounced around the system for a few years, then I wound up in a group home."

Ivy paused to take a breath and a sip of wine, and Ethan had to stop himself from smashing his glass after hearing her story.

"Anyway. Enough about me. I understand why you don't want to see your uncle. He sounds terrible. But your parents—" her voice cracked. "Did they know how he treated you? Were they that hard on you too?"

"No, they were never like him. They weren't around much, but they never pushed me past my limits the way Lawrence did. Or Marshall. My dad used to call Lawrence a crackpot sometimes, but the teams he coached always won, so I never questioned his methods. I thought I had to do what he said to win."

"What do you think they would have done if they'd known? Would they have made you stay?"

"I don't know. I don't think so, but it's been so long, and I never thought of it that way. Hell, I assumed they knew. But what if they didn't?"

For a moment, Ethan sat there, staring blankly into his glass. Would things have been different if his parents had known?

"Hearing you chose to leave... well I guess I understand why, but at the same time, I don't." Ivy continued, draining her glass.

"Ivy." Her name cracked out of his lips. He'd upset her, and he hated it.

A tear fell, dripping onto her cheek and leaving a silvery trail over her freckled cheek.

The table was small enough for Ethan to reach out and

touch her, to cross the space between them and take one of her hands in his. With the other, he swiped his thumb along her cheekbone, erasing the track of the tear, nearly losing himself in the warm hazel of her eyes.

Finally remembering her food, Ivy picked up her fork. Ethan watched anxiously as she took the first bite, gratification and something else flooding through him as she closed her eyes in ecstasy. Ethan wanted to watch her eat and let himself enjoy her enjoyment of the food, but he didn't want *his* stomach growling later and interrupting. Ethan tried to enjoy his food as much as Ivy relished hers, but he didn't think he had ever appreciated anything as much as she did her pasta. Enraptured, he watched her as she ate. He caught her eyeing his bread, so he wordlessly handed it to her, and she swiped it over her plate, soaking up the remaining tiny droplets of sauce.

"Do you want dessert?"

The gold flecks in her eyes sparkled even brighter.

"Always." She took a sip of her wine and gazed at him over the rim of the glass. Her excitement lit the visible portion of her face like a spark.

"I didn't have time to make anything, but I thought, if you wanted, we can... go out and find something?"

"Yes! Let's do it." Ivy was so enthusiastic, Ethan forgot to be nervous during the whole dinner, even when he was baring his soul.

Before they left, Ivy sent her second check-in text to Lily, and after a few moments, she made an exasperated sound. Ethan glanced at her as a deep blush stained her cheeks.

"Everything okay?" he asked.

Ivy bit her lip.

Ethan wanted to bite it for her.

"Oh, yeah, it's just Lily...being Lily."

"How so?"

Ivy let out an amused, if exasperated, breath. "Lily asked if we— and these are her words, by the way— but she asked if we'd," she paused, and Ethan glanced at her again. Her cheeks were redder, and she'd squeezed her eyes closed. "She asked which base we'd gotten to. She says she hopes at least second, but she's hoping for a home run."

"Wow. She sounds...fun?"

"She is." Ivy chuckled. "She has no filter."

"It must be nice having a friend looking out for you."

"She might be looking out a bit *too* much."

"What did you tell her?"

"I told her to mind her own business, which, in retrospect, means she'll ask about it *more*. I should've lied and said yes."

Ethan's face grew hot, thinking about...*bases*.

When they burst out laughing at the same time, he realized she'd had the same thought.

As Ethan drove to a nearby bakery, Ivy asked him about his favorite music, movies, and tv shows while he navigated the river district. Ethan had a raging sweet tooth he rarely indulged because eating dessert alone was like drinking alone: both were better when enjoyed with other people.

A heavenly scent wafted through the air when they pushed open the bakery doors, and Ivy bounced on the balls of her feet in excitement. Ethan nearly did the same; it smelled that good.

"It's kind of cold in here, don't you think?" Ivy shivered, and without thinking, he held his arm out. With a grateful look, she pressed herself against his side, aligning her body with his. *Don't look down, don't look down, do not look down her shirt,* he had to remind himself, because he was still only a man. The softness of Ivy's body pressed against the hardness of his, and he couldn't think about it, or he'd have her pushed up against a bakery case feeling just how soft she was. But then Ivy reached up to twine her fingers with his. Their joined hands drew his eye like a moth to a flame, and how well her hand fit in his did *something* to him. Ivy pressed her cheek to his shoulder and smiled up at him, and Ethan didn't know if he'd rather drown in her eyes or the hollows of her dimples. In his distraction, he mutely pointed at several random desserts in the cases and walked out of the shop with no idea what was in the box.

"It's so nice out. Let's walk down to the river." As they strolled along the water, she pointed out things he never would have noticed on his own: a couple swinging a toddler between them. Unusually bright coral-colored flowers dotting the riverbank. Several bench-style swings at regular intervals along the sidewalk. She brought him to one, sitting and tucking one foot under herself, gently pushing the swing with the other.

Ivy opened the bakery box and contemplated the assortment of tiny desserts. It seemed like she didn't know where to start. When she turned her face up to his, the fairy lights along the riverwalk sparkled like stars reflected in her eyes.

"Let's start with this one." Ethan pointed at random, unable to break eye contact until she did it first, stabbing her fork into a creamy white custard dotted with fruit. She brought it to her mouth but paused halfway when she saw how closely Ethan was watching her.

"What? Is there something on my face?"

Ethan's cheeks and ears burst into flame.

"Sorry." He ran his fingers through his hair and bit the inside of his cheek. "I— umm. You make a little moaning sound when you eat. It's cute."

Ivy ducked her head, letting her hair fall forward to hide her face.

"Wow. Okay. I guess you shared, so it's my turn now." A long exhale sent tendrils of hair flying. "I *love* trying new foods. It's my favorite. I told you about the group home. It... wasn't great. It was too full, and sometimes..." She paused again, longer. Her eyes went glassy, probably getting lost in old, painful memories. "Most of the time, it was okay. We didn't get much variety, definitely nothing special." The tip of her finger rested on the glossy green bakery box. Another deep exhale. "Sometimes there wasn't enough for all of us, so some nights I just didn't go home. Someone at school figured out I was living in the locker room and library and reported me. They labeled me as 'troubled'. I never did drugs or slept around, but I can see why some of the others did. Taking control of your life the only way you can, you know?"

Ethan could relate to that, taking control in whatever minuscule ways you could when everything else was in someone else's hands. "Yeah. I get that."

"I was almost sent to a halfway house for juvenile delinquents, but a spot opened up in another foster home, with a lady who had a good track record with 'troubled kids'." Ivy paused, letting out a sardonic bark of a laugh. But then she gave a real smile, erasing some of the sadness in her eyes. "Maya. She was so *different*. So amazing. The day she picked me up, she handed me a backpack full of little things. Things you wouldn't think twice of unless you'd never had them. And I hadn't. She gave me snacks, like Oreos and chips, and she made sure I knew they were for me. *Only for me*." Her voice wobbled. "A pack of gum, toiletries with nice scents, not just bars of the cheapest soap at the supermarket. And tampons." Ivy paused again, meeting his eyes and smiling. Ethan remembered the day they'd met when her bag had spilled. Her story explained so much about her, and it sent a pang through him how much she'd struggled at such a young age. "So, anyway, Maya picked me up, let me choose a restaurant, and told me to eat whatever I wanted. I was so nervous and excited, I just pointed at the menu, and it ended up being ham and pineapple pizza. Maya gave me the same horrified look you're giving me now. But she let me get it anyway and brought me home. I still get it sometimes, just to remember."

"I'm sorry, I didn't know. About any of it."

Tears turned her eyes silvery again, but at least they didn't fall. Ethan didn't think he could bear it if she cried again.

"Of course, you didn't." Ivy's smile was watery. "It's okay, now. It was a long time ago."

"Still. I wish there was something I could do. Kids don't deserve that." His hands clenched around the box he held, crushing the cardboard with a loud crunch.

"Oh!" She gave a little cry, her body jerking back.

Shit, he'd scared her.

"Ivy, I'm sorry. Maybe we should go." He began to close the box and gather their forks, but her hand on his stopped him.

"Okay, we can go if you want. But why?" She looked concerned and...sad?

"I can't do this," and it sounded anguished, even to him. "I can't not be angry over what happened to you, and to your kids. I can't fix it, and I scared you, and I'm sorry. So, if you want to go, I understand."

"It's not your fault." Her voice was gentle.

"But I still wish I could help."

"No. Ethan, what happened to *you* isn't your fault."

Inside, Ethan was reeling, but he tried to keep his face neutral. He'd never considered that before, but after a moment's consideration, he realized she was *right*.

"Ethan." Her voice was even. "Look at me." He hadn't heard her be commanding before, and his eyes snapped to hers. "What happened, happened. I learned from the past, and I moved on. And I'm here with you, now. You can move on, too." Ivy stared intently into his face. She squeezed his hands in emphasis, sliding her fingers between his.

She was right.

He needed to let the past die.

"I'm sorry," he said again.

"Ethan, it's *okay*. I'm okay. Now, will you eat this with me?"

She held up her fork with a bite of the fluffy-looking dessert in front of his face.

They ate more of the desserts and talked about college. She told him how she'd graduated from Central University and had then gone on to complete a master's degree in biology last December. She explained more about the job she'd told him about, telling him how worried she was, and what would happen if she didn't get it.

"I keep checking my email, waiting for the update that must not be coming." When she reached into her pocket and came up empty, the delicate arches of her brows pinched together, forming a crease in the center of her forehead.

Ethan wished there was some way he could help, but what could he do short of paying off the board? He had a feeling she'd hate that solution.

"Anyway." She pointed her fork at the box. A single truffle remained. "You have it," Ivy said. "I probably ate more than you, anyway."

Ethan broke the truffle in half and held it out to her, expecting her to take it from his hand.

Instead, she leaned forward and let him place it in her mouth, her lips barely brushing his fingertips, and then she moaned, keeping full eye contact. She arched an eyebrow at him and smiled when she'd finished the chocolate, the pink tip of her tongue flicking out to lick her lips. Ethan's blood turned to fire in his veins.

"Will you be okay if we walk more? It's so pretty with the lights on the water."

The fairy lights strung on either side of the river sparkled on its surface and made her skin glow.

"Yeah, pretty." But he was looking at her, not the water.

A delicate blush swept across the apples of her cheeks as she eased off the bench and offered her hand. His laughter—

light and unexpected— rang out through the night air when she tried to pull his oversized frame to his feet.

The moment was perfect until she rose on tiptoes and brushed a kiss on his cheek, and Ethan wondered what could be past perfect. Was it possible to implode from how *good* it felt? As they strolled along, fingers interlaced, Ethan nearly forgot about his injured knee, though she hadn't. He nearly forgot about anything that wasn't her.

After Ivy declared Ethan walked enough, he drove them back to his apartment. He'd planned to take her straight home, but she left her phone at his place. She apologized a hundred times, but Ethan chose to think of it as a sign. Because he enjoyed being with Ivy. And he didn't want the night to end.

Ethan Ford having fun with a woman. Who would've thought?

And then her words about moving on came back to him.

"Ivy," he said while they were stopped at the red light nearest his apartment.

"Hmm," she said dreamily. She rested her chin in her hand, leaning her head against the window.

"My real name is Ethan Fisher."

"Fisher? Not Ford?"

"Yeah. Ethan Fisher."

"Is this a Marshall thing?" Her nose crinkled in confusion.

"Yeah." Ethan ran his right hand through his hair, driving one-handed with his left arm braced against the door. "Yeah, he said if I wanted to earn my place, I had to make my own name. Literally. So, I became Ethan Ford."

"I like Ethan Fisher better." She looked at him with big sad eyes and reached over to take his hand where he'd laid it on the center console. "Ethan. Ethan Fisher." She said it a few more times, and hearing his name, his *real* name on her lips loosened something inside him he hadn't realized he'd locked away. "Thank you for telling me."

"I wanted you to know, in case this—" he trailed off, not willing to finish that thought. "But I don't know if I'm ready for the rest of the world to know. Who I am, I mean. The team might be weird about it." Ivy gripped his hand tighter.

"Okay, *Fisher.* I'll be sure not to tell anyone, *Ethan Fisher.*" She chuckled. "Where did Ethan Ford come from anyway?"

"You're going to laugh."

"I might not. Okay, I probably will. But come on, tell me anyway." Ivy jabbed him in the arm with a finger, then winced and shook her hand.

"Fine." Ethan rubbed the back of his neck. "My dad had an old sixty-six Mustang we'd tinker with sometimes, and it was the first thing I thought of when Marshall told me to choose a new name." He didn't look at Ivy as he spoke. It'd been years since he'd thought of that car. "My name was almost Ethan Mustang."

"You're not serious."

"No, I'm not."

She doubled over in laughter, her forehead nearly resting on her thighs. It felt so *good*, knowing he'd been the one to make her laugh.

"It's not *that* funny." Ethan scowled.

"It kind of is, I mean, it's on your *jersey*. It's in programs and shows up on the giant screen. And you named yourself after a *car*?"

"Okay, fine. It's a little funny." He still scowled half-heartedly as he pulled into his parking space in the apartment's garage, put the car in park, and turned to look at Ivy.

Wide, blazing, hazel eyes stared into Ethan's as she slowly unhooked her seatbelt and leaned toward him. Her face was a breath away from his as she reached with both hands and slid her fingers through his hair. She cupped his face, her thumbs tracing lightly over his cheekbones. Gently, she pulled his face to meet hers and pressed her lips to his. He tried to restrain himself, he really fucking did, but she was so warm and soft when he ran his hands down her neck and over the soft skin of her shoulders that he slid his hands to her waist to hoist her over the console into his lap.

Instantly, Ivy moved closer, pressing her body into Ethan's, chasing his lips when he backed away to look down at her. Too gently, he pressed his lips back to hers, and seeming to want more, Ivy gripped his hair to keep him in place as she ran her other hand up his chest. He made a sound deep in his throat, and he didn't know if it was a groan or a plea, but *oh god* she was everything he needed her to be, and he needed more of her.

His hands sank into her hair and wrapped around her nape as she molded the softness of her body to the hard angles of his. Without breaking the kiss, she moved to bracket his thighs with hers, and with her on his lap, they were the same height. It was nice, he thought, being on even ground with her. A soft sound escaped her, and taking it as encouragement, Ethan slid his tongue along hers. She sighed as she opened for him. His tongue swept into her mouth, devouring her, and she gave it right back to him, her tongue dancing with his.

Ivy tasted like wine and chocolate. Kissing her was watching the fireworks after scoring a winning run on the Fourth of July. Kissing her was the scene in *The Sandlot* where the night sky was lit only with stars and sparks, and the whole neighborhood watched in wonder.

Shifting again, Ivy's legs eased further apart as she leaned closer to fist one hand in his hair and trace the other down his chest. Heat radiated from her center as she molded her upper body into his, and he let his hips rock against her. She gasped his name against his lips, so he did it again.

He slipped his hands beneath the green silk of her shirt, slowly tracing his fingertips up her back, feeling the smooth softness of her skin under his calloused hands. Reluctantly, he removed his lips from hers and kissed the soft spot behind her jaw, then nipped his way down her neck to suck a bruise below her collarbone. He groaned her name.

"Ethan," she breathed as she ground against him again.

He backed away for a moment, and she leaned forward with him like she didn't want to lose contact.

"Is this okay? Can I—" he brushed his fingers along the lace resting over the tops of her breasts. She shivered and nodded.

"Ivy, I need to hear you say it."

"If you're going to make me say it, you have to say it too," Ivy purred, peering at him through her lashes.

"Say what?"

"What do you *want*, Ethan?"

Fuck, that's hot.

"I want," he nipped at her jaw, "to see you." He kissed his way down her throat. "I want to touch you. Please, Ivy." Ethan nuzzled at her collarbone, unable to pull away.

"Such a gentleman." She laughed in his ear, her breath sending even more blood rushing south. "You can, but only if I can too."

Ethan only had enough control over his body to nod.

Reaching between them, Ivy began unbuttoning his shirt, slipping her fingers beneath the fabric as she worked her way down. His hands rested on her upper arms, his thumbs sliding beneath the thin straps of her top. With movements so slow they were painful, Ethan gently pushed the straps over the curve of her shoulders. When they fell around her arms, she impatiently opened the final button on his shirt before tugging her top lower, giving him a soft, vulnerable look as she did.

And holy shit.

Warm, soft breasts that looked like they would fit perfectly in his palms came into view, and a soft moan escaped her lips as he swiped a thumb over a rosy nipple. Perfect couldn't describe what she was. *Marvelous, stupendous, divine,* his brain helpfully supplied. *Shut UP,* he told his brain.

Ivy's hands found his chest, and she traced over his pectorals with a feather-light touch, pushing apart the sides of his shirt.

"Damn, Ethan. You're, like, a statue or something."

He huffed a laugh in her ear, preening at her praise.

"And you're so beautiful. So perfect. Such pretty..." It was probably best not to call them tits, right? But they were so perfect. He should at least *try* to be respectful. "Breasts."

Shit. Stay focused.

Ethan leaned forward, kissing his way from her collarbone to the tip of her breast where he swirled his tongue around her nipple before pulling it into his mouth and tugging lightly with his teeth. Her body arched against his, her hips grinding against his aching length, which he tried desperately to ignore.

He was about to repeat the movement when headlights illuminated the garage, and Ethan wrapped his arms over her back, crushing her body to his to hide her semi-naked state from whichever of his neighbors chose *right now* to return home. Ivy was shaking beneath his arms, and her heart hammered against his chest. When the other car's lights dimmed and its driver's shadow disappeared, Ethan relaxed, and Ivy sat back. Hastily, he pulled her shirt back up before they had another mishap.

"Oh, hell, we're like a couple of teenagers. The windows are even fogged up." Ivy laughed so hard tears ran from the corners of her eyes.

"We should probably get you home before Lily comes after me."

"She would, too. It's been a while since I checked in."

"Lily is kind of terrifying."

"It's what makes her such a great friend."

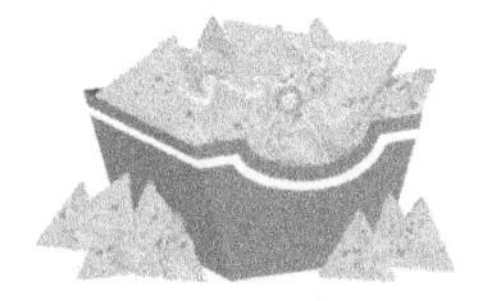

The living room was lit by the glow of the TV, and Lily and Jase were sitting on the sofa when Ivy opened her front door. Janna must have already fallen asleep.

"You're back!" Jase cried and ran to wrap his arms around Ivy. She was surprised; he usually wasn't so affectionate.

"I told you I'd come back," she whispered, squeezing him. "Go to bed, okay? I'll come to tuck you in in a minute."

Lily's eyebrows rose as she took in Ivy's rumpled appearance, but she waited until Jase was in his room before speaking.

"Looks like you had fun." Lily's eyes flicked from Ivy's messy hair to her swollen lips to the mark below her collarbone.

"A little," Ivy said primly.

"Spill," Lily commanded.

Flopping onto the threadbare couch, Ivy removed the shoes she'd borrowed and tucked her sore feet beneath a throw pillow.

"Well, between the two of us, we have enough problems to fill a psych textbook, but Lily, he's so... sweet. I mean, I knew after how he was with Jase, but he asked—" Ivy paused, realizing she'd said more than she meant to.

Lily rolled her eyes.

"We're all adults here, ma'am."

"He asked to touch me, *and* he said breasts instead of... whatever else you would call them. Who *does* that?"

"Respectful groping. What a gentleman," Lily said in an

overly dramatic rendition of a Southern belle, clutching imaginary pearls at her throat. "But get to the good stuff!"

"That *is* the good stuff. We didn't get past the groping. We were in the car like teenagers, and one of his neighbors almost saw me without my top. It killed the mood."

"Hmm," Lily hummed. "I'm going to need details when you actually do the deed! You have to tell me all about his enormous monster cock."

"Lil! Monster cock? Really?" From what she'd felt, Lily wasn't far off with her assumption, but she didn't need to know that.

Lily waggled her eyebrows suggestively. "I've seen the man, and he has to be packing. Right?" When Ivy didn't answer, Lily gave her an evil grin. "Busted. Be sure to remember all the details when you see it, so you can tell me, okay?"

"Damn it, Lily, I am not telling you anything about anything, monster-sized or not. Go home and charge your vibrator." Ivy shooed her friend out and went to bed, dreaming of hard muscles and soft lips against her skin.

12

Three weeks later, Ethan grew tired of the endless meetings and reviews and physical therapists. He'd been on the injured list for almost a month and was itching to play again. Too long with nothing to do, he'd been bored out of his mind, spending entirely too much time thinking of Ivy and trying to ignore the apprehension that trickled through his nerves at being off the field so long.

He regretted not being able to see Ivy more than the handful of times she'd brought Jase and Janna to Hawks games. They'd watched the Friday fireworks together, and because he was free to do what he wanted, he flapped their blanket down right in the middle of the grass and held her hand as the lights went out. But it'd been a few days since he'd seen her, so he invited her and the kids to the park near his apartment. Her response was a photo of Jase with an enormous smile, his Hawks hat jammed on his head, with two thumbs up. It warmed his heart to see the boy so excited. He still didn't know what Jase's life was like before he'd been placed with Ivy, wasn't sure if he wanted to know, but she was right. Nothing he did would change the past, but he would do *everything* to help right now.

On Friday night, Ethan couldn't sleep. The warmth of Ivy's body and the vision of her tugging her top down for him plagued him since their date, and he felt blood rushing south in appreciation at the memory. Mentally, he slapped himself and ducked into a frigid shower to stop torturing himself over her.

In the back of his mind, Marshall's voice told him to stay away, but as he found himself doing more and more lately, Ethan ignored it.

After their soul-baring conversations, Ethan was amazed when Ivy stayed, much less allowing him to touch her.

Rolling his eyes at the euphemism, he realized they'd gotten to second base, and her reactions to him clearly indicated she wanted him. She'd made the first move for fuck's sake, but whatever evil seeds Marshall planted in Ethan's mind took root, telling him they couldn't be together, and he didn't deserve a relationship—didn't deserve to be happy.

With Marshall out of the picture, though, Ethan found himself reevaluating his life and his priorities.

Were his dreams ever his own, or were they Marshall's all along?

The old man's claws dug into Ethan's mind longer and deeper than Ethan realized, but the damage was done. Now, those scars needed to heal.

If he asked Ivy, Ethan knew what she would say. She'd say he needed to figure out what he wanted. She'd say he should contact his family, to see where they all stood, and maybe repair the relationship, if one still existed. Either way, at least he'd *know* and be able to move on.

Would they even want to speak with him, let him be in their lives again? Those bridges were burned.

Weren't they?

The vibrating of his phone pulled Ethan from his brooding.

> Lil it's shark week and I am HORNY and DYING

Can you like throw some chocolate down the stairs?

Shark week? Wasn't Shark Week in August? And she wanted chocolate?

Oh. *Oh.*

Ethan responded to the text she'd meant to send Lily saying he'd be over in half an hour to deliver chocolate. After racing through the aisles of the nearest supermarket, he found himself outside Ivy's door with an armload of bags. She looked beautiful as always, but also tired and wan. Dark half-moons colored the skin beneath her eyes, and she was pale and wobbly on her feet. Tendrils of hair stuck out from her loose bun, and an oversized hoodie hung halfway down her thighs with duck-printed pajamas beneath. A sweet smile curved across her lips, but it turned watery when she saw the bags in his hands.

"You brought all this for me?" Her lower lip trembled.

"Of course, I did, sweetheart. I wasn't sure what you wanted, so I brought a little bit of everything."

Ivy threw her arms around Ethan, nearly knocking him to the ground, then she backed up and doubled over with her hands pressed to her lower abdomen. Ethan immediately dropped the bags and knelt with her.

"You are clearly not okay. Can I do anything?" He was at a complete loss; her pain worried him.

Air hissed slowly through her clenched teeth. "I just need to get back to bed," she groaned, curling up even more.

Looping one arm behind Ivy's back and one beneath her knees, Ethan scooped her up in a bridal carry, maneuvering them down the hallway. Gently, he placed her on the bed and her arms squeezed him tighter before she whimpered and curled up again.

"What do you want first? Pizza?"

"Ice cream. Please?" Squeezing her eyes closed, she tugged the blankets up to her chin.

When he returned with an armload of snacks, she'd abandoned the blankets and removed the oversized sweatshirt, leaving her only in a soft bralette and her duck pajama bottoms.

"Is it always this bad?" Ethan asked as he handed over the food.

Before speaking, she took an enormous bite of the cinnamon-and-sugar-coated pretzel and patted the other side of her bed. Ethan froze, eyebrows raised. Still chewing, Ivy rolled her eyes and smacked the bed harder, so he toed off his shoes and slid onto the bed beside her, leaning on the headboard and staying on his side.

"It's not always *this* bad." Ivy sighed. "I didn't get my period until I was seventeen, and now I guess it's like my body wants to make up for lost time. I never know when it's coming, and sometimes I'm okay, but sometimes it feels like I'm dying." She began spooning ice cream into her mouth at an alarming rate.

"Is there anything else I can do?" Ethan asked, both awed and frightened at the rate at which she was consuming the ice cream.

"It's nice not being alone." Her voice was small as stared up at him from beneath her lashes.

"You're not alone now. I'm here."

That elicited a smile, then Ivy went back to the ice cream. When she'd finished, she looked down at the empty pint cup, her brows furrowed and lips turning down.

"I didn't offer you any," she said sadly, dropping the empty cup and spoon on her nightstand.

"I brought more," he whispered into her ear in a seductive voice.

"And that, Ethan Fucking Fisher, just earned you infinite brownie points."

"My middle name is technically Cable, but I like fucking better."

He was proud of the double entendre, but she scoffed at it.

"I bet you do. But Cable? Where did that come from?" She nudged him with an elbow.

"My mom is a film nerd. She dresses up like Princess Leia every Halloween. Or she used to..."

He paused, remembering the white dress and silly cinnamon bun wig. He'd dressed up as Chewbacca with her for more years than he cared to remember. He scraped his hand through the short hair on the back of his neck, conflicted. They were good memories, but reliving them felt like prodding a bruise.

"And Cable...?" Ivy prompted.

"It was supposed to be Caleb, but the day I was born, my mom was, understandably, exhausted after she had me. I broke some hospital records."

Glancing down the length of his body, Ivy nodded, unsurprised.

"Mom said she'd been watching the Empire Strikes Back when her water broke, during the scene on Hoth with the big walker things? Anyway, she said that scene kind of got stuck in her head, and when it came time for Dad to cut the umbilical cord, she yelled 'cable detach' like they did when they were tripping the walkers. And then she misspelled Caleb on my birth certificate. Dad thought it was so funny, he didn't tell her until later. He joked I should be glad they didn't name me Chewbacca instead."

"I *love* it! That's the corniest, cutest thing I've ever heard!"

"It's ridiculous."

"Yeah, but it's sweet. I don't even know if I have a middle name." With her eyes downcast, she toyed with the edge of her sea-green sheets. "I thought about trying to find it, but then it seemed pointless."

"Don't be sad, you could have a stupid one like Cable." Ethan bumped her with a shoulder.

Easing forward, Ivy moved until their faces were only a breath apart, slid her fingers into his hair, and slanted her lips over his, evacuating any traces of lingering anguish. Her upper body pressed against his, and she held him with surprisingly strong arms. She rained soft kisses to the corner of his mouth, along the line of his jaw, and Ethan wrapped his arms around her, needing her closer to him. Sighing, Ivy pressed her lips to his again and ran her fingers through his hair, tugging lightly and making a soft, pleased sound when he kneaded his hands into the tense muscles of her lower back. Her tongue slid against his, sweet like ice cream, and it was *everything.*

She was everything.

When Ivy leaned back to look at him, her eyes went dark, the green-gold halo of her irises nearly eclipsed by her pupils. His breath caught in his throat as she reached to hook her thumbs beneath the band of her bra—

And promptly doubled over, nearly smacking their foreheads in the process as she groaned and wrapped her arms around herself. Shivering, she rolled off him and folded her body around a pillow.

"Do you want me to leave?" Ethan asked.

"No! Can you," and then she mumbled under her breath, too low for Ethan to hear.

"Anything. What do you need?"

"Can you just hold me?"

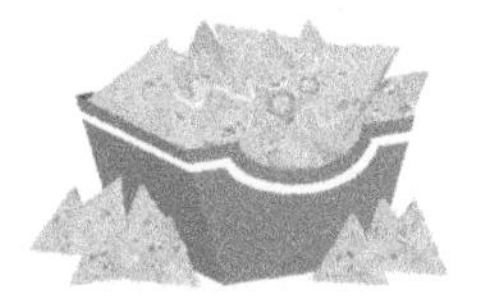

Tears pricked Ivy's lids again; she couldn't believe Ethan came over for her. No, that was believable. It was unbelievable that she'd *asked* him to stay when she was like this. Helpless. Miserable. *Needy*.

Groaning as the pain in her uterus tore through her with a wave of nausea, Ivy snuggled into the circle of Ethan's arms as he settled deeper in her nest of pillows. He was so *warm*. She tucked her head under his chin as he pulled her against his chest. He wrapped his arms around her and *damn he smells good,* she thought.

Ethan's cologne was sweet and salty and a bit citrusy, like golden sunshine and cerulean waves. Ivy nuzzled her face against his neck, letting out a long exhale, enjoying the closeness, and Ethan's body relaxed against hers.

"Ethan?"

"Yeah?"

"Thanks." Her voice sounded small.

"What for?"

Tipping her head back, Ivy gazed into his dark eyes.

"Everything? Bringing me food? Staying with me?"

His arms tightened around her.

"I do things for you because I like to. You know that, right?"

Tears filled her eyes. Having to take care of herself for so long with so little made asking for help nearly impossible. And her current state made it worse.

"Oh, shit, are you crying? Ivy?"

"This, whatever we are, is so new, and I don't want to be the girl who *has* to be taken care of, and I don't want you to feel like you *have* to take care of me. I don't want to be a burden."

Ethan's fingers were gentle but firm beneath her chin as he lifted her face to meet his eyes.

"Ivy. Sweetheart." His eyes were deep brown on the outer edges, but green and amber in the center as they stared into hers. "You are not a burden. I *want* to take care of you. Will you let me?"

"I can't promise it'll be easy, but I'll try."

He pressed a kiss to her forehead and swiped her tears away. As her legs tangled with his, she wondered if there was a not-awkward way to ask him to take his shirt off.

Not for any inappropriate reason. Of course not. He was so warm, and she wanted to snuggle up to him, skin to skin.

If she happened to see his perfectly sculpted chest and stupidly ripped abs, well, so be it.

"Ethan?"

"Mmm?" he hummed, his fingers tugging her hair out of its bun.

"Oh, fuck, that feels so good." The tips of his fingers found her scalp. "Umm. I seem to have on slightly less clothing than you do?" She squeaked the last bit as a question rather than the statement she'd intended, and she hoped her cheeks weren't too red.

"Oh, yeah?" His voice deepened.

"Yeah, so, umm... can we maybe rectify the situation?"

"Hmm? How so?" His voice was a delicious purr in her ear and a deep rumbling against her chest.

Shit, he was going to make her say it.

"Would you, umm, take your shirt off?" Just saying it felt lecherous, and she wanted to crawl into a hole in mortification.

"Why, Ivy?"

She heard the pleased smile in his voice, but she couldn't make herself look at him.

"Damnit, Ethan, I'm fucking freezing, and you're a furnace." Not to mention those freaking abs.

"Well, you know, if you had on more than those PJs and a bra, you might not be so cold." He was outright laughing at her now.

"Fine, if they bother you so much, I'll cover up, then." And she whacked him on the arm before rolling over to get out of bed.

Or she tried to.

Two solid arms wrapped around her, keeping her in place.

"Don't you dare." Ethan's breath tickled her ear, sending tingles lower.

He pulled them both into a sitting position and glared at her mockingly before releasing her.

"Stay put." Ethan's fake scowl was too adorable for words, and she wanted to kiss it off his face.

With movements so slow Ivy knew he did it on purpose, he crossed his arms and tugged the hem of his shirt up, and with every inch of solid flesh revealed, Ivy was more and more convinced he *was* a marble sculpture because there was no way a real, human man looked like *that*.

When he finally pulled it off, he stood over her with his hands on his hips.

"Happy now?" The faux scowl was still in place, so Ivy rose on her knees to kiss her way up the planes of his stomach and over his pecs.

"I guess so." She smirked and fell backward onto the bed.

He grumbled, folding his shirt into a neat rectangle before pulling her to him, resting her chest against his again. Everywhere his skin touched hers burned, sending flickers of heat pooling low in her belly, and the sensation was so delicious, she wanted to *lick* him.

She shifted, hooking one leg over his, trying to get more comfortable and *closer*, always closer to him. Suddenly, Ethan went still.

"Ivy?" His voice was a hoarse rasp.

"Mmm?" She hummed, still trying to find the perfect spot against his chest.

"Umm, what you're doing is making... things hard."

Okay, that was bluntly honest and kind of unexpected. Oops. Some primal part of herself she hadn't been aware of purred, happy to have such an effect on him. The rest of her was slightly embarrassed.

"Shit, fuck! I'm sorry!"

"Don't be, I didn't want to alarm you."

"Alarm... me?" She blinked at him and squirmed again. "What do you—"

He hissed as she pressed her hips closer and-

Holy shit.

"Ethan?"

"Yes?" His eyes were closed, and he appeared to be doing breathing exercises. Inhale one, two, three. Exhale three, two, one.

"Wow."

"Well, that's nice to hear." She felt his chest, and possibly something else, swell with her praise.

Lily was right.

And then he was kissing her, rolling them so she lay on top of him. Her brain filed that away for later, the way he looked up at her before tugging her lips down to meet his again.

Ivy reveled in the feel of him beneath her, filing that away for later. Ethan groaned her name as he kissed his way down her throat and over her collarbones to the top of her bralette.

"Ethan?"

"Hmm?" His lips closed over her nipple through the thin fabric, and he tugged lightly with his teeth.

"*Shit*. Ethan."

Pulling the lacy strap down over her shoulder, he freed her breast and kissed his way down to the tip, which he traced with his tongue.

"We can't do anything," Ivy gasped as his thumb and forefinger found her other nipple and pinched. "At least not yet. Period, remember?" He grumbled against her skin, and she laughed. "Cramps make it hard to...you know."

With a pout, he gave her nipple one last kiss and pushed the strap back up on her shoulder. "Well, we definitely want you to...you know." A wicked little smile tugged the corners of his mouth, making her shiver in anticipation.

"Ethan?" She pulled the bralette back in place.

"Yeah?" His face was still dangerously close to her boobs.

"Up here." She tipped his head up with one finger. And he obliged her, coming back up to kiss her until she forgot the cramps, nearly forgetting her own name.

THE SMELL OF BACON PERMEATED IVY'S BEDROOM WHEN SHE woke the next morning.

Rolling over, she found herself reaching for the empty spot beside her, the night before replaying in her head.

She'd asked Ethan to stay, and he'd said yes.

And now he was cooking bacon in her kitchen, which was more than enough to get her out of bed despite the cramps still wracking her body.

Ivy brushed her teeth and pulled on a hoodie before padding into the kitchen. Ethan was stirring something in a large bowl while simultaneously flipping strips of bacon in a large pan Ivy forgot she owned. Jase sat at the table listening while Ethan explained something to him about butter and vanilla.

"Morning," she said sleepily, padding over to rise on her toes and kiss him on the cheek.

He turned and kissed her lips, and Jase made fake gagging sounds. Ethan grinned at Ivy.

"There's coffee." He waved at the pot.

"Bless you." She sighed, searching for her favorite mug.

"And there's going to be bacon, eggs, and pancakes up in a few minutes."

"God, you're amazing," she mumbled with sleepy happiness. "I think I'll marry you."

Ethan's back went ramrod straight at the stove.

Ivy poured her coffee.

And then what she'd said hit her.

"Eventually, I mean. When we've had three dates instead of two." She giggled nervously.

Ethan remained silent.

"I'm sorry," she whispered, panic setting in. Too much, too fast. She should've kept her stupid mouth shut.

"Don't be," he said quietly. "I feel it too. It's...intense."

He held his arm out for her, and she tucked herself beneath, catching her breath and leaning against his side as he expertly made the most amazing breakfast she'd ever eaten. He kissed the top of her head, then steered her to the table where Jase was pointedly ignoring them by pouring orange juice into a glass.

After her second cup of coffee, Ivy heard a screech and saw Janna racing toward Ethan. Ivy stopped her before she rampaged into the stove and burned herself.

"Mister Ford!" Janna yelled, scrabbling to escape the circle of Ivy's arms.

"Actually, Janna," Ethan replied without looking at them as he skillfully flipped a pancake in the skillet, "my real last name is Fisher. I'm Ethan Fisher. You can call me that instead."

Ivy's heart stopped.

Sharing his real name was so personal, and his wanting to share it with her kids nearly overwhelmed Ivy. A tear leaked from the corner of her eye.

"Ethan Fisher?" Janna's nose wrinkled. "Then who's Mister Ford?"

"I'm Ethan Fisher," he said. "Um. Ford is a name I made up."

"Well, that's silly." Janna stared up at him, considering. "Hmm. Ethan. Okay!" And she wriggled away from Ivy to crawl into a chair.

"Ivy?"

"Yes, Janna?"

"Did you know he's Ethan Fisher?" The little girl was serious, her eyes wide.

"I do now." Ivy laughed.

"I already figured it out. I know how to use Google." Jase shrugged.

Of course, he would've figured it out, with all the research he'd done after meeting Ethan.

"Right. Google. I'm impressed with your research skills."

Breakfast cooked by Ethan was the most delicious thing Ivy had ever eaten. His pancakes were light and fluffy with crispy edges, and there must have been some kind of magic in the eggs and bacon because she'd never had anything more wonderful.

She wondered what it would take to have Ethan Fisher cook her breakfast every morning.

13

A few weeks passed with the assistant coaches doing their best, but the team floundered without proper leadership. Whether out of guilt or actual concern, assistant coaches steered clear of Ethan, leaving him to sit out games in the bullpen except when he ventured out with the team before games began.

That only made his mood darken further. Returning to the scene of his torment with nothing to do but sit and watch sent his mind back down those old paths of self-loathing and doubt. Darkness overtook him, and the mean, broken version of himself tried to rear its ugly head, despite the lightness Ivy had brought him.

The rest of the team, at least, seemed less tense around him; not friendly, exactly, but less standoffish than before. They didn't seek him out, but the outright avoidance was gone.

Another Monday came around, and Ethan wandered through the halls without purpose, lost and out of sorts.

"Ethan!" Derek's voice sounded far away, and Ethan realized Derek had been calling him for a while.

"What?" Ethan heard the old sharp edge in his voice, exhausted with putting on a front but unable to curb his tone.

"How are you? You've been out of commission for a while." Derek seemed genuinely concerned.

"Yeah, I'm good. I saw Ivy a few times."

Derek bounced on the balls of his feet, grinning from ear to ear. "She told me. I'm happy for you guys. You both seem... different."

Jen's platinum head poked out of a door.

"Johnson, Ford, team meeting. Now."

Both men followed Jen into the meeting room where the rest of the Hawks were already seated and waiting. Gregory Marshall was, thankfully, not present. They'd heard from an assistant about his suspension and subsequent dismissal.

Now, a woman with silvery hair and a well-cut suit waited at the front of the room. Stern, but not unkind, blue eyes watched them like their titular Hawks as Ethan and Derek slid into the final remaining chairs.

"Ah, good. Everyone is here." Her voice was familiar and authoritative, and Ethan wondered if they'd met before. "I'm Emily Harkness, team manager of the Hawks."

He knew that name.

Shit.

"As you all may have discerned, Gregory Marshall has been released from his position as head coach after the incident with Mr. Ford, and the Hawks are under new coaching leadership. Mine."

When her piercing blue eyes narrowed at him, Ethan knew she remembered him, too. He didn't have time to process the information because Emily Harkness wasn't finished.

"We've also traded for a new relief pitcher."

Oh, no. Ethan had a bad feeling about that.

"Everyone, please welcome Isaac Reyes. As you may know, he used to pitch with the Tornadoes."

A smattering of welcomes sounded through the room as Isaac jumped up from his seat in the front row, turned to wave at his new teammates, and smirked his signature cocky smirk.

Beside him, Derek perked up and paid attention to Isaac. Interesting.

"Hi, guys. I'm so excited to be here!"

Ethan slid low in his seat to avoid catching Isaac's gaze, tugging his hat low over his eyes to hide his face.

"Thank you, Reyes." Harkness patted his shoulder. "So, I've looked at Mr. Marshall's stats and notes, and I have to say, I disagree with his philosophies and ideas about baseball. But we'll get to that later. Right now, I'd like to meet with all of you individually in my office. Ethan...Ford, you're up first." She beckoned with a manicured hand, and Ethan followed reluctantly as she left the meeting room and headed down the hall to the office formerly belonging to Marshall.

Already, Harkness had claimed it as her own. Framed art and certificates adorned the walls, and potted plants lined the top of the bookshelves. A large photo of college-aged Emily and Laura Lorne sat front and center on her desk, and Ethan felt a pang at seeing his mother so young and happy.

Behind the desk, Emily sat in the imposing black leather chair, steepling her fingers before her with her elbows resting on the desk, holding Ethan hostage with her icy gaze.

"So, Ethan."

"Yes, Coach?"

"I assume you remember me."

"I do." Emily Harkness was one of Laura's oldest, best friends. Fierce like Ethan's mother, Emily was now the only female head manager in the League.

"Your mother did not send me here, which, I assume, is what you're thinking."

"I— oh." Well, she wasn't wrong.

"I applied through proper channels and received this coaching position on my own merit. However. Your mother is aware I'm here now. And she's worried about you." Emily sighed.

Ethan scowled.

"How long has it been since you've spoken?" Harkness's icy blue eyes stared at Ethan across the desk.

Ethan did the math in his head, and the realization was... a lot.

"Five years."

"Ethan Cable Fisher." Ethan winced at his full name. "Call your mother."

"No offense, Ma'am, but I don't think you can tell me to do *that*."

"I'm not saying this in any official capacity, but I am practically family, and Laura misses you. Have you considered how much your absence is hurting her?"

Ethan rolled his eyes.

"Perhaps consider how much it's hurting you, then."

He scoffed instead of answering.

"Ethan." Emily's eyes narrowed. "Jimmy was in a car accident. Did you know?"

"I did not."

"You would if you called your mother."

Ethan sighed.

"I just so happen to have her number. Here." Harkness pulled a sticky note from a drawer, wrote the number on it, and held it out to him.

His fingers shook as he reached across the distance and took the paper.

"And Ethan? After you call Laura, get your knee checked out again. I'd never forgive myself if you further injured yourself on my watch."

Bristling, Ethan left the office. Call his mother. After all the shit with Marshall, with the injury, and now with a new coach who happened to be his mother's best friend?

It was too much too fast.

With his breaths coming too quickly, Ethan practically ran

down the hallway to find a secluded place to hide and think.

Except he couldn't.

The images swirling through his mind left him detached, unable to cement himself in reality. Too many voices from the past were appearing in the present.

Pounding heartbeat, too-quick breaths.

Shaking hands and ice-cold sweat trickled down his spine.

He was too big and too small in his skin.

He wanted to scream or cry or break something.

Whether or not his mother had sent her best friend to be his coach, it seemed like she was meddling. Even if she hadn't, the flare of anger and confusion remained, and a roiling pit of fear at a new coach.

Ethan's track record with coaches was currently zero for two, and this one wasn't looking great either.

He called Ivy.

It rang three times. No answer.

Fuck.

He tried again. Still nothing.

Shit.

When his fists clenched, the tiny paper rectangle crumpled in his hand. Unfolding it with still-shaking fingers, he read the number, and before he changed his mind, he dialed.

"Laura Lorne speaking."

"Oh. Um. Mo— Laura?"

"Yes?"

"It's Ethan."

"Ethan?"

There were noises in the background, so maybe she didn't recognize his voice.

Hearing her voice after so long sent needles of pain through his veins.

"*Mother.*" He ground out. "It's Ethan."

He couldn't say Ethan *Fisher* out loud. Not now.

"Oh." Her tone shifted, unreadable. More noises and other voices in the background "My son, Ethan Fisher?"

"This was a bad idea."

"I'm sorry." Laura's voice sounded rougher. Older. Ethan wondered how much she'd aged in the past five years. "This isn't a great time, Ethan, but I can—"

Of course, it wasn't a great time. When had it ever been?

"Right." He cut her off. "Well. Sorry to have bothered you. Bye."

The painful squeezing in his chest tightened further as he disconnected the call.

Ethan should've known better.

He called Ivy again. Still no answer.

Laura didn't make time for him, and now Ivy couldn't either. He'd thought he could count on *someone*.

He should've known better.

Maybe Marshall was right. Maybe he shouldn't have gotten attached. Maybe—

The vibrating in his hand was so startling, he dropped the phone. Once he'd recovered enough to pick it up, he answered.

"Hi!"

For the first time, the bright warmth of Ivy's voice both soothed and grated his nerves.

And he hated it. Didn't want to be annoyed with her. But right now, everything else was at the forefront of his mind, and anger and annoyance crept into his voice.

"Hi." The word was as harsh as the snap of a whip as it left his mouth. It stung like a whip, too.

"Oh, sorry, is this a bad time? Did you call accidentally? I saw the missed calls and— "

"No, it was on purpose."

"What's up?"

"It's nothing."

"Oh. Umm. Okay?" Ivy sounded taken aback.

"Fucking hell."

She didn't say anything for a few seconds, the silence echoing with his pounding heartbeats. Would she hang up? Be done with him for good?

"Are you okay?" Concern tinged her voice.

Fuck, he didn't want her pity.

"I am fucking awesome," he snarled, hating the sound of his voice. "The new manager? The one who replaced Marshall? She's my mother's college roommate. Her best friend."

"Oh. Wow."

"Yeah, it's a fucking delight."

"That sounds...difficult."

"It was, yeah. So, I called you, but you didn't answer."

"Yeah, I was calling the school again. I saw on Facebook that someone I went to grad school with got a job at the same school I'm waiting to hear back from, so I was trying to get in touch with the assistant principal. Not that it worked."

Shit, he was such an asshole for not even considering she might be busy, and realizing it made him feel worse.

"And," he went on as though she hadn't spoken, "I called my mother. And she didn't have time for me. I should've realized things never change."

"Damn, that's— wow. Do you want to talk about it?"

"Not now I don't."

"O—kay... I'm here if you change your mind."

"Are you though?" Fuck, he was being such a dick. He hated it, but the words just slipped out.

"What the hell, Ethan? I missed your call and now—what, you're mad at your mom and your coach and taking it out on me? Are you the only one who gets to have a bad day?"

"Maybe this was a mistake."

"What, calling your mom? It sounds like you weren't ready to talk to her."

"No, I mean— yes, but this. Us. A mistake."

She inhaled sharply, the small sound like a stab to his already aching chest.

"Do you really think so?"

He hadn't, but once it was out there...maybe...

"I don't know what to think, Ivy."

"Maybe you should take some time to figure out what to think. I don't— I can't— I just— ugh. I am not doing this with you right now. If you decide you want to talk about it in person, like adults, fine. We will. Figure out when and where. If you don't, then this wasn't going to work if you'd give up so easily anyway." Exhaustion coated her voice. "I have to go. Let me know if you want to talk. Or don't. I guess I'll know your decision either way."

And she hung up.

Immediately after she ended the call, Ethan knew he'd fucked up.

Despite the tone of the call and their argument, he realized his heart rate had slowed, and he could breathe again.

He had to fix this.

But first, he had to do his job.

Slipping his phone into his pocket, Ethan slumped through the hallway to collapse into the chair outside Dr. Chadna's office. His leg bounced of its own accord, and he didn't know what to do with his hands. Still, his skin seemed both too large and too small, and it was infuriating to be so helpless and uncertain.

Marshall had Ethan convinced he was a worthless piece of shit, nothing more. But Ivy had shown him he wasn't. And now he'd fucked everything up.

How could he make it up to her?

And did he want to talk to his parents?

The only thing he could pin down was his feelings for Ivy. Whatever was happening between them was something he'd never expected, and he had no intention of letting it go.

Unless she wouldn't forgive him.

But then Dr. Chadna called him into the exam room, and Ethan had to shove everything else aside.

When Dr. Chadna cleared him to play, albeit with stern instructions to immediately see her if he had *any* problems, Ethan joined the rest of the team in the clubhouse where they'd begun conditioning.

Harkness hadn't yet arrived on the field, and the other players had formed small, insular groups, talking while they prepped for the warmup and team meeting. Ethan's routine was solitary, but he decided to join Derek and Jen and regretted the decision immediately when Isaac Reyes's curly head popped up out of nowhere.

"Ethan! You good?" Derek called, dragging Ethan's attention to the ball about to break his nose.

Ethan had never been so grateful for Derek's enthusiasm, both for throwing the ball and for diverting him from his thoughts.

"Yeah, Chadna says I'm good to play." Ethan scowled, shrugging as he readjusted his hat lower over his eyes after tossing the ball to Jen.

Isaac ambled over and stuck his hand out to Jen.

"Hi! I'm Isaac."

The blonde woman narrowed her eyes at him before gripping Isaac's hand in what Ethan knew would be a death grip.

"Jen," she said, still glaring. Jen was not one to be overly friendly to strangers.

Derek, on the other hand...

Ethan watched as Isaac tried to shake the blood back into his fingers after Jen's handshake when Derek approached him.

"Hi, Isaac, I'm Derek Johnson." Derek nudged Jen out of the way with his shoulder and held out his hand to Isaac. "And it is *very* nice to meet *you*."

Ethan was completely shocked when Isaac blinked and

swiped his forehead on the shoulder of his neon green hoodie, but he hadn't moved fast enough to hide the hint of red staining his light brown cheeks. Derek's grin grew wider.

"So, tell us about playing for the Tornadoes. I've heard they're one of the *best* to play for. Lawrence Lorne is a legend." Jen butted in before Derek began flirting.

Very pointedly, Ethan ignored Isaac's side-eye.

"Oh, yeah, I guess it was fine."

Now, *that* was interesting. Ethan had known Isaac well enough in their youth to know his tone was more telling than his answer.

"So why did they trade you?" Jen's pale blue eyes narrowed. "Mitchell wasn't *that* good."

"Well, actually," Isaac started, but Ethan interrupted before the pitcher shared information that wasn't his to share.

"He probably talked their fucking heads off," Ethan muttered, annoyed, but with a hint of their old, friendly ribbing.

It was weird. But not *bad* weird.

Isaac beamed at him.

"Wait, do you know each other?" Derek said at the same time Harkness spoke.

"Language, Ford." She'd appeared out of nowhere and had changed into clothing more suitable for a baseball field, dark athletic pants with a team t-shirt, and a red Hawks hat sat neatly atop her silver bob.

"Hawks!" she barked in all her commanding glory.

All the players halted their warmups and gathered before Harkness.

"I don't know how Mr. Marshall ran practices, but what I see now, I don't like. Too much separation. We must work *together*. Together, we're better. Remember that."

Biting the inside of his cheek to keep from speaking, Ethan

still had to restrain himself from rolling his eyes. He understood why the woman was Laura's best friend.

"Today," Harkness continued, "we're going to start with something a little bit different." She gestured to a large pile of black rolled rubber cylinders piled in the shape of a pyramid. "Everyone, take a mat and meet me in the outfield."

Mat?

No, she wouldn't...

"You don't think she's going to make us do yoga, is she?" Ethan said under his breath to Derek.

With a grimace, Derek replied, "Dude, I think she is."

"Fuuuck," Ethan groaned. Muscular he might be, but limber he was not. But how hard could yoga be? "I assume you know what's going on?" Ethan asked Isaac, who'd dropped his mat beside him.

"Not a clue," Isaac replied, folding his legs into a pretzel.

Surreptitiously, Ethan tried to copy the pose and nearly fell on his face in the process.

"Since we're all here, I'd like to lead you all through a beginner mind-body yoga session. We're going to begin by standing at the front of our mats, in *Tadasana*, or mountain pose. Please ground yourselves through your feet, and inhale."

That didn't sound too bad. He could stand on a mat and breathe.

Forty-five minutes later, Ethan was drenched in sweat, aching in places he hadn't even known had muscles. And on top of that, Isaac Reyes, of all people, had managed to manipulate his body with seemingly no effort, holding poses and breathing like it was nothing.

Even inimitably cheerful Derek was scowling and sweating after the torture session.

The rest of the day was unlike any other he'd experienced in his twenty-odd years of playing baseball in some form or another. Harkness was authoritative, but unlike Marshall, she did not belittle or pit the team against each other. Her methods were *exhausting,* though. Ethan could barely hobble to his car after the horrible yoga session Harkness had proclaimed would be their new warmup, and she requested the team spend time doing "mindful meditation" on their own time. Ethan shuddered at the thought. Close proximity to too many pieces of his past left him raw, and he wanted nothing more than to see Ivy, to wrap her in his arms and apologize, then bitch about his day with the new coach.

How domestic and mundane *that* sounded.

It also sounded *amazing.*

Without thinking, Ethan climbed into his car and drove on autopilot straight to Ivy's apartment. Once he'd parked on the street in front of her building, he realized he should've called her first. He tried, but it rang once and went to voicemail. A text came in a few seconds later.

Can't talk. it's story time at the library.

I want to talk. Please. I'm sorry. Can I come over later?

Ok

Shit, a two-letter response from Ivy, who usually at least spelled out the word. She must still be pissed.

Restless and unwilling to be alone after the day he'd had, Ethan fidgeted with his phone, debating with himself whether it would be worth it to text Jen and Derek to see if they wanted to get dinner.

Scrubbing his hand over his face, Ethan opened a text thread with them. Jen suggested a new restaurant downtown, and Ethan and Derek agreed.

A short, glassed-in counter and cones of spinning meat greeted Ethan as he pushed through the shop doors. Delicious aromas left his mouth watering, and Ethan almost didn't wait for the others to arrive to place his order. But they'd wait for him, and since they were all apparently friends now, he had to do the friend thing.

In a few minutes, though, he wished he hadn't bothered because when Derek arrived, Isaac Reyes walked in with him.

Well, shit.

This is turning out to be a hell of a day, he thought, trying not to bare his teeth in a grimace.

"Yo, Fisher," Isaac called, holding up a hand for a fist bump.

"Who's Fisher?" Derek asked, looking around the shop.

"He's Fisher." Isaac pointed at Ethan.

"What?" Derek still appeared confused.

"He's Ethan Fisher."

Isaac fucking Reyes, ladies and gentlemen, Ethan seethed silently.

"Huh," Derek didn't seem bothered. "Cool. So, food?"

Ethan thanked the stars for Jen's lateness because she would not have let it go.

Jen came in after a few more minutes; she'd brought Ryan the announcer with her. Introductions were made, then they ordered and found an outdoor table.

The evening was pleasant, with the scents of the other restaurants downtown floating through the air along with the sounds of families playing at the nearby playground and music from the bars dotted along the street.

They'd begun eating and chatting about music and tv when Derek stiffened and turned to Ethan, pointing at him open-mouthed.

"Ethan *Fisher*?"

"What?" Jen's laser focus zeroed in on Ethan's ducked head and reddening ears. Ryan looked around curiously.

"As in *Jimmy* Fisher?"

"Yep! That's his dad? Cool, huh?" Isaac answered for Ethan.

"Damn it, Isaac." Ethan snapped. "Did you think I kept that to myself for a reason?"

"So you *do* know each other." Jen looked between Isaac and Ethan. "Also, what the fuck? Jimmy Fisher? Your dad is *Jimmy Fisher*? Legendary pitcher? Hall of Fame inductee? Why *the fuck* didn't you tell me?"

"Seriously! Why the hell not?" Derek was bouncing in his seat, not unlike Janna. "If my dad was in the freaking Hall of Fame, I'd tell the world!"

Ethan looked down, twisting his napkin between his fingers, while Isaac looked the tiniest bit embarrassed.

Ethan ran his hands through his hair and decided to come clean.

"To make a long story short, my dad and I don't get along, and after I left home, I didn't want people to think I was handed my position because of who my dad is."

Jen nodded, a cool expression sliding over her face.

"But—" Derek tried to interrupt.

"I had been thinking of using my real name again, though. But now my mom's best friend is the coach, so maybe not."

And he'd shared more information than he'd meant to. Fuck.

Jen and Derek stared at him for a moment, and Ethan saw the gears in their heads whirring.

"Isn't Jimmy Fisher married to—" Derek began.

"Laura Lorne, David Lorne's daughter. Yep!" Isaac interjected again, damn him.

"So your mom is a big-time agent, the owner of a billion-dollar sports agency, and your dad is in the Baseball Hall of Fame? And you don't want people to know?" Jen asked, arching a brow at him.

"Bingo." Ethan pointed at her. "I fucking hate it. I might be a decent pitcher, but I'm not Jimmy-Fisher-level good. I never have been, and Marshall never let me forget it. It's a lot of pressure, and it's exactly what I was trying to avoid when I started going by Ethan Ford. I didn't want anyone to expect me to *be* Jimmy Fisher."

Abruptly, he stood, knocking his chair over in the process, but he didn't bother to right it.

"I need some air," Ethan said, not looking back at them as he walked away.

"But we're outside!" he heard Derek call helpfully.

Reluctant to head back to his apartment, and having heard nothing from Ivy, Ethan drove back to the stadium, despite it being at the heart of his problems. He'd always been able to think more clearly when letting muscle memory take over, the movement of his body freeing his mind to sort through his problems.

The empty baseball stadium was eerie in its peacefulness. With no lights or sounds other than his footsteps and the creaking of the metal gate as he swiped his key fob to get in, Ethan felt like he was in a horror movie.

And maybe he was because as soon as he stepped behind the gate, every light in the stadium blazed on, blinding him. Blinking, Ethan peered through his fingers but saw nothing other than the stadium, lit up as if it were a game night.

Must be a glitch in the system, he thought.

Spinning the bat in his hand a few times before tapping it on the instep of his shoe, Ethan settled into a batting stance before swinging it lightly to loosen his shoulders and wrists. He heard a faint rustle of fabric, but when he looked up and saw nothing, he chalked it up to the wind rustling one of the stadium's many sponsor flags in the breeze.

There didn't seem to be much of a breeze, though.

Deciding to ignore it, he pressed the button for the automatic pitching machine and squared up his hips and shoulders for the first pitch.

Thunk.

Hit. If he'd been on the field, it would have been a perfect shot to left.

Thunk.

Hit, dead center.

It was dark in the alcove, but Ethan would have sworn he'd seen something move behind the machine.

Maybe it was a shadow.

Thunk.

Left again.

The barrel of the pitching machine shifted, seemingly of its own accord.

Ethan straightened out of his stance and walked toward it.

He saw the ball coming toward him and turned fast enough to avoid being hit straight in the stomach; it rammed into his flank instead.

Instant numbness and then intense pain radiated from the place of impact, and Ethan folded to the ground, landing on his hands and knees, gasping for breath.

His instincts screamed at him to get up but moving seemed impossible.

Another sound, glass maybe, and an ugly, rasping, mirthless laugh.

The machine moved again, its barrel pointed toward his head, and looking past it, Ethan noticed the figure of a man hunched behind it.

What the fuck?

"I should have left your useless ass to rot with your uncle." Marshall's voice projected from the shadows, punctuated by the crash of him tossing a glass bottle over his shoulder. "You're *worthless*," the old man taunted. "You were nothing! I made you! And now I've lost everything, and it's *your fault!*"

Ethan stayed on the ground, silent, as he watched Marshall stumble out. He shouldn't have been surprised. Ethan had been the recipient of angry drunken messages and calls from the man for years now, plus all the poisonous words at games and practices. He edged his fingers toward the bat he'd dropped, slowly grasping it, but remaining flat and otherwise motionless. Tensing his muscles, he hoped he wouldn't have to defend himself against the angry old man stumbling toward him but expected the worst anyway.

"What do you want?" Ethan asked, the effort of speaking sending a white-hot knife of pain through his side. He wondered if it was worth trying to pull himself back to the gate of the batting cage. Marshall was unpredictable at best, volatile at worst, and Ethan wouldn't have put it past him to do something worse than hit him with a ball.

"I built this team. I *made* you. It's all mine, and I am not leaving! *You can't take it away from me!*"

Marshall was close enough that spittle flying from his trembling lips sprayed Ethan's face.

Each movement sent lightning bolts arcing through his body, but he refused to let Marshall see his pain as he hauled himself to his feet, glaring at the old man straight in the eyes.

"Just because *you're* worthless," Ethan growled, "doesn't mean I am. I believed all of your bullshit for *years* because *you* were never good enough, so you blamed it on me. You're done, old man."

Marshall snarled in Ethan's face.

And punched Ethan right where the ball had hit him.

The adrenaline spike was enough for Ethan to swing the bat up to block the knife Marshall had pulled out of his belt. Sharp metal skidded across the bat, burying itself in the wood, and Ethan pushed the bat, and Marshall with it, away from himself before the knife hit him. The old man scrabbled backward and tripped over a stray ball, falling flat, splayed out before Ethan.

Chest heaving, Ethan glared down at Marshall, and for a moment, he considered how easy it would be to hurt the old man the way he'd hurt Ethan. An image of Marshall's face, beaten and bloodied, swam in Ethan's mind. It would be *so easy*. Marshall had attacked him after all, and Ethan had no illusions the old man had come for any reason other than murder.

But *Ivy*.

All the words he'd said to the coach echoed in his ears. Because of Ivy. And he knew he needed to tell her. Apologize. Grovel at her feet if he had to.

"I. am. not. worthless." Ethan spat each word with the pent-up pain and anger of the past five years.

And then he noticed the flashing red-and-blue lights and the sirens at the same time Marshall froze.

"Ethan, are you all right?" Harkness's voice echoed over the stadium's sound system.

Knowing she couldn't hear his response, Ethan held out a thumbs up.

"The police are coming into the batting cage, and you need to come out."

After Ethan had given a statement to an officer and been directed to an ambulance by an EMT, Emily pushed her way through the small knot of officers and security guards to stand by Ethan.

"Well, this has been a more exciting first day than I expected." Her tone was laced with sarcasm as she rolled her eyes and adjusted the hem of her knitted cardigan.

"How did you know I was here?"

"Security called." Harkness waved her phone in front of his face. "They saw Gregory Marshall on the cameras and notified me, and I figured he wouldn't do any harm prowling around, but then you showed up. We'll talk about that later, by the way." She patted him on the shoulder. "You'll need an x-ray before you're cleared to play. I've informed your mother you're on the way to the hospital."

For fuck's sake. His mother?

"Emily," he began, but she glared at him and arched a perfectly sculpted silver brow. "*Emily,*" he continued, staring right back, "I am an *adult*. Why the fuck did you inform my mother?"

"Language, Ethan. Laura and I were on the phone when I got the security alert. She was already at the hospital with Jimmy."

"Fine, I'll go." He fished his keys out of his bag, but Harkness stopped him.

"Absolutely not. You will ride in the ambulance."

"Isn't that kind of overkill?" Ethan snapped.

"You were almost *overkilled*, Ethan."

He rolled his eyes and scowled.

"Hanging out with Jimmy, too, I see. Sounds like one of his bad jokes." And *he* sounded like a surly teenager.

"You will adjust your tone, Ethan Fisher, or you might find yourself on the bench for another week." And *she* sounded like his mom.

Marshall had used those same words against him hundreds of times, but Harkness's version lacked the venom Marshall's had.

"Yes, Coach." He was chastened by her threat, but more so by her tone. It sent him coasting on a ride through memories. Jimmy and Laura laughing together after wins, stone-faced after losses. Jimmy's old teammates treating Ethan like their own. Laura, berating Ethan when he punched a bully at school or stayed out all night with his teammates. Moving in with Lawrence, the excitement of making varsity in high school. Laura, yelling at Ethan that he was better than this, than Marshall, and to *stay*.

Oh.

He'd forgotten she'd told him to stay.

14

We're home now if you still want to talk.

Hey, I'm sorry, I can't talk right now. I'm at the hospital. There was an incident at the stadium. I'll call you later and tell you, okay? But I've got to leave my phone for a while because of the X-rays. But I need to talk to you. Please. Did I already say I'm sorry? Because I'm sorry.

"The hospital?" Ivy squawked, spraying fried rice.

Ethan wasn't the only one who'd had a bad day; a packet of paperwork she'd mailed to Nayomi never arrived, and she'd had to scramble to get a copy together. It wasn't even a big deal, but every time she made a misstep, chilling fear raked its claws down her back. Because no matter what she did, the thought that Jase and Janna would be taken away was paralyzing. And she would *not* let them be taken away, to lose their home because she'd fucked up. So, she'd panicked and spent the day going back and forth between the library and her apartment, printing documents in triplicate.

And then at lunchtime, she'd mindlessly scrolled for a few minutes only to find that J. Simpson had hired one of her former classmates. Her only consolation was that the new hire was to the English Department, so maybe there was some sort of hold-up with the Science Department funding.

Few things were better at the end of a long day than Crab Rangoon, so they'd taken a trip to her favorite Chinese buffet.

Jase's face echoed Ivy's worry after she read the texts aloud, no matter how mad she was at him or how idiotic their argument had been. Janna was oblivious, trying to maneuver her kiddie chopsticks.

"Ethan says he's okay. So, he's okay." Let her pretend to be okay, too. "Can you hand me the sweet and sour sauce?"

"What do you think happened?" he asked. His knuckles turned white around the tiny ceramic bowl as he slid it to her.

"I don't know." Ivy sighed. "All he said was 'there was an incident'."

"What does that mean?" Jase morosely prodded a piece of sesame chicken with his chopsticks.

"I'm not sure, buddy. Maybe something else to do with his knee?"

"Maybe." He scowled deeper while he methodically swirled the wooden spoon.

"Okay, after dinner, we'll call him and see what we can find out. Deal?"

"Deal." He nodded, tapping the spoon on the pot.

Never mind the fight with Ethan earlier. He'd said he wanted to talk, so they would talk. When, she didn't know. But she'd try.

She had to, for both of their sakes.

Heaving a sigh, Ivy tried to carefully scoop up a dumpling from her soup, but it slid off her spoon, splattering the table and her phone with broth.

After wiping off the screen, she called him.

"Hey, Ivy."

Relief flooded through her as his voice, at least, sounded normal.

"What happened? Are you okay? Why do you need X-rays? *What happened?*"

"It's okay, I'm fine. I'll tell you what happened in a second, but first, I'm so sorry." His voice cracked. "Ivy. I didn't mean... I had a bad day, and I took it out on you. You were right. I hate myself for it. With my mom and everything— I'm so sorry. I was panicking, and I couldn't stop."

"I'm not going to say it's okay because it's not." Ivy heard his sharp inhale through her phone. "But I forgive you. I understand. I want to help, if—if you'll let me."

His relieved exhale whooshed through the speaker.

"God, Ivy. You helped already. I went to the stadium for batting practice after a shitty day, and somehow Marshall broke in. He hit me with a ball from the pitching machine. I'm waiting for the doctor to show up to read the X-ray."

"Why do I get the feeling there's more to it?" Her voice came out in a rasp, and she had to remind herself to breathe. "Which hospital? We're coming to you."

"Ivy, you don't— "

"Which. Fucking. Hospital. Ethan."

There was silence for a moment.

"Sacred Heart."

"Good. Text me where you'll be. We'll be there soon."

As she drove through the darkened city, Ivy did her best to avoid thinking about where Ethan might have gotten hit by a flying baseball and what kind of damage that might do to a person. Derek told her pitchers often pitched at speeds of ninety miles per hour or higher, and it stung when he caught them with a glove on, so imagining it hitting Ethan— no. *If I lose it, so will Jase.*

Jase was wide-eyed when they entered the hospital; his hands clenched and unclenched by his sides in a gesture oddly reminiscent of Ethan. The boy looked pale, and Ivy threw her arm over his shoulders, squeezing him. Genuine surprise washed over her when he wrapped his thin arms around her waist and squeezed her back.

The elevator opened and they exited, looking for a sign to point them to the radiology department. Ivy didn't bother to stop at the desk when the nurse offered help. Instead, she marched straight past the round nurses' station in the middle of the hall, mumbling about someone waiting for them. The long hallway stretched before them, empty except for a well-dressed middle-aged woman pacing at the far end. When she caught sight of them, the woman paused and peered in their direction for a moment before sharply turning on a heel and pushing open the door to the stairwell.

Only one room appeared to be occupied, and Ivy stepped in to find Ethan lying on the hospital bed with his eyes closed. She smothered a gasp when she saw him. The harsh hospital light cast a sickly pall over his face, and he wore a hospital gown draped loosely over his torso.

When Ethan sat up with a groan, Ivy flung herself on him, trying not to sob into his shoulder.

"Ow, shit!"

She backpedaled. "Sorrysorrysorry!"

"Shit! Um, uh, crap! Sorry. It's okay." Ethan grinned sheepishly at Janna, who clapped her hands over her ears. "C'mere." He waved Ivy over to him and squeezed her with one arm.

"I'm so sorry," she breathed, blinking back tears and tucking her head into his shoulder. "I didn't mean to hurt you."

"I hurt you, too."

"That's different. You're *actually* hurt."

"Ivy," his voice carried the slightest hint of a laugh. "I got hit by a baseball; I'm not dying."

"But isn't that bad?" Ivy's lip wobbled, and she bit it to make it stop.

"Ivy, sweetheart, it's just a bruise."

With a worried look, she murmured, "Promise?"

He kissed her in the space between her furrowed brows. "Promise."

"Good." She smacked him on the shoulder. "What the hell happened?"

Ethan glanced sidelong at the kids, and Ivy's eyes followed. Janna had discovered the remote to the tiny tv and was pushing buttons, completely absorbed in changing channels at lightning speed. Jase stood beside the door, staring intently at Ethan.

"Marshall showed up, drunk. He messed with the automatic pitching machine, and I got hit."

Jase flinched.

There was more, but Ivy realized Ethan didn't want to say more in front of Jase, so she changed the subject.

"Tell me about your new coach. You said you had a bad day? Did something else happen?" Ivy stopped for a moment, and Ethan didn't speak. "With the new coach?" she pressed.

Ethan sighed.

"Yeah. She made us do *yoga*, Ivy. It was *horrible*."

A chuckle sounded from the door.

"Emily's methods have always been questionable, but they do get results." The woman from the hallway stood with an older man in a worn-looking robe and slippers sitting in a wheelchair, trailing a rolling IV rack.

The pair looked familiar, but she'd never met them. Except...

His face was so like the man's, and his eyes were almost identical to the woman's.

Holy shit those were his *parents*.

This was happening *now*?

"What are you doing here?" Ethan's voice was flat in a way Ivy had never heard.

"We came to see you." Ethan's mom's brows pinched in the middle; the same way Ivy had seen Ethan's pinch together.

"Why?"

"What do you mean?"

"Why did you come to see me? You didn't have time earlier."

Oh, shit, this was happening. Should Ivy take the kids and leave? When she began to move away, Ethan's arm tightened around her waist, keeping her beside him.

"What? Oh, Ethan, no. Your father crashed the Mustang last week, did you know? And he was transferred here in an ambulance, and of course, they wouldn't let me ride with him, but they couldn't find him when I arrived, and that's what was happening when you called. We were trying to find out if he'd been dropped off or if the ambulance had been delayed. I thought, well, anyway it's all been sorted now."

"Oh." And then Ethan crumpled, leaning on Ivy for support.

"Ethan." As if sensing something had happened, the older woman gave her son a curt nod, but her eyes were soft as she looked at him, then at the two children, and finally they landed on Ivy. "Are you going to introduce us to your family?"

"Um. What, Lau- Mom?" Ethan didn't seem to follow, and he stared at his mother.

"Your family, dear." Ethan's mom gestured around the room while he sat in silence, still staring.

"Um. They're not? I mean maybe one day, but—" Ethan's ears turned bright red, and Ivy could have kissed him right there in front of his mother for being so adorably socially inept.

"But—" Laura gestured limply at Jase, and it fully clicked for Ivy.

With his dark hair and eyes, and his ever-present Hawks hat, Jase could easily be mistaken for Ethan's son.

"Oh, no, uh—ma'am," Ivy interjected. Unsure what to do, she nearly dropped into a curtsy. "This is Jase. He's my foster son. And his sister, Janna."

The woman turned her gaze onto Ivy.

"And who are *you*?" Her question wasn't rude or condescending, just curious.

But Janna chose that moment to jump in.

"Are you a queen?" The little girl gestured at the older woman's impeccable coiffure and perfectly tailored silk suit. Janna *did* do a curtsy.

"She is to me." the man in the wheelchair chuckled and wheeled himself over to where Janna was glancing back and forth between them. When he reached the small vinyl-covered couch where she sat, Janna peered at him for a moment, then went to stand beside him, eyeing the IV tube warily.

"Does that mean you're the king?"

"Me? I'm a scoundrel." The man grinned at her.

Ethan snorted.

"Got something to say, kid?" The old man's tone was still light, but there was an undercurrent to it Ivy couldn't interpret, and she didn't like not knowing what it meant. Ready to jump back into the conversation, Ivy started to speak, but Ethan beat her to it.

"Why are you here?" Ethan repeated the question, running a hand through his hair, then wincing.

"Emily told me you were coming for x-rays, so I came down to meet you, and then I saw—well-- I saw what I thought was your family, and I brought Jimmy so we could meet them. I'm Laura Lorne," she said, turning to hold her hand out to Ivy.

"Ivy Johnson. And this is Jase and Janna."

"And I'm Jimmy Fisher." He winked at Janna, who still sat in his lap. "Not the king."

Ivy glanced back at Ethan. His face was pale, and he looked as though he might be struggling to breathe. That may have had something to do with the bandage wrapped around his waist, though, because once she'd gotten closer, Ivy noticed it beneath the gown he wore. She threaded her fingers through his and squeezed, and he bumped his shoulder into hers in silent thanks.

"It was lovely to meet you all, but I think we should go.

Ethan, do you need me to call you a car?" Laura turned her gaze to her son.

Ivy bristled.

"He's going home with me, Ms. Lorne."

Laura's unreadable face flickered, and Ivy couldn't tell if she was angry or amused. Ethan's lips twitched as he looked between the two women. It looked like he was trying not to laugh.

"Call me Laura, dear."

Dear? Ivy was uncertain if the endearment was genuine or insulting, but she tried not to glare at the older woman. But when Laura offered a warm smile, Ivy tentatively returned it.

Laura looked at Ethan for a moment, then eased over to brush a lock of hair off his forehead before rushing out of the room, leaving Jimmy behind.

"Guess I better go after her." He winked at Janna, who wrapped him in a hug and gave him a smacking kiss on his cheek before climbing off his lap. "Good to see you, kid." He nodded at Ethan. "I like her." Jimmy jerked his thumb at Ivy as he followed his wife out. "Wait for me, Your Majesty," he called after her as he wheeled out of the room.

After his parents left, Ivy saw Jase still hovering in the corner, so she called him over to where she was still tucked under Ethan's arm.

"You okay, buddy?" she asked him.

His shoulders ratcheted up to his ears, but he didn't answer.

Ethan flicked the bill of Jase's hat, knocking it back on his head.

"What's wrong?"

Ivy heard the concern in Ethan's voice, and she kissed him on the cheek before sitting on the awful couch with Janna.

With his head still down, Jase's words came out as a mumble. The only word Ivy caught was 'drunk', and a pang shot through her.

Ethan patted a spot beside him, and Jase perched on the edge with his head still down.

"Jase," Ethan said, and it was a jolt because he so rarely used the boy's name, "don't be scared. Marshall got arrested, and he's gone now." He paused. "Everything is going to be okay." It sounded as though he were speaking to himself as much as the boy.

Slowly, Jase nodded, his shoulders loosening. Ethan bumped Jase's fist with his own, and while Ivy didn't comprehend male bonding rituals, somehow it seemed to have worked. Jase was calmer, so Ivy didn't question it.

The doctor entered a few minutes later, and Ethan was cleared to leave with instructions to take pain medication as needed, as the injury had only been a nasty bruise.

They all packed into her small car, with Ethan awkwardly folding himself into the front seat. The ride home was mostly silent, with Janna falling asleep in her seat almost instantly. When they arrived at Ivy's apartment, Jase and Ivy carried Janna in while Ethan held the door for them. Ivy saw Ethan's pain in his tight eyes and clenched teeth, so she reminded him to take his medication. He scowled, and she laughed softly, remembering the last time.

"I'm only taking half this time," he whispered.

Once Ivy was certain Janna and Jase were in their rooms, she found Ethan sitting on the edge of her bed, looking down at his shoes.

"So," Ivy said, sitting beside him on the bed, careful not to jostle him, "you ready to talk?"

"God, this day."

"Yeah, I get it. But..."

"You're right. I'm sorry." Ethan's dark eyes met hers, and Ivy saw everything in them. "I didn't mean to snap. And take it out on you. And I guess I misunderstood with my— with Laura, too." His voice cracked when he said 'my'.

"Hey." Tangling her fingers with his, she squeezed his hand. "It's okay to have a bad day. But if this—" Ivy moved their joined hands back and forth between them, "is going to work, we have to talk through things together, okay? You shut me out."

"I'm sorry. I'm not used to having someone to talk to."

"I know, and it's why I'm trying not to be hurt. But you can't give up so easily, Ethan. It was hard to let you in, you know that, right? Not just for me, but I have Jase and Janna to consider, too. Letting you into our lives is a *huge* deal. And I thought...I thought if you were so committed to helping Jase, maybe a relationship wouldn't be so much of a stretch. I like you a lot, Ethan. Jase and Janna do too. But if you're going to duck out the second there's any kind of trouble, you need to leave. Now. I can't...I *won't* be abandoned again." The air between them shifted, and she looked away.

"Ivy. I'll do better."

"Good." She sniffled. "Thank you. I'm sorry I wasn't there for you when you were upset."

"You helped anyway. I was going to tell you earlier, but..."

"Your parents, yeah. What a way to meet them."

"I know right? But I wanted you to know. When Marshall was there, he said... what he always said. But I told him he was wrong about me. And I think for the first time, I believed it."

A lump formed in her throat, rendering her speechless. On her lap, he wrapped her hand in both of his, her fingers completely engulfed by his.

"Ivy."

"Mmhmm?" She didn't want to burst into tears, but she was perilously close to that outcome.

"Thank you. I wouldn't have said it before. Before you. I wouldn't have thought it might be true."

Biting her lip, Ivy leaned her head on Ethan's shoulder.

"I'm glad."

It was a relief to say those things aloud and to hear what

he'd said. It hurt, but it was like a good stretch after being on a plane for hours. Maybe a little tense, and hard to get through, but worth it in the end. After sitting in silence for a few more minutes, Ethan shifted and groaned.

"Can you help me?" he asked, tugging on the hem of his shirt. One dark eyebrow arched, and his lips twitched, but he still managed to look mostly serious.

Pretending to be exasperated, Ivy stood and rolled her eyes but stepped between his spread knees to lean down and pull his shirt up over his head, letting the tips of her fingers skate over his uninjured side, the smooth, warm skin covering rippling muscles until her fingers came to the band around his middle.

"The bandage too?"

The stretchy bandage covered most of Ethan's abdomen, and Ivy reached to unroll it, her fingers brushing his warm skin. Ethan shivered under her touch. The bruise was already dark and ugly where the ball hit him, and she expected it would only get worse. Ivy placed her hand on his chest but didn't dare touch the bruise.

"Is this okay?" she murmured.

He nodded.

"It's not as bad as it looks."

"Are you going to tell me how pretty I am again?" Ivy grinned at him. "Because Pain Meds Ethan was fun."

Ethan huffed, cradling Ivy's hips in his hands and pulling her forward to rest his chin on her sternum and look up into her eyes.

"Maybe I will." His voice was rougher than usual. And he smiled lazily, sending sparking heat over Ivy's skin. Ethan's eyes went dark as he looked at her and worked his hands from her hips to her lower back before cupping her rear. "Maybe I'll show you how pretty I think you are."

Goosebumps pricked her flesh at his touch, and she let out an involuntary groan.

Ethan's eyes went darker.

He slid his hands higher on her back until he grunted, audibly gritting his teeth. Ivy froze in his arms.

"I can't lift my arm, it pulls too much," Ethan grunted, lowering his arm, then pink spread over his cheekbones. "I need a shower, but I can't reach high enough." His voice was too deep to squeak, but it went much higher than its normal low octave.

It was adorable.

"Do you think you can help me?" He leaned back, looking down. "I can't wash my hair by myself."

"Ethan Fisher, are you trying to trick me into showering with you?" Ivy pretended to be shocked and scandalized, narrowing her eyes at him. Not that she minded the idea of showering with him.

"No! No! You can stay outside the curtain and reach in or something! Or I'll figure it out!" Ethan was stammering, and Ivy glared down at him in mock seriousness, then pressed her forehead to his.

"Of course, I'll help you. Go on. I'll be back in a minute."

Blood pounded in her ears as she watched him go into her bathroom. Shivers racked her body, a side effect of her earlier anxiety, and Ivy made her decision.

It felt momentous. A turning point to something deeper in their relationship, even after the landmark of their trauma sharing. Ivy knew suddenly she needed the intimacy of *being* with him, and she was pretty sure he needed closeness, too, after the night they'd had.

Taking a deep breath, Ivy undressed and entered the tiny bathroom's steamy warmth.

"Hey," she said shyly. "Do you still need my help?"

The curtain shifted aside enough for Ethan to poke his

head out, and when he saw Ivy naked, his mouth fell open. His eyes raked over her body, and she wondered if spontaneous combustion was a possibility.

Still gaping, he nodded.

"Can I come in?" Ivy shivered despite the heat.

He pushed the curtain aside enough for her to step in.

"Hi," she breathed, and for a moment, Ethan stood there with water coursing over him, tracing paths over his gorgeous muscles and down to his-

Nope. Eyes up, Johnson, Ivy thought. *No shower shenanigans while he's injured.*

Ethan maneuvered them so Ivy stood beneath the spray, their bodies close but not touching as the water coursed over her hair and skin. The water was cooler than she preferred, and she squeaked and shivered, crossing her arms over her torso for warmth. Ethan chuckled and reached past her to turn the tap to the warmer side. The smooth, warm heat of his body slid against hers, and Ivy wished her arms weren't blocking the slide of her nipples over his chest.

"So, you need help with your hair?"

"Mhmm."

"Okay." Breathlessly, she squeezed the travel-sized bottle, a handful of his minty shampoo squirting into her palm.

Then she glanced up to where his head was about a mile above her reach.

"Ethan?"

He took a moment to answer, seeming more interested in tracking the rivulets of water running over her chest and down her stomach.

"Yeah?" He was slow to answer.

"I can't reach your hair."

"Hmm."

"Eyes up here, Ethan."

He reluctantly dragged his gaze up again, his full lips forming a pout.

"What were you saying?"

"I can't reach your hair, you fucking redwood."

He grinned at her, then slowly lowered to his knees so he was kneeling on the bathtub floor before her. Now his face was perfectly even with her breasts; if she breathed deeply, his face would go right between them.

"How 'bout now?" His voice reverberated through her, sending heat shooting through her belly. Lower.

"Yeah. Yeah, that's good."

Maybe Ivy took longer than necessary to work the shampoo into a lather between her palms, but she was too distracted by the dark gleam in Ethan's eyes. After a moment, she remembered what she was supposed to do and pushed the frothy mess into Ethan's hair. He closed his eyes and leaned forward, placing his forehead between her breasts, groaning as her nails scraped his scalp. The sound echoed through her, feeding the flickering desire building in her bones. His hands wrapped around her ankles and slowly traveled up the backs of her legs, tracing light circles over the sensitive skin behind her knees. As she scrubbed his long hair, his hands traveled higher, pressing into her thighs and eventually kneading into the roundness of her backside. They groaned at the same time, and he leaned his head back to look at her then pressed a kiss to her breastbone. Could he hear her heartbeat, so close to it?

When Ivy turned to detach the shower head, Ethan's hands rose higher, his thumbs stroking over the curve of her waist. Ivy pushed his head back with one hand, rinsing out the shampoo with the other, scrubbing until the foam disappeared. His eyes were closed, and the rumbling in his chest told her how much he had enjoyed her help. It was new, that feeling of being bewitched by pure sensation, so attuned to his every movement. Turning back to hang the shower head, Ivy felt Ethan's tongue flick out to trace a stripe across the underside of her breast, and she stifled a moan. He smirked but didn't do it again. Instead, he found his shower gel and squeezed some into his palm before rubbing his hands over her shoulders and down over her breasts and stomach. His slow strokes stoked the fire in her belly, and she had to remind herself he was injured, and they *couldn't have sex*.

Yet every nerve ending Ivy possessed sang for him beneath his touch. Did he know how strongly he affected her?

If he didn't touch her where she needed him soon, Ivy thought she might expire on the spot.

His hands drew a light path over her stomach and down her legs, then back up her calves and the backs of her thighs to her rear. He was tall enough to wrap his arms around her and scrub the soap up to her shoulders and upper back one-handed, so he didn't stretch his side. When he finished and Ivy was about to beg him to either stop teasing her or to fucking *touch* her already, Ethan gently pushed her back under the spray of water until all traces of the soap were gone.

Every touch burned and teased and *ached*, and when his fingers found the crease of her thighs, she shivered despite the scorching heat of the water. Gripping her hips, Ethan pulled Ivy back until their bodies were pressed together, with him still on his knees before her. The shape of his body through the steam burned into her brain, all haloed and cloudy, soft around the edges like an old photograph. With one hand, he traced his fingers over her belly to reach up and palm one breast while he pressed open-mouthed kisses to the underside of the other. His other hand drew lower to the juncture of her thighs before dipping between them at the same time he sucked a nipple into his mouth.

She gasped his name as Ethan's mouth seared her skin, and Ivy nearly collapsed when a finger brushed gently over her clit before dipping lower to swirl over her entrance. His other hand

and his mouth moved in the same rhythm, with his thumb and tongue flicking over her nipples before he pinched and sucked at the same time. Slow-burning ecstasy built, flickering in time with his fingers. His other hand painted slow, lazy circles over the swollen bundle of nerves at her apex before he slid a finger inside her. Gasping, Ivy's inner muscles clenched around his finger as he curled it *right* where she needed it. Her thighs began trembling.

Then Ethan's hand and mouth stopped laving at her nipples as he sat back on his heels to look between her face and where his finger stroked inside her. So slowly, he removed his finger, and when he pushed it back into her, he added another, crooking his fingers just enough that her whole body trembled, and if he kept it up, she was going to—

"Don't come, Ivy," he said against her skin.

"What?" She groaned, grinding against his hand where his fingers remained inside her because it was too fucking good, but he *stopped.*

"Don't come." His free hand gripped her waist, squeezing to keep her from grinding, from searching for any source of friction.

"Why?" she pleaded.

"Because, Ivy," and oh god, the way he growled her name was almost enough to send her over the edge even with his fingers stilled inside her, "when I make you come for the first time, you're going to come on my tongue."

Oh.

Oh.

And then he dipped his dark head forward to lick a stripe over her center as his fingers began pumping again. Ivy couldn't control the sounds coming out of her mouth as she reached down and threaded her fingers into his wet hair. His tongue circled over her before he used his left hand to gently spread her, sucking her clit into his mouth, and swirling his tongue over the sensitive bud.

Stars erupted behind her closed lids, and Ivy lost track of what Ethan was doing with that sinful mouth. All she knew was how good it felt to have his mouth on her, his fingers inside her.

Ivy swore and moaned his name again. Her hips bucked, and her upper back pressed into the cold tile, but she didn't notice because *holy fuck* it was so good. Wave after wave of pleasure crashed over her until she almost collapsed to the floor with him. Gently, she tugged his hair to pull his attention away from where he was still sucking and laving at her over-sensitive clit.

Ethan rose slowly, kissing his way up her body to finally land at her lips, melding their bodies together. With a sigh, Ivy opened her mouth at the glide of his tongue over her lips and wrapped her arms around his waist.

"Ow!" Ethan yelled, and Ivy jerked herself back into the cold tile. "Come back, it's okay," he panted, eyes still dark and wild.

"Are you sure?" Ivy stayed away.

He grabbed her, pulling their bodies back together. His hard length pressed into her belly and without thinking, she slid one hand between them to wrap around him. His shudder was enough encouragement that she pumped her fist, slowly increasing pressure and speed. A growl left his lips in the form of her name. His hips jerked against her hand, and she watched in fascination, wishing he was rutting into *her* instead of her hand. But they'd have time for that when he wasn't injured. When he pressed his face into the hollow of her neck and shoulder, Ivy pressed her face to his chest, and then he came on her belly after a few more powerful thrusts.

When he was spent, he took a cloth and gently cleaned her, then wrapped his arms around her, and they stood for what felt like hours beneath the cooling spray.

15

When sunlight filtered through the gauzy white curtains, Ethan groaned and tried to turn away from the brightness. But he couldn't. What the—

A freckled arm and leg draped over him, and when he shifted, Ivy's chest pressed tightly against his back. He huffed a laugh at *her* spooning *him*. Gently, he disentangled her arm and leg and rolled them both over to wrap himself around her instead. She mumbled in her sleep, and Ethan blissfully went back to sleep with her head tucked under his chin and her hair in his face.

When he woke again, it was to a pair of sleepy brown eyes and mussed curly hair peering at him over Ivy's head.

"Janna?"

The little girl stared at him wide-eyed, so Ethan jostled Ivy's shoulder. She groaned but didn't wake up. Ethan took a moment to make sure he was fully clothed, bemoaning his early morning plans, shoved the covers back, and slid out of bed to follow Janna into the living room.

His bruised side was still stiff and sore, but he ignored it when, after Ethan sank to the couch, the little girl immediately crawled into his lap.

"You okay, kiddo?" Ethan wasn't sure what to do.

She sniffled, wrapping her two tiny arms around his bicep as though he was a teddy bear.

"Had a bad dream."

Ethan snuggled her closer, debating on dropping a kiss onto her furrowed forehead. He knew plenty about nightmares; they'd plagued him as a child, too.

"Want to tell me about it?"

"Bad people wanted to take us away from Ivy. I don't want to leave her house. I like it here, and I love Ivy. Do you love Ivy, too?"

He chuckled against the top of her head.

"Maybe one day, Janna, but I haven't known her long enough to know yet. But I do like her a lot."

Janna considered him for a minute, and determining his answer was satisfactory, asked, "Can you make me breakfast?"

"Come on, let's see what we can find."

Eventually, Jase joined Ethan and Janna as they rummaged through the cupboards for ingredients. Thankfully, they found eggs and bacon, but the frozen waffles were irredeemably freezer-burned. The kids decided spaghetti was an acceptable replacement for waffles or bread, so he obliged but not without trepidation.

"Good morning?" Ivy's voice came from the hallway.

She was adorably sleepy still, with messy hair and wearing an oversized shirt she'd swiped from his duffle bag. She rubbed her eyes and stretched, and Ethan wanted to carry her back to the bedroom and have his way with her.

"You have good timing."

"I smelled bacon." Ivy squinted at the stove. "What's this?" She tapped a spoon on the pot as she peered down into its depths.

"I'm not sure," Ethan said. "Breakfast spaghetti? It was their idea." He pointed to Jase and Janna, who looked supremely pleased with his creation. Can you help me?" He huffed out a breath to lift a lock of hair out of his eyes and shook his head, letting the dark waves fall over his eyes for emphasis, before pouring the eggs over the noodles, cheese, and bacon.

"You want me to..." She tugged a red satin scrunchie off her wrist and flapped it at him.

"Yeah? It's getting in my eyes."

Blinking a few times, Ivy came over behind him and reached up, making grabby hands at his hair, and Ethan squatted down for Ivy to scrape back the top half of his hair into what felt like a half-bun.

"Thanks, sweetheart."

"Welcome."

He shook his head a little, testing her work. When it didn't move, he smirked. "I kinda like it. I'm keeping this."

"Oh yeah?" She stepped closer.

"Yeah."

Her hands traveled down his neck and shoulders, caressing gently down his back until she lightly swatted him on the ass.

"Did you just feel me up?" Ethan asked. "There are children present."

"I don't know what you're talking about." He heard the grin in Ivy's voice and the drip of coffee into her mug.

He scooped the finished concoction into bowls, and Ivy stared down at hers.

"Huh." Ivy took a bite. " 's good." She spoke with her mouth full and continued chewing before swallowing audibly and taking a sip of her coffee.

Everyone dug into the food, and while the ingredients weren't something he'd have chosen to put together, Ethan had to admit it had turned out better than he'd expected. The meal perfectly encapsulated what he had now that he'd found Ivy, unexpected and maybe a little offbeat. And he loved it. Breakfast spaghetti would become a tradition if he and Janna had anything to say about it.

"So," he said, leaning back against the counter after they'd finished eating, "you met my parents."

"That I did," Ivy replied. "Not what I expected."

What did she mean? Had meeting his parents so soon been too much?

But, no, she'd still brought him home with her last night and let him...

"Ethan?" her voice broke through his thoughts.

"Yeah?"

"I can hear you thinking. Stop it."

Ivy came to face him and positioned herself between his legs, pressing her hands into his pecs and tilting her head back to look at him.

"Meeting the parents is a typical thing to do in a relationship?" She made the last word a question.

"Are you sure you want that?" Ethan's voice came out softer and sadder than he'd intended.

Are you sure you want me?

She bumped her hips into his and dimpled up at him, biting her lip when he grabbed her ass to keep her there.

"I think I've made it pretty clear that I do, Ethan. The question is, is this what *you* want?" She gestured around her at the messy kitchen with crayon drawings on the fridge, stacks of plastic plates and cutlery covered in cartoon characters, and a lone teddy bear peeking out of a lower cabinet.

And he didn't realize it until she pointed it out, but it *was.* There was a family, ready-made and waiting for him.

His answer was a kiss that began soft and chaste but quickly turned searing, with teeth and tongues and grasping.

The doorbell rang.

Shit, he'd forgotten Jen was coming to pick him up.

Ivy nipped the soft spot beneath his jaw, and he had to physically remove her from his space because she seemed intent on staying there.

"Stop it, you." He pointed an accusatory finger at her, and she pouted.

Ethan bit her pouting bottom lip, but the doorbell sounded again, longer and more insistently.

"Damn it," he growled against her mouth.

After he said his goodbyes, Ethan followed Jen to her silver Range Rover.

"That was all very domestic," Jen said as she reversed the car out into the street.

"What?"

"That... *that...* that I just witnessed." She waved her hand vaguely in the direction of the apartment building. "Kissing the wife and kids goodbye."

A vision of the future popped into Ethan's head: waking up to Ivy every day. Making breakfast. Kissing her goodbye. Would she want that too?

"Dude. What happened yesterday?" Jen slid mirrored sunglasses up her nose.

After the perfect night he'd spent with Ivy, Ethan had forgotten about his parents and...everything else. He scrubbed his eyes with the heels of his hands.

"It's a shitshow, Jen."

"Do you want to talk about it?"

"What is this, Therapy with Jen hour?" Ethan kept his tone light as he deflected.

"Shut up, asshole, you know what I mean."

"Yeah, I guess I do, Dr. Jen." Ethan ran his hands through his hair, staring out the window.

"So, Ethan Fisher, huh?"

"That's me."

"You going to tell the team?"

"You think I should?"

"I think they're going to find out eventually, and I think it would be better if it came from you, especially with all this 'team building' shit of Harkness's."

Fucking Harkness.

"Do you think we'll have to do yoga and meditate again?" He hoped not, but fully expected the torturous practice to be added to the rotation in team meetings.

"Probably. Guess we'll have to get used to it."

They groaned in unison.

When they reached the stadium, Isaac appeared and grabbed Ethan by the arm, uncharacteristic seriousness casting a shadow over his dark skin.

"Look, I'm sorry man. About oversharing yesterday."

Ethan rolled his eyes. Isaac had always been horrible at secrets.

"It would've come out eventually. Does the whole team know yet?" Ethan asked.

"I kept my mouth shut. This time. You've got a scary reputation around here, and I didn't want big, bad meany-face Ethan Ford after me."

Ethan rolled his eyes again.

"Shut up, Isaac." But it lacked venom.

Isaac danced around Ethan, singing, "Who's afraid of Ethan Ford? Who's afraid of Ethan Ford?"

"Reyes." Harkness's voice cut through the singing like a knife. "Must you be so juvenile? We have a visitor."

Ethan turned to look past Harkness, and sure enough, there was Laura Lorne, who nodded curtly at them both.

"Boys," she said, and Ethan needed to stop rolling his eyes, or he'd wind up with a migraine.

Isaac bounded over to Laura and hugged her while Ethan remained wary. Last night aside, he was still uncertain how to be around his mother after so long.

"Can we talk?" she asked softly.

Ethan nodded.

"Emily, may we borrow your office?"

"Of course," Harkness said. "Reyes, with me."

Reluctantly, Ethan followed his mother to Harkness's office, where Laura seated herself behind the large desk. Resting her elbows on its surface and steepling her fingers before her the same way Harkness had the day before, Laura watched Ethan in silence for what seemed like a decade. Being under her intense scrutiny sent him back to his teenage years when all he did was disappoint her.

"How are you?" she finally asked.

"Fine," he bit out.

"And the x-rays?"

"Fine," Ethan repeated.

Laura pinched the bridge of her nose.

"Ethan," she began. "I would like to get to know you again, but I can't do that if you're going to act like a surly teenager."

Ethan sighed too.

"Fine," he said again, and she glared daggers. "Sorry." He ducked his head. "How—how is Dad?"

Seeing his parents in the hospital had been unexpected. But seeing how old and frail Jimmy looked in the wheelchair had been unsettling.

"The doctors say he'll be fine after a round of antibiotics and some physical therapy. It's not as bad as they initially thought. But he's not as young as he thinks he is." Then Laura rolled *her* eyes.

"Hmm." He was relieved but unsure what else to say.

"Ivy seems nice." Laura changed the subject.

"She is."

"How did the two of you meet?" She still peered at him over her steepled fingers.

"She's Derek Johnson's foster sister, and he gave her tickets a few weeks ago. I signed some balls for the kids."

"And what is she to you? Have you been together long?"

Ethan barked a laugh.

"No, we haven't been together long."

But it seemed like forever. There was no way he was letting that tidbit of information slip to his mother, though.

"Hmm." Laura looked at him for a long moment. "Jimmy is smitten with the little girl."

"Janna? Yeah, she's a cute kid."

"What's the boy's name?" she asked.

"Jase."

"He looks like you did," she said quietly.

Ethan said nothing, but he understood what she meant.

"So, we thought—well *I* thought— you...I thought you had a family and didn't tell us."

And it stung, to hear the hurt in her voice, even if the slight had been imagined.

"Mom, I wouldn't have..." he paused. "Ivy has..." but that didn't feel right, either. "I think...I want to start over. Being with Ivy has... shown me that."

"I'd like to start over too. We've missed you, you know. Lawrence has been keeping tabs on you."

Ethan's hackles rose at the mention of his uncle.

"I don't want to talk about Lawrence."

"Ethan," Laura started, but he interrupted.

"No, I won't. I'm not ready."

For a moment, Laura's face froze, and Ethan knew she was trying to hide whatever she was feeling.

Just as he always did.

"Okay," she said, sounding defeated, and Ethan wondered just how tired she was. Laura Lorne was *never* defeated. She was infamous for that. "Oh, and Ethan?" she added. "I'd like to meet Ivy. Officially."

Ethan grimaced as he left the office.

The day's team meeting was more of Harkness's team-building bullshit. After running drills he and his teammates hadn't done since high school, she made them do *trust falls*. It was *terrible*. Ethan hadn't given his teammates cause to trust him, nor had he ingratiated himself with them enough to trust them, so it seemed as though Harkness had chosen this as a specific, hellacious torture meant for him. Derek, of course, loved it. He laughed while falling and stayed leaning back in Isaac's arms a smidge longer than necessary. Jen went through her turn silently and efficiently, falling without flinching and immediately walking away after she was pushed back up. Ethan's turn came too soon, and when he turned his back on his team, he had to count down to his fall to hype himself up. When several pairs of hands caught his arms and back, and unfortunately, his bruised side, Ethan was surprised. He realized he'd *expected* them to drop him. That they hadn't felt like another stitch falling into place, tugging the shattered remnants of his broken self back into place.

Eventually, they proceeded to a more standard practice: conditioning and strategizing in preparation for the next stretch of home games. Harkness's coaching methods, other than her weirdness, were efficient, and after practice, Ethan was confident in his pitching in a way he hadn't been in a long time.

And maybe it was the endorphins, or some residual painkillers in his system, but as he left the stadium parking lot, Ethan decided to drive to the hospital.

It wasn't where he'd expected to see his father again after so long—not that he'd thought much about the *where* so much as the how. The *how,* he expected to be...bad.

But Jimmy hadn't seemed angry last night, so maybe...

Ethan hovered outside the door when it flew open beneath his hand. A nurse in blue scrubs stepped out and held the door for him, so Ethan had no choice but to go in unless he wanted to look like an asshole.

. . .

"Hey, kid." Jimmy looked old. Beeping machines and wires surrounded him, and he seemed small.

At least his voice sounded the same.

"Umm. Hi." Ethan did an awkward wave.

Jimmy snorted.

"Dad, I'm—" Ethan began.

"I know."

And that was it.

It was enough.

When Franklin Soto sauntered in half an hour later, Ethan and Jimmy were discussing baseball, of course. Ethan had been surprised and pleased to learn Jimmy had been keeping up with Ethan's stats, and they were discussing Harkness's methods compared to the good old days of Jimmy's coaches half a lifetime ago. A deep grunt sounded from the doorway, and Ethan looked up to see a large, hairy man leaning on the doorframe.

"Hi, Frankie."

Another grunt.

"How's it going?" Ethan stood and held out his hand, which Frankie used to jerk him into a hug smelling of motor oil and aftershave. Frankie still towered over Ethan, and he rubbed his knuckles into the top of Ethan's head like he had when Ethan was little.

"Ow, dammit! Knock it off, Frank," Ethan groaned, dodging a swipe of his godfather's huge hand.

Frankie grunted and muttered something that sounded like "dumbass kid" under his breath.

"That dumbass kid's got a girlfriend," Jimmy supplied and grinned at Ethan, who promptly started spluttering.

"Oh yeah?" Frankie said. "She cute?"

Ethan bristled.

"She's beautiful."

"She also comes with two foster kids," Jimmy said.

"Kids, huh?" Frankie gazed down at them, waiting to see what Ethan had to say.

He shrugged.

"It's different, but they're good kids. They've had a hard time. Ivy gave them a home."

Jimmy and Frankie shared a knowing look.

"When's the wedding?" Jimmy asked, and Frankie let out a barking laugh.

"Shut up, you miserable busybodies." Ethan rolled his eyes and tugged his hat lower, hopefully before they caught his burning cheeks and stupid grin.

"How are you, old man?" Frankie asked Jimmy.

Jimmy snorted.

"Ready to bust the hell outta here," Jimmy muttered.

"Got the 'Stang fixed up and ready to go when you do," Frankie said.

"How has that piece of junk not been scrapped yet?" Ethan asked, only half-joking.

Both Jimmy and Frankie glared.

"I bet you're still driving those new, flashy, piece of shit, spaceship-looking cars, aren't you?"

"Hell, yes, I am. At least the floorboards don't fall out whenever I hit a bump."

Jimmy chose to ignore that, and Frankie covered his laugh with a cough.

Their conversation felt so familiar and... *normal*...the joking and ribbing. Ethan's chest squeezed, and he looked over at Jimmy, who grinned at him with sparkling eyes.

When Ethan was little, his nightmares had been all violence and danger, the sort of things children are afraid of. As an adult, his nightmares were different: shadows and darkness and emptiness.

Ivy seemed to keep them at bay, but Ethan wondered about her dreams, too. He'd heard her talk in her sleep. Nothing coherent, just jumbled words accompanied by tossing and turning. When that happened, he pulled her against his chest, and she relaxed.

Ethan hoped she'd let him stay again, for both their sakes.

When he parked in her apartment's lot, Ivy, Lily, and the kids clustered around the picnic tables, and Derek pulled into the lot behind him.

As soon as he exited his car, Ethan was mobbed by Jase and Janna. Unsurprisingly, Janna used her brother as a ladder, and Ethan scooped her up, depositing her on his shoulders. He felt her arms resting on top of his head as he walked to where the other adults were hanging around a grill, Jase trailing behind. Ivy didn't notice Ethan at first, and he enjoyed watching her while she gestured excitedly to Lily, waving her beer bottle around.

"Hello, sweetheart," he whispered in her ear as he wrapped his arms around her from behind. She jumped and laughed, squirming in his arms to try to turn around, but Janna wrapped her arms around both his and Ivy's heads, squishing their cheeks together and cackling like a tiny tyrant.

Lily took pity on their predicament, reaching up to remove Janna from Ethan's shoulders. Ivy turned and kissed Ethan, twisting her fingers in the fabric of his shirt to tug him closer, resulting in a wolf whistle from Lily.

"Ladies," Ethan said to Lily and Janna when Ivy released him.

"No one has ever accused me of being a lady, Sasquatch." Lily paused, snapping her gum. "And you probably shouldn't start now."

"Me neither," Janna chimed in.

Ethan saw Jase watching the exchange, and he pressed a

kiss to Ivy's temple, setting his beer down before joining the boy.

"Hey, buddy."

Jase grinned and held out a hand for a fist bump.

"Are you going to get to play this week?" Jase asked.

Ethan watched Jase roll a ball in the fingers of one hand, a nervous tic he was all too familiar with.

"Probably. The bruise is ugly, but it's just a bruise. I've played through worse."

Jase scowled.

"You shouldn't have had to play if you were hurt. Why did your coach treat you like that?" he looked sadly up at Ethan.

And it broke Ethan. He had to consider his answer before he gave it, and what he came up with broke him more.

"I shouldn't have let him treat me so badly, but honestly, it's because I thought I deserved it." Ethan threw an arm over Jase's shoulders. "But nobody deserves it."

And as soon as he'd said it, he knew it was true. A weight he hadn't realized he'd been carrying fell from his shoulders.

Jase scraped the toe of his shoe in the grass but didn't speak.

"Come on, let's get Derek to play catch."

Derek and Janna joined in the game, and Janna surprised Ethan with her deadly, precise aim. Ivy watched while Lily flipped burgers on the grill, and he took the opportunity to savor the moment; nothing special on the surface, but so profound for him. When he caught Ivy watching him, he flexed his chest and biceps more than necessary to make her laugh, watching her eyes go large. He nearly took a ball to the face for his effort, but it was worth it to see her scrunch her nose and stick her tongue out at him.

And it felt so...good. Normal.

And fuck if that wasn't exactly what he wanted.

16

Waking up to Ethan Fisher in her bed was the best way to start the day, Ivy decided.

Sleeping with Ethan was comforting in a way she hadn't known existed. Something about a large, warm body lying next to hers all night was exhilarating. Ivy didn't even feel the need to sneak out of bed to brush her teeth like she'd heard others did. Derek, for instance.

When she woke up, she and Ethan were parallel, facing each other. A lock of long hair fell over his eyes, and Ivy brushed it away before pressing her face into his chest. A heavy arm and leg fell over her, pulling her closer, and he mumbled something against her hair. Ivy wriggled back a little, but Ethan's arm held her in place, and his erection pressed against her stomach. He stopped her before she rubbed against him more.

"Woman," he growled sleepily, "if you don't stop, you're not leaving this bed for the rest of the day. And I don't think *they'll* be too happy about that."

On cue, the door creaked open.

"Ethan! Ethan! Can you make us more breakfast spaghetti?" Janna sang, bouncing on the edge of the bed.

"You have to feed them on time, or things get dicey," Ivy said, smiling as he groaned into her hair.

"I don't wanna," he groaned.

"You created monsters," she laughed. "Come on, let's see what we can find."

When Ethan emerged, awake and showered, hair still dripping onto his shirt, Ivy was reminded of the shower they'd shared and almost purred at the memory of his mouth on her.

"Morning," he said, brushing his lips over hers with a grin before lightly flicking his tongue out and walking away. He knew what she was thinking, and he was *teasing* her, damn it. And since she was looking, she noticed he'd changed out of his shorts into gray sweatpants, and seriously, was so much flexing required to retrieve a mug from a cupboard?

Two could play his game.

"You good for a few minutes? I need to get dressed."

"Hmm? Yeah, go ahead." He was distracted; Janna had latched onto his arm, trying to pull him to the stove to cook for them.

Ivy dressed faster than she ever had in her life. She chose her white shorts, knowing they set off her tanned legs, and a soft black tee loose enough to hang off one shoulder and gap open if she leaned *just so.* And she conveniently forgot to put a bra underneath.

Then, when she emerged, she made sure to stretch and arch her back to reach the milk in the refrigerator and to stay doubled over longer than necessary when searching through the bottom drawer. She knew her plan had worked because there was a crash and a curse from Ethan's direction. Smirking, she sauntered over to him and bumped him with a hip to move him away from the sink to unnecessarily wash her hands, then she leaned past him to grab a towel, and his breathing hitched.

"Ivy," he growled low in her ear, drawing out her name, the syllables a caress against her skin. "If you don't stop, the first time I fuck you will not be what I had planned, and it'll just be me throwing you over my shoulder and bending you over the bed like a caveman. And you don't want that, do you?"

Ivy did. She really fucking did.

"Plans?" she deflected.

"Rose petals and candles and wine and shit."

"Ethan?" She hooked her fingers into his pockets and pulled him forward.

"Yeah?" Ethan's eyes were dark from where he towered above her.

She put her face against his neck, tracing her tongue along a vein, and canted her hips into his.

"You owe the swear jar. Double." Then she laughed, ducked under his arms, and ran away.

Eventually, they'd both calmed down enough for Ethan to convince the kids he would cook for them the next time he stayed over, and they settled for cereal instead.

"So, we're playing at home for the next few days. It'll be my first game back. Will you be there?" Ethan asked, dumping more Froot Loops into his bowl.

"Yes!" Jase yelled before Ivy answered.

"Do you want us to come?" Ivy asked, poking her spoon into the sugary dregs of her cereal.

"I always want you to come, Ivy." Ethan's voice lowered, and a flush crept up her chest. He chuckled. "I mean, of course, I'd like for you to be there."

Somehow Harkness tricked me into telling her you'll be at the game. And if Harkness knows, my mom knows. Which means she'll probably be there too.

OMG I've never hung out with someone's mom before 🙃

It's just my mom. It's no big deal.

Just his mom, Ivy thought, scoffing. *No big deal. Right.* Laura Lorne had been so lovely and put together. And she was...not. Ivy had no clue what to talk about if she tried to start a conversation. If they'd even come in contact.

Ugh.

Not to mention she'd never met the parents of a man she'd dated, particularly under such awkward circumstances. Even if the word 'dating' seemed anticlimactic for what they were doing.

And Ivy was spiraling.

I've never met parents before, much less hung out with them.

I don't know what to do!

She's just a person.

SHE IS NOT JUST A PERSON ETHAN SHE IS YOUR MOTHER

WHAT IF SHE HATES ME

If she hates you, you'll know it immediately.

But she won't hate you. She'll love you.

I AM FREAKING OUT

If you stop freaking out, I'll make pizza this weekend...

And I'll make you come, too.

HOMEMADE PIZZA?!?!😱

if I lie and say I'm not freaking out will you do it anyway?

Maybe...

okay deal😘

How though?

How what?

how will you make me come?

Which time?

Ivy had to put her phone down to catch her breath or she'd do something indecent at the park.

Ethan?

Yeah?

Thanks. This helped. this is why I keep you around.

You only want me because I make you pizza? Thanks. 😂

not just that! you're pretty too. 😈

That's encouraging.

Why are you REALLY freaking out?

She didn't want to tell him. It was stupid, but she felt how she felt. It had always been there, that tiny, nagging feeling. Of not belonging, of not being good enough. Particularly being with Ethan, especially after seeing his mother, who happened to be the owner of a massive sports agency and a fucking *heiress*. And it wasn't Ethan making her feel that way, that was all Ivy.

But it stung, nonetheless.

Ivy typed and retyped her answer, knowing the three little dots disappearing and reappearing on Ethan's end must have been driving him crazy, not wanting to give him her answer, but also wanting to relieve the aching pressure gathering in her chest.

She sent her answer knowing Ethan would hate it.

After a few minutes, her phone vibrated with a call. When she picked up, Ethan's voice was rough in a way she'd never heard before.

"Ivy, don't talk down to yourself. If anything, *you're* too good for *me*."

"Don't you start," she snapped. "Nobody's too good for anybody. That's not how this works."

"You're right. It's not."

"Don't you mind-trick me, you...you mind-tricker." Ivy sighed at the poor insult.

He chuckled in her ear, the low sound sending sparks down her spine. Lower.

"Seriously, Ivy. Don't ever feel like you're not good enough. It's how I've felt all my life until..." he stopped mid-sentence.

And she thought she knew what he meant, but she needed to hear him say it.

"Until...?" she pressed.

"Until you," he said simply.

Her eyes burned with unshed tears.

"Thank you for that," she said, her voice sounding watery. "Do I still get pizza and orgasms?"

"Anything for you, sweetheart," he rumbled.

God, she loved when he called her sweetheart.

"Sorry, I'm— "

But he stopped her.

"Don't apologize," he interrupted. "I get it. But I've got to go. I'm hiding in the bathroom, and we're supposed to be meditating and manifesting, whatever the hell that means. Harkness is...something else."

"Okay. Think about me while you meditate."

"I was."

TO JASE'S IRRITATION, THEY SKIPPED THE PREGAME WARMUP, BUT Ivy didn't think Janna would last through that *and* the game. A sweet, white-haired man with high-waisted khaki shorts, high white socks, and black Velcro-closure shoes led them to their seats. Ivy wanted to hug him. When the man announced they'd arrived at their seats, they were greeted by Laura, who managed to look quite regal in jeans and an expensive-looking red tee.

"Hi," Ivy said shyly.

Laura seemed almost as uncomfortable as Ivy; her hand trembled when they shook.

Jase had brought a pair of Lily's birdwatching binoculars, and even though their seats were on the front row directly behind home plate, he had them trained on the players.

Laura nudged Ivy with her elbow.

"Ethan was just like him. He lived and breathed baseball. He'd bring his program to every game and write down every single hit and pitch."

Ivy caught Jase listening. He didn't look their way, but he'd *love* being compared to Ethan.

"Jase only recently discovered baseball, but he's already so into it. I'm going to check out the rec center teams for him for next season," Ivy offered.

He beamed at her from his seat.

Janna, feeling left out of the conversation, plopped down beside Laura, a blue ice pop dripping in her hand.

"Queen Laura?" she said.

Laura looked bewildered to be addressed so. "Yes, Janna?"

"Are you Ethan's mommy?"

"I am."

"I like Ethan. Do you know why he's so sad?"

Laura blinked, nonplussed.

Music echoed through the stadium, breaking the tension.

Until Ivy's phone rang. An unknown number. She answered with her heart in her throat.

"Ivy, hi, I just wanted to let you know I received your paperwork, and everything is all straightened out."

The voice was familiar, but she hadn't even received an email from the school with her paperwork yet, how could they have gotten it back?

"Sorry, who is this?"

"Nayomi Harrison. Sorry, this is my cell, not my office phone. I'm on the way out, but I know you were worried, so I wanted to let you know ASAP."

"Oh." Relief washed over her at the same time as irritation. What the hell was taking the school so long? "Thank you. Have a good night." She tried to keep her tone even; Nayomi wasn't the problem.

"Is everything all right?"

Ivy let out a rough exhale, explaining the whole ordeal again. "I got a one-line email last week, reminding me that my application would expire in thirty days if nothing happened. So, there's that." She took a sip of her soda, crunching on a piece of ice.

"Too bad everyone I know on the school board retired." Laura patted Ivy's arm affectionately. "Maybe a donation would help move them along."

"Ethan said the same thing. It's good to know I can hit you both up for fundraisers in the future," she joked.

"You think he'll want us around in the future?"

"I think that's something you'll have to work out together. But I think he's willing to try if you are." She wondered if Laura knew how lonely Ethan had been as a child. His background wasn't the same as Jase's, and it wasn't her place to share either of their stories. But she hoped Ethan and his parents were able to sit down and hash out their past, for better or worse. So many things remained unsaid between them.

Then Ethan was at bat, and as he settled into his stance, Ivy appreciated the curve of his rear in those tight white pants, the width of his shoulders. His jaw worked as he chewed, and he puckered his lips slightly to snap the gum between his teeth.

Breathing out a sigh, Ivy daydreamed about those lips and imagined the ripple of his back muscles as he swung the bat for a foul.

With the swivel of his hips, Ivy got an intense visual of him swiveling those hips into *her,* and she sighed again, biting her tongue to keep any more noises from escaping.

"I remember the early days," Laura said, raising one eyebrow. "Jimmy in those pants...well... you get it."

Ivy let out a squeak at being caught ogling him by his *mother*.

"Don't be embarrassed," Laura laughed. "I know exactly how you feel. Jimmy and I were intense in our younger days. Did you know— well you wouldn't because we never told Ethan. But remind me one day to tell you all about why you should never use stadium seats for," and she paused to peer at the kids, "ah, adult activities."

If Ivy had been drinking, she would have sprayed it halfway across the field. As it was, she gaped at Laura before breaking into a howling laugh.

"I'm surprised," she said.

Ivy, panicking, ran through everything she'd said in the past hour. Nothing embarrassing came to mind, though.

"If I were you," Laura continued, "I'd be asking for all the dirt on Ethan. Embarrassing stories, baby photos..."

"Oh! I..." Ivy trailed off, uncertain how to explain. "Did Ethan tell you about me?"

"Not much. Why?"

Ivy held her breath for a moment.

"I was in foster care for most of my life. I don't have any photos or embarrassing baby stories, so I hadn't considered them." Laura's face blanched, and her eyes grew wide. "It's okay," Ivy added hastily. "I'm...okay. I just...didn't think about it." After a few moments of silence, she added, "I would *love* to hear embarrassing baby Ethan stories though. And pictures! I bet he was the cutest baby."

Laura's eyes shuttered before she blinked, offering Ivy a bright smile.

"Of course! I found a few I thought you might like to see."

Then they pored over photos of tiny Ethan in an oversized baseball hat propped on top of ears too big for his little head, perched on his father's shoulders. Toddler Ethan running across the infield in only a diaper. Elementary Ethan in a Little League uniform, covered in dirt and Gatorade, holding a shining trophy.

"He was so cute!" Ivy squealed, handing the photos back to Laura.

"Jase reminds me a lot of Ethan at that age." Laura nodded to where Jase stood behind Janna, waving to the mascot, but still more solemn than the other kids his age. "Always so serious."

INSIDE THE DUGOUT, ETHAN HAD TO RESIST THE URGE TO casually observe Ivy and Laura together. Instead, he resorted to pacing in a tight line behind a rack of unused gear.

"Fis— ah, Ethan," Harkness said. "You're up."

Shit, he was next on deck. Quickly, Ethan tugged off his hat and jammed on his helmet, grabbing the bat Jen handed him on his way out of the dugout. He tried to catch a glimpse of Ivy and Laura since their seats were right behind home plate, but he took too long, and the umpire glared at him from behind the plate. Shaking his shoulders, Ethan stepped up to the plate. After two fouls, he knocked one down the center, far enough to get whichever teammate was on third all the way home. He had no idea who was on third, but they scored, so it didn't *really* matter. Ethan knew he shouldn't try to see them, but he wanted to know how it was going.

Ethan was astonished to find Ivy and Laura deep in conversation as Janna happily devoured a cotton candy cloud. Jase had binoculars trained in his direction, and he gave the boy a sharp nod, just like Jimmy did when Ethan was young.

Readjusting his hat, Ethan trained his eyes on the pitcher. The shortstop moved nearer, and when the second baseman edged a few steps further away in preparation for Jen's hit, he saw his chance.

Slowly crouching so the movement drew less attention,

Ethan edged as far as possible while remaining on first, taking advantage of his long legs. When the pitcher set his back foot on the rubber, Ethan's fingers twitched, and he took off, making it a third of the way to second before the other team was even aware of his movement. He dove, sliding into second, and the umpire called him safe. The crowd on the home side went wild, with popcorn flying and fans screaming. To the side, Ethan saw Jase jumping and screaming too, but he resolved not to let himself get distracted by Ivy again.

Ethan watched and waited until Derek hit a home run, pulling the Hawks even with the Brewers, tying the game.

And when he jogged home, Ethan took the opportunity to glance at the stands. Ivy and Jase were jumping up and down together, waving at him, and Janna held Laura's hands, doing a silly dance with her. They were all grinning like fiends and screaming at him as his teammates crowded around Ethan, Jen, and Derek.

Ethan grinned, accepting the 'good games' and fist bumps from his teammates without glowering.

And having someone waiting for him, watching his games, actually feeling like a part of the team? It was electrifying, making him want to be the best, not just out of obligation, but for the *team.*

At the top of the sixth, raindrops splattered over his forearms where he stood on the mound, watching and waiting as Derek signaled him from where he squatted behind home plate. Rain was fairly uncommon this time of year, and Ethan squinted past the stadium lights into the now dark, cloudy sky.

It was as though the sky split open, and both teams raced back to their respective dugouts, though they were already soaked. Ethan jogged in from the mound and gratefully accepted a towel from a bat boy. It did nothing to dry his soaked uniform, but at least he was no longer blinded by raindrops.

"Freak rainstorm, huh?" Derek leaned over the rail, holding out a hand to catch drops in his palm.

Isaac slung an arm around Derek's shoulders.

"It's fun, though, right? Makes me feel like a kid again, playing in the rain."

After a few minutes, music poured from the speakers, and the stadium cameras began panning over the seats, looking for fans entertaining themselves to wait out the rain.

Ryan's voice interrupted the music, informing fans the local weatherman had assured him the rain should end shortly, so the game should resume in about half an hour, and the music returned. Applause burst out, and on the screen, Ethan saw the fans getting more into the music, dancing in the aisles and on the throughway.

Isaac jumped over the dugout railing, landing with a splash as he danced to the music, some song with a fast beat about thunder, and Derek followed, leading Jen. Isaac bopped over to Harkness, beckoning for her to join them. More of their teammates joined in, and Jen and Derek splashed their way over to Ethan, who reluctantly let them drag him into their dancing. And then, the whole team, coaches, trainers, and bat boys and all, danced on the sidelines while they waited out the rain.

When the song ended, Ethan returned to the dugout. Harkness sat the next song out, too, so they watched the JumboTron, with Harkness laughing at the crowd's antics, and Ethan hoping for a glimpse of Ivy.

Someone in the tech department decided it was time for a KissCam. The camera panned over couples, many of whom put on a big show for the camera. A twinge of jealousy hit Ethan since he'd never participated in that particular baseball pastime.

As though thinking of her summoned her, Ivy appeared on the screen. She was dancing in the uncovered area in the front row of seats behind home. She was soaked, but she sang while she twirled in the rain. Ethan guessed she saw herself on the screen because she winked and blew a kiss to the camera. Behind her, Janna gave Jase a smacking kiss on his cheek. He rolled his eyes.

"That's your girl?" Harkness asked from her seat beside him.

"Yeah. Ivy." He couldn't take his eyes off the screen, where the camera lingered on her dancing. A few others joined her, taking her hands or dancing together in the aisle. Ethan watched while Ivy held Janna's hands as they spun around each other.

"Go get her. Dance with her."

Ethan, sure he'd misheard, glanced over at Harkness, who made shooing motions at him.

"Go on. We'll be here for a while."

"Thank you?" he said, and then he was out of the dugout and vaulting himself over the rails into the stands. And there she was in all her rain-soaked glory. The last notes of the song she was dancing to floated away, and a new one began, slower, with a stronger beat. Ivy's hips swayed, rocking into the rhythm. He crossed the final few steps and she saw him right before he crashed into her.

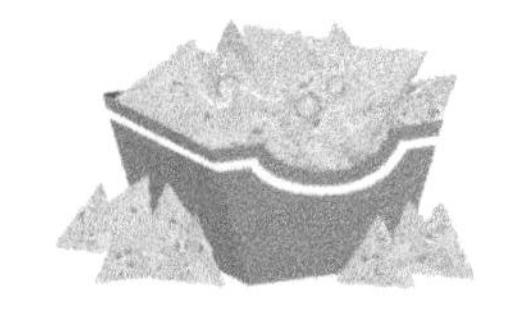

IVY NOTICED THE SOAKING-WET BASEBALL PLAYER BARRELING toward her a second before she sensed the warmth of his body through his wet uniform. Ethan's lips pressed into hers, and she thought he might devour her in front of the whole stadium filled with baseball fans, and oh God, his *mother*. But she didn't care as he wrapped her in his arms and lifted her, somehow managing to keep their mouths tangled together. Ivy laughed as he finally lowered her to catcalls and wolf whistles from the fans. She hid her face against his chest, reveling in his warmth as she realized the camera was still on them, with their faces showing on the enormous screen beyond the outfield.

"Hi," she managed to say, her voice muffled against his chest.

She still tasted his peppermint gum, and her heart seemed like it might beat out of her chest.

But she felt his heart hammering beneath her fingertips, too.

"Hi," he whispered back. "Come with me."

"What?"

"Come on!" The giant, besotted grin on Ethan's face was nothing compared to what pounded through her chest as he grabbed Ivy's hand, tugging her toward the stairs where he helped her climb over, then he was running with her again, pulling her toward the rest of the team. A slower song began, and Ethan dragged Ivy right to the middle of his teammates, pulling her body against his and wrapping his arms around her. They were *dancing*.

Ethan Ford, dancing on the field for thousands of people to see.

Ivy *loved* it, the heat of him against her, swaying with the music, each raindrop drawing cold trails over her skin. With a smirk, Ethan dipped Ivy, bending her back over his arm. The sudden change in altitude had her gripping his arms for balance as Ethan's torso folded over hers.

"I won't let you go." His voice was low in her ear, the stadium lights reflected like stars in the deep brown of his irises.

And then they were upright again, and Ethan was spinning her, their movements splashing through the falling rain.

"This is fun." Ivy grinned at him, a little breathless. "How inappropriate would it be if I groped you in front of all these nice people?"

"Very, very inappropriate." His voice dropped an octave. "It's the pants, huh?" Ivy nodded. With a low chuckle, Ethan lowered his forehead to rest on hers. "I'll wear them for you later. You can grab whatever you want then." Then he slanted his lips over hers again, much to the enjoyment of his teammates.

"Promise?" Ivy asked, pressing the curves of her body against the hardness of Ethan's and swinging her hips against his in time with the music, all while grinning wickedly up at him.

"Anything for you, sweetheart," he said, and she melted against him.

Eventually, the umpires called the game over when the rain didn't stop. Ethan grumbled about the tied score, but Ivy had seen a whole new side of Ethan, and for her, it was worth it.

17

After coming out on top of three of their last four games, the Hawks had a day off before a week of away games, and Ethan intended to take full advantage.

Anticipation got the best of him, so he went straight to Ivy's apartment after buying flowers, wine, and candles, just like he'd joked. Derek's car was parked in the lot already, but Ethan was early, so he wasn't surprised when Derek opened the door, silently gesturing over his shoulder at the shrieking laughter and loud music coming from the direction of Ivy's room.

"Dude," Derek said, "you do *not* want to go back there. They threatened me with a curling iron. A *curling iron*. It would ruin me." Derek shuddered at the prospect of hot tools, patting his hands protectively over his perfect fade with longer curls on top.

Ethan shuddered, thinking of the amount of product in his own hair, and was grateful no one was tall enough to attack him with a curling iron. After fist bumping with Jase and hoisting Janna onto his shoulders, he decided to brave the chaos.

"Actually," Derek said, following Ethan but hiding behind him, "you might have to rescue Ivy. There's no telling what kind of torture Lily's inflicted on the poor girl."

"Oh no!" Ethan said in a mockingly serious voice. "Can we

rescue Princess Ivy?" He jostled the giggling girl on his shoulders before bumping his knee against Ivy's door in a semblance of a knock.

More shrieking ensued from behind the door. Lily's head poked out, and she brandished the curling iron at them.

"You're here early! Go away!"

Ethan tried to peer past her but couldn't see past the cloud of what he hoped was steam from the shower. But it smelled a lot like hairspray.

"Save me, Ethan! You're my only hope!" Ivy's laughing voice came from somewhere amidst the cloud.

"Has anyone ever told you you're a rudely large man, Sasquatch?" Lily yelled from somewhere near his sternum. "Scram. We'll be done soon."

If a half-hour was soon, they were done soon.

Ivy emerged into the living room where Ethan and Derek were playing with the kids, and since he feared the giant wrath of tiny Lily, he refrained from telling her they were late.

"Hi," Ivy said, almost shyly, and Ethan tried to ignore the rush of blood that left his brain and went south when she blushed and dimpled up at him.

She was *stunning*. The light-blue dress she wore wrapped around her upper body before flowing down from her waist, stopping halfway down her thighs. The v-shaped neckline crossed over itself and shifted when she moved, and Ethan had to grit his teeth to keep his jaw from going slack when he realized a ribbon tied in a bow around her waist was the *only* thing holding the dress together.

Lily gave him a knowing smirk.

"Like what you see, Squatch?"

Derek elbowed him in the ribs, and all he got out was "Ow. I mean—wow."

Ivy laughed at him, and her dimples grew deeper, the

sunlight bringing out the gold in her hazel eyes as she stared up at him.

"Gross. Get a room, you two," Lily called, then laughed at her joke. "I guess that's the plan, right?"

"Shut up, Lily," Ivy hissed before kneeling to hug Janna. The blue dress split over her thigh, and Ethan had to remind himself how to breathe. Somehow, though he'd seen every inch of her, this new glimpse of skin had his blood boiling like a Victorian man having seen his first bare ankle.

They said their goodbyes, and Janna wouldn't let him go until he promised to cook for them the next time he stayed over. Lily made them take awkwardly staged photos on the way out, and as they drove away, Ethan commented that it felt like they had been sent to prom by their parents.

"I have a feeling you hated prom," she said.

"I didn't even go to prom."

"Why not?" she asked, peering up at him after sliding on large sunglasses.

Ethan shrugged.

"Never had time to. Not that I would have been brave enough to ask anyone anyway."

She put her hand over his where it rested on the gear shifter.

"Too bad. I would have loved to see pictures of baby Ethan in a tux."

He snorted at her but grinned.

"I had the *worst* haircut at eighteen, and I was too skinny and all ears." He scowled at the memory.

"I *like* your ears." She pouted at him. "So, what would I have to do to get you in a tux *now*?"

"Aren't you a little old for prom?"

"I meant, aren't there other reasons to wear a tux? Some kind of formal baseball event? Baseball prom?"

Ethan scoffed.

"Yes, but I've never been."

Ivy gaped.

"There's a baseball prom?"

He laughed, flipping his hand over on the shifter to thread her fingers through his.

"It's a formal party after the season's over, given by some of the League's sponsors." He paused, thinking. "There are various hosts every year, one of the largest of which is my mother's agency. So basically, my mother is throwing a party for my teammates." He groaned.

"So, you don't want to go?" Did she sound disappointed?

"Do *you* want to go to a party like that?" he asked.

"Well, I *would* like to see you in a tux," she simpered at him.

"If I just wear a tux, can we skip the party?" He tried to keep his tone light.

"Oh, come on, don't you think it'll be fun?"

"A party, thrown by my mother, for all of the teams in the League? No, I don't."

"Maybe I can go with Derek then," she offered in a small voice as she looked out the window.

"Shit, I'm sorry, sweetheart. I didn't realize you wanted to go. Want to go to the dumb fancy party with me?" he said in his best apologetic voice and raised their hands to his lips to brush a kiss over her knuckles.

"Will there be food?" She shivered at the touch of his lips against her fingers.

"Of course."

"Hmm," she hummed, peeking at him out of the corner of her eye.

"*Fancy* food. Laura Lorne is known for her excellent taste in hors d'oeuvres. And wine."

"Will you dance with me at baseball prom?"

"Do you want me to?"

She nodded almost bashfully.

"Then I will dance with you."

The brightness of her smile rivaled the sun glinting off the river as they drove past.

"This is an interesting location for a date," Ivy remarked, peering out the window at the sign for the specialty supermarket.

"I thought you'd like to pick out your own pizza toppings," he said, grinning at her.

"And you are absolutely right! Let's go!"

And even though it was unconventional, it was probably the most fun he'd had with Ivy, at least with their clothes on. He already had basic ingredients for pizza, but they wandered through the aisles, choosing toppings for what Ethan estimated would be about ten large pizzas if they used them all. Ivy, naturally, tried every sample and loudly proclaimed her love for each, except the funkiest cheeses. They bought enough food for an army and enough desserts for two.

The whole time they wandered through the store, he couldn't keep his hands off her, his fingers itching to untie the ribbon of her dress to discover what lay beneath. Instead, he limited himself to tucking her under his arm as he pushed the cart haphazardly with one hand. She sneaked an extra box of Lucky Charms when he wasn't looking. Ethan pretended not to notice, and Ivy pretended to not notice his pretending. Every few aisles, she would slide her hand in his back pocket and dig her nails into his backside while keeping a straight face and pointing out something silly, and he barely avoided throwing her over his shoulder and driving straight home. Her little game was going to send him into cardiac arrest.

Ivy didn't speak again until they were in his apartment. She toed off her shoes and perched beside him on the counter in her usual spot, a glass of wine in hand, occasionally adding flour or water to his dough as needed.

"Ethan?" Ivy took a large gulp of wine, swinging her legs where they dangled over the edge of the counter.

"Yeah?" He dabbed the tip of her nose with flour.

"I'm kind of— I mean I don't—" and then she groaned and downed the rest of her wine in one go.

"What's wrong, sweetheart?" he asked as he dumped the kneaded dough into an oiled bowl to rise.

He was washing the residual flour off his hands when she sighed deeply.

"The wine helps, I guess."

"Helps what?" Ethan stood in front of Ivy, wedging himself between her knees. With her on the counter, and him between her thighs, he barely restrained himself from tugging the dress apart, but since something was clearly bothering her, he knew he shouldn't. Instead, he compromised by placing his hands on her waist.

"I'm...I'm nervous," she admitted, a blush blooming over her cheeks and chest.

His head snapped up to meet her eyes.

"Nervous? Why?"

She was so kind and so sweet. So perfect. What could she possibly be nervous about?

Ivy buried her face in her hands.

Ethan stroked his thumbs along the curve of her waist. "We don't have to, if—if you don't want to." He might expire, but if she was nervous...

Her breath caught before she spoke.

"I've just never been with someone like you."

Then his mouth was at her collarbone, and he traced it lightly with the tip of his tongue.

"Someone like me?" He nipped the base of her throat and sucked a mark into her skin, smiling against her neck as she writhed.

"Ethan," she said. "Pay attention."

"I am." Working his mouth up her neck to the soft spot beneath her ear, he bit down lightly, and her back arched, thrusting her body against his.

Ivy leaned back and placed a hand on either side of his face, pushing him away from where he was contentedly marking her neck with his teeth.

"Ethan."

His eyes met hers, but the look on her face was incomprehensible.

"What is it? What can I do?" He wracked his brain, trying to figure out what he'd done wrong.

She thought for a moment and sighed. "I don't know how to *be with* someone like you. You're so attentive and so good to me." She looked down, away from him. "I don't want to disappoint you," she said in a small voice.

It occurred to him that the conversation was no longer just about sex. How could she possibly believe she'd disappoint him in *any* way? Ethan resolved to hunt down anyone who'd ever hurt her.

"Ivy," he said, trying to keep the growl out of his voice. "You *can't* disappoint me." He paused. "Look at me." She did, slowly. "I want to be with you. Do you want to be with me?"

She nodded.

"And I care about you, Ivy, a lot. Have I done anything halfway with you?"

Ivy shook her head.

"I guess the real question is, do you trust me to take care of you? To stay?"

Her thumbs grazed over his cheekbones before she leaned forward to rest her forehead against his.

The silence of a few seconds stretched for millennia.

"I do," she whispered.

It was all he needed to hear, putting wings on the shards of his heart that she was slowly piecing back together.

Ethan scooped Ivy off the counter and into his arms. She remained quiet as he carried her, nestling her face against his chest as he walked them down the hallway before kicking open the door to his bedroom and setting her gently on the floor.

Her lips were soft and warm as he molded his to hers, and she relaxed beneath his touch. And then his words from earlier in the week came back to him.

"Shit!"

Ivy fluttered her eyes open, looking confused. "What's wrong? What happened?" Her body went rigid in his hands.

"I forgot the fucking flowers!"

"What flowers?" she asked, still confused.

"The flowers! I told you there'd be wine and flowers, but I forgot to do the thing with the flower petals on the bed. Fuck. They're still in the fucking kitchen!" Ethan raked his hands through his hair, berating himself for being so ready to see her, he'd completely forgotten his plans for romance.

Ivy blinked a few times, then turned around, shoulders shaking. "Ivy?"

She turned back to face him, tears streaming down her face.

She was *laughing* at him.

"I don't need flowers. I just want *you*." She wiped her eyes, then pressed her body into his and reached her face back up to his. His heart took flight, soaring in his chest.

"Are you sure?" he asked. "I promised you flowers."

"Later," she said, her voice husky. "Don't you think we've waited long enough?"

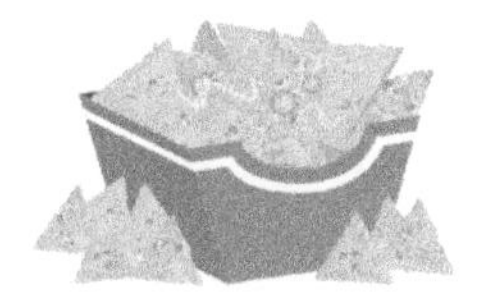

Tired of waiting, Ivy stepped back from Ethan, easing their bodies apart. She wanted this; had wanted it for so long, and she was warring with herself. Did she want to go slow, savoring each lingering touch? Or did she want to feed the fire he'd fueled inside her, to let that inferno take over?

She held up a hand between them when he began to follow her and with her free hand, untied the ribbon holding the dress together. Ethan's breathing paused. The two halves of the dress remained together, despite being untied. Frustrated, Ivy tried to reach up to push the two pieces apart, but Ethan's hands stopped her. He took half a step closer, and with agonizing slowness, slid his hands beneath the fabric to trace his fingers over her ribs and chest to her shoulders, where he gently pushed the sleeves of the dress down, finally making it fall open to reveal her body. Ethan let out a breath and pushed the dress the rest of the way off her arms.

Standing before him in nothing but scraps of lace, Ivy finally dragged her eyes up to meet Ethan's.

It wasn't the first time he'd seen her, but the moment was heavier, weighted with something she couldn't quite name as his dark eyes roamed over her like he didn't know where to start. Her earlier reaction had been silly, she knew, caused by nerves and insecurity more than anything he'd shown, and every ounce of trepidation left her body as Ethan stared at her.

The light pink, barely-there lace of the bra did nothing to hide the darker pink of her nipples. Ivy saw the moment Ethan noticed they were already pebbled and waiting for him to draw them into his mouth because his eyes went nearly black.

"Ethan?"

"Mmm?" He pulled her closer, lowering his mouth to hers.

"You remember the first time you slept over and you had too many clothes on?"

His eyes were still on her as he murmured his assent.

"You're doing it again."

Ivy reached between them to unbutton his shirt, exposing the exquisitely muscled planes of his chest. Slowly, she pushed the sleeves down his arms, enjoying the feel of hard muscle beneath her fingertips. Ethan remained surprisingly still, and when she looked up at him, he was studying her as if she were prey. When their eyes met, Ivy's fingers trailed down the notches of Ethan's abdominal muscles, through the line of dark hair disappearing beneath his jeans, and further to unbuckle his belt and unbutton his jeans. He groaned as she pushed his jeans past his hips, and he quickly kicked them off.

For a few moments, they each stared at the other's mostly naked state, then something between them snapped into place, and Ethan pulled Ivy to him, threading one hand into her hair and placing the other on the juncture of her neck and shoulder, staring into her eyes. Their heartbeats thrummed in unison as she rose on her toes, pressing her body against the hardness of him and slanting her lips to fit his. His hand at her neck gripped tighter, and he used the hand in her hair to tug her tightly against him. She marveled at this, at him, how much he made her *feel* from just a kiss. His hands were barely on her, and she was already melting at his touch. His tongue flicked over the seam of her lips, and she gladly opened to him, letting him in, needing to be closer. He pushed a thigh between her legs, and she ground against him, little sparks of pleasure blooming as she moved. He made a sound deep in his chest and moved his hands from her neck to reach behind her and unhook her bra.

Before she could make a quip about how easy it was for him, Ethan kissed his way down to a nipple and bit down, hard, harder than he ever had before, and all thoughts left her head as his tongue swirled over the stinging, reddening skin to ease the slight pain. Then his other hand left her hair and trailed down between her breasts before splaying out over her belly and dipping beneath the pink lace covering her sex.

Ethan let out a satisfied growl against her skin when he found Ivy drenched for him. One finger slipped between her folds and sank into the wetness there, and Ivy nearly keened at how good he felt.

She gasped his name as he pressed the pad of his thumb over the hidden bundle of nerves there and slowly curled his finger inside her. Ivy's hips bucked as he moved his mouth to her previously neglected nipple and bit down again. "More," she panted, grinding against his hand.

He obliged, slowly pressing another finger into her, stretching her inner muscles. Ivy reached between them to wrap a hand around his length, slowly pumping her fist.

"Now feels like a good time to mention that I have a birth control implant, and—*oh*—" Ethan's body jerked, his fingers sliding deeper, and she gasped, "my last blood test was clear. So if yours was too, we can..."

"Fuck, *yes*, Ivy. I'm clear, too."

She'd able to feel him, *all* of him.

"I need you. Now," she hissed against his skin. Ethan *growled* and stalked forward until the backs of her thighs touched the softness of his bed, and she crashed down, bringing him with her. His body caged her in, and for a moment, the darkness of his eyes and his body towering over hers made her feel, and oh, how she needed him to devour her.

Slowly, with a final twist of his fingers inside her, Ethan moved both of his hands to her hips to draw the lace down over her hips, flinging the scrap of fabric behind him. Hooking her fingers into his boxer briefs, Ivy tugged the waistband down to free him. And she hummed in delight at the sight of him staring down at her, chest heaving and hair wild.

Hooking an arm beneath Ivy's knee, Ethan slowly pulled her leg up until it pressed into her chest, resting his hand beside her head. She felt him at her entrance, so she flexed her hips to brush herself over him. The hand gripping her hip flexed, pushing her back down into the mattress, and his eyes closed as he leisurely rocked his hips.

"Ethan," she pleaded, aching with how much she needed him. "Tease me later, for fuck's sake."

"Such a dirty mouth, Ivy," he said. "Don't you want me to take it slow?" He pushed a single inch into her waiting warmth.

Not enough. More.

"I want you," she said through gritted teeth, "to *fuck me.*" Wrapping her free leg behind his hips, she used it for leverage to pull herself up, impaling herself on his cock.

Ohhhh, shit.

The stretch was almost too much for her, and she was so full of him, she couldn't *breathe*. But her hips moved of their own accord, and suddenly Ethan was moving with her, thrusting so deeply inside her that a sound more animal than human tore itself from her lips.

And then they were gasping together, and it was *so good, just what she needed—*

Until Ethan stopped. And eased himself out of her.

"Stand up, Ivy." His voice was commanding, deep, and husky, and Ivy found herself scrambling to obey him. He walked behind her, fingers brushing lightly from her hips up to her nape and around to cup her breasts, thumbs flicking over her nipples. Then he slid one hand down to grip her waist.

"I said I wasn't going to fuck you bent over the bed like a caveman." His breath tickled her ear, and sparks spread through her body at his words. "But I think you liked the idea, didn't you?"

Ivy didn't have time to nod as Ethan shoved her upper body down on his black sheets, his hand pinned beneath her. Ethan's fingers found their way lower, spreading Ivy's folds before he plunged back inside her. They moaned in unison when he bottomed out, his hips slamming into the globes of her ass. His wandering fingers found her nipple and pinched hard, sending Ivy's eyes rolling back as the beginnings of release crashed through her like waves in a hurricane.

Ivy growled Ethan's name when her inner muscles started fluttering around his cock, and he pressed his chest to her back, fucking her through the orgasm that *wouldn't stop coming.* She went limp when she felt Ethan's muscles seize against her back, and he shuddered, spending himself inside her.

He collapsed over her back, resting his weight on his arms, and brushed a kiss over the back of her neck as they lay panting.

"I really did plan for flowers and candles and shit," he whispered.

"You can make it up to me later," she whispered back, turning to nuzzle against his neck.

"Wait here," he said. "I'll be back with wine and snacks."

Is it too soon to be in love with him, she asked herself, sighing happily as she watched his gorgeous backside disappear through the door. Contentedly, she fell back against the smooth coolness of his pillows, sated and smiling.

Ivy must have fallen asleep because when she jerked upright, Ethan was nowhere to be seen, but two glasses of sparkling wine and a tray of fruit and cheese sat on the nightstand beside her. A faint sound of running water came through a door she hadn't noticed earlier, so she padded over to it and toed it open to find Ethan leaning over an enormous, jetted tub, dumping what looked to be an entire bottle of bubble bath into the rolling water. Every flat surface in the room was covered with candles and flowers, and Ivy took it all in as she leaned on the door frame.

"Candles and flowers and shit, huh?" she asked, smiling down at him.

Ethan jerked upright, dropping the bottle in his startled haste to stand.

"Oh, um. Yeah." His stammering was adorable, especially after the way he'd fucked her. Her toes curled just thinking about it. "I mean, I promised." He shrugged and ran a hand through his hair.

"Ethan Fisher," she said, crossing to him and wrapping her arms around him. "I only ever wanted you."

18

"Get in," Ethan ordered. Ivy stared at him, one eyebrow raised. "Please?" he amended.

"Only if you bring me the food," she said coyly.

"Deal." He trailed his fingers down her back and watched her shiver before stepping into the steaming water. She hissed at the heat but moaned once she slid beneath the frothy layer of bubbles.

"Ethan?"

"Hmm?" he asked lazily, watching her lean against the tub's angled back and rest her head on the lip of the white enamel.

"Snacks." Ivy made shooing motions with her hands.

This woman and her food. Ethan chuckled and retrieved the tray, returning to place it within reach on a small folding table he moved closer to the tub.

"This thing is amazing, but why do you have it? I can swim in here." Ivy had submerged herself up to her chin and blinked up at him lazily as he offered the glass of wine.

"I don't know if you've noticed, but I'm rather large."

"Oh, I've noticed." She eyed him lasciviously.

Ethan smirked at her, flexing his pecs to make her laugh again. She did laugh, but her eyes grew darker as she took him in.

"*Anyway*," he continued, "I put it in when I bought the apartment. I needed a big tub for soaking after some of the more intense practices."

Ivy's brow furrowed.

"It's nice to see someone else enjoying it." He glanced to where her breasts were visible beneath a layer of bubbles and quirked his eyebrows.

Ivy flicked water at him.

"Get in," she ordered in a mockery of his earlier words.

"Yes ma'am. But first, more wine?"

Ivy held up her empty glass in answer, so Ethan retrieved another bottle.

When he returned, she was chewing happily and waved at him to get in. Ethan stared down at her for a moment, enjoying the view, then went to stick his foot in the water and nearly yelped at the heat. He flinched but lowered his body into the steaming water, leaning back to look at Ivy, who peered at him over the rim of her glass.

He arched a brow at her.

"Just enjoying the view." She smirked at him and raised her glass in a toast.

Rolling his eyes, Ethan took his glass from the table, downing half of it in one go.

"So, it is going to be a party," Ivy purred. She finished her drink and slid her foot up the length of his calf. She leaned forward, and Ethan didn't resist the urge to look down at where her breasts had emerged from the water, glistening and covered with a light layer of bubbles. It looked like frosting, and he seemed to want to lick it off.

"I wouldn't," Ivy said, reading his mind. "The bubbles are bitter."

"Did you...eat the bubbles?"

"Well...no. But I dropped a piece of cheese into the water."

"And you ate it anyway?" He already knew the answer.

She gaped at him. "Of course, I did. It was just a little cleaner after I dropped it."

"Hmm," Ethan hummed. "C'mere." He used his glass to gesture for her to come to his side of the tub.

Ivy scooted closer until she was a few inches away from him, between his spread knees, reveling in the heat of the water and proximity to *him*. She sat back on her heels and reached to refill their glasses.

"Turn around," Ethan ordered, and Ivy tilted her head at him but did as he asked. She turned around on her knees so her back faced him, and he pulled her back to lean against his chest. His free arm wrapped around her waist as she nestled into the comfort of his hold on her.

Ethan leaned forward to rest his chin on Ivy's shoulder, enjoying the feel of their skin together in the steaming heat of the water. For a while, they lounged in the bath, with him occasionally feeding her bites of fruit and cheese until they'd finished all the food and wine. A pleasant buzzing filled his head from the wine, and the rolling jets kept the water warm and bubbly. Lazily, Ivy turned her face to press a kiss to his neck, and while he knew he probably should be sated, he wanted *more*.

More of her. Always.

Gently, Ethan tipped Ivy's head back to rest her head on his shoulder, exposing the column of her throat. Working his hands from her collarbones down her shoulders and arms, he massaged small circles into her slick skin. Moaning as his thumbs pressed into a sore spot at the base of her neck, her entire body tightened and relaxed against his with each press of his fingers. Her eyes were closed, and Ethan took full advantage of it, staring down at her soft body curving against the hardness of his. The tips of her breasts peeked through the bubbles, and

Ethan couldn't resist trailing his hands down to palm the soft mounds and flick the rough pads of his thumbs over her taut nipples. Her moan shot straight to his cock, and Ethan began hardening against her backside.

Ivy rolled her hips to press back against him.

Giving her a warning nip beneath her jaw, Ethan returned his attention to her breasts, tracing his knuckles over the soft skin underneath. He dipped his hands beneath the soapy water, dragging bubbles onto her skin and sliding his fingertips through the slickness there. Her impatience began to take over; she squirmed beneath his touch. So, Ethan clamped one arm over her hips to hold her in place while he dragged his free hand slowly up and down the length of her body from her chin to her thighs. Her breath hitched as he drew closer to her more sensitive areas, but he ignored them, feeling her body tense and sag in expectation of his touch and then his denial.

Grinning into her hair, he whispered in her ear, feeling her shiver as his breath caressed the shell of her ear.

"Tell me what you want, Ivy."

Her irritation was clear from the intensity with which she dug her nails into his skin, but the slight pain was worth it to watch her tremble beneath his touch.

"I think you know what I want," she growled. But her voice was breathless, her eyes shuttered.

If he kept teasing her, she'd beg.

Ethan eased the very tips of his calloused fingers into the crease of her hip and thigh, lower, skimming over her folds, and up the other side and over her stomach and the curve of her waist. Back to the soft underside of her breasts heaving slightly with her labored breathing.

"Say it," Ethan said, drawing a half-moon beneath the dark pink of her nipple.

"Please," she gasped, trying to grind back against his cock.

"Please what, Ivy?" His tone seemed to undo her.

"Please touch me. Ethan, *please*."

"Since you asked so nicely," Ethan said and obliged her, moving both hands to pinch and roll her nipples between his fingers as he sucked a mark into the soft skin where her neck and shoulder met. Ivy let out a breath, and he moved his fingers lower, to press into the swollen bundle of nerves hidden there. She moaned and pressed her ass into his achingly hard cock.

His middle finger slid inside her to stroke the spot he knew would make her eyes roll and her toes curl.

And they did.

Ethan loved watching Ivy come undone from his touch. He loved the sounds she made, and he loved the way her body moved as he stroked and teased her.

He loved *her.*

Ethan let the realization wash over him, then he examined it and accepted it for what it was.

"Ivy, I—" he began but didn't know how to tell her. Couldn't bring himself to voice it yet. "I need you."

Ivy keened in affirmation, and Ethan gripped her hips to lift her onto his cock, pushing inside her with one swift stroke.

Softness and heat enveloped him, and his eyes closed in ecstasy as he stilled to allow her body to adjust to him. And when she moved, rocking her hips upward, he moved with her, finding a place deep within, deeper than he'd been so far.

It felt so good, so warm and soft, and so *right* being with her.

As they moved together, Ethan found the words closer and closer to escaping the closer he came to climax.

And when they found their pleasure together, he whispered the words into her hair.

"I know," she said.

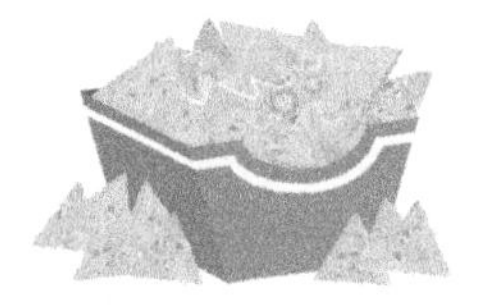

Ivy knew her response was concerning for Ethan. But she hated the knee-jerk reaction of saying 'I love you' for the first time in immediate response to the other person saying it first. Not that she'd ever told anyone she'd dated she loved them. Because she hadn't loved anyone the way she loved Ethan.

Ivy was determined to *show* him before she told him.

After the slow, sweet sex in the bath and Ethan's revelation, Ivy was ravenous, and she said so. Ethan kissed the tip of her nose and returned to the kitchen for more food. Ivy wandered naked into his closet intending to borrow a button-up and maybe swipe a few other shirts to smuggle home when she saw his uniform hanging toward the back. Giggling, she grabbed the clothes off the hangers and sauntered back into his bedroom, where she pulled the jersey over her head, unbuttoning all but two buttons in the vicinity of her belly button.

Ethan was tossing the pizza dough in the air when Ivy found him in the kitchen like he was some kind of ripped pizza god. And he didn't drop it or toss it into the blades of a spinning ceiling fan. He seemed good at it. Because of course, he was.

"Now *that* is sexy," she said, watching him concentrate on tossing the dough. He'd pulled on a pair of grey sweatpants before he got started with the pizza, muttering something about "cooking naked" and "dangerous".

Ivy leaned toward Ethan, lazily resting her elbows on the cold, dark marble counter, and drank in the sight of him in the sweatpants as he tossed the dough in the air for a final time.

When he finally looked at her, his mouth dropped open.

"I think that's blasphemy against the baseball gods," he said, staring at the fabric barely hiding her breasts.

"I thought you'd like it." Ivy looked away, biting her lip.

"I do, and now I'm going to fantasize about you wearing it every time I put that jersey on, which might be problematic for my teammates."

With an angelic smile, Ivy rounded the kitchen island and leaned past him, opening a cabinet for a glass, letting the jersey ride high on the back of her thighs. Ethan let out a sound somewhere between a snort and a grunt, and Ivy felt his hand tracing the letters written across her back in bright red.

"I'd rather you wore my real name," he said, his voice holding a hint of melancholy as he trailed his hand over the letters and down her back.

Not too much melancholy, though, because when he reached her bare ass, he swatted a cheek and ducked away before she could retaliate. After a moment, he returned to the dough, easing it onto a pizza stone as Ivy perched in her usual spot beside him, stirring the pizza sauce.

"I'd rather have your real name, too," Ivy muttered absently, belatedly hearing the implication of her words, and wondering if Ethan had too.

He blinked down at her from his absurd height, and she dimpled up at him before sticking her finger in the sauce and bringing it to her mouth to taste it.

"Have you talked to Harkness about changing it? Do your teammates know?"

"Just Derek, Isaac, and Jen." Ethan gently flattened the dough on the pizza stone, smoothing the bumpy edges and pressing out air bubbles.

"Do you think Harkness would let you change it?" She broke a piece off the ball of artisanal mozzarella and popped it in her mouth.

"Probably," Ethan replied, "but do you think it's a good idea in the middle of the season?" Ethan handed her another bite of the cheese before moving it to the opposite side of the stove so there would be *some* left for the pizza.

"Do you think anyone will care?" Ethan cocked an eyebrow at her. "I don't mean it in a bad way. Just...you've earned your place, and you put up with all the shit from Marshall for so long. Do you think anyone will begrudge you the right to your name?"

"I don't know," he admitted. "It's something I hadn't thought about until recently." He finished arranging the third and final circle of dough on a stone. "Ready to build these?"

"Yes! I've never done this before." She slid off the counter. He dropped an apron over her head, tying it at her waist. "What do I do?"

Together, they built their pizzas, and while they baked, Ethan and Ivy sat on his couch, flipping through his Netflix queue. It occurred to Ivy that in their time together, they'd never hung out and watched tv, and she watched him as she slid the remote from his hand, clicking through his recently watched videos.

"You can learn a lot about a person from their watching habits," Ivy said mock-seriously.

Ethan scoffed.

"Not from mine." He sighed, not looking at her. "I never had time to do the things I enjoyed. And I guess I was so tired and... it got to the point of never enjoying anything, so it felt pointless to do...anything." He offered that truth so succinctly that Ivy didn't catch his meaning at first.

Ivy looked at him for a moment, an ache forming in her chest at how broken he must have been.

"Well, that's completely idiotic. I am an expert on Netflix. What do you like? Comedy? Drama? Horror? Anime?"

"I don't know?" He offered the words as if in question. "It's been a long time."

Ivy took it as a personal challenge.

"Good. We're going to watch *everything*."

"Everything?" Ethan sounded skeptical.

"Yes, everything."

"Sounds like it'll take a while." Then, he sounded hopeful, if uncertain.

"Yep. Let's start with this one." She clicked over to the bright yellow icon of The Good Place. "Pure comedic brilliance, with a moral to boot." Looking over her shoulder to the kitchen, she called, "We need nachos."

"We're making pizza." Ethan chuckled.

"Oh, I know." Ivy pointed the remote at him. "But we need nachos."

"We didn't buy tortilla chips."

Ivy sighed long-sufferingly.

"We just had sex, now we need nachos. Trust me, it's the best. Make a list. After pizza, we're going shopping again. This time, I'm taking the lead."

"Didn't you take the lead last time?"

"Yeah, but we didn't get *snacks*. It's *different*."

IVY'S METHOD OF WANDERING AIMLESSLY WAS FUN UNTIL IT GREW exhausting, but Ethan patiently wandered back and forth with her as their cart grew ever heavier. He enjoyed her enthusiasm at picking out junk food, even if she did wander around like a lost little kid on a sugar high.

"Tomorrow, we should go feed this to the ducks at the park near your place." She pulled a bag of frozen vegetables marked for clearance from the freezer. "Do you want to take the kids with us? We don't have to; I just think they'd like to go. But not if you don't want to."

Ivy didn't look at him as she wandered further down the aisle, peering through the glass cases in her search.

"Yeah, that sounds fun. What snacks do they like? We should get something for them, too."

Ivy ducked her head, spun on her heel, and marched back to where he stood, launching herself at him at the last second.

"I love you, too," Ivy whispered in his ear while she squeezed the air out of his lungs.

Ethan felt warmth surge through him at her words but...

"I mean it's nice to know, but why tell me now?"

"It's just, you're so perfect anyway." Was she crying? Ethan soothed his hand over her back. "But you want to get snacks for the kids?" Ivy was definitely sobbing into his shirt. "Sharing food is one of our love languages, mine and the kids', and it just... means so much to me. That you care about them, too." She sniffled.

Ethan wrapped his arms tighter around Ivy and kissed her temple in the middle of the frozen vegetable aisle.

"I love you, Ivy," he whispered into her hair. "And they're your family, so I love them too. Even Janna. Especially Janna."

Ivy let out a watery laugh.

"Ice cream?" he asked her.

"Only always." She met his eyes and smiled, and he brushed away her tears.

Somehow, Ivy managed to talk Ethan into buying one of

every pint of Ben and Jerry's, and he didn't even care about the amount of sugar she was persuading him to eat because it was Ivy and *she loved him too.*

AFTER HIS TIME WITH IVY, ETHAN FELT AS IF A PIECE OF HIS SOUL had fallen back into place, and he rode that high right into Monday morning.

He pulled into the stadium lot behind Derek, and they parked in adjacent spots. He wasn't wholly unsurprised to see the catcher exit his car with Isaac on the passenger side.

"Good day off?" Ethan asked, offering a genuine smile. They both grinned back at him.

"Looks like yours was pretty good too. Or you had a run-in with a vampire." Attempting to look concerned, Isaac leaned forward to peer at a mark on Ethan's neck, but he couldn't keep his face serious.

The marks Ethan had sucked into Ivy's thighs the night before were much worse than the ones she'd left on his neck, but he wasn't sharing that information with his teammates. Some regressive part of his brain was proud of having marked her, and she, him. As Ethan walked through the halls of the stadium's underground labyrinth of offices and meeting rooms, he smiled and nodded at his teammates, noting and blissfully not bothered by their shock at his abrupt change of temperament. After changing into workout clothes, Ethan wandered into the gym, shoving his wireless earbuds in and finding the playlist Ivy had made for him. Bright, upbeat music that was a musical representation of *her* filled his ears. Ethan went through his warm-up stretches, feeling tighter than usual thanks to some particularly acrobatic positions Ivy had suggested. His muscles were pleasantly sore as he stepped onto a treadmill, adjusting the speed and incline.

He started off slowly, letting his body get warm, not paying attention to the pop music in his ears, but enjoying the background sounds anyway. He was about to head to the batting cages when --

"Ethan. We're leaving."

Ethan jumped a mile, nearly losing his footing, having completely missed Harkness appearing beside him. He yanked the earbuds out and turned to face her.

"Perhaps you'd like to join us?" She gestured a manicured hand to where the team waited outside the bus. He followed her to join them.

Something in him shifted, needing to get the weight off his chest. Tell the truth and let them judge him. As he stepped toward his usual seat, he cleared his throat and waved for attention.

"Guys, can I say something?"

The bus went silent, and Ethan winced. Anxious thoughts skittered through his mind as he searched his teammates' faces, but he wasn't discouraged by what he found there. He mostly saw confusion, so he looked at Harkness in question.

She nodded at him with one corner of her mouth tipped up.

He cleared his throat again. "Some of you may know this, but I wanted to clear the air. My dad is Jimmy Fisher, who you've probably heard of." A few nods affirmed him. "And my grandpa was David Lorne, pitcher, elite agent, and trash human. And my mom is the CEO of one of the largest sports agencies in the country. So...yeah. Umm. Hi, I'm Ethan Fisher. Ethan Ford was..." he paused. "Ethan Ford was entirely Marshall's creation."

Ethan saw a lot of furrowed brows and scowling, but none of it seemed directed at him.

"Hiiiii, Ethan!" Isaac winked and waved wildly at him.

Ethan rolled his eyes at Isaac but still felt his lips curve into a half grin.

"So, Fisher," Harkness said, finally speaking. "Are you ready to leave with the rest of the team?"

19

On a rare summer morning off, Ethan found himself with Lily, Jase, and Janna at the park. Ivy was having brunch with his mother, and Ethan had volunteered to hang out with the kids while she was out.

"So, Sasquatch," Lily said as they walked through the grassy area between the parking lot and the park's entrance. "What are your intentions with Ivy?"

"My what?" Ethan blinked down at her.

"Your intentions. You know, like in all the old movies, someone asks the brooding, scowling man who's after the girl what his intentions are." Lily waved her hands in the air while she spoke, her dark bangs swaying on her forehead.

"Umm." Ethan's face and neck grew hot. They'd already slept together and declared their love, what other intentions did there need to be?

Unless she meant...

"You mean, like, getting married?" A man with a voice as deep as his should *not* have been able to squeak. But the m word came out in a much higher pitch than he'd ever heard out of his mouth.

Lily grinned like a she-devil.

"Well, you've had mind-blowing sex, you told her you loved her, and she loves you, so that's the next step, right?"

Could she read minds?

"No, I can't read minds, but Ivy is like a sister to me, and I know things, okay?" Lily leaned down to re-tie her sneaker. "Have you thought about it?"

Ethan would have been lying if he said he hadn't considered it. Well, *being* married, not the *getting* married part. He knew he wanted to be with Ivy; she was it for him. But a big ceremony with tons of people watching sounded terrifying. Which, when he thought about it, was even more ridiculous since his job was playing a game for people to watch. He sighed through his nose and ran his hands through his hair. Their talks of the future hadn't included a *wedding*.

Lily eyed him with one brow raised.

"I just want to be with her, okay?" Ethan said desperately.

"Hmm." Lily stared up at him, her dark brown eyes assessing him. "That works for now." Then she scampered off as if she were one of the kids and joined the group on the playground.

Ethan followed behind her, helping Janna empty sand out of her shoes and then hovering while she climbed the tallest slide. Jase wandered off and found a couple of boys his age to play with, and Ethan made sure to text Ivy because he knew how excited she'd be.

Seeing Jase acting like a child was a far cry from the solemn, nervous boy he'd been a couple of months ago. He was so proud of how far the boy had come since he'd invited Jase to the stadium. He knew Ivy was too, and he made a mental note to mention it somehow without embarrassing Jase.

When the sun got too high, Ethan invited Lily to lunch and extended the invitation to Derek as well. They met at a local burger joint. Lily bullied Ethan into ordering cheese fries, then proceeded to steal half of them since she'd ordered sweet potato fries instead. Derek kept giving him a side-eye until Lily spoke.

"I've already given him the intentions shakedown," Lily said, popping a particularly cheesy fry into her mouth.

"Hmm." Derek considered him, then swiped a fry from Ethan's plate. Derek had ordered a chicken sandwich and had been stealing bites from Lily and now, apparently, Ethan.

He didn't mind, though.

"But is he taking care of her?" Lily waggled her eyebrows, letting him know she didn't mean 'putting bandaids on a paper cut' caretaking.

Thankful for the surrounding children, Ethan crammed his burger into his mouth to hide the heat creeping over his cheeks.

He knew he took care of Ivy; the sheer number of orgasms he prided himself on giving her accounted for that, but he was *not* sharing that with Ivy's best friends.

"You are *taking care* of her right?" Lily glared, pointing a butter knife at him.

"Mmf," Ethan said through his burger.

"I'm not sure if he is, Lil." Derek's deep brown eyes bored into Ethan's.

But then he caught a look pass between the pair, and— *they were fucking with him.*

So, he decided to play their game.

"Oh, well, actually, Ivy takes care of me. There's an apron, pearls, heels, a whole bit." He paused to wipe his mouth and to look up to see their glowers before he continued. "She cooks, she cleans, it's delightfully archaic."

Lily's eyebrows furrowed, as though she knew something he'd said was wrong, but she didn't quite catch it. Derek glared. Ethan raised his eyebrows at them, waiting for the pieces to click.

"Wait a minute," Lily said, grinning. "Ivy can't cook for shit."

"She sure as hell can't walk in heels. The cleaning is questionable too." Derek threw his head back and howled with laughter, smacking Ethan on the shoulder.

"She cooks and cleans? Oh, my stars." Lily chortled. "Sasquatch, you had us going for a second. You have now earned our approval."

After they returned home, Janna was napping in her room when Jase quietly asked Ethan to play a game on the Wii.

"Sure, what did you have in mind?" Ethan hoped it wasn't bowling.

"Umm. Baseball?" Jase cracked a grin.

Ethan groaned, but they played, and Ethan was spectacularly bad at it, worse even than he'd been at bowling.

"But you have to account for things like the angle and the wind!" He shouted at the tv. "You can't flick your wrist to pitch! It's just *wrong*!"

He was so caught up in the wrongness of Wii baseball he didn't even register Ivy entering the room.

"Lemme show you how it's done!"

Ethan blinked, and Jase laughed.

"Oh, boy," Jase whispered, "here we go."

Ivy flounced over and took the white controller from Ethan's hand. She stood in front of the tv, gripped the controller, set her feet, stuck out her butt, and slung her arm forward in a horrible imitation of pitching.

And she somehow threw three strikes in a row. The indignity of the game was entirely negated by watching her shake her ass, though.

Nope, Ethan hadn't minded at all.

When Jase won the game and went to his room, he left Ethan and Ivy alone for the first time all day.

"Hey," she said, dimpling up at him with a wide smile and slightly unfocused eyes. She twined her arms around him, resting her head on his chest.

"Hi," he replied, kissing the top of her head.

"So, I have news."

After spending the day with his mother? Not good news, then. When she didn't speak, Ethan realized whatever she had to share was going to take some prompting.

"That sounds ominous."

"It's about the job."

"And...?" He didn't want to assume, but since she wasn't showing her usual excitement, his mind immediately went to the worst.

"I told them I couldn't take it. It's been so long. I'm so tired of waiting."

"Oh, no, sweetheart, I'm so sorry."

"Don't be. Honestly, with how much they've been dragging their feet all year, I'm not sure I want to work with them. Anyway, that's not the news. After the last time I spoke with them, I got fed up and started searching for other jobs."

That was a good idea; he'd wanted to suggest it to her, but she'd been so certain that the teaching job would be hers.

"That was a week or so ago. The next day, I got an email offering a phone interview, and they called me today to tell me I got the job! I'll be teaching middle school instead of high school, but it's at Jase's school! Isn't that so awesome? He'll be too cool to hang out with me, but that's okay. Anyway, I got a job!" A wide smile wreathed her face, her dimples deeper than ever. "It's such a relief."

"I'm proud of you, sweetheart. You'll do great."

She sighed and pushed her face against him, rubbing her cheek against his sternum.

"What're you doing?" he asked, amused by this vaguely cat-like motion.

"You smell nice." She sighed happily into his t-shirt.

"Okay." Ethan resolved to wear cologne more often. For a while, they remained in the embrace, with Ivy resting her head on his chest. After a few moments, Ethan scooped her up and carried her into the bedroom, depositing her on the bed. Ivy yawned and stretched, then stood and began removing her clothes, tossing them into her closet.

Enjoying the show, he kept watching her, and when she caught him, she grinned, her movements becoming more deliberate. It took *years* for her to reach behind her to unhook and slowly remove the lacy bra, and because he was only a helpless man, Ethan's eyes immediately dropped to the expanse of skin she had uncovered. Ivy's nipples pebbled under his gaze, but she continued, slowly undoing the button of her jeans and sliding them down over her hips, revealing plain black underwear.

Why the plain black underwear got him hard so quickly, Ethan didn't know. Maybe it was the way she looked at him as she slid her clothes off. Maybe because he knew what was beneath the scrap of black cotton. Either way, his eyes trailed down her belly, between her legs, and he instantly wanted to take them off. Put his mouth on her and make her moan.

And then she sauntered over to her dresser and pulled open the drawer she'd designated as his, rifling through it to find one of his black tees. She pulled it over her head and disappeared into the bathroom. Ethan swiftly changed his clothes to something more comfortable, trying desperately to ignore the raging hard-on the love of his life had caused and then abandoned. He heard water running and tried to focus on those sounds instead of how badly he wanted her. When he heard her opening the door, Ethan scrambled under the covers to at least attempt to hide his erection.

Which was unnecessary, as the second Ivy emerged from the bathroom, she pounced on him, pinning him beneath her.

"Hi," she said between kisses to his face and neck. "I needed to wash my face and brush my teeth. It has been a *day*."

"Hmph." Ethan grumbled, but he caught the sparkle in Ivy's eyes, knowing she saw through it.

"Well, if you wanted me to stop," she said, pretending to misunderstand him, "you could have said so."

Ethan curled his fingers into her hipbones, rolling over with her when she rolled off him. Then, he hovered above her, staring down into her face.

"Do you think I *ever* want you to stop?"

Ivy smiled up at him, reaching up to twist her fingers through his hair, brushing his cheek.

And again, how much he loved her hit him full in the chest, as hard as he'd been hit by that errant baseball, and it was hard to breathe.

In the next moment, he was kissing her, hard, trying to put all of his emotions into the simple act of pressing his lips to hers.

But it wasn't enough. It was never enough. He would always want more of her. His tongue flicked against hers, and he felt her legs fall open beneath him. Smiling against her lips, Ethan traced his fingers over the waistband of her plain black underwear. But not beneath them. Not yet. His lips moved over her neck, gently; he didn't want to mark her too visibly. When Ethan found the spot over Ivy's heart, he heard her heartbeat, and he sucked a mark there. Her hands slid beneath his shirt, tugging the hem up, and he lifted himself for her to pull it over his head.

The sense of male pride Ethan always felt when Ivy stared at him flooded his senses even as he watched her eyes darken. Grabbing the hem of her shirt, Ethan pulled it over Ivy's head, and they gazed at each other, both drinking the other in.

Need for her burned through him; he needed her more than oxygen.

He fumbled in his haste, tripping as they scrambled off the bed to undress, and they laughed as their foreheads knocked together, each trying to disrobe the other. Eventually, their clothes fell to the floor in a heap, and he picked her up, wrapping her legs around his waist. Ethan carried her to the bed, falling back and landing so hard, his breath was nearly knocked out as she sprawled out atop him.

With Ivy's spread knees bracketing him, her hot center slid against him, and Ethan couldn't stop himself from slipping a finger between her legs, stroking her to draw out even more of her arousal. Touching her was like setting a match to gasoline, and he felt her fire licking over his skin when she rocked her hips and moaned. So, he added a second finger, tracing over her clit and sliding inside her.

"I need *you*, Ethan," she panted, throwing her head back and closing her eyes tightly. But her words and her actions were contradictory. She rocked herself into his hand, and Ethan stared up at her, watching the ecstasy wreathing her face. "Ethan, *please*," she whispered.

Ethan stroked inside her one last time before removing his fingers, and Ivy hissed at the loss. With both hands, he gripped her hips, holding her still, holding her above his aching cock.

She writhed, trying to push down, but he managed to keep her above him.

"Go slow, sweetheart, for me? Please?"

He did *not* want to go slowly, but this was different, somehow, like they needed to be slow and sweet, no matter how much they just wanted to *fuck*.

Nodding slowly, Ivy met his eyes, her breath catching as Ethan loosened his grip on her hips to lower her down.

Inch by agonizingly slow inch, she sank onto him, enveloping him in her wet heat, and Ethan wanted to growl in pleasured frustration at how good she felt around him. So soft and wet and *his*.

He told her, then said it again.

"You feel so good. I'm so glad you're *mine*," he whispered when he had finally, *finally* bottomed out inside her.

Her face crumpled, and she fell forward onto his chest with a sob.

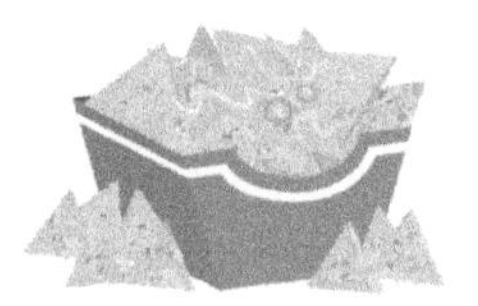

IVY HATED CRYING DURING SEX. BUT ETHAN WAS SO *PERFECT*, AND she loved him, and she felt so *good* with him, she couldn't help but cry.

"You're mine, too," she whispered into his now tear-stained chest.

He'd frozen beneath her when she began crying, and then he stroked his hand over her hair.

He must not have heard her.

She braced herself, using his arms to push herself up off his chest.

"You are *mine,* too," she said fiercely. She sniffled and looked down at his face.

"You're crying because...?" He looked up at her, his dark eyes fearful as if he were waiting for an ax to fall on his neck.

"I am *crying*," Ivy dug her fingers into his biceps and rocked her hips, "because I love you."

"Okay?" Ethan grunted as she bucked harder against him.

"Sometimes," she grunted, with a particularly hard grind, "I get emotional when I love someone." Ivy watched Ethan's eyes roll back as she began to speed up, timing her thrusts with her words. "And when someone loves me back," she paused, waiting for him to look back up at her.

"When someone loves you back," he repeated, bucking his hips up into hers so hard she saw stars, "you get attached," *thrust*, "and then you worry you're too attached and they'll leave."

He'd taken the words right out of her mouth.

They rocked together, finding their rhythm. Ivy slid her hands up so their fingers threaded together as their slow, sweet sex turned more intense. Ivy lowered her chest to Ethan's, clenching her inner walls around him as she felt the climax building inside her.

"I'm not leaving," he breathed, squeezing her fingers tighter. He said it again, pounding into her after every word. "You're not alone anymore."

She began sobbing again.

They climaxed together, and when she was settled into the crook of his neck with his arms wrapped around her, she whispered it too.

"Neither are you."

20

Three months later

"—And up next we have the managers of the Hawks and Tornadoes, sharing their thoughts on their teams' chances for winning the— "

Harkness clicked the tv in the team meeting room off, sending the room into complete silence despite being full of people.

"I love a speech, as I'm sure you've all figured out by now." A few soft laughs scattered throughout the room. "But I don't think one is necessary now. Look at how far you've come as a team. When I arrived, halfway through the season, this team was...not a team. But now you are. And that means we can work hard, work together, and win."

From his seat in the back of the meeting room, Ethan saw his teammates nodding their agreement. All he could do was sit, fists clenched in his lap, trying to focus on anything other than finally having the chance to have everything he'd ever wanted.

Everything he'd wanted before Ivy, though.

Before, he hadn't even considered what he'd want to do

after winning. Any future had always been a blur, every path he'd ever considered led to the World Series and stopped there.

Meeting Ivy had completely upended his life. All of his priorities and goals had shifted, he'd made room for so many new people, but he hadn't taken the time to consider what he wanted. Because what he'd wanted before hadn't even been his desire, it had been Marshall's voice whispering in his head. Before that, his uncle's. Never his own.

The meeting continued, but Ethan suddenly saw the path before him as clearly as if he were watching it on a screen. He knew what he had to do.

With a jolt, he stood, intending to act on his plans, but with another jolt, he realized the meeting hadn't ended. Sheepishly he sat as Harkness paused to give him a stare, and Ethan threw himself back into his seat, fumbling in his bag for gum before shoving a piece in his mouth.

The past few months with Ivy did wonders for his nervous habits, but with the season ending at the *World Fucking Series*, and his new plan of action, Ethan couldn't contain his nervous energy. Chewing gum helped him avoid biting the inside of his cheek to a bloody ruin; already he was working his jaw into a steady rhythm. A hand appeared before his face, and Ethan handed the pack over to Derek who passed it to Isaac, who handed it to Jen, who took the last piece.

Ethan sighed.

He ran his hands through his hair, bracing his elbows on his knees to keep his legs from bouncing. It didn't work; it made his entire body bounce, too. It felt like his brain might vibrate out of his skull, and the waiting was torture. Harkness was taking her sweet time explaining the travel and lodging arrangements, along with the various other obligations once they would arrive onsite. The whole ordeal sounded like a nightmare.

"Well," Harkness finished. "We're going to the World Series."

Around him, his teammates had varied reactions. Some, like him, seemed anxious, with their frenetic energy displaying itself in tapping fingers or bitten nails. Derek, on the opposite end of the spectrum, was excited, gesticulating wildly to Isaac, who seemed to be in the middle of the anxious and excited crowds. He smiled, but he seemed more subdued than normal.

"Right, well, we'll meet back here again tomorrow for travel, so... carry on." Harkness seemed distracted. Ethan thought she was probably already mapping out strategies in her head.

He was eternally grateful the World Series coincided with Ivy's school district's autumn break. Over the past few months, Ethan and Ivy had rarely spent the nights when he'd been home apart, and he seriously considered buying her a new bed because his large frame didn't fit comfortably in her full-sized one. So as soon as he got a free moment, Ethan scoured the internet for a rental house large enough for Ivy, Lily, Jase, and Janna.

After their weird interrogative dinner, Lily and Derek officially accepted him into their strange little family. Lily still called him Sasquatch, and Derek had begun teasing Ethan even more, but now they had the easy camaraderie of siblings, or at least what he imagined that would be like. The same with Isaac, though Isaac was overly friendly to everyone anyway.

Soon, everything had fallen into an easy rhythm, and Ethan loved the simple domesticity of their lives now. Ivy had even gotten better at cooking — she had surprised him about a month earlier by making him homemade Alfredo sauce *and* homemade bread. She'd fretted over the vaguely phallic-shaped bread loaves, but he'd praised her and the slightly misshapen bread anyway because it had been delicious.

Ethan knew the team members were required to all stay in a block of rooms at a hotel near the stadium, which was standard. But he also knew he'd sleep better knowing Ivy was nearby, so he rented a house on the beach for Ivy, Lily, and the kids.

As he wandered the clubhouse, Ethan noticed many of his teammates doing the same, nervous energy still rippling off most of them.

When Ethan encountered Isaac, the shorter man was pacing and alternately running his hands through his hair and scrubbing his hands over his face, leaving him looking ragged.

"Are you okay?" Ethan asked warily.

Isaac grunted, still pacing.

"Isaac?"

Isaac paused his pacing, finally looking at Ethan.

"We're playing the Tornadoes," Isaac said.

"Yes?" Ethan wasn't quite certain where the conversation was going.

"We're playing the *Tornadoes*," Isaac repeated.

Right, Isaac used to play for them. The pitcher had been on the Hawks team for at least half of the season, and Ethan had nearly forgotten where he'd come from and who he'd played for.

"Ah." *Lawrence.* Ethan shifted uncomfortably. "What did he say to you?"

"He said if I left, I was a traitor and to never come back, even though it wasn't my decision," Isaac said through a scowl.

"That sounds familiar," Ethan scoffed, shoving his hands into his pockets.

For a while, they were both silent, ruminating on the past, but then Isaac asked, "Why didn't you play for the Tornadoes after college?"

Ethan snorted. "Lawrence."

Isaac arched a dark eyebrow at him in question.

"You know I lived with him for a while in high school," Ethan began, and Isaac nodded. "My parents sent me there when I started getting more attention from scouts. Living with him was like being some kind of monk. He lived and breathed baseball; it was the *only* thing for him. It was never like that for me, but I was young and didn't know any better, so I followed along with what he taught me." Ethan's shoulders curved inward. "I thought my parents didn't want me when they shipped me off to him, so I thought I had no other choices. I thought what he said was law. He always wanted to be better, to outshine all the things his father had done. Become more famous than my mom, the socialite-heiress-CEO." Ethan scowled again, shaking off the rising memories. "Lawrence always pushed me, harder and harder, always breaking me down, but never building me back up. He said he saw how much I was like my grandfather, his dad, and I think he was trying to keep me from going down that road the only way he knew how."

Isaac frowned.

"What *did* happen with your grandfather?" Isaac asked. "I've heard a lot over the years, but it was before my time."

"It was before mine too, and no one would ever give me a straight answer," Ethan replied. "I tried to piece things together, though. He started gaining attention from a young age. He was a great player, even in high school, but his upbringing was kind of rough. Single mom working two jobs situation, I think. Scouts started watching him when he was a high school freshman, I think, and at some point, all the attention got to him. He went to college to study engineering, but he left early to be a free agent for the Tornadoes. There were rumors of partying and drugs, but the college covered it all up, especially when he did well in the Majors. He married my grandma and got clean for a while, but then more rumors started. Steroids and cheating, and he began having these...outbursts. Picking fights with teammates and umpires, throwing punches and screaming, and getting kicked out of half his games. But for a while, he still played too well for them to kick him off the team. He did a lot of gambling in the off-season, and he won big. Big enough to buy out the agency representing him. And I think he got addicted to power since he'd been ordered around his whole life and had never made his own choices. He drank and gambled more, and more cheating rumors went around. Grandma left him, and it all got worse. And then his car crashed." Ethan shrugged. "He was a good player, but I think he was lost a long time before it all went bad for him.

Isaac's dark eyes were wide.

"Wow," Isaac said. "And Lawrence thought you'd be...like that?"

"I guess," Ethan answered. "I used to watch old replays of his games to analyze his playing style, but I think Lawrence misinterpreted it. I think he thought I wanted the power and notoriety, instead of trying to learn the way he played. And then when I got angry over him treating me like shit, his reaction was to kick me out. When I was eighteen, he threw me out on the street after a bad practice, and I was so broken down that Marshall finally got to me. He'd been skulking around, scouting me for a while. When Lawrence kicked me out, Marshall took me in and got me tryouts at colleges. Then once he was sure I was good enough, he started pressuring me to go into the Majors. That was the only time I stood up to him, and I paid for it. Once he signed me on with the Hawks, he started in with the same shit Lawrence did. Crazy training, ranting and raving about legacies, always telling me I'd never be good enough to live up to any of the other players in my family."

"And Jimmy and Laura let him treat you that way?"

"I don't think they knew. They were both so busy, always traveling when I was younger, and when I gained more attention, I lashed out at them for only paying attention when I was playing well. Then Lawrence offered to coach me, and they shipped me off. I didn't have anyone to talk to, so I did whatever he said to do. And then with Marshall, it was more of the same, but by then, it was all I'd known for so long, I let it happen. Thought it was what I deserved."

"Ethan," Isaac said, not angrily, but not weakly. "Why didn't you tell me? I thought we were friends."

Ethan's shoulders pulled in further.

"I didn't think anyone would care."

"If I had known..." Isaac let the words trail off.

"Well, it's better now anyway." Ethan wasn't sure why he'd shared so much, but Isaac at least looked like he felt better.

But Ethan was...unsettled, off-kilter.

The team was scheduled to fly out the next day, so he headed home to Ivy, exhausted. They fell into bed after dinner, and for once, they went straight to sleep, Ethan wrapped around Ivy.

ETHAN JERKED UPRIGHT, DRENCHED IN SWEAT, WITH IVY smoothing her hands over his upper body.

"Ethan. Ethan? Breathe. It was a nightmare."

Her soft voice was a balm after the rough rawness of the dream.

"I'm here, it's okay." She was still touching him, wrapping her arms around him, holding him as close as possible.

Inhale, exhale.

Ethan curled himself around her, still struggling to breathe and calm himself. Shudders wracked his body, and he buried his face in her hair.

When Ethan's mind finally returned to the present, the tension in his body released enough for him to fall back against the pillows, pulling Ivy against him on his way. For once, she was the one who was warm while he shivered, and he pulled her closer, needing to touch her, to be sure she was real.

"Do you want to talk about it?" Ivy asked, threading her fingers through his where they rested on her shoulder.

"I talked to Isaac today." And he told her all of it, the memories he'd dredged up about his uncle and Marshall and everything else.

It was the first time he'd said it all out loud. How he'd let himself be used, how he'd treated his teammates.

"I think," Ivy paused to look him in the eyes, and Ethan knew what was coming, "I think you should tell your parents."

His free hand slid through his hair, catching in the knots made by his tossing and turning.

He sighed. "You're probably right." His eyes squeezed shut at having to deal with it, talk about it all *again*. "But then I'm done with it, okay? It hasn't bothered me since..." and he trailed off.

But she knew.

She pressed a kiss into the skin of his chest, and they drifted back to sleep, tangled together.

Ethan woke abruptly the next morning, the stark reality of playing in the World Series finally settling over him. Ever since he was little, he'd dreamed about the World Series, before he'd truly known what it meant for a team. And even if his priorities had shifted, Ethan couldn't help but be excited. He dragged his free hand over his face and lamented the lack of feeling in his other hand. Ivy had wrapped herself around his arm and leg in the night, and he was loath to move her, particularly since it was unlikely they'd get to sleep together again until the series was over. He ran through his mental checklist for what he'd need to bring and groaned at the thought of putting on a suit for the press conference. Ivy huffed in her sleep, burying her face in his shoulder against the light peeking through her curtains.

Her arm stretched across his torso, and he held her small hand in his, tracing her fingertips with his thumb, pondering-

Ivy sat bolt upright.

"Breakfast!" she screeched, throwing off the blankets.

"What?"

"Breakfast! We were going to make you breakfast!"

Sleep left her eyes bleary, but she jumped out of bed and raced into the kitchen. Ethan chuckled at her enthusiasm, and at the banging sounds and cursing he heard from the kitchen. He also heard a chorus of "swear jar!" and pulled himself out of bed to join them.

Jase set up the Keurig and took out mugs, and Ethan nodded gratefully and ruffled Janna's hair as he pressed the switch to brew coffee. The nightmare and lost sleep had left him with something akin to a hangover, and Ethan would prefer to be coherent before he left for the press conference. Ivy ushered him to a seat, refusing to let him see what she was cooking, though the smells and number of things cooking on the stove gave him a good idea. Jase and Janna helped her cook, and Ethan smiled into his coffee mug while they did more singing and dancing than actual cooking.

Ethan was not surprised when Ivy plunked an enormous bowl of breakfast spaghetti in front of him and mouthed "sorry" and gestured at the kids. Having pasta combined with breakfast foods was still weird, but he enjoyed it because they'd made it for him, and he said so. Janna grinned through her noodles, and Jase tried to pretend he wasn't proud of himself. As usual, Ivy tucked into her food with gusto, praising the kids and asking Ethan questions about the upcoming games.

Once again, Ethan was struck, as he had often been over the past few months, at the simple domesticity they had settled into. Shared smiles with Ivy over morning coffee, conversations with Janna that he never quite followed about princesses and dragons, discussing stats with Jase. Sometimes he and Ivy cooked together. Sometimes the kids helped them. And every time he had to leave, his heart constricted and wouldn't loosen until they were back together.

When they'd finished, he dragged himself out of his seat to help do the dishes. Ivy had a distant look in her eyes Ethan knew meant she was trying to hide her sadness at him leaving.

"It's only for a few days, sweetheart," Ethan said into her hair.

"It could be a whole week!"

Ethan prayed to the gods of baseball, if there were any, that it would not be a week. Facing Lawrence again in his nightmares had been unpleasant enough, and he'd rather not have to do it again for a week straight.

"Can we at least see you? Before or after games?" Ivy's hazel eyes peered up at him hopefully.

"I don't think Harkness minds," he said, "but it'll probably be limited. We'll have press conferences and meetings and shit."

Her nose scrunched up at him before she rose on her toes to kiss him.

"Swear jar," Ivy whispered against his lips, and Ethan barked a laugh against her mouth.

Once he'd loaded his bags into his car, Ethan came back into the house for final goodbyes.

"Bye, Daddy!" Janna screamed, kissing him on the cheek when he leaned down.

Ethan kissed her back and stood before her words hit him. He looked up into Ivy's widened eyes and watched the tendon in Jase's jaw tighten in a painfully familiar way.

Well, shit.

"Jase, can we talk?"

Leading Jase to the stairs outside Ivy's apartment, Ethan settled down on the bottom step and let Jase sit beside him.

"You okay, buddy?"

The tendon in Jase's jaw ticked again as the boy clenched his teeth.

"Did Ivy tell you anything about before? Before we came to live with her?"

"Just that it was rough for you."

"Yeah. It was...."

Letting the boy work out whatever was bothering him, Ethan sat in silence, listening to the whir of the building's air conditioning units.

"My mom was sick for a long time. She got sick when Janna was a baby, and it was hard for my dad. Mom was in the hospital a lot, and it got to be expensive, so my dad sold our house, and we moved closer to the hospital. Before we moved, I took Janna to our neighbors' house, but after, there was nowhere to go. And then my mom." Jase swallowed hard, blinking. "My mom died, but we still stayed there. Sometimes, my dad would stay gone for days. I didn't know when he would be back, and sometimes...we ran out of food. I had to steal stuff a couple of times. I didn't like it, but Janna was so little. She didn't understand."

The roiling, burning anger he'd felt when Ivy had told him about her childhood burned through Ethan again, his heart breaking for the boy who'd had to grow up too quickly.

"Sometimes," Jase continued, staring down to where his shoes scuffed the concrete stairs, "when my dad did come home, he was okay. He didn't want to see me, and said I looked too much like my mom, but he took care of Janna when he could. But then he stayed gone longer. Didn't pay bills, didn't pay for Janna's daycare. She was too little for school, so I had to stay home with her. Someone from the school came looking for me after a while, and when my dad didn't show up at all that night, they took us away. After a few weeks, we went to live with Ivy, and we got to stay together."

"I'm sorry, Jase. I hate that you had to go through so much.

That your father couldn't get enough of a handle on himself to take care of you. But I hope what Janna said didn't upset you." Ethan slid down the steps to sit beside the boy.

"No. It's good, I think. Maybe she's forgetting what it was like."

"Can I ask you a question?"

Jase looked Ethan straight in the eye and nodded.

"I'm going to ask Ivy to marry me. Would you...do you think you and Janna would...what would you think if we adopted you? Is that something you'd want?"

For a moment, Jase's face went slack. Then he wrapped his arms around Ethan's neck.

"That would be *so cool*."

21

Worry washed over Ivy; Jase had been doing so well over the past few months, but she hadn't seen him look quite so startled, either. She wasn't sure if the boy was upset because of what Janna had said, or if it was because Jase thought Janna had forgotten their parents altogether. And she wasn't sure which was worse.

Sighing, Ivy gathered their things for a trip to the library, hoping to cheer Jase up. Janna ran around like a demon with a face covered in peanut butter, though Ivy had no idea how it had happened, and Ivy had nearly forgotten the whole incident when Ethan and Jase returned from their talk.

They both looked considerably happier than when they'd left for their chat, and Ivy was again grateful for Ethan's calming influence on both her and her kids. She thanked whatever lucky stars had sent him into her life as he smiled at her. They all walked out to his sleek black car for another reluctant goodbye.

"I love you," Ivy said into his skin before pressing a kiss against the column of Ethan's throat.

"I know." He grinned and kissed her forehead before she scowled at him. "I love you too," he whispered into her hair as he wrapped her in a tight embrace.

Ivy sighed into his tight black tee, pressing her face into his chest.

"You need to go."

"I do." He made no move to leave.

"Ethan!" She poked him in the ribs, earning a grin and a sore finger for her efforts.

"Fine, if you're so eager to have me leave," he said, scowled, but dropped the expression quickly, pressing a kiss to her temple. He eased into the car and drove away.

WITH CONSIDERABLE EFFORT, IVY AND LILY MANAGED TO MAKE IT to their rental house, despite the four-hour drive and a truly exorbitant amount of bathroom breaks. Ethan had rented a gorgeous house on the beach with enough rooms for Ivy, Lily, and both kids, and Ivy hoped Ethan would be able to visit between games. The sound of waves crashed through Ivy's open window, and she imagined what it would have been like in summer. All blazing sun and laughing children, the scent of sunscreen, and tropical drinks.

Once their things were unpacked, everyone piled back into their rented van and drove to the stadium. Laura, as CEO of an agency, owned a skybox in most stadiums and had invited Ivy and her cadre to join her and Jimmy for the games. When Ivy, Lily, Jase, and Janna arrived, they presented their passes to the gate attendant who led them up a few flights of stairs into an enormous glass-and-chrome box. The view was *incredible*. The bank of windows overlooking the stadium drew Jase's attention, and he peered down at the field and began spouting off trivia about it, but Ivy only half listened while she corralled Janna and Lily away from the glass so they didn't leave fingerprints on it. Several large screens lined the walls, and Ivy pointed out Ethan on one; they could see the whole stadium from the box, but they were so high up, it was impossible to see the players' faces, except for when they were shown on screen.

Ivy introduced Laura and Jimmy to Lily, and they all settled into their fancy reclining chairs to watch as the game started.

As the game progressed, Ethan seemed...off. His usually graceful movements, surprising for such a large man, were tight and jerky and not like himself. Beside Ivy, Jase hissed through his teeth and clamped his jaw shut every time Ethan made a play, and even with her limited understanding, Ivy guessed the game was not going well. The scoreboard would agree with her: it was seven to four at the bottom of the eighth, and the Tornadoes fans were going wild in the stadium below. Laura and Jimmy shared glances in a "we've been married so long we can speak telepathically" kind of way, and Ivy wondered what they were thinking. As for Ivy, she was worried for Ethan. His shoulders rounded after every out, and even from a distance, she knew enough to see his form was off. Derek jogged out to the mound a few times, more than he'd done all season combined.

Thankfully, Ethan's uncle wasn't present on the sidelines, so Ivy assumed Ethan's odd behavior stemmed from nerves.

When the game ended, even Janna was subdued by the loss.

"Cheer up, guys, there are at least two more games left," Jimmy offered in a lame attempt to bolster their spirits. Laura glared at him, and he raised his hands in defeat. "I'm just sayin'. They'll do better tomorrow. The first game is always the worst."

When Ethan arrived at the beach house, with still-wet hair and a duffel bag slung over his shoulder. Janna was already asleep, but he quietly kissed her on the forehead after depositing his bag in Ivy's room. Jase was awake and reading, and Ivy overheard him and Ethan having a low conversation in the other room.

Fidgeting with the hem of her oversized black tee, Ivy waited on the edge of her bed for Ethan to find her. When Ethan finally came back in, he flipped the light switch off and flopped down on the bed beside her, throwing an arm over his eyes. Only the faint glow of the hallway light outside her door lit the room.

"Ethan?" Ivy asked. He hadn't even kissed her hello.

"Yeah?" Ethan's voice was hoarse and faint, distant.

"You okay?" She nudged him with her knee.

He sighed in response.

"Want to talk about it?"

Ethan sat up.

"You saw the game."

"Yes," Ivy replied, "but there are more—"

"I know." He cut her off and slid off the bed, kneeling beside the duffel he'd dropped earlier to unlace his running shoes. "It's just..." Ethan trailed off, looking up at her. A crease formed between his brows, but otherwise, his face was unreadable.

"It's just... what?" So unlike Ethan, this reluctance to talk to her. A slow, creeping sensation of cold slid up Ivy's spine.

His brows creased while the tendon in his jaw flexed as if he was practicing the words in his head before saying them aloud. He stared down at his hands.

"I don't want to do this anymore."

And Ivy's heart plummeted to the floor.

"It's been so much harder lately, and I don't know if this is even what I want now." It was freeing for Ethan to finally say the words out loud. He'd been unsettled for a while, and he'd realized what he had to do on the flight. "I feel like this is a good time for it to end, you know?" Unzipping the duffel bag, Ethan placed his shoes in their mesh pocket. "It's been a good run, but I think it's over." He let out a sharp exhale.

Ivy sniffled above him. Ethan raised his eyes to meet hers, and she was...crying?

"What happened?" Ivy whispered. "What did I do?"

"What do you mean?" He blinked up at her, confused.

"I said," she snapped as a tear fell onto her freckled cheekbone, "what did I *do*? Why is it over?"

What was she—

"Ivy, sweetheart, *no.*" Ethan eased over to where she still sat on the edge of the bed and rested his chin on her knees before reaching up to brush her tears away with his thumbs. "Ivy," he said, "I want to *retire*."

"You— what?"

"I think now is a good time for me to retire. I only ever wanted to make it to the World Series, and now we're here. Go out on top, you know?"

"I just- *what*?"

"Ivy. *Ivy*." He sat back on his heels and ran his hand through his hair. "You didn't think I—"

Then *she* cut *him* off.

"You were being so weird!" Ivy's voice quavered. Angry tears dripped onto her cheeks. "You didn't even kiss me, and you said," and she made air quotes around his words, "you 'don't want to do this anymore'! What else was I supposed to think?" She crossed her arms over her chest and inhaled shakily.

For a moment, Ethan thought maybe he should wait, he had *plans* for this, dammit, but he wanted to reassure her.

Needed to.

Pulling the bag closer, he removed the gift he had for her and straightened the fabric before placing it on her lap.

Nonplussed at the pile of fabric landing on her lap, Ivy arched a brow at him in question. He smiled at her, watching her unfold the tiny black Hawks jersey.

"That's nice, but—"

"Turn it around."

He knew what she'd see when she turned it. His number printed in gleaming white, and—

She inhaled sharply.

"*Fisher*? Ethan, what does this mean?"

"Tomorrow, at the game, they're honoring dad, and..." he paused for a breath, "I did an interview, a whole reveal thing. The League is okay with it, so I'm going to be using my real name for the first time."

"But this is *tiny*," Ivy said, holding up the jersey for inspection.

"That one's for Janna. I got one for each of you."

"You— but— for all of us?" She looked like she might cry again.

"Of course. Jase's going to flip his shit." Ethan chuckled at the thought. "You should try yours on, though."

Ivy unfolded the other jersey before finally getting to hers. Ethan's heart was pounding out of his chest, and his breath caught as he watched and waited.

Because it was Ivy, she flapped her jersey out in front of her rather than unfolding it, so she didn't hear the small thud of the velvet box hitting the carpet. Ethan bit back his laugh and retrieved the box to hold it out in front of her, waiting while she pulled the jersey over her head rather than fiddling with all the buttons.

"It's more comfortable than I expected," she said, smoothing her hands over the fabric. "I love it!" And then she *finally* looked back at him after an eternity and gasped.

"Ivy?" Ethan had thought his hands would shake when he proposed to her. He'd thought he'd be nervous or awkward, but it was *Ivy*, so how could he be? “I want the name on that jersey to be your name too.”

Ivy gaped at him.

“I never imagined that sliding into you that day at the stadium really meant I was sliding into love.” He took a slow deep breath, gazed into the eyes he couldn’t live without, and said, “Ivy, will you be my wife?”

Ivy’s hand shook when Ethan slid the ring over her finger, but then her hands were in his hair, and she threw herself on him so hard, he fell backward on the carpet. She kissed him hard, her hands tugging at the hem of his shirt, then sliding beneath it when he didn't remove it fast enough. Her hips rocked into his, and she moaned against his mouth before trailing her lips over his jaw and down his neck. When she finally succeeded in getting them both undressed, Ivy hovered over Ethan, pressing just the head inside her, and he groaned, resisting the urge to push her down further. Ivy pulled on his hands, threading their fingers together. Ethan watched the muscles of her thighs tighten as she held herself above him, sliding back and forth, using him to spread her arousal over them both. Her hands gripped his tightly as she lowered herself, fully sheathing him inside her. Ivy’s head tipped back as she rode him, flexing her thighs and rolling her hips.

The ring glinted on her finger, and the caveman part of his brain crowed *mine forever*.

Ethan jerked his hips up to meet her, and Ivy pushed his hands over his head and leaned down, bringing their chests together. Their skin burned where it met, and Ethan had to fight not to flip her over and pound her into the floor.

Ivy’s thighs tightened over his hips, and her internal muscles gripped him tighter when she climaxed. She was so undone, it sent Ethan over the edge with her. They collapsed back to the carpet in a sweaty heap, panting and spent. He loved seeing her disheveled and undone knowing he'd been the cause of it.

"Ivy?"

"Hmm?" It sounded as though she might already be asleep.

"You never actually said yes."

Ivy let out an enormous sigh and rolled her eyes theatrically.

"Yes, *fine*, I'll be your wife." She pulled his head down and pressed her forehead to his.

"The jerseys weren't just for this, you know." Ethan sat up to look at her properly.

"You mean you want to—" Emotion caught in her throat.

"Of course, I do. I know we haven't talked about it, but I know you wanted to adopt them, and they're my family now, too."

22

Cars were backed up for blocks in all directions when Ivy and the others arrived at the stadium, and tensions were high as they all trooped out of the car and through the lot. Jimmy and Laura met them at the gate with no mention of the engagement or the ring. So silent were they that Ivy suspected Ethan hadn't told his parents. Despite her developing relationship with Laura and Jimmy over the past few months, Ivy was nervous about announcing she and Ethan were now engaged. They hadn't had time to discuss anything the previous night, so Ivy wasn't sure if Ethan wanted to be the one to tell them, or if he wanted to talk to them together.

As they picked their way through the rapidly filling stadium, Ivy decided to remain silent, although, with Laura's attention to detail, she doubted the ring would go unnoticed for long. Probably because Ivy couldn't stop herself from looking at it. The antique marquise cut diamond was surrounded by smaller stones and set in a scrolling halo with a delicately scalloped pavè band. It was *exactly* what she would have picked for herself if she'd ever allowed herself to dream about such things.

But she never *had* dreamt about it. On the rare occasion the thought of marriage or even *permanence* entered her mind in any other semblance of a relationship, she had promptly shut the thoughts down.

Nothing had been permanent. Not her parents. Not Maya. Not even her foster children would have been permanent. They likely would have been transferred to new families, or taken in by relatives, leaving her like everyone else. She hadn't loved any of them any less for it, but she just...expected everyone to leave.

But now that big, beautiful, *amazing* Ethan Fisher had crashed his tight-pants-wearing ass into her life, everything had changed. Their broken pieces fit together in ways she'd never considered, and they were getting *married*.

And he wanted to adopt Jase and Janna.

All those things meant forever, and Ivy was still reeling.

In the seat beside her, Lily kept looking over at Ivy and grinning like a loon, waggling her eyebrows when she looked down at where Ivy's hand was linked with Janna's. As she had done every ten seconds since the night before, Ivy looked down at her left hand and the faint sparkle of the ring made her breath catch in her throat.

She needed to get a grip.

The walk across the stadium took *years*; years in which Ivy imagined every possible way to break the news to Ethan's parents. "Hi, guys, your son wants to spend the rest of his life with me, hope you're okay with that." Or "Oh, by the way, Laura, Ethan asked me to marry him, and then we had sex on the floor until he had to go back to the hotel to stay with the team because of your friend's weird rules".

The sound of Jase's footsteps as he ran the final few yards to the door of the skybox broke her from her reverie. Ethan, already in his pristine white uniform, waited outside the box, grinning at Ivy and greeting Jase. Janna ran to him too, so he knelt to pick her up. Behind Ivy, Lily snickered audibly and poked Ivy in the ribs.

"It's your *fiancé*, Ivy."

Ivy rolled her eyes and gritted her teeth before smiling up

at Ethan. She was glad to see him, even if she hadn't expected to see him before the game began.

"Hi?" she said, more of a question than a greeting.

Ethan gently set Janna down, then pulled Ivy into him. For some inexplicable reason, he'd sprayed cologne on his uniform, and the familiar scent of citrus and bergamot and *Ethan* was comforting as her cheek rested against the smooth fabric of his jersey.

"I'm sorry for what's about to happen," he whispered into her ear. "I should've known better, but I wasn't thinking when I texted her last night."

"Wait, what?"

From somewhere behind her, Laura spoke.

"Are we going to stand here, or are we going inside?" Ivy heard a hint of something in Laura's voice, but as she turned to look at the older woman, Laura gently pushed her forward as Ethan opened the door.

Balloons erupted from the door in a cascade of red, black, and white. The kids and Lily darted forward to push through the mass of mylar blocking the door. Ivy glanced at Ethan who sighed good-naturedly and nodded toward Laura. Turning to face Laura, Ivy found herself suddenly enveloped in a rose-perfumed embrace.

"I'm so happy for you two!" Laura squeezed Ivy, then stepped back and took both of Ivy's hands in her own. "When Ethan asked me for the ring, I knew it was coming, but he didn't tell me anything else." At Ivy's confused look, Laura clarified. "The ring was my mother's."

Something warm and soft welled up inside Ivy's chest at the family heirloom she now wore. The ring meant even more to her knowing it had belonged to someone in Ethan's family, and she loved *him* so much more for offering it to her, for trusting her with something so important. Something she'd never have from her birth mother.

"I didn't know." Ivy choked back a sob and tried to hide it by hugging Laura again. Ethan hadn't told her the ring was his grandmother's. It made her feel closer to him, closer to his family in a way she'd never have with her own. "Thank you for trusting me with this."

"My darling girl, you are more than welcome to it. Thank you for bringing my son back to me." Laura's voice cracked, and she held Ivy's hands tightly.

"I didn't—"

"You showed him the way. None of this—" Laura waved around them, at the food and balloons, the people gathered in the box, "would have happened if it weren't for you."

Bittersweet emotion overtook Ivy until she felt Ethan's fingers thread through hers as he led her inside.

"Let's see if they left any food for us," he said, chuckling.

"Ha! I'd be more worried about Lily getting into what appears to be an entire case of champagne." Ivy pointed to the tables laden with food and drinks, awed at Laura's dedication.

"How did this," Ivy waved vaguely, "happen?"

Ethan grimaced.

"After I left last night," and Ivy was pleased to see the tips of his ears turn pink where they peeked through his hair, "I called my mom. I thought she'd want to know."

"And she did all of this that quickly?"

"Ah, no. I imagine her assistant did most of the work." Ethan rolled his eyes fondly. He pulled down a particularly large balloon shaped like a ring and handed it to Ivy.

She lightly bopped him over the head with it, then dashed away to hide behind a column of balloons. Ethan rolled his eyes again, grinning at her.

Jase and Janna were distracted by the balloons and treats, and the adults were distracted by the champagne, so Ethan and Ivy hid together behind the balloon column, sitting on the floor and sharing the food. Ivy noted Ethan being extremely careful with the food, going so far as to spread napkins over his lap, so she flicked one with a finger and quirked a brow in silent question. He scowled.

"These white fucking pants. They're going to be covered in dirt later, but Emily would be out for blood if she saw me start the game with," he paused to inspect the plate, "whole grain mustard and blackberry jam on my pants." He sighed. "I hate these things. They show everything."

Ivy stuffed an artisanal sesame cracker spread with sheep's milk cheese and jam into her mouth before responding. "Yeah, they *really* do." Her muffled words came out somewhere between wistful and flirtatious. She looked up at Ethan who was grinning widely at her, the gold in his eyes catching the bright lights and sparkling.

"Oh, yeah?"

Ivy's cheeks burned, even though she was going to marry the man.

"Yeah." She tried to be sultry, but it came out more like a squeak.

"What exactly do they show, Ivy?" Ethan's voice dropped an octave when he said her name.

Ivy gulped champagne. The bubbles tingled on her tongue.

"Did you know I *still* don't understand baseball?"

"Don't change the subject."

"I'm not. Do you know *why* I don't know anything about baseball?"

"Feel free to enlighten me." He smirked at her from behind his glass. Water, though, no champagne for Mister Major League.

Leaning in closer, Ivy gave him a long once-over, trailing a finger over his shoulder and down his arm to where his hand rested on his thigh.

"Mostly, I focus on you. You have *great* form, did you know? I mean I guess you do. You look good, anyway. My favorite is when you set up to bat and tap your shoes three times each before you do this little shake. It starts in your shoulders and goes all the way down to your hips. Then you take a couple of practice swings that stretch your jersey. Sometimes I wonder how it doesn't split. When you swing for real, you *really* put your back into it. And then when you run…" She trailed off, grinning at the delighted surprise on his face. "Did you know you have a great ass, Ethan? And those thigh muscles. You're like a fucking tree in the *best* way." Her hand trailed over his thigh, feeling the muscles beneath the fabric tense at her touch as she dragged her hand higher. "I also spend a lot of time trying to see what else is under there, too. But those damn compression shorts kind of block the view." Ivy pretended to pout at Ethan, whose eyes were still widened in surprise.

"Nice job on the ring, Sasquatch."

Ivy scowled up at Lily, who had appeared out of nowhere and winked suggestively as she stared down at them. Turning back to him, she saw Ethan hauling himself to his feet.

"I should probably go anyway."

Ivy watched as Ethan said his goodbyes, and she followed him to the door of the skybox, where she stood on her toes to kiss him.

"We'll pick up where we left off later, okay?" She grinned up at him when his hands slid down her waist, dangerously close to the swell of her ass.

"Definitely," Ethan growled against her neck before he tugged a hoodie over his jersey and took off down the stairs to join the team for their pre-game rituals.

When the cameras panned over the teams before the game, Ivy saw Ethan smiling and laughing, and it looked like the goofy grin was still on his lips when he jogged to the mound as the game began. So much had changed from when she'd first seen him, with the black paint smeared over his face and a perpetual scowl, and she made a mental note to remember to tell him what she'd thought when they'd first met.

Until she saw him look directly into the camera with an evil smirk that had her practically melting in her seat.

As always, when she watched him play, Ivy paid more attention to Ethan than the game he played. She loved watching him roll his shoulders and tap his bat on his cleats before squaring up to swing, loved the brace of his large hands on his muscular thighs between pitches. And she especially loved the white pants. Though she couldn't see them, she knew exactly how the muscles in his back would ripple every time he swung the bat. Ivy imagined those muscles bunching beneath her fingertips, and she had to clench her thighs *and* her jaw to keep from making a scene. Tonight, it seemed like he was being more... vigorous than usual. Finding excuses to jog more, or to lean over bracing his hands on his knees, and occasionally looking directly into the camera while he did it. Ivy cursed herself for sitting beside his mother, who pretended not to notice. Trying to focus more on the game, Ivy occasionally asked Jase what was happening or played with Janna. *Thank the stars we're getting married,* she thought, *or I would have to turn into a baseball groupie.*

23

After Ethan proposed with the jerseys, Ivy purchased a full Hawks uniform: hat, black-and-red striped tall socks, tight white pants, and black running shoes. She'd splurged and bought one for Janna too since Jase already had the whole setup. Ivy had *plans* for the uniform, and she cackled with glee every time she thought about it. Seeing her wearing his name would drive Ethan wild, and her ass in the curve-hugging white pants? He'd go feral.

Laura, Jimmy, Frankie, Derek, and Ethan were waiting for them when Ivy and crew arrived at the gate. When her group met the others, Jimmy, Laura, and Frankie stopped to greet the kids, and Ivy stood on her toes to kiss Ethan before he saw what she was wearing. As his hands slid down her back, he stiffened against her when his hands came across the belt and dropped down to her hips. She felt him shift to look down her back, past the black and red letters of the jersey. Holding her breath, Ivy waited for Ethan to slide his hands over the white-clad swell of her ass, but Janna ran up and tugged on both their hands.

"Ethan! We match! Look!" Janna shoved her hands in the pockets of her pants which were a smaller copy of the ones Ethan wore. Ethan took in Janna's outfit, and Ivy watched as Ethan registered her and Jase's uniforms too.

"You have to take a picture!" Lily screeched, running over to grab Ethan and Ivy's other hands, tugging them toward the others.

Lily whipped her phone out and snapped several photos, offering directions and rearranging them like a despotic photographer. Eventually, she dragged Jimmy into the photo because he'd donned *his* uniform too. Then she dragged Derek into the shot, and finally, everyone was all grouped around Ivy, Ethan, and their kids, and Lily handed her phone to a stranger for a group photo. Ivy couldn't stop the tears welling in her eyes at her *family*.

Until Ethan's hand slid into her back pocket and squeezed.

"Nice outfit, sweetheart," he growled into her ear. "Let me see the back."

Ivy shivered at the order in his voice, and she spun around for him, cocking her hip out at a provocative angle. Heat radiated off Ethan when he turned her back around and pulled her against his body.

"God, I love seeing my name on you, but I'm going to enjoy taking this off."

They were interrupted by Jimmy teasing Laura, who giggled and swatted at him, and Jimmy immediately picked her up and spun her around before planting a big, sloppy kiss right on Laura's lips. At that moment, Ivy was struck by the similarities between Ethan and Jimmy. The way she caught Jimmy looking at Laura when Laura wasn't watching, the same look she'd seen on Ethan's face when she caught him looking at her. Warmth spread from deep inside Ivy, and she smiled even wider, glancing between Ethan and his father. Ivy saw Laura eyeing Jimmy the way she knew she stared at Ethan, and Ivy had to look away from the private moment. Swinging her gaze back to Ethan, she saw he'd been swarmed by fans and was somehow wrangling them all at once while still managing to hold a conversation with Jase and Derek, probably about the game.

Eventually, though, Derek, Jimmy, and Ethan had to return to the dugout, and all the others made their way down into the stadium.

Because Laura was Laura, she'd arranged for Jase and Janna to take part in all the usual activities. Dizzy bat race, t-shirt cannons, joining the mascots to pass out various junk food to fans between innings, everything. Everyone's energy ran high, fresh off last night's win. Derek did a bouncing dance while he squatted down behind home plate, and even Ethan was acting a little cocky, showing off on the mound.

And it drove Ivy *wild*. She couldn't stop staring.

"Keep it in your pants, Johnson," Lily sang at Ivy over her extra-large stadium cup of tepid beer.

"I don't know what you're talking about," Ivy answered primly, sipping her warming beer.

Lily and Ivy watched the kids and Jimmy rolling around in giant hamster balls and bouncing off each other, trying to cross the finish line.

"I see you making googly eyes at Sasquatch over there," Lily said, gesturing with her cup. "I'd tell you to jump on that, but he looks kinda busy." Ethan was on second, glancing between Harkness and the Tornadoes' pitcher.

"Yeah," Ivy sighed. "Later, though." She raised her eyebrows at Lily, who cackled loudly enough that two older men in Hawks hats in the row ahead of them turned around to stare.

"She's gonna get it later!" Lily called, wiggling her hips suggestively in her seat and pointing at Ivy.

The old men blushed and whipped back around.

"Bet they never had a good fu—" Lily sniped under her breath.

"Okay, you have had enough of this." Ivy leaned over to take Lily's cup and deposited it in her cup holder.

Lily blew a big, wet raspberry at Ivy, and then stood to dance wildly to the music blasting over the speakers, pulling

Ivy up to dance too. Ivy was leaning against the green railing in front of the dugout watching Lily's antics when her phone vibrated in her pocket.

Come to my hotel room and keep the uniform on.

You like that, huh?

After the game, you'll see how much I like it.

Ivy gulped, wishing she hadn't finished Lily's extra-large beer. Heat pulsed through her, and she crossed and uncrossed her legs, trying to ignore the empty ache between them.

Game three was another win for the Hawks, though the Tornadoes managed to snag a few runs, and the Hawks returned to the hotel in high spirits. Ivy kissed her kids and sent them with Lily, who gave her a knowing smirk. Her rideshare delivered her to the hotel as the final stragglers of the team piled into the elevator. From the corner of her eye, Ivy saw Ethan rise from a chair before stalking over to her. Damp waves clung to the sides of his neck, and he'd changed into street clothes. When he reached her side, Ivy had to fight the urge to climb him like a tree at the look in his eyes.

The next elevator arrived, and Ivy and Ethan were alone until an arm shoved through the closing doors. Derek and Isaac burst through the doors, looking nearly as desperate as Ivy. An awkward silence settled over the elevator as all four inhabitants avoided looking at each other.

Until Derek snorted. Ivy bit her lip, trying not to dissolve into punch-drunk giggles as she met her brother's gaze. His warm brown eyes sparkled with amusement, and Ivy rolled her eyes heavenward as she mouthed *shut up.* Behind her, Ethan was so close, his chest pressed into Ivy's back with every breath, and her breath hitched in anticipation.

And of course, they all got out on the same floor, but Derek's and Isaac's rooms were on opposite ends of the hallway.

Outside his room, Ethan took Ivy's hands in his, pulling her close, and deftly shifting her hands to hold both of her wrists in one hand while he unlocked the door with his keycard. Once they were finally inside his room, Ethan backed Ivy into the wall, still holding her wrists and pinning her hands up by her shoulders. His body invaded her space, heat rolling off him as he slammed into her and claimed her mouth. At some point, Ivy was too lost to have noticed when Ethan managed to slide his free hand between them, making fast work of her belt. When his hand slipped beneath the white fabric, Ethan growled, and Ivy gasped.

"No underwear *and* you're this wet?" He kissed and bit his way down her throat. "You're going to kill me, Ivy. How am I supposed to focus on a game when you look like this?"

"Like what?" Ivy's eyes rolled back at the sensation of his fingers stroking inside her and his thumb strumming her clit, and her voice was more breath than words.

"*Fuckable,*" he snarled into her ear.

Ivy gasped Ethan's name as he continued to work her with his hand, the wet noises of his fingers moving inside her the only sound other than their breathing.

Withdrawing his hand from her pants and making her whimper at the loss, Ethan roughly turned Ivy so her front pressed against the wall. One hand still pinned both of hers above her head, and from the sounds behind her, he was undoing his jeans. Ethan shoved Ivy's pants down past her knees and spread her legs further apart.

And then Ivy felt him nudge against her entrance, and without meaning to, she rocked back against him, trying to fuck herself on him, her need like a live wire inside her, sparking more and more with every touch.

"Fuck, Ivy," Ethan hissed in her ear as he rammed his hips

forward until he was fully sheathed inside her. His hand slid beneath her jersey, rolling a nipple between his fingers, but he didn't move.

Electricity scorched through her veins, and she hissed, circling her hips, anything for more of that sensation. When Ethan remained still, she decided to use him, bracing against the wall to push back against him. Ethan released her hands to wrap his fist around the ponytail sticking out from beneath her hat, tugging her head back so she saw him out of the corner of her eye. That little bit of tension and the slight change of angle nearly whited out her vision. Once her hands were free, Ivy reached behind Ethan, digging her nails into his backside to wrench his hips forward. Finally releasing whatever hold he had on his self-control, Ethan snapped his hips, pushing her harder against the wall.

A strangled sound left her throat as her body pressed harder into the wall, the cool paint achingly smooth against her burning, over-sensitive skin.

"Fisher?" Someone called Ethan's name outside the door.

Ivy froze, almost screaming in frustration, expecting him to stop. But Ethan kept moving, pressing his face into Ivy's shoulder to muffle his groaning.

"Fisher, we have an early morning. Lights out in ten." Harkness.

"You got it," he called toward the door. His voice sounded aggravatingly normal, and he let out a low chuckle against the back of her neck, his breath sending goosebumps down her spine. "I'm sorry, sweetheart, but we've got to be fast." Ethan's whisper sent more skitters of pleasure along her skin, and she was *so close*.

Then Ethan released Ivy's ponytail and shoved his hand between her legs to roughly circle his fingers over her clit until her inner walls gripped his cock. Stars burst behind her eyes, and she forgot how to breathe. He finished quickly after and collapsed with a grunt against the wall, bracketing her body with his. After planting a soft kiss and a scrape of his teeth on the back of her neck, Ethan moved to rearrange himself and straighten his clothes while Ivy did the same.

"I guess I should go."

"Mmm." Ethan turned her around, nuzzling her neck. "You could stay and sneak out in the morning."

"Emily Harkness is a terrifying woman, and I do not want to face her wrath."

Ethan's hands found their way beneath her jersey, sliding up over her waist to palm her breasts.

"Ethan!" Ivy hissed.

He pouted.

"Fine. You can go. You're going to keep these though, right?" He slid a hand into her back pocket and tugged the fabric.

"If they make you act like this, you can bet your sweet baseball-playing ass I'm keeping them," Ivy said and kissed him before sliding out the door.

Where she walked directly into Jen, who sauntered down the hall.

"Looks like someone rounded the bases and made it all the way home." The blonde snickered at Ivy. "Nice."

When Ethan awoke, he groaned and rolled over to pull Ivy close. Except her side of the bed was empty.

Right. He was in a hotel. Because he was playing in the World Series.

And today was the day he'd been dreading. The joint press conference with the Tornadoes' players and staff.

With Lawrence.

Anxiety at having to share air with his uncle scraped through Ethan's body, leaving his muscles aching and in need of relief only the warm touch of Ivy's soothing hands could give.

Instead, he had to settle for a shower just short of volcanic.

After the shower, Ethan buttoned himself into the suit he had brought for the press conference, black on black with a red tie. Ivy had laughed while she'd smoothed the lapels of the jacket when he'd tried it on for her at his apartment, muttering about wearing colors for once under her breath. Ethan had reminded her his tie was red, and black *was* a color, thank you very much. And then he'd enjoyed wrapping the red tie around Ivy's wrists to pin her hands over her head until she'd breathlessly agreed that black was a color.

With those memories bolstering his mood, Ethan joined his teammates for the press conference and did his damndest to ignore the asshole who used to call himself his uncle and coach.

Ethan was ready for the game and the whole World Series to be *over*. He wanted to get married and settle into domestic bliss with Ivy and their kids. Maybe when this was all over, he'd finish school and be a teacher. Ivy would love that, he thought, trying to conceal his smile and stay serious for the cameras.

With one foot firmly planted on the bag, Ethan kept his eye on Jen as she strode to the plate. Her confidence gave Ethan a boost; Lawrence's shit at the press conference still rang in Ethan's ears. No matter how little Ethan valued his uncle's words as an adult, the sting of hearing the same things over and over in the past hadn't fully healed.

It was the bottom of the fifth, and Ethan hovered near third while Derek did the same on second, both men in nearly identical positions as they waited for

—crack—

Jen hit a foul into the seats behind third, and the Tornadoes' catcher called a timeout to confer with the opposing pitcher.

In the handful of seconds it took for the catcher to jog to the mound, Ethan found himself in too close proximity to his uncle. The nasty look on Lawrence's face nearly made him back away, but he wasn't about to take his foot off base. It was better to pretend he wasn't there.

"What the hell is wrong with you?" Lawrence muttered, barely audible.

Ethan's breath came in short pants like he'd been caught between bases and had to sprint and dive beneath a ball. Instead of responding, he adjusted his helmet for probably the fifth time, and as it had so frequently in the past few months, Ethan's mind blurred the past and present into a single, murky image. This time, he shoved it aside, and for the first time, he let the stadium sounds fill his ears rather than listen to his uncle.

The dull roaring of so many intermingling sounds drowned out Lawrence's tirade enough that Ethan's mind yanked itself back into the game just in time to jog to the dugout to gather his hat and glove and return to the mound after Jen got tagged out at first.

Ethan managed to stay focused as the innings progressed, somehow maintaining the speed and placement of his pitches on muscle memory, never following his train of thought to the past, never ruminating on his uncle's bullshit. Until the final inning when he found himself in an almost identical position as before. Gritting his teeth, he did his best to ignore the words of his uncle, but Lawrence kept moving closer, taking a half step nearer with every foul Jen hit.

And she *kept* hitting fouls.

Still, Lawrence grew closer, close enough for Ethan to see the redness staining his cheeks and bloodshot eyes. Was Lawrence drunk?

Seriously? Another drunken coach attacking him? What the hell was his life?

Again, Ethan tried to drown out Lawrence's muttering. It worked, at least for a few more fouls, until a few stray words caught Ethan's attention.

"—that girl and her brats—"

How does he even know about Ivy?

"Shut up," growled Ethan through clenched teeth. At his sides, his hands clenched and unclenched, fisting the fabric of his pants. One eye twitched.

"You know she's just using you, trying to get close to you for a payday."

"What the fuck?" Ethan yanked his helmet off, turning to fully face his uncle. "Don't talk about her." His fingers dug into the foam lining his helmet, his knuckles going white with the force as seething anger flashed through him like lightning.

Crossing the last few feet between them, Lawrence got as close to him as possible without touching him. "You can't possibly think anyone would want to be with someone like you —you with your anger issues and—"

Harkness and an umpire appeared to one side, but Lawrence didn't seem to care as he continued ranting. "And another thing—a fucking female manager? What is the league coming to if they're letting *women* in now." Lawrence spat on the red clay lining the white chalk of the third base line. "My father—"

"Okay, that's enough out of you," the umpire, a tall man with an impressive mustache, called over Lawrence's yelling.

Startled at the sudden appearance of people around him, Ethan looked around to find his teammates standing in a semicircle around the unpleasant scene. Like they had his back. Like they were a team.

Still reeling, Ethan watched the home umpire striding toward them, taking his place with the others. After conferring for a few minutes with both managers, the umpires stood to one side until they returned to the group that had since grown to include most of the Tornadoes.

With a press of a button to the mic clipped to his collar, the head umpire's voice reverberated throughout the stadium, cutting through the confusion. "After review, Tornadoes Manager Lawrence Lorne will be ejected for unsportsmanlike conduct." A laugh bubbled up Ethan's throat, but he clamped a hand over his mouth before it escaped. Lawrence reacted about as well as one would expect—more cursing and yelling, and two umpires had to practically drag him off the field.

A wave drew his attention to the area behind the dugout. Ivy, Laura, and Frankie stood in a row. Worry creased Ivy's face. Laura looked pissed. Frankie cracked his knuckles ominously as Lawrence was led away.

When the game resumed, it was clear that both teams were ready for it to end. Ethan watched from the bullpen as Adams, the relief pitcher, ended the game with the fastest three strikeouts he'd ever seen. Then it was over, and Ethan was so relieved that he didn't bother looking at the score.

Post-game was a blur of reporters and questions he didn't listen to. Exhaustion gripped his limbs, slowing his movements, and he wanted nothing more than to leave the stadium behind.

Ivy, his parents, and everyone else waited for him as he

exited the locker room. Being Laura Lorne and Jimmy Fisher came with certain perks, Ethan thought ruefully. He wasn't sure if he wanted to be alone or to be with them for the comfort that came from surrounding himself with family. Either way, he was glad to see them as they gathered around him.

"You okay?" Ivy whispered in his ear as she wrapped her arms around him.

He didn't know how to answer.

Everything he hadn't had the opportunity to process throughout the night settled over him, its weight heavy and draining.

"I'm not sure." His voice sounded tired, even to him. "Lawrence said awful things about you and Emily, and—"

"What did he say?" Laura's voice cut through, sharp and cold as a knife.

"It doesn't matter, now. He's gone, isn't he?" The umpires had pulled him aside after the game for more clarification, and it was humiliating enough to tell them his history and his uncle's words. He didn't want to go through it all again.

"It matters." Laura spun on her heel, marching toward the exit, her phone in hand.

What was she going to do?

Ethan and Ivy followed while Frankie, Jimmy, and Lily stayed behind with Jase and Janna. Jen, Isaac, Derek, and a few other team members filed out of the locker room and joined the procession.

"Look." Laura pointed to her phone screen. "He's ranting on Twitter. I'm sure he's still here somewhere."

Was she going to hunt down her brother? And for what? Not that Ethan wanted to be a part of what was likely to be a pretty intense showdown, but he was captivated by the thought of his mother giving her brother a verbal lashing.

Emily Harkness strode toward them, a handful of official-looking suits in tow. She made brief eye contact with Laura, who gave a slight nod but didn't break stride. Ethan assumed from the set of her jaw that Emily would love nothing more than to join them but valued her position too much to do so.

Ethan and Emily were bound by the League's rules of conduct, but Laura had no such restrictions and could do what she wanted.

"What is happening?" Ivy caught up to him, whispering so Laura wouldn't hear.

"I'm not sure." Ethan had never seen his mother so angry, and he was glad he wasn't the recipient of her ire.

"This is going to be fucking awesome," Jen said in an undertone as they exited the stadium into the back lot. "Lorne just tweeted about the loss and how they'll come back tomorrow, blah blah blah. Didn't mention getting thrown out, though," she called in a louder voice for Laura to hear.

"You follow him on Twitter?" Derek asked.

"He knows how to tweet?" Isaac sounded skeptical.

"He always did have a flair for the dramatic. He gets it from our father."

Ethan heard the eye roll in her voice without having to see it.

Outside, the halogen lights cast puddles of yellow over the parking lot, bathing Lawrence Lorne and his dejected-looking team in half-shadows where they waited, leaning against the concrete exterior of the building.

"Oh, shit," Isaac muttered.

"Oh, shit," Ethan agreed.

Lawrence turned toward them, a nasty look on his face.

"You!" Lawrence's hair was mussed like he'd tugged on it several times.

"Oh, shut up." Laura pushed past the few Tornadoes who didn't scramble out of her way fast enough.

Lawrence stared at her as if surprised to see her there. Ethan was struck by their similarities, then. Close in height and build, though his mother's hair had always been darker than Lawrence's sandy locks. Despite Lawrence's bullying and belittling of the past, though, at the moment, nothing was more terrifying than Laura in her stony, seething anger.

"What the—"

"I said, 'Shut up.'" Laura advanced on her brother, who had the good sense to take a startled step back. "What the hell is wrong with you?"

"I—"

"I'm not finished. How dare you speak to my son that way? How dare you speak to him at all after the way you 'trained' him?" She drew air quotes around the word, her fingers making claws that were frighteningly close to Lawrence's face. "You shouldn't be allowed on a baseball field after that! He was a *child*, Lawrence."

"He said wanted to be the best! And he was obsessed with our father! Always watching those old tapes. I was trying to keep him from turning out that way."

"*You* kept the tapes. You watched them as much as he did, or don't you remember idolizing dear old Dad when you were younger? And now look at you."

Lawrence blanched.

"And don't get me started on the way you spoke to Emily, you misogynist piece of—"

Beside Ethan, Ivy tensed, her fingers digging into his arm. He was torn between gleeful fascination and vague horror as the situation unfolded.

"Misogyny?" Lawrence interrupted. "It's not misogyny if it's true. Women should not manage baseball teams! Or play on them."

Jen's molars ground audibly in the mostly-still night air.

"And another thing—" Lawrence was really on a roll now, and Ethan wondered what else the man could possibly have left to shout about. "The agency should be mine. It was *my* legacy. Mine!" Lawrence's scowl deepened as he raised his voice. The few team members who'd been pretending to ignore gave up the pretense and turned to watch the spectacle. "It should have gone to me!"

"So you could run it into the ground the way you've ruined your team?" Laura scoffed in her brother's face.

Ethan winced. His mother certainly knew where to land her verbal blows to inflict maximum damage.

"Bitch." Lawrence spat the word with as much venom as Ethan had ever heard.

"Asshole," Laura fired back.

If it hadn't been so terrible, Ethan might have laughed at seeing his mother and uncle behaving like stereotypical siblings.

"And you," Lawrence's attention shifted to the door where Emily stood, having taken half a step out. "You're the problem here. Why don't you take this mess you call a team and go home before you embarrass yourself, huh, honey? Let the men handle this."

Emily bit back a smile, which Ethan found rather startling, given the situation, until she pushed the door completely open and stepped out, the League officials still on her heels as they filed out behind her.

"Mr. Lorne, we need to have a conversation," one of them said, gesturing for Lawrence to follow them back inside.

"Well, that was fun," Derek said conversationally.

"I'm sorry you all had to see that," Laura called to the small crowd that remained after Emily, Lawrence, and the suits went back in. "I apologize to both teams. The Lornes were in fine form tonight." She gave a contrite smile.

"Nothing to apologize for." Jen's voice was gravelly as she glared toward the door.

Ethan worried that she might go after Lawrence too. And

while his uncle deserved whatever he got, Jen was too good to get suspended before the final game.

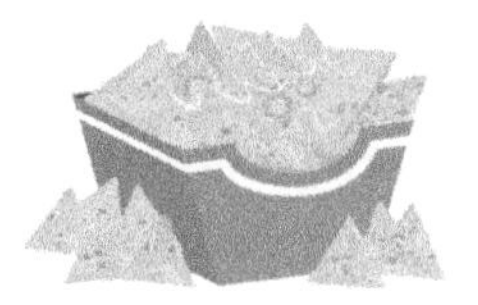

"Do you want to talk about it?"

They'd returned to a meeting room inside the stadium, where Jimmy, Frankie, and Lily waited with Jase and Janna. Janna was nearly asleep, curled up on Jimmy's lap.

Ivy still didn't quite know what happened on the field, but Ethan was still so pale and tense, she knew it was bad. He looked at her gratefully as she rubbed circles over his back in an effort to calm him.

"I'm okay."

He didn't sound okay.

With a sharp tug, he pulled her against his chest and buried his face in her neck. Definitely not okay, then. His muscles were taut beneath her hands, but his breathing began to slow after a few moments.

"What happened?"

"Just...Lawrence. Being awful, as always." Ethan clamped his jaw closed so hard, Ivy thought he might have cracked a molar.

"He's a sad old man," Ivy said, glaring at him over Ethan's shoulder. A trainer had brought a towel, and Lawrence held it pressed to his face. “I thought your mom was going to punch him.”

“Wouldn’t be the first time,” Jimmy interjected. Frankie nodded in agreement, still looking a bit menacing.

“Good.” Ivy’s voice was vicious.

Ethan backed up a step to stare incredulously at her.

“What? Sounds like he deserved it.”

Ethan gaped.

“Too bad I didn’t get to him first. But it’s probably for the best." She gestured at the kids.

“That’s terrifying.” She heard the laughter in his voice.

Squaring her shoulders, Ivy poked him in the chest. “He doesn’t get to say awful things about anybody, but especially not you.”

“Oh, I’d pay to see you go after him,” Ethan said, laughing outright and pulling her close to his side. “Let’s just hope you never run into him in a dark alley.” He pressed a kiss to her temple before they joined the others. Ethan squatted down to talk to Jase and Janna.

“Is everything okay?” Jase’s eyes were wide as he glanced between Ethan and Ivy.

Her heart ached, knowing how scared he must have been.

“Everything is okay,” Ethan said, “Gramma Laura is just a little riled up. Her brother wasn’t being very nice.”

Janna’s eyes widened to match her brother’s. “That was her *brother*? But Ivy says we have to be nice to each other! Especially *family*!”

“Well,” Ivy began, but Ethan stopped her with a look over his shoulder. He leaned forward to whisper something in the little girl’s ear, and when he was done, she nodded solemnly. Ivy glanced at her fiancé curiously, but he just winked.

Several minutes later, when Laura, Harkness, and the umpires returned, Harkness gave a piercing whistle that immediately silenced the room. Ivy gathered the kids to leave, but Ethan stopped her, nodding to the umpire to tell her to wait.

"In light of the unprecedented behavior, Tornadoes Manager Lawrence Lorne will be suspended for the remainder of the World Series." He said more, but Ivy wasn't listening.

Still seething, she had half a mind to hunt down Coach Lorne and give him a piece of her mind, but she didn't want to traumatize her kids further. *One day,* she thought, *one day, he'll get an earful from me.* Ethan looked at her as if he'd heard every thought crossing her mind, so she smiled sweetly and took Jase's hand.

"You okay?" His hand was ice cold, and his jaw was set in a grim line mirroring Ethan's.

Jase didn't seem to want to talk, but he nodded stiffly. Ivy squeezed his hand, and he squeezed back. They'd need to talk it out later, but hopefully, it wouldn't have any lasting effects. Janna, on the other hand, appeared to have forgotten the incident already.

"Laura, you were a badass," Jen called. "We've all seen what a shitty leader can be like, and none of us stood up to Marshall before, so there's no way we would let Lawrence Lorne talk to one of our own that way." The blonde spat the name as if it were acid. "You're just lucky I didn't get to him first. Who knows what would've happened."

An awkward chuckle went around the room.

Jen didn't laugh.

"You're right, though, Jen. We should've seen how Marshall was treating Ethan sooner and stopped it." Derek shed his usual grin for something fiercer. Around them, the rest of the team nodded their agreement.

Beside Ivy, Ethan stiffened. She looked up and his eyes were bright at Jen and Derek's defense of him.

"Still wish I'd broken his nose," Ivy muttered.

Ethan barked a laugh and rolled his eyes.

"Get in line," Jimmy quipped from the back of the room.

WHEN THEY RETURNED TO THE RENTAL HOUSE FOR THE NIGHT, Ivy waited until Janna was asleep before piling two mugs of cocoa with marshmallows and knocking on Jase's door.

"Come in." His voice sounded too tired for a ten-year-old.

Ivy nudged the door open with her toe and sat on the edge of his bed before handing him the mug. Jase took it and wrapped his thin fingers around it but didn't look at her.

"Ethan's okay," Ivy said, blowing the steam off her mug. "Are you?"

Jase's thin shoulders curved inward.

"I will be. I just— it was like my dad, you know? Always muttering mean things under his breath." Jase squeezed the mug tighter. "I couldn't hear him from our seats, but I just *knew*. He had that look, and it made Ethan act all weird."

"I know." Ivy set her mug down on his nightstand and edged closer to him. "I saw it too. But you know what?" She nudged Jase's shoulder with hers. "He didn't let it get to him. It used to bother him, and not very long ago. But I think finding a family...finding *us* helped him a lot. It showed him that he didn't deserve that. That he deserved to be happy, he deserved to have love." Ivy gently took Jase's mug and placed it beside hers. "You deserve that too, Jase. Whatever your dad used to say to you, he was wrong. We love you. We are your family now, okay?" Her eyes burned and her chest ached as she pulled Jase into a tight hug. "Ethan and I plan to adopt you and Janna, so it'll be official. If—if that's what you want." She looked down and twisted the ring on her left hand.

"I know," Jase said, grinning. "He asked me if I wanted you to adopt us before he asked you to marry him. He asked me if I wanted to be an official family, with name changes and everything." Jase bounced on the bed. "Jase *Fisher*." His smile grew even wider.

Ivy was dumbstruck that Ethan thought to ask Jase and knew how much it meant to the boy. Her...son.

"I love you, kiddo," she said, planting a kiss on top of his head.

"I love you, too," he said, ducking away.

FINALLY, THE END WAS UPON THEM. ETHAN DRESSED IN HIS uniform, only to wait in the eerily silent locker room. His mind went completely blank. An hour or a week could've passed and he wouldn't have known the difference.

This was it—the culmination of his entire life's work, and this, the final game, would determine whether or not everything he'd been through to get to that point was worth it. Ethan had no illusions about himself as he flipped through memories like Polaroids. At times, especially in those early seasons with Marshall, when he'd still been reeling with shock and hurt and confusion, he'd been an obnoxious little shit. Even thinking about it made his skin crawl with embarrassment, and he wondered if it was too late to apologize or make up for it somehow. Maybe winning this game would be enough. *My last game,* Ethan thought. *Better make it count.*

When a noise brought him out of the slideshow of memories, Ethan glanced up to find a room full of greasepaint-streaked faces staring at him, wearing the same old mask he'd worn to terrorize their opponents. Wordlessly, Derek handed him the stick of eyeblack, and Ethan swiped it beneath his eyes and smeared it over his cheeks. Solidarity—that's what was happening—with his teammates. Because it was clear they'd done it for him—for his finale.

An overwhelming rush of affection for these people, most of whom he barely knew, trickled through him as he stared out at their painted faces. Pretending to need to wash the paint off his hands, Ethan stole away rather than let them see how much it meant to him.

When he found himself at the mostly abandoned bank of sinks located in the locker room, Emily Harkness stared back at him, her blue eyes flinty in the mirror. She appeared to be staring herself down, giving a silent pep talk.

"Fisher," she called as he turned to leave her to it.

Ethan took that as permission to stay.

One silvery eyebrow rose as he stepped into the puddle of light and she saw him, but she made no remarks about the black paint streaking his face.

As Ethan reached for soap, Emily fished in her pocket and retrieved a small gold tube.

"You know," she said conversationally as Ethan scrubbed his hands, "I heard what he said." She leaned closer to the mirror, applying a layer of bright red lipstick that he would bet perfectly matched the Hawks red lettering on his jersey. "It's not the first time I've heard it. Probably won't be the last." She didn't scowl in the mirror, but her eyes narrowed at her reflection. "Female coach." She let out a barking laugh. "'Go home and cook for the men. Be a secretary. There are no women in baseball.' That's what they said to me."

"That's disgusting." Ethan wondered what other horrible things she'd heard.

"It is. And it's weird, but," she paused, angling her head to swipe a finger along her bottom lip, smoothing out a nonexistent flaw in the red lipstick. "The loudest ones always seem to be the most bothered when I look like this." She gestured to the flawless perfection she'd created on her face. She looked like she meant business, with a tiny flick of black winged liner that looked sharp enough to kill and the slash of red drawn on her mouth. With a smirk at her reflection, she glanced to Ethan. "I call it 'blood of my enemies red.' It's nice to imagine a bunch of men being bothered by something so menial as makeup. Plus, it matches the uniform."

With a sharp nod, she walked out the way Ethan had entered, the weight of the final game seeming to slow her step just enough to be noticeable.

When he reentered the room where the team waited, Emily began to speak.

"Well, I see you all have your game faces on." That got a low chuckle from most of the team. "Me too." She gestured at her face, and someone, Jen, probably, let out a piercing whistle. For a few moments, she stood before them, briefly making eye contact as she looked out over her team.

A familiar sense of excitement jangled through Ethan's nerves as he waited for her to continue.

"I should probably light a fire under your asses, but I'm not going to. I could talk about the other team and their coach and a million things, but I've watched you all grow from a bunch of assholes who played baseball together to a team. And that is why *we* will win."

The team roared in unison, banging their batting helmets together with a terrifying clash. The effect was...striking. Greasepaint-streaked faces grinned ominously around Ethan as he joined in.

"Well, I don't know what you'll do to the other team, but you scare the hell out of me. Let's do this!"

. . .

ETHAN'S HEART POUNDED IN HIS EARS IN TIME WITH THE fireworks booming overhead.

They *won.*

His last season, his last game, his only World Series, and they *won.*

He held out a hand when Harkness motioned for the team to put her down, and she gripped it tightly to steady herself as she climbed down from all the hands and shoulders supporting her.

Out of the corner of his eye, Ethan saw a bright orange cylinder sloshing toward them, and he knew what was about to happen, so he ducked away from her in time to *mostly* avoid getting splashed with gallons of red Gatorade.

Harkness was not so lucky.

Her hair was plastered to her face as she spluttered and laughed, trying to see who'd doused her.

Derek and Isaac, naturally.

The crowd had begun to spill onto the field with the team, and Ethan signed a few balls for fans as he looked for his family.

He saw Janna first; she was small enough to slip through gaps in spectators and escape the adults. She raced toward him but skidded to a halt when she was about a yard away, a horrified look on her face.

"Why do you look like *that*?" She pointed at his cheeks.

He had forgotten about the eyeblack. It had been Jen's idea, an intimidation tactic and a last goodbye to the old Hawks all in one.

Ethan squatted down and held his arms out.

"It was to keep the sun out of my eyes."

Janna squinted up at the night sky.

"But there's no sun." She crossed her arms to glare at him,

and he had no choice but to laugh. She was like a tiny Ivy, not taking his shit.

"You're right. It was mostly to look scary to the other team. Do I look scary?"

"Nuh-uh. You look silly. Take it off." Janna the tyrant, as usual.

"Sure thing. Want to help me?" Ethan scooped her up and pretended to rub his cheek over hers.

"Daddy, nooooo!" she shrieked.

His heart squeezed at the name.

Ivy appeared, and Ethan deposited Janna back on the ground, then stood and scrubbed at his face with the wipe Ivy provided. She bounced on her toes, nearly as excited as Jase. But *nobody* was as excited as Jase, and seeing him jumping up and down and howling in delight transported Ethan back in time. Ethan blinked away the fog of memories and looked up straight into his father's eyes. Jimmy winked, and Ethan felt a final piece click into place.

24

Laura's friend Andrew was a tall, thin, bald, bronzed man who had seen the business end of a Botox needle one too many times. He was fidgety, fretful, and had an annoying tendency to spout trivia, but Laura trusted him with her wardrobe, so Ivy would as well.

Ivy now found herself in Laura's palatial dressing room. *I should have expected as much,* Ivy thought as she took in a room the size of her entire apartment. Shelves of shoes and bags lined the walls, with racks of clothing organized by style and color on the opposite side. Full-length, silver-framed mirrors reflected her unusually pale face at her beside Laura's serene one and Andrew's shiny one. And there were not one, but three chandeliers.

"Just relax and enjoy yourself," Andrew said. "This is my favorite part!"

But Ivy found relaxing difficult when the man came at her with an armful of dresses and an impossibly high stack of shoe boxes in his other hand. "And of course, we'll schedule a full spa treatment, nails, waxing, hair and makeup, the works." She winced.

Laura, who had joined them in the dressing room, winked at Ivy, toasting silently with her glass of champagne. Ivy tried to disguise a snort as a cough as Andrew unloaded his burdens, deftly shifting the velvet-flocked hangers from his arm to the clothes rack and stacking the shoe boxes beneath.

This was her Cinderella moment, Ivy realized as Andrew clapped his hands together gleefully. She had found her prince, and now she had to go to the ball.

Or wait — was that backward?

Months ago, when Ethan had told her about what she'd jokingly called baseball prom, the idea had sounded fun — dressing up, drinking, dancing. Now that the time for the infamous Lorne Major League Base(Ball), with all proceeds going to local inner-city youth leagues had come, Ivy realized she was unbelievably nervous.

This was her first event as a soon-to-be Fisher, and the name Fisher meant something in baseball land.

Ethan was descended from sports royalty; hell he *was* sports royalty, having won the World Series, and Ivy was nobody from nowhere who had accidentally wandered into a dynasty. It was a Cinderella story, she thought, taking a long sip from her glass of champagne.

"Just call me CinderIvy," she muttered into the glass, then snorted again, the bubbles burning her nose.

"What was that, dear?" Laura lowered her glass to the marble-topped table between them.

Briefly, Ivy considered making an excuse or flat-out lying. But she knew the guilt would crush her.

"Just call me CinderIvy," Ivy repeated, sinking into her plush chair. "It's just... it's overwhelming. All of this." Waving around generally at the room, Ivy stared down at the scuffed toes of her sneakers. In stark contrast to the floor, which inexplicably looked like gold spun into carpet, Ivy started to tuck her feet under her bum, but then she realized she'd probably ruin the chair, so she crossed her ankles uncomfortably, trying to avoid Andrew's bronzed gaze as he flitted about in his search for accessories. "Sometimes... sometimes I don't feel good enough for Ethan. We come from such different backgrounds. I'm nobody, and he's *Ethan Fisher*, and his—your—whole family is rich and famous. I just don't know if I fit in with... this." Ivy pointed in turn at the lighting and full-length mirrors of the room. "And what if I do or say something to embarrass him at the charity ball? I've never been to a charity event, and I can't remember the order of the silverware, and I've never even used silverware with more than two forks and I just—" she trailed off.

"I'm not going to say you don't come from different worlds, because you do. Very different."

Despite the softness of Laura's voice, Ivy's chest tightened, and her face crumpled, but Laura put up one finger.

"But that's a good thing. Did you know Jimmy lived in his car before he was signed?"

Shaking her head, Ivy felt her eyes grow wide in surprise.

"He did. He had lost his scholarship due to poor academics and decided to be a free agent in the next draft. Before he played baseball in college, he lived with his dad in a tiny silver Gulf Stream until he was seventeen, and his dad up and left while he was in school. Jimmy couch-surfed for a year and no one realized, not his coaches or teachers or friends. And then when he got his scholarship to Central University, he focused so much on baseball, his grades dropped, and he lost his scholarship before his second year. He lived in that beat-up old clunker for a few months and somehow managed to impress the coaches at his tryout.

"And then I met him." Standing and crossing over to the bar cart, Laura refilled her glass and brought the bottle over to fill Ivy's as well. "When I met him, I was hotheaded and ready to make a name for myself. And he was some hotshot baseball player who might as well have been from a different planet. Jimmy broke all my rules. He took me on dates to dollar movie matinees and two-for-one street-cart hot dogs and walks in the park. Nothing like the wining and dining I was used to. I was a spoiled princess with no real-world experience, and he was a scoundrel with too much. We taught each other a lot, you know. Just like you and Ethan have. I guarantee he never would have seen himself being a father to two children. But you gave him something he didn't even know he needed. And Ethan... he completed the family you built.

"I don't want to hear about not being good enough or whatever bullshit is going through your head. You're going to have a lovely gown because I am buying one for you—"

"Oh, no, Laura—" Ivy tried to interrupt, but her future mother-in-law would have none of it.

"I am buying you a gown, Ivy. I'd buy you the moon for how happy you've made my son, and for bringing him back into our lives. And don't even get me started on two grandchildren where we thought we would never even get to meet one. Not to mention a wonderful future daughter-in-law. So please, let me do this for you, Ivy. Let me buy you a ridiculous gown to knock my besotted son off his feet. Let me say thank you the best way I know how."

Bright, unshed tears lined Laura's eyes, and Ivy's eyes burned as she shoved herself out of the chair and practically into the older woman's lap.

Andrew, who had busied himself behind the clothing rack during Ivy and Laura's heart-to-heart let out a sob and threw his arms around both women.

"Oh, I just love this mentor-mentee soul-searching bonding we've got going on," he said with a sniffle. "It's just like a movie. Now it's time for the makeover montage!"

UNEASE SETTLED OVER ETHAN AS HE RETURNED HOME AFTER dropping Jase and Janna off at Lily's apartment. Like something out of sight, or a non-existent wind raising the hairs on the back of his neck.

All day, he'd been… off. But he couldn't quite place his finger on it and chalked it up to nerves.

Ethan planned to officially announce his retirement soon, so maybe he was anxious about letting it slip at the ball. He raked his hand through his hair. Anxiety, that was it.

Anxiety made sense.

But Ethan reminded himself there was no accounting for what made someone anxious, so he imagined what Ivy would tell him.

"Deep breath. In…good, hold it. Now out."

In, out, Ethan breathed the way she'd taught him. It helped ease the tension pulling his shoulders toward his ears, but he still couldn't shake the uneasy feeling.

Eventually, he shoved his earbuds in his ears and went about his preparations for the charity ball trying to ignore the sensation, retrieving his tuxedo from the dry cleaner and chuckling as he imagined Laura's gasp of horror at his procrastination. After showering, he pulled out his arsenal of travel-sized hair products, and for the thousandth time, groused about Ivy's bargain bin hair dryer. Somehow Ethan's haircare collection disappeared during his transition from his apartment to Ivy's. Each time he bemoaned her lack of adequate styling gear, Ivy teased him about his regimen. But it didn't stop her from running her fingers through his hair or commenting on how soft it was, so he was not going to stop.

Once his hair was styled to his liking, Ethan carefully loaded his tux into the back of the BMW, casting wary glances around the parking garage.

Again, the feeling of being watched. Prickles of apprehension spider-walked across his skin, but nothing seemed out of the ordinary. Much too quickly, Ethan peeled out of the garage and drove toward his parent's home to finish prepping for the gala.

Thundering bass and wailing guitar reverberated through the car speakers, and the knot between his shoulder blades eased slightly. Cracking his neck at a stoplight, Ethan saw a small, dark vehicle in his rearview mirror. It was vaguely familiar, though he couldn't place it, and the hair on the back of his neck prickled again. When the light turned green, the car rode his bumper for several minutes before taking a tiny opening to speed around him and cut him off before burning rubber to get away. The windows were completely blacked out, rendering the driver invisible.

Swearing, Ethan yelled that the driver was a fucking asshole and felt slightly appeased.

When he finally arrived at the Lorne-Fisher domicile, the incident was all but forgotten. Jimmy was the first to greet him, shoving a lowball glass of bourbon into Ethan's hands.

"Just trust me," Jimmy said, raising his glass in a salute.

Ethan downed the glass, relishing the burn of the alcohol as it eased his anxiety. But only slightly. Silently, he held the glass out to Jimmy, earning a raised eyebrow from his father before Jimmy gestured for Ethan to follow him. Together, they went to the liquor cabinet where Jimmy refilled both glasses. Double, this time.

"That bad, huh?" Ethan asked after a sip of the bourbon.

"I can smell the hairspray from here." Jimmy winced. "I'm still worried Andrew will come after my hair with that shit one day."

Ethan choked on his sip of bourbon and let out a hacking cough as the alcohol burned his throat. Jimmy eyed his son's hair.

"Not that he needs to come after *you* with it," Jimmy joked with a wink.

"Ivy likes my hair," Ethan shot back, rolling his eyes. "Do you know how long they'll be?"

"Not a clue," Jimmy replied, peering upward, toward the second floor that held Laura's closets and dressing room.

"Should I..." Ethan trailed off, also staring up at the ceiling.

"Not if you value your safety. The last time I checked in on them, about an hour ago, Andrew threatened me with tweezers and moisturizer." With a shudder, Jimmy drained his glass.

Grimacing, Ethan mirrored the movement, then set his glass on the sideboard. Maybe it was the whiskey or some weird masochistic curiosity, but he retrieved his tux from the coat rack near the door and headed up the stairs in search of his fiancée.

Soft piano music trickled down the stairs, along with a flowery scent he associated with Laura, and Ethan paused, praying Andrew hadn't doused Ivy in the same perfume his mother wore.

Hell, he'd be scarred for life.

Ethan was reaching for the doorknob when it was wrenched open from the other side and a shiny, bronzed pate poked out.

"Go on, you. She'll be ready soon." Andrew waved his thin

fingers in Ethan's face before pointing behind him at the stairwell.

Following orders and swearing under his breath, Ethan turned back to the stairs, but went up instead of down, heading to the library.

Ethan picked up and set down about a dozen books, eventually giving up and changing into his tux. When the door opened, he was brooding silently on a wingback chair. He'd left the overhead lights off, with the only illumination in the room coming from the hallway.

The soft yellow glow cast Ivy in silhouette, hiding her face. He couldn't see what she wore, but the outline of her body was sinful.

And then she stepped out of the light into the duskiness of the room. As his vision adjusted, Ethan realized sin was indeed the correct word. Her hair was neatly pinned to fall over one shoulder, with a structured wave nearly hiding one eye. Ivy's eyes were lined with a black much more dramatic than her usual soft brown, and as such completely changed the angle and color of her eyes. And her mouth...dark red, nearly black, like liquid sin, had been painted on her lips. Ethan could only think of her pretty, painted mouth wrapped around his cock.

"Ahem," Ivy cleared her throat pointedly, and Ethan's ears burned.

"Fuck, Ivy."

"Thank you. I think." Ivy chuckled nervously, taking a step forward so he could see the dress.

Black velvet skimmed over her arms and to the floor, the hem draping around her almost demurely. But the cut of the dress was anything but demure. The bodice fell over her torso in a deep v, with soft golden skin and a hint of the curve of her breasts peeking from beneath the black fabric. As she took another step forward, the dress fell open to reveal a slit to her mid-thigh, and Ethan nearly swallowed his tongue.

"Fuck, Ivy," he rasped out.

"You said that already."

"Yeah, but it's accurate. You look...fuck." Normally, he prided himself on being fairly articulate for an oversized professional athlete, but the sight of his fiancée in his signature color had rendered him a monosyllabic caveman.

"You like it?" Ivy asked, reaching up to touch her hair but stopping her hand halfway.

"Like it?" Ethan replied, closing the distance between them and smoothing his hand over her waist. His fingers brushed over the bare skin on her back, and he had to remind himself to breathe, and not to shove her up against the bookshelves and ruck the skirt up around her waist and—

"Fuck, Ivy." He dragged his eyes away back up to her face. Her eyes were dark and half-lidded, her mouth open in a pant.

"You've said that a few times now."

"Would it make you happy if I said 'goddamn' instead?" he grunted. "Because *goddamn*, Ivy. Holy shit, Ivy. This dress is... *you* are breathtaking."

"No one has ever said that to me before." A little crack in her voice broke him.

"I should tell you every day. You've taken my breath away a million times since the moment I met you."

"You better kiss me before I cry and ruin this makeup." But she made the first move, grasping his lapels and pulling him closer.

Carefully, he kissed her until something about the velvet dress beneath his hands turned him wild, and he pushed her back against the shelves, kissing her senseless.

He longed to press his fingers between her legs, to slip into her soft, wet heat, but there was no time for all the things he wanted to do to her. Reluctantly, he backed away, taking in the sight of her, all heavy-lidded and disheveled in the half-dark.

Ethan really, *really* wanted to skip the gala. To stay home and take his time with her.

"We should probably go." He eased a finger into the neckline of the dress, tugging it back into place with a brush over a nipple for good measure. Ivy snorted a laugh.

"You're probably right." She smiled softly, straightening her dress. "I love you." She stood on her toes to press a softer kiss to his lips.

"I love you, too. You sure you don't want to stay?"

Grinning, she took his hand and led him downstairs, where they found a note taped to his phone.

Leave it to Laura to write a note and stick it to his phone rather than send a text.

"Well, they left already, but a car should be here...now?" As he held the note out to her, tires crunched outside.

"Nice timing. Let's get this over with."

The ride to the gala was uneventful, if a bit handsy, but the moment they left the car, that odd sense of being watched settled over him again. Beside him, Ivy shuddered.

"Do you feel—"

With her brows furrowed, she nodded.

"I feel it too." Her hazel eyes peered at him, concerned, and Ethan wrapped an arm over her shoulder, pulling her against his side as if he could protect her from whatever was coming.

25

Booming heartbeats pounded in Ivy's ears as she and Ethan stepped through the double glass doors into the party. Inside, the amount of noise was constant and almost calming. At least it drowned out the rapidity of her pulse and didn't leave any room for intrusive thoughts.

Isaac and Derek appeared as Ivy and Ethan ventured further inside. Both wore tuxedos, but Isaac flouted convention in bright Hawks red, which perfectly matched Derek's tie.

"Hey, Ivy," Derek called, throwing his arms around her. A calm, different from what she felt with Ethan, settled over her as she hugged him back. "You clean up nice!" He held her at arm's length, eyeing her appreciatively. When she met his eyes, a lot of unspoken words passed between them, and Ivy knew he was remembering their shared past and where they'd found themselves now.

"You don't look too bad, either," Ivy said, squeezing his hand and blinking back tears.

"What about me?" Isaac pouted, dramatically snapping his lapels before sticking his hands in his pockets and spinning around.

"You know you look good." Derek reached out as if to take Isaac's hand but cuffed him on the shoulder instead. "Which I have already told you six, now seven times. You don't have to fish for compliments, dude."

Ivy laughed as Isaac stomped a foot in mock indignation, but the slight unease remained in her chest.

"I was aiming for ten," Isaac groused.

Ethan, who had paid attention to precisely none of the conversation, looked at them, confused.

"Ten what? Drinks?"

"No, but that's a good idea too!" A waiter passed by with a tray of champagne glasses, and Isaac flagged him down, passing the delicate glassware into Derek, Ivy, and Ethan's hands.

Champagne in hand, Ivy reminded herself to breathe and appreciate the soiree. The massive open space was filled with hundreds of people in formal clothing. Some, like Derek and Isaac, sported fashion in their teams' colors. Every corner of the room had pockets of the same team colors, but enough were dispersed throughout to make a scattered rainbow, and Ivy enjoyed the intermingling when the teams were usually separate by default. Lines had formed near the various food stations and around the cases with the items up for auction, many of which had been donated by the Lorne-Fisher family.

The decorations were simple and lovely to avoid clashing with the brightly colored fashion, cream-colored floral arrangements with small silver and gold accents. But Ivy's favorite part lay around the edges of the space. Each Major League team had a station with white-coated chefs serving tasting menus from the teams' hometowns. Ivy interrupted Isaac to point out the various types of foods of which there were entirely too many for them to try alone.

"Divide and conquer?" she asked, grinning.

Ethan still seemed uneasy, casting his eyes around the room, but he walked away to join a queue.

Ivy continued to wander through the regional offerings,

grateful so few people here knew her, allowing her to skip the socializing. Frequently, she cast her eyes over her shoulder, searching for Ethan in a sea of unknown people. With his distinctive height and hair, it was hard to miss him, and each time Ivy found him, her anxiety eased, and she was able to wander again for a few moments until she was nervous again.

Until she looked and couldn't find him.

Plate in hand, Ivy frantically scanned for Ethan in the crowd. He wouldn't have left her here alone, so something must have happened.

Laura. Laura probably needed him.

But, no, there was Laura in a white and silver gown, dancing with Jimmy.

So where was Ethan?

A flash of red silk nearby, and Ivy questioned Jen, but she hadn't seen him. Shoving her plate into a bewildered Jen's hands, Ivy mumbled incoherently as she pushed through the crowd.

She wondered if Ethan just needed air, because she did, so she slipped through the crowded entrance until she felt the cool wind on her over-heated cheeks and sucked it down in gulps.

The sound of Ethan's voice reached Ivy before she saw him, his voice low, but deep enough to cut through the street sounds. He spoke quickly, and she couldn't make out the words, but Ivy instantly knew something was wrong. When she spotted him, he was half-hidden in shadow, gesturing before turning to walk away when an arm reached out to grab him, yanking him fully into the darkness of an alley.

Before Ivy was aware of what she was doing, she hiked her up dress with one hand and raced toward the spot where Ethan disappeared, shoving people out of the way if they didn't clear out fast enough. The bad feeling she'd had all day reached a fever pitch in her head, and all she could think was *no no no* until she rounded the alleyway and Ethan was there.

So was another man, someone she'd never officially met but recognized. He was dressed immaculately, in a crisp, well-made suit, as if he were planning to attend the gala and happened to find his protege on the way inside.

"Marshall." Ivy hissed the name, and it tasted like ash on her tongue.

"Ah, and here's the little bitch who's caused so many problems." Marshall's voice was cold and unctuous, sending chills down her spine. A strangled sound came from Ethan, and Ivy felt waves of fury toward the awful old man.

"Leave, Ivy, please." His voice shook.

"Yes, that's right, girl, do as you're told." Marshall shifted as he waved dismissively, and Ivy saw a shadow beneath it and froze. Ethan, distracted by Marshall's words, didn't see the gun and tried to shove past Ivy.

But she couldn't let him be shot, so Ivy, small and defenseless, and without any sort of plan to extricate herself from the situation, stepped in front of Ethan, putting herself between the two men. Never had she felt smaller than she did standing between the two towering men.

Marshall stared her down with bloodshot eyes. Before, when he'd attacked Ethan, he'd been drunk, Ethan had said.

Now though, the man's eyes were eerily clear. Cold rage twisted his already grotesque features, and Ivy understood the man was truly unhinged.

"Move, girl," he ordered again, looking past her to Ethan.

Behind her, Ivy realized Ethan was frozen in place, nearly vibrating with panic and rage.

"No," she said, standing her ground. "Leave him alone. You're done hurting him."

"Ivy, no—" Ethan's voice was hoarse, croaking.

A dark chuckle ripped from the old man's throat.

"Who's going to stop me, girl? You?" He laughed again.

"Actually," a new voice called from the entrance to the alley. "I am." A figure was wreathed in shadows until they stepped forward, and Ivy tensed further when she saw the owner of the voice.

"Lawrence Lorne, how nice of you to join us."

As he picked his way through the narrow alley, Lawrence completely ignored Marshall, peering beyond Ivy to stare intently at his nephew. Ethan released Ivy and shifted, to run or get between her and his former coaches, she couldn't tell, so she stepped backward, pressing her back into his chest. The usual wash of heat from Ethan's body didn't seep into Ivy's skin, but his racing heartbeat did.

"You okay?" Lawrence still ignored Marshall, causing the other old man's face to grow even redder and more twisted than before.

"What do *you* want? Haven't you done enough already?" Ivy spat when Ethan didn't answer, narrowing her eyes and shifting her feet to position her body and face both men at once.

"To atone," Lawrence said and smiled sadly, then turned to face Marshall. "Gregory."

"You're a disgrace to your name!" Marshall hurled the words, spittle spraying. "Both of you!"

Slowly, Lawrence took a few steps toward them, narrowing the space between himself and the other man. "That was always your problem, Gregory. Too focused on the past, never in the here and now." With a final step, Lawrence closed the distance between himself and Marshall, creating a triangle and forcing Marshall to choose which of his opponents to face.

It would have been funny, like a scene in a movie, if Ivy weren't afraid of what Marshall might do. Because he still had the gun tucked into the waistband of his crisply pleated slacks.

And Lawrence didn't know.

As slowly as she could, Ivy began to turn her body, and by

extension, Ethan's, sideways, to shift them away from whatever was about to go down between Marshall and Lawrence.

An uncanny calm settled over Ivy. It was jarring after the anxiety of the day, being on edge and waiting for lightning to strike. Whatever happened, afterward, she knew it would all be over.

A blink and it was as though she'd been separated from her body, looking down at the scene from above. Marshall, still agitated and ranting about names and winning and blaming everyone but himself. Lawrence, glancing between Ethan and Marshall. Ethan, frozen in a way she'd never seen him before. And Ivy, in the center of all of them.

"-vid Lorne would never have let some *girl* come between him and winning!"

Ivy came back to herself in another blink, with Marshall still spewing bullshit.

"Ethan did win you colossal fuckface." Ivy snapped, speaking directly to Marshall.

"He didn't lead *my* team to victory!" Marshall snarled.

"Maybe if you'd tried, I don't know, *leading* instead of pitting players against each other or forcing them to play while injured, you might have won more often. And you might have coached the Hawks to the pennant. But it's too late now."

Marshall's placid face devolved into a mask of pure rage.

"David Lorne died alone and angry. And so will you." From behind her, Ethan's voice was quiet, but it cut through Marshall's hissing and spitting. "*You* are the one who's useless." His voice grew stronger, and he gently pulled Ivy to his side, emerging from behind her. "What did you ever do? How many years of coaching, and already people have forgotten your name?" Marshall tried to speak, but Ethan wasn't finished. "You — what— you heard my name and thought you'd ride it to the top? I'm not my grandfather. I'm not going to cheat and fight my way to winning."

Marshall shifted, casting an uneven shadow onto the brick wall behind him.

"Nice speech, boy." Crooked yellow teeth split into a frightening grin. "Did you practice in the mirror? Did she tell you what to say?"

"Shut up, I'm not done." Gravel coated Ethan's voice. "And you." Turning to face Lawrence, he came out from behind Ivy. "You." His voice was raspy with rage and sadness, and Ivy's heart cracked at the pain she heard.

"I know." Lawrence's voice was low, but it carried in the brick-enclosed space. "I know." Louder, this time. "I saw how angry you got when you were younger, and I thought..."

"I was a hormonal teenager! With the constant pressure you put me under, what did you expect?" Lawrence tried to speak, but Ethan kept going. "I AM NOT MY GRANDFATHER! I DID NOT MAKE HIS MISTAKES!" It was as if Ethan had exploded after so many years of taking every vile thing they'd thrown at him. Now, he stood in front of Ivy, his fists balled up at his sides, and a sick awareness surged through her.

Ethan still didn't know about the gun.

With Marshall's focus fully on Ethan, Ivy waved her fingers low by her side to get Lawrence's attention.

Gun, she mouthed when he shifted toward her. *He's got a gun.* She made a gun with her fingers to emphasize. A fraction of a nod was the only confirmation that Lawrence understood.

"Marshall!" Lawrence shouted, pulling the other man's gaze away from Ethan. As slowly as she could, Ivy reached out to grab his hand and squeezed. Hard. Hard enough to convey something was wrong. He squeezed back, but Ivy still had no way to explain with his back to her.

A streetlight on the corner flashed out with a loud pop and a shower of sparks, sending more weird shadows skittering down the alley.

Startled, Marshall did what Ivy had expected from the

beginning — he pulled the gun and pointed it point-blank at Ethan's chest.

"Gregory." Warning tinged Lawrence's voice, but it was as though Marshall only saw Ethan.

Ethan acted as if he didn't even see the gun. Heaving breaths shook his back, and he shifted further in front of Ivy, spreading his arms wide—to grab Marshall or hide Ivy from him— she didn't know.

From behind Ethan, Ivy could no longer see Marshall, but Ethan shifted, readying to move. Muscles tensing, Ivy settled into a crouch, ready to tackle Ethan around the knees to keep him from lunging at Marshall when she saw a flutter of movement out of the corner of her eye and

— WHAM —

Then — BANG —

Screaming echoed throughout the alley along with footsteps as people flooded in, and Ivy realized the screaming was coming from her own mouth.

"Ethan!"

Several heartbeats drowned out the noise before Ivy realized the dark wall in front of her wasn't a wall. The wall was her fiancé, shaking and confused, but whole.

"Ethan?"

A groan came from the ground. Two bodies lay there—Marshall and Lawrence. Marshall lay startlingly still, a slow trickle of blood dripping from a wound in the back of his head. Lawrence, however, was not still. He lay sprawled on the ground, clutching his arm to his chest.

"What happened?" Ivy breathed.

"It's over," a new voice said.

Jimmy. Ivy turned to find Frankie close behind him.

"What happened?" Ethan echoed.

"Well..." Jimmy ran his hand through his hair in a gesture

identical to the way Ethan did it. "You know the auction?" Ivy and Ethan glanced at each other before nodding at Jimmy, unsure how the auction was relevant. "Well, I realized I forgot the bat in the car. The one I hit that grand slam with in the bottom of the ninth in ninety-four. So, I went to get it out of the car before your mother realized I forgot it, and what do I see but this bozo," here, Jimmy aimed a sharp kick at Marshall's ribs, "walking past, muttering, and sticking a gun in his waistband. Thought I'd see what was going on, but I didn't want to spook him with so many people on the sidewalk. Who knows what would have happened? Then I saw him dragging you in the alleyway, but Ivy showed up and I couldn't get closer. I started coming down the alley, and when the light went out, I took my chance."

"So, you hit him. With a baseball bat." The bat in question had a large, sloping signature along the barrel and a small bloodstain, but seemed otherwise undamaged.

"He was threatening my family." Jimmy inspected the bat, spinning it in his hand in a familiar casual gesture.

"And you?" Ethan stared down at Lawrence.

"I was trying to grab the gun away while he was distracted with you. Bullet grazed my shoulder."

"And your speech?"

"I was wrong. I know that now. Hell, I knew it a long time ago. I was too mad and proud to admit I fucked up. The drinking didn't help." Frankie and Jimmy helped Lawrence get to his feet. "I'm sorry for all of it. And you, too." Turning to Ivy, he continues. "I'm sorry for...what I said."

"You're damn right you're sorry!" Laura appeared, shoving through the crowd like a haughty queen come to glare at her subjects. "If you weren't bleeding, I'd punch your stupid face. I'm still considering it!" The tiny woman fumed at all the larger men around her until her face softened. "Are you okay?" She hadn't directed the question at anyone, so they all murmured their assent, except for Lawrence, who muttered about his shoulder.

"It's over." As though he hadn't any strength left to hold himself up any longer, Ethan sank to the ground.

Alarmed, Ivy dropped with him, taking his hands in hers and holding them close to her body. But when she looked into his face, it was lighter than she'd seen it. Any hint of lingering darkness and tension remaining had disappeared.

A smile spread across Ethan's face, broader than she'd ever seen.

"It's over," he repeated, crushing Ivy into his chest. He repeated the words again while he held her, and it hit Ivy how deeply he'd still felt the trauma dealt by the man lying dead on the ground.

And the one still beside him.

"It's over," Ivy echoed into his ear, then stood, holding her hand out to him. Laura went to him at once, squeezing him with small, strong arms before waving at the others to join them. Frankie, towering over everyone, wrapped his long arms around them all, even Lawrence, who, along with Ethan, looked wary.

"I'm leaving."

"What?" half the people in the circle shrieked.

But Ivy knew what he meant. It *was* over. He could be finished and put the past behind him.

"I'm...I'm leaving the team. Retiring."

"You sure about that, kid?" Jimmy spoke first.

"Didn't you always say it's best to go out on top?" Ethan's voice was so...light. She'd heard him happy, but this was different. So much weight had been lifted from his shoulders.

Jimmy laughed, and Laura fussed, but Ivy knew she'd ultimately agree with whatever Ethan decided, and her heart melted as he continued.

"I want to finish my degree and...and teach. Or coach

maybe. But I want to do something good. Help people—kids—maybe. Like me. Or like Jase."

Jimmy and Laura's eyes softened, and Lawrence nodded solemnly.

When the police arrived, they took statements from everyone involved and all those who'd witnessed the events of the night. Ivy explained about searching for Ethan only to see him get pulled into the alley. Ethan said he'd received a strange text from someone pretending to be Lily borrowing someone's phone, saying something was wrong with one of the kids. When he'd gone outside to call the number, Marshall had appeared.

Bile rose in Ivy's throat over how closely Marshall had watched them, and she wondered how long he'd followed Ethan. Watched her and the kids. Prickles of fear slid down her spine, and Ivy shivered until Ethan pulled her close against his side.

After what felt like years, they were all released to rejoin the gala, which had devolved into a full-blown rager. Ivy asked Ethan if he wanted to go home, but he must still have been riding the adrenaline high because he wrapped his arms around her and whispered in her ear that he owed her a dance.

Someone—Isaac probably—had unearthed a smoke machine and lowered the lights to near darkness, and when Ethan and Ivy stepped onto the dance floor, it was as though they were the only people left in the room. Ethan's arms wrapped around her, pulling their bodies against each other. Dark hair tickled her cheek as Ethan let his forehead fall to rest against hers and they slowly swayed to the music. Warmth and peace settled over Ivy, and she leaned back to brush her lips over Ethan's.

"Mom! Dad!"

Tucking her head under Ethan's chin, Ivy continued to sway

with him in time to the music while his hand stroked over the bare skin of her back.

"Mom! Dad!"

Through the blissed-out haze of the fading adrenaline, Ivy heard what sounded like a kid yelling for their parents. But there weren't any children at the gala. Weird. She settled in closer to Ethan, closing her eyes and blocking out the world again. Ethan made a sound of contentment deep in his chest, and it rumbled in her ear as someone yelled again, closer this time.

Then Ivy was surrounded by people wrapping their arms around her, and she realized her kids had arrived, and Jase had called her *mom*.

In all the time Jase and Janna had lived with her, they'd never called her mom. The last of her adrenaline rush faded, and she collapsed to the floor, bringing Jase, Janna, Ethan, and Lily down with her.

"What are you doing here?" she hissed to Lily, trying to hold back tears.

"Ah, I might have texted her. Asking about the weird text I got. And then I told her about what happened," Ethan supplied helpfully, tugging his hand through his hair. Janna settled on his lap, and Jase sat cross-legged on the floor, one of his knees touching each of them.

"And Jase was still awake, so I told him, and...here we are?" Lily shrugged. Both her and Jase's faces were bone-white, with eyes like saucers.

Jase slid his hand into Ivy's, and his fingers were like ice as she squeezed them. His gesture sent her over the edge into full-blown sobbing.

"It's okay, we're okay," Ethan chanted as he gathered all of them into his arms— even Lily, who still looked sick.

When they were all calmer and without tears, Ethan launched into an explanation, with Ivy filling in her side.

Others joined the little knot of people on the floor; Derek and Isaac with cocktails for the adults and lemonade for the kids; Jen with plates piled high with the regional delicacies. Jimmy, Laura, and Harkness hovered on the edge of the group, listening in silence while the whole ordeal was recounted for them all.

To Janna, it seemed more like an adventure story, something to be in awe of before moving on to the next exciting thing. Jase grasped the gravity of the situation more than his sister, and he was rattled, but the adults who'd joined them were all speechless and stone-faced.

Eventually, the police called, and Ivy, Ethan, Jimmy, and Laura had to go to the police station to provide their statements. Lily took Jase and Janna home after eliciting promises that everyone would keep them updated on the situation.

Behind the glass panels of the station doors, Ivy heard a distant, tinny yelling and turned to see a tv with a video of Marshall playing in a glass-enclosed office, but the sound disappeared when the door closed, and Ivy shuddered. Statements were given, papers were signed, and Ethan and Ivy were released.

They slowly descended the steps in front of the station when Ethan tugged on her hand to stop her.

"Look," he said, pointing ahead.

The sky was a deep blue, tinged with pink and gray, the first hints of sunlight peeking between the buildings, with the rays reflecting off the glass and metal, casting shattered patterns on the cracked pavement in front of them.

"Ivy, it's a beautiful new day." He drew her to him, and when she looked up, his smile was the most beautiful thing she'd ever seen. "Let's go home."

EPILOGUE

It is a truth universally acknowledged, Laura Lorne thought, *that one with children will always be late*. She, Jimmy, and Frankie were waiting outside the new restaurant where they were to meet Ethan, Ivy, Jase, and Janna. To celebrate the big win, Ivy had said. Beside Laura, Jimmy kept grinning down at her with his lopsided grin, as if he knew something she didn't. What he knew, Laura couldn't possibly imagine. Out of the corner of her eye, she thought she saw Frankie nudge Jimmy with an elbow, and Laura sighed, pinching the bridge of her nose.

The unmistakable deep laughter of her son reached her ears as she was considering asking the host for a curbside cocktail. Bright peals of laughter echoed all the way down the street from Janna and Ivy, like bells ringing through the brisk morning air as they rounded the corner together. Laura's heart nearly burst at the happiness her son had found.

Janna wore a poofy dress and those silly, lacy socks little girls wore. Even Jase, whose standard outfit was athletic shorts and a tee had changed into nice clothes. Laura thought he looked like a mini version of Ethan, which was accurate, as Ethan wore a black button-down and slacks.

A faint inkling of an idea began to form at the back of

Laura's mind, but by then, the children were upon her and the distraction got the better of her.

"Hi, Mom, Dad, Frankie." Ethan's voice was quiet compared to the kids' yelling, but Laura couldn't miss the soft smile he gave to Ivy, who returned it tenfold.

One of the long, white-belled sleeves of Ivy's dress tangled in Laura's purse as the two women embraced, and that hint of an idea shifted further forward in Laura's mind. Holding Ivy at arm's length, Laura took in the white dress and flowers braided into Ivy's hair. Ethan and Jase's nice shirts and Janna's dress.

"Is this—" Laura began, but Ivy couldn't contain herself any longer.

"We're getting married!" she exclaimed, throwing her arms around Ethan and smiling sweetly at him.

For a moment, all the secret planning and private Pinterest boards Laura had made flashed through her mind. Then she reminded herself she had only recently gotten her son back after so many years, and she would *not* interfere.

Still standing beside her, Jimmy threw his arm over her shoulder.

"You knew!" she said, smacking him lightly.

"Ethan is terrible at secrets," Jimmy shrugged. "He's too jumpy."

Ethan scoffed.

"You're doing it now?" Laura asked. "Here?"

"Not exactly." Ethan shoved his hand through his hair, and Laura noted how long it had gotten, waving to his shoulders.

"There's a courthouse two blocks away!" Ivy still held onto Ethan as if her life depended on it.

A courthouse wedding? Save us, Laura thought, and Jimmy squeezed his arm tighter around her shoulders as if he'd read her mind. But she held her tongue, grateful to be included in the event.

"We're getting a daughter!" Jimmy quipped, and Laura's eyes clouded with tears. She waved away everyone but Ethan. She tugged his ear down to her level and whispered.

"This was what I wanted for you." Her throat was tight. "To be so happy."

Ethan squeezed her tight before letting her go and taking Janna's hand.

"Let's go! We don't want to miss the reservation," Frankie said in his rumbly bear voice.

Of course, Frankie knew too, Laura thought, falling into step beside Jase.

When they arrived at the courthouse atrium, Ivy gleefully snatched a number from the machine, despite Ethan gently reminding her they had an appointment. She shoved the tiny slip of paper into a purse, which Laura was thankful to see was considerably smaller than her usual massive tote.

Derek, Isaac, and Lily waited for them in the lobby, all three bedecked in autumn colors to offset the bouquets of cream-colored flowers they carried. Derek looked almost somber beside Isaac's burnt orange suit and cravat. Laura smiled as Ivy squeezed Lily's arm, exclaiming about not needing flowers.

"Shut up, it's your wedding day," Lily said, rolling her eyes. Laura coughed lightly to cover her laugh. "Of course, we brought you flowers."

Together, the group took up most of the waiting room, but at least they'd only arrived a few minutes before their allotted time.

The wedding was exactly as Laura should have expected and nothing like she would have planned. It was short and sweet, with simple, standard vows, perfect for Ivy and Ethan, who'd stared into each other's eyes as though no one else was in the room.

Ethan Fisher nearly had to pour his wife into the backseat of the car, not out of drunkenness, but out of exhaustion from spending the day in incandescent bliss.

His *wife*.

He still couldn't quite believe the words and the frisson of pleasure they caused him.

Ivy peered at him through lowering lashes before wrapping both of her arms around his bicep and throwing her legs over his lap.

"Ethan?"

"Hmm?"

"We're married." Her voice was muffled by his arm.

"Yeah, sweetheart. We're married."

"Ethan?"

"Hmm?"

"I like being married."

Ethan chuckled.

"We've been married for about four hours."

Ivy leaned her head back and scowled in mock affront.

"Are you saying after four hours, you *don't* like being married?"

"I am *saying*," Ethan tapped the tip of her nose, "four hours isn't long."

"So now you're saying once we've been married longer you won't like it?" Her hazel eyes sparkled at him in mischief.

"What I am saying, Ivy Johnson-*Fisher*," he made sure to growl her new name at her, "is you are stuck with me for the next...forever."

"Forever, huh?" Ivy squeezed his arm tighter.

"Forever," Ethan agreed. He made to slide a finger beneath the hem of her dress, but she swatted his hand away and tugged the dress lower.

"Ethan Cable Fucking Fisher. We are in public." Her eyes twinkled up at him, reflecting the streetlights shining through the window.

"Technically, Ivy Johnson-Fisher," he said, leaning down to kiss the soft spot beneath her ear, "we're in a car."

"And there is another person in this car!" Ethan couldn't tell if her hiss was from his words or the scrape of his teeth over her pulse point.

"He's driving," Ethan offered, sliding his fingers over her arm and watching the goosebumps form in their wake.

"Yes, and what happens when he looks in the rearview mirror and sees...everything?" Ivy's back arched despite her words.

"That is an excellent point. No one else will be seeing... everything...but me." Ethan couldn't quite help the hint of a possessive growl creeping into his voice.

Rolling her eyes, Ivy threaded their fingers together tightly enough to keep his hands from wandering more.

After a few more minutes, and despite her earlier words about privacy or propriety, or whatever she was calling it, Ivy slid even closer to him and began pressing open-mouthed, almost biting kisses up the side of his neck before nipping at his earlobe. Ethan shifted in his seat, to get away or give her better access, he wasn't sure.

But when he cupped her cheek to kiss her back, she wriggled out of his grip and tapped two fingers on his lips.

"Nope. Save it, Baseball Boy."

"Baseball Boy?"

"New nickname," Ivy said. "Like it?"

"I hate it. I'm retiring, remember?"

"Yeah, but until that's official...Baseball Boy." Her smile sent warmth shooting through him, and he couldn't help wrapping his arms around her and tucking her head beneath his chin after pressing a kiss to the top of her head.

Sleep took Ivy quickly once she finally let her body still against his, and Ethan lost himself in marveling over the new life he had.

A year ago, during the depths of his training with Marshall, if anyone had told him he'd find love, reunite with his family, and find a family of his own, he would have laughed in their face.

A soft sigh escaped Ivy's lips as he stroked her back, and Ethan thought of the first time he saw her, with her sun-kissed smile. The first interaction with her, imagining her in his shirt, which happened regularly since Ivy had laid claim to the entirety of his closet, but Ethan couldn't complain. Not when seeing the length of her bare legs in *his* shirts still sent electricity coursing through his veins even after months of experiencing it.

But it was not her loveliness, all golden and gleaming soft skin, and the scent of her, all vanilla and sunshine.

No, it was her presence, soothing, a balm for a part of himself that had always been cold and lonely and miserable. Being there for her, for her kids, *their* kids, had pieced him back together, filling in the shards of his shattered soul and then some.

For now, though, it was just the two of them on their honeymoon. Which, naturally, Ivy started by falling asleep on his arm.

When the car finally rolled to a stop outside their hotel, Ivy opened her eyes sleepily and stretched sinuously, arching her back to its full extent. Reaching over him to open the door, Ivy slid her body across his, pretending not to notice as she shook her ass right in his face. Of its own volition, or so he'd swear, Ethan's hand deftly swooped beneath the hem of her dress to squeeze the soft curve there, humming in pleasure to find it nearly uncovered, save for a tiny scrap of lace that felt more like decoration than functional underwear. A gasp left her throat, and she wriggled under his hand before sliding the rest of the way out of the car. And then he heard another gasp, this one in shock.

"Ethan?"

Slowly, he unfolded himself from the depths of the car, cracking his neck once he reached his full height.

"Do you like it?"

Before them stood the most exclusive, pretentious hotel in the city. The massive building took up an entire city block, climbing dozens of stories into the sky and glittering in the pink and orange light of the receding sunset.

"I didn't—I don't— Ethan, it's so *expensive*." A hint of frantic energy stole over her again as she twisted her hands together.

"Ivy." Ethan cupped her chin in his hands and turned her face to meet his eyes. "Major league pitcher on the heels of a World Series win." He pointed at himself. "Did you forget?"

"It's still too much!" Ivy said in a small voice, blinking up at the behemoth of a building.

"It's not too much. Nothing is too much for you. So, I want you to enjoy it, okay?" Ethan meant every word.

"Okay," Ivy said faintly, turning a small smile up at him. "Do you think there's a pool?"

Containing his self-satisfied chuckle, Ethan wrapped his arm around her.

"Let's go find out."

THE BACK OF IVY'S NECK ACHED FROM CRANING HER HEAD UP AND from side to side to take in the sleek metal and glass interior of the hotel, though she'd tried to be stoic and solemn at first. But when the hotel manager emerged from her office with a tray of champagne and gold-dusted chocolates, well, Ivy couldn't help herself. Never had she had the opportunity for such self-indulgence and luxury, and Ivy was determined to enjoy every second, whether it was the way one should behave or not.

Now, on the way to their room—their *suite*— Ivy felt every single one of the bubbles in the champagne coursing through her veins to pool low in her belly, leaving her tingly and wanting.

Ivy was *married*, this was her *honeymoon* with her *husband*, and while they'd planned a longer vacation with Jase and Janna for their winter break, right now, she planned to take full advantage of the handful of days they had to themselves before they had to return to the reality of their life.

As they walked, Ivy made her plan for their first night of married bliss. The small suitcase she'd packed was in the hands of a teenage bellhop, but she'd brought a bag Lily had shoved into her hands as they'd left the reception.

"For tonight," Lily had said with a leer.

Ivy hefted the bag higher on her shoulder and tried to surreptitiously feel around inside. The texture of lace slid over her fingertips and a small cardboard box. Perfect timing, she realized, as they approached a door. The manager swiped a key and pushed the door open, and Ivy lost all sense of manners or propriety as she threw herself past the bemused hotel manager and nearly knocked the woman down in her haste to enter the room. Once inside, Ivy barely noticed what was probably the height of luxury as she cast her eyes around in search of a spot to investigate the contents of her bag without drawing attention to her action. Ethan and the manager were having a low conversation at the door, so Ivy slid the bag off her shoulder and tugged the straps apart, easing open the magnetic clasp.

Inside the bag, Ivy saw a pile of black and red lace and ribbon, which, on further inspection, was a corset. Her mouth went dry, considering the sexy implications of the garment. *It is your wedding night,* her inner voice intoned.

Her inner voice sounded a lot like Lily's.

But she agreed with Lily, or her inner voice, or both, and plunged her hand back inside the soft brown leather bag. The cardboard box was revealed to be...under-bed restraints? Ivy's mouth went dry.

Were they for her or Ethan?

Was she supposed to *restrain* her mountain of a husband?

Fingering the red lace cups of the corset, Ivy decided to go for it. One last time, she shoved her hand back in the bag and pulled out a clear bottle with pink holographic writing.

Cherry-flavored lube.

Immediately her cheeks went pink. Virgin bride she was not, but this felt so delightfully naughty, she couldn't help but giggle.

Which drew Ethan's attention like a cat to a mouse.

One dark eyebrow quirked at her, and she dropped the bottle back in the bag, hoping he hadn't seen it. Hastily, she closed the bag as Ethan said his goodbyes to the manager.

Ivy's heart beat in her ears as she formed her plan.

"Darling," she said, and even she could hear how corny and *suspicious* she sounded. "Uh, Ethan. I think there's a coffee shop downstairs. Would you mind terribly if I troubled you for a coffee? I'm dreadfully tired," she said sweetly, like a dame in a black-and-white movie.

Ivy knew Ethan was onto her, biting his full lower lip to hide a smile.

"Sure, I'll get coffee for you. But I made sure there was an espresso machine in the kitchen. I can make espresso if you want." He gestured to a closed door she hadn't noticed.

"Espresso sounds lovely!" Too shrill, even to her ears.

"One espresso coming up," he said, leaning over to brush his lips over hers before turning toward the kitchen.

"Ah, make mine a double," she called, "and for you too!"

"Are you sure you want caffeine, sweetheart? You seem a little...jumpy."

"I just need lots of energy! Ha ha ha." Ivy groaned internally at the halting, fake laughter.

As soon as the door swung closed behind him, Ivy grabbed the restraints and raced for the bed. Of course, it was a king-sized bed, and of course, it had pristine white linens that would immediately reveal she had tampered with the bed. Nothing could be done to avoid it, though, and Ivy used her full body weight to shove the enormous mattress over enough to slide the long straps into place, leaving the black circles of the wrist and ankle straps dangling at the edges of the bed. She straightened the duvet as best she could and practically leaped across the room to retrieve her bag before bounding into the bathroom and slamming the door closed.

Once inside, Ivy took a moment to breathe and calm her pounding heart. Excitement and a hint of nervous energy flooded through her as she stared at her flushed face in the mirror. She giggled at herself before putting on a serious face, one more befitting of the corset. Naturally, she broke down into more giggles. Letting out a whoosh of a breath, Ivy tugged the corset free of her bag, and two faint clinks sounded as something wrapped in the folded fabric fell to the marble-tiled floor.

Three somethings, actually.

The first item Ivy retrieved was a tube of deep red liquid lipstick, with a sticky note in Lily's handwriting reading: "it's long-lasting — trust me." The second was an airplane-sized bottle of vodka, which Ivy set on the counter to drink after the lipstick set so she didn't smear red across her face. The third item was a small black triangle lined with red lace with dangling strings, and Ivy rolled her eyes at the tiny, ridiculous garment. Quickly, she disrobed, and fully naked, glared at her reflection while applying the lipstick.

Red wasn't a color she wore often, and the brightness of her lips was startling, though she assumed that was why Lily had given it to her.

Next, Ivy fumbled quickly with the silly triangle thong, until Ethan knocked at the door. An ankle tangled in a strap, leaving Ivy hopping on one foot and screeching, "just a minute," before she finally set the damn thing to rights, sliding it over her thighs, with the back part of the garment sliding between the globes of her ass.

Somewhere between feeling sexy and empowered, but also awkward and uncomfortable, Ivy looked at herself in the mirror once more before tackling the corset.

With a determined grit of her teeth, Ivy managed to hook three of the front hooks together before the bottom half of the corset split wide over her navel. Grunting, Ivy unhooked the top and tried to start from the bottom. The same thing happened again but in reverse; now the damn thing fell open over her boobs. Stamping her bare foot and swearing silently, she managed to get the hooks lined up and in their places after a lot more swearing and stomping. Except it still didn't quite fit properly. It was too loose over her boobs and hips, so she reached behind her back and tugged at the red ribbons laced up the back.

After tugging again at the strings with no luck, Ivy gave up and called in reinforcements.

"Ethan? Could you come in here but keep your eyes closed?"

"Um. Yes? Why?" He rattled the doorknob.

"Are your eyes closed?"

"Yes."

"Are they really?"

"...yes?"

Opening the door but only poking her head around the edge, Ivy saw his hand covering his eyes, so she grabbed him by his other wrist and led him in.

"Okay, keep them closed," she said, "I need your help."

"How can I help you if my eyes are closed?"

"I need your hands."

"I can do that," he grinned, taking his hand away from his eyes.

"Down boy," Ivy laughed, "not yet. I need you to give me your hands but keep your eyes shut and here, tie this." She turned around to have her back to him, reaching behind her back again and dropping the ends of the ribbons into his waiting hands.

Professional athlete that he was, Ethan yanked on the ribbons as though tying his cleats before a game, and all the air in Ivy's lungs was forced out as the metal rods encased in the lace squeezed her torso.

"A little looser," she wheezed, and they worked together to get the ribbons tied in a bow, with the length of the loops draping down her back.

"Can I see now?" Ethan's hands lingered on her hips.

Ivy took in their reflection in the mirror: Ethan, so tall and calm behind her, his eyes still closed, and Ivy, smaller and flustered. She stifled a chuckle at the visual representation of their relationship.

"No, you may not. Go in the bedroom, strip, and lie on the bed." Ivy's tone surprised her, and it definitely surprised Ethan, who cocked his head and tried to sneakily crack one eye open.

"No!" she shrieked but laughed as she shoved him out the door. "Let me know when you're ready."

Ethan mumbled something about always being ready, and she swatted him on the rear before closing the door behind him. The vodka beckoned from the counter, and Ivy grabbed it and downed it in one stinging gulp before eyeing the mirror again.

Bright-red lipstick? Check.

Boobs adjusted? Hmm. She scooped her breasts higher in the cups of the corset, adjusting her cleavage. Boobs? Check.

Husband?

"Ivy?" Ethan called.

Husband? Check.

Before she could lose her nerve, Ivy straightened her shoulders and stepped through the door.

As always when she saw him like this, Ivy was struck by how large and beautiful this man she'd married was. She paused, taking in the sight of him. All the smooth skin and broad planes of muscle, long dark hair and full lips.

Ethan drank Ivy in as well; his eyes couldn't seem to settle on one place, jumping from her lips to her breasts, to the tiny lacy triangle between her legs. His cock, which had been half-hard when she'd opened the door, sprang to attention, resting thick and hard and heavy on the lower plane of his abdomen.

Ivy almost forgot herself and jumped on him right there.

Almost.

But she had a plan.

"So, Ethan." She gripped the door frame to keep herself on track.

"So, Ivy." He wasn't mocking her, but she could hear the amusement in his voice.

"Um. So." Ivy tossed her hair back over a shoulder and ran her hand over the lace at the top of the corset. It wasn't the most comfortable thing she'd ever worn. "So," she tried again, "we have, um, this thing."

"I noticed, actually," Ethan said.

Ivy's eyes flew open, and she made herself look no lower than his chin.

"You did?"

Ethan hummed in response, putting his hands behind his head, the muscles of his upper body rippling with the movement.

"And you want to use them? The... restraints?" Ivy tried not to let her voice crack.

"Well, about that."

"What?"

Ethan's voice lowered, all rough and husky. "Do I get to restrain you too?"

Oh, shit. For a moment, Ivy considered it. Using him as she wanted, him using her, both of them wringing every last ounce of pleasure from the other until they were begging.

Biting her lip, she nodded.

"Well?" Ethan moved his hands and spread his arms wide across the mattress.

With a deep breath, Ivy eased herself onto the bed, assessing the best way to attach the Velcro cuffs to his wrists and ankles. Straddling him seemed easiest, so she did. His skin was scorching against her already heated sex, and she slowly dragged her lace-covered center over the naked, silken heat of his skin. Ethan groaned, the deep rumbling sound reverberating in his chest, but before he could move his hands to touch her, Ivy pounced. Wrapping her hands around his wrists was out of the question, but she did the best she could.

"Be still," she commanded in her best semblance of a growl.

To her astonishment, Ethan instantly stilled beneath her.

"Good," Ivy praised, and a rumbling, almost purring sound emanated from Ethan's chest as she leaned over him to wrap the cuff around one wrist, then the other. The rough section of Velcro barely touched the soft side, but it seemed to be enough to hold him in place. After a moment of consideration, she decided not to attach the ankle cuffs.

Below her, Ethan slowly moved his head, barely brushing his lips over the soft skin of her breast where the corset had pushed it up into a high mound. His mouth was warm and soft, and Ivy wanted to lean into the touch, but she'd told him not to move.

"Ethan," she said in warning, and he smiled innocently as his lips touched her again, trying to pass his movement off as him adjusting the angle of his head.

With a quick press of her lips to his, Ivy straightened, sitting upright while still straddling him. Lightly scraping her nails over his chest, Ivy watched as he squeezed his eyes closed in frustration, enjoying her newfound power over him. Leaning forward again, Ivy nipped at his earlobe before kissing her way down the column of his throat and biting harder in the place where his neck and shoulder met, sucking a bruise into his skin. She continued this way, biting and kissing her way down his torso until he was breathing hard and shuddering beneath her.

Bracing her weight on her arms, Ivy slid her body slowly along the length of Ethan's until her thighs were spread over his. With one finger, Ivy stroked the hot, hard length of him. Every muscle in his body jerked, but her weight held him in place. Again, Ivy stroked him with one finger, circling over the sensitive head before running her finger back down to its base.

"Ivy, please—"

"Please what?"

"I don't know, I just— *fuck*," his words cut off with a groan as she wrapped her hand around him and leaned forward to swirl the flat of her tongue over the thick, ruddy head of him, mimicking the movement she'd made with her hand.

And then she remembered.

"Stay here," she said, then laughed at his pout and the jerk of his head toward where his wrists were above his head.

Sliding off him, Ivy scampered into the bathroom and returned with the bottle of lube. Ethan watched in fascination as she dripped a small amount of the liquid onto her palm before wrapping her hand around his shaft again. He was impossibly thick and hard in her hand, and she hummed in pleasure as she leaned forward to taste the flavored lube. It tasted *exactly* like her favorite cherry hard candy, and Ivy lapped at him enthusiastically, sucking him in further to swirl her tongue. Looking up at him, Ivy watched his eyes zero in on the pretty red circle of her lips wrapped around his cock.

"Shit, fuck, *goddamn*, Ivy—"

He'd had such a dirty mouth when they'd met, though he'd tried to temper it around the kids. Now, though, Ivy wanted to find that side of him again, so she bobbed her head up and down, hollowing her cheeks and sucking every drop of the cherry-flavored liquid off him. He was so hard, his pulse throbbed on her tongue, and when his body tensed and she knew he was about to come, she just...stopped.

Ethan stared at her, panting and wild-eyed.

"*Fuck*, Ivy, *please*, I need—"

Ivy eased her mouth off his cock, and he *whined*. Ivy delighted in having made him fall apart so much he could barely breathe. Ethan's chest heaved and his pupils were so large, his eyes appeared black.

Good, Ivy thought, sitting back on her heels, taking the

bottle of lube in hand again, making sure he saw every move she made.

This time, when she dripped the liquid onto her fingertips, she touched herself rather than him, sliding her fingers beneath the tiny scrap of lace hiding her sex from view. Unsurprisingly, Ivy found herself already drenched and ready for him, and she moaned at the feeling of the cool liquid on her fingers mingling with her arousal to coat her clit. Their eyes met as Ivy touched herself. Ethan's jaw worked in obvious frustration, and his hands clenched and unclenched above the black bands keeping them in place. When she'd decided they'd had enough teasing, she stood and walked to the head of the bed. Ethan's eyes tracking her every move, and his body jerked as she eased the tiny thong down over her hips and thighs before dropping it to the floor. Slowly, Ivy climbed onto the bed beside Ethan's head and slung one knee over him to rest beside his outstretched arm, the other mirroring it. It was difficult to maneuver with her legs between his arms, but somehow, she managed until she had herself positioned above his mouth. She didn't lower herself to his lips, though, until she'd leaned forward and rested on one elbow, taking him in her other hand. Then she shifted her hips and knees enough to lower herself onto his tongue, and nearly in unison, both Ivy's and Ethan's tongue stroked over the other.

Ethan's tongue was wet and hot as he laved over her, sucking her clit between his lips and swirling his tongue over the swollen bud. Ivy moaned as she sank her mouth lower onto his cock, and below her, his hips shifted, bucking and shoving himself deeper into her throat, making her gag. Ethan stopped at her discomfort, but Ivy circled her hips and ground down on his mouth, so he kept licking and sucking at her, drawing out her pleasure until, as she had before, he...stopped.

Ivy hissed a curse; she was so *close*.

"Ethan, *please*."

His deep chuckle vibrated against her, and it was almost enough to send her over the edge.

But not quite.

"Ethan."

Then, bending his knees and digging his heels, he pulled, his biceps bulging, until Ivy heard a cracking, tearing sound, and suddenly his arms were wrapped around her waist, heaving her off his face.

"Shit!" Ivy squeaked as he snatched her off the bed.

"Your turn," he whispered in her ear, sending delicious shivers down her spine and causing even more heat to pool in her center.

Except...except he didn't put her back on the bed.

Instead, Ethan placed his hands on Ivy's shoulders, his thumbs rubbing over the muscles and tendons in her neck, making her relax into his touch. Until he slid his hands down the length of her arms, when, reaching her wrists, his hands encircled and quickly drew them behind her back. With one hand, Ethan held her wrists together behind her back, and with the other, he tugged...on her corset ribbons? When the silk looped over her wrists, understanding settled over her. He drew the ribbons tight, testing to be sure her circulation wasn't cut off, but she couldn't escape the way he had. When he was satisfied, he leaned his chin on her shoulder.

"You good?" he whispered against her neck.

Ivy nodded her assent, and almost instantly his hand was between her shoulder blades, pushing her upper body down on the bed so she had to turn her head in order not to suffocate in the sheets.

His knees pushed between her thighs, spreading her legs wider.

"Did you have fun teasing me?" he growled, placing his hands on her hips, thumbs tracing over the tension of her lower back.

"Yes." She wiggled her hips, and his fingers dug into her skin. Ivy whimpered when the heavy heat of him came to rest on the cleft of her ass and one finger dipped into her, dragging her wetness over swollen, heated flesh. She whimpered again as the tip of Ethan's finger swirled over her entrance, teasing. Ivy's back arched at this new intrusion of unexpected pleasure, and Ethan rumbled a deep laugh as he bent over her, pressing his finger deeper.

It was all too much, his body over hers, holding her in place, her nipples pressed against the smooth sheets, his hand teasing her.

Too much but not enough.

"Ethan, *please,*" Ivy begged.

Ethan removed his hand to grip her hips again.

"Please, what, sweetheart?" Ivy was somewhat gratified to hear his voice sounding nearly as desperate as hers.

"Oh, *fuck*, Ethan, please, I need you inside me. *Please*." Her voice pitched to a high keen by the end of the sentence.

Ethan pushed into her in one stroke. Ivy sobbed in relief as he pulled out and shoved himself back into her, again and again, gripping her arms to pull her back harder as he slammed into her.

Whatever control he possessed evaporated as the rhythm of his hips grew erratic, and he folded his body over hers, sliding one strong arm beneath her body to stroke her clit. Pleasure erupted through her, sending stars shooting across her vision, and Ivy's inner muscles gripped tight around him as he fucked her harder until he shuddered and collapsed on top of her.

"Fuuuck," they said in unison, and they laughed together, too.

"So that's married sex," Ethan mumbled into the pillow.

"It was, but it is *not* going to happen again if you don't untie my wrists," Ivy griped from where she still lay face-down on the bed, flapping her elbows like wings.

Ethan tugged the ribbons apart and gently turned her over to pull her to her feet. He brushed his lips over hers, then crushed her to his chest, and she was home.

The End

ACKNOWLEDGMENTS

To you, dear reader. Thank you, thank you, thank you from the bottom of my heart for reading this book. I hope you love Ethan and Ivy as much as I do.

Megan, thank you for alternately holding my hand and mostly keeping my self-destructive tendencies at bay. Nothing I've written would exist if it weren't for you encouraging me literally from the very beginning of this journey. Thank you for being a soundboard for all my wild ideas. We've already been friends forever, and now it's in print so you're stuck with me EVEN LONGER MWAHAHAHA.

Stacy, you were the first to read this in its new form. Thank you for believing in it and me. I'm absolutely not sorry for your new romance novel addiction.

Michelle and Jaina. I can't fathom how we found each other because of a movie that definitely doesn't exist, but I'm so glad it brought us together. We've (remotely) been through so much together, and I've loved our weirdness and this place we've created for ourselves. You've been the loudest cheering section on this journey. Thank you for that. I'm glad the space wizards got to kiss.

Brittany and Lake Country Press. You gave me a chance when I'm not sure I would've taken it elsewhere. Your enthusiasm for my characters and story has given them the best home, and I am unbelievably grateful for you and how you made my dream come true. I can't thank you enough for what you've done for me and this story.

To my LCP author sibs: y'all are like the long-lost family I wish I had. I'm so glad we've all got a home in LCP.

Tara, you don't know how much I appreciate your insight. It's been immeasurably helpful, not just for SIL but in general. You gave me confidence in my writing, and that is a feat in itself.

Eve, you created the most delicious illustrated nachos of all time. Thank you for the art of my dreams.

To Emily and Lisa and everyone in the fandom spaces who followed along with this story in its earliest iteration and screamed in my DMs and comments about how much you loved it, I wouldn't be here without you. Y'all mean the galaxy to me. Liana, I wouldn't be here without 3,2,1...Write. Thank you for creating this space where I've found so many new friends and learned so much about writing and publishing. Maude, you don't know how much your help means to me. Again, thank you all.

To my husband, your support has been the singular column holding up the crumbling ruin that is my fragile psyche. Thank you for the hours you've spent distracting our kid so I could get the words out of my frazzled head. Thank you for never wavering in your support, even if you don't quite comprehend my vehement love for fictional characters. Thank you for listening to my rants about those fictional characters. Thank you for the red pens. I love you to the moon and back.

To my child, thank you for graciously agreeing to watch Bluey while I wrote and edited this book. Thanks for the encouragement, kiddo, and thanks for all the times you said you believed in me. I love you.

To Harper, thanks for being by my side for almost every word I've ever written. You're the best pup.

To my parents, you always said I'd write a book, and you were right. This may not look like what you thought, but it *is* a book! Thank you for supporting me even if you didn't quite expect the direction I took.

ABOUT THE AUTHOR

Juliet has been reading voraciously as long as she can remember. She began writing around age seven. Her first stories about horse girls have been tragically lost to the ravages of time. An avid fangirl, Juliet loves everything from hobbits to dragons to magic and everything in between. The nightmare of 2020 brought back her love of writing, and she's been immersed in creating her own worlds ever since. When not reading, writing, or mom-ing, Juliet can be found daydreaming about a galaxy far, far away or enjoying second breakfast with her husband, spawn, and an anxious golden retriever.

ALSO BY JULIET BRIDGES

Coming Soon...

Puck to the Heart

Milton Keynes UK
Ingram Content Group UK Ltd.
UKHW031917050224
437294UK00007B/353